marry lies

Ravaged Castle Book Two

USA TODAY BESTSELLING AUTHOR

AMANDA RICHARDSON

Marry Lies
Amanda Richardson
© Copyright 2023 Amanda Richardson
www.authoramandarichardson.com

Copy/line editing: Victoria Ellis at Cruel Ink Editing & Design
Cover Design: Moonstruck Cover Design & Photography
Cover Photography: Rafa G Catala
Cover Model: Fabián Castro

BLURB

He never wanted a wife, but for her, he'd spin a web of lies.

Miles

The idea of seeking a wife to salvage our family's reputation starts as a joke... until it spirals into a desperate reality.

Before I know it, I'm lying my way into a marriage of convenience with a woman who is everything I'm not. Estelle Deveraux radiates warmth where I'm shrouded in darkness, exudes vibrant colors while I dwell in shades of gray, and irritates me with her maddening cheerfulness.

I find myself entranced, watching... *craving*.

Before I know it, she's not just my *wife* but an all-consuming obsession—one I didn't anticipate.

And one I can't let go.

Stella

Being presented with an opportunity to kickstart my clothing line is a dream come true.

The only caveat? I have to stay married to Miles Ravage for a year and sing his praises to anyone who will listen.

Bad-tempered, unsmiling, and cold, Miles is exactly the kind of man I loathe.

However, beneath the ice, I uncover an enticing complexity—a veiled darkness that lures me in, begging me to discover his secrets.

One watchful secret in particular... with *me* as his sole obsession.

Marry Lies is a marriage of convenience, opposites attract/frenemies-to-lovers romance with a voyeur hero and Beauty and the Beast themes. It is book two in the Ravaged Castle series. All books can be read as standalones.

Warning: This book contains a grumpy hero who hates everyone but her. It also contains explicit sexual situations and strong language. There is no cheating, and there is a HEA.

There once was a castle, so mighty and high,
With large, gilded gates, it rivaled Versailles.
To all those below, it was splendid and lush,
But to those inside, it was ravaged and crushed.
Five Ravage boys born amongst old, rotted roots,
Their father ensured they'd all grow to be brutes.
Some said they were cursed, sworn off of desire,
But they turned into men and found what they required.
Forbidden, illicit, they had to work for that love,
They questioned that castle when push came to shove.
The curse and the rot gave way to unsavory tastes,
Dark proclivities and sick, messed up traits.
Five stories of five men with sinfully dark tales,
The Ravage brothers prove that love does prevail.

TRIGGERS

Triggers: Voyeurism (with and without explicit consent), cock warming, edging, DIY porn, depression (on the page, detailed), anxiety, burns/scars and negative thoughts about them, death of a grandparent (not on page), PTSD.

*Please note that Marry Lies is *not* a dark romance. Happy reading!

For all the girlies who preferred the scarred beast before he became a prince.

PROLOGUE
THE FOUNTAIN, PART ONE

Miles

One Year Ago, Paris

You'd think taking a three a.m. stroll around the Eiffel Tower would lend me some solitude and quality alone time. Instead, there's a naked woman a hundred feet away from me, traipsing through the Fountain of Warsaw at Les Jardins du Trocadero. I'd watched her with interest from a couple hundred yards away as she set her things on the ground and quickly stripped down to nothing. Averting my gaze like a gentleman, I began walking in the *other* direction, but then I stopped.

I suppose you could say my curiosity got the best of me, as it always does.

My opinion of the general public is low. People are unreliable, insatiable, and self-interested. Of course, that also includes me, but I'm *just* delusional enough to consider myself smarter than most people. It's rare for something to pull me out of my structured routine—rare for something to pique my interest. Once it does, I have to see it through.

If I gave into every whim, I'd never get anything done.

Which is why I'm both fascinated and irritated with the naked woman in the fountain—especially because she's leaning her head back and smiling.

I'm not naive. I know every large city has its fair share of miscreants. Still, something about that large, infectious smile has me taking a few steps toward her. There are a couple of other people passing through the Jardin, but otherwise, it's just me and this lunatic. As I get closer, I realize she's submerged past her neck, so I feel less like a voyeur as I walk closer. The first thing I notice is that she's young. Pretty, but in an objective sort of way. *Not my type.* She has curly, blonde hair piled up on top of her head, and she looks carefree and at peace.

The way she's floating, completely still in the water, uncaring...

I could never do that.

I could never do something so stark raving mad.

A flurry of emotions pass through me: wonder, intrigue, envy... and then that envy twists around inside of me and turns into resentment. I will never get that luxury, even if I wanted it.

I could never let people see *me.* All *of me.*

When I'm about twenty feet away, I stop walking. A small part of me wants to get closer to ask her what the hell she's doing. Surely there must be a reason. But the other part of me is telling me to walk away.

What could I possibly have to say to her?

And more importantly, why does a very small part of me *want* to talk to her?

This is the problem with my curiosities. I'm focused and eagle-eyed. No one else is looking at the naked woman. The people around us haven't noticed. But when something catches my attention, I can't forget about it. I can't help but look. I can't help but *want* it.

As a little boy, I once saw this teddy bear in the shops of Beverly Hills. It was small, and it had a little red beret on its head. I thought about that bear for days. *Weeks.* I begged my mother to take me back so I could get it. Chase, one of my younger brothers, kept trying to show me all of his shiny, new toys to make me feel better.

I didn't want more toys.

I wanted one *special* toy.

So in a way, whenever I feel that same tug of longing, that same burning hunger, almost nothing can stop me from pursuing it.

And yes, I went back for that bear. It was my favorite toy for years. I'm sure a therapist would be able to connect the dots between my quiet, scheming mind as a child, and becoming the CEO of my own firm by the time I was twenty-five. I never settle for less.

"Aren't you boiling in that suit?"

Her voice startles me—the British accent is soft and lilting. I press my lips together and refuse to tell her that yes, I've been boiling all day. Paris isn't usually so hot in October, and yet it was abnormally warm today.

"I'm fine." I rock back on my heels as she tips her head slightly backward, exposing her neck.

Just as I open my mouth to ask about the fact that she's skinny dipping in a very public—and probably very germ-infested public fountain—she speaks.

"Let me guess," she says brightly. "You're American?"

I nod. "What gave me away?"

"The suit, as well as the general air of importance and arrogance." I open my mouth to argue, but she beats me to it. "Here on business, then?"

"I guess you could call it a business trip," I tell her, walking closer.

If you can count visiting my father as a business trip.

"What brings you to the Eiffel Tower in the middle of the night?"

I step closer, letting my eyes rove over her. The dark water is hiding anything indecent, but the light from the Eiffel Tower highlights the softness of her exposed body, the way her skin glows with pale gold undertones.

I can't stop staring at the way the shadows fill the hollow of her neck. Her smile grows with each passing second, like she knows I'm captivated against my will. There's both a delicacy and a strength in her smile— like I shouldn't be watching her.

Which, of course, makes me want to watch more.

"I can't sleep," I tell her honestly.

"Me either." She stares at me as she floats in the water. Her eyes wander over my suit. "I don't see a wedding ring, so I'm going to assume you're single." I open my mouth to retort but she continues down her list of assumptions. "And you've walked over to me, which is a red flag. If there weren't other people around, I might find it creepy. But... based on that forehead crease and the way you're frowning, I'm going to assume you often wallow in melancholy, hence the middle-of-the-night stroll."

"I don't wallow in melancholy—"

"Well, maybe not entirely. You're here talking to me, so there's *something* interesting about you somewhere underneath that stuffy suit. Am I right?"

My lips twitch but I don't smile. I don't particularly enjoy that she was able to size me up so easily. Normally *I'm* the one sizing people up.

"I can neither confirm nor deny your assumption."

She snorts. "You sound like all the posh blokes in London. *I can neither confirm nor deny...*" she trails off, mocking me.

"Do you enjoy hearing yourself talk?" I ask briskly.

"Some people lack the ability to laugh at themselves. That's where I come in," she teases.

I stare at her and clench my jaw. Is she serious? *She's* the one swimming naked in a fucking fountain.

If anyone has the right to judge, it's me.

"I hear there are public showers at the train station," I bite back. "In case you didn't know that. I can only assume you're either without a home or completely unhinged."

She laughs. "Of course you would think that. It's called *having fun*. Have you ever heard of it? Try not to spontaneously combust."

I glower at her. "You're ridiculous, do you know that?"

"I'm well aware."

My eye twitches. I slowly walk closer until I'm at the edge of the fountain, and I glance over to the pile of hot pink clothes on the ledge. *Such an assaulting color, just like her personality.*

"Well, I'll leave you to your *fun*," I say quickly, glaring at her before turning around.

"Isn't there anything you want to do before you..." she trails off. "Some big adventure, or something simple like getting a tattoo?"

I spin back around to face her. "Oh, so we're getting deep now? Alright. The answer is yes, of course there are still things I want to do. And how do you know I don't already have a tattoo?"

She laughs again, pulling her hair out of her bun and dipping it into the water so that it floats behind her. "Do you?"

Before I can bark a response, she stands, exposing her top half.

I immediately avert my eyes and listen to her wet footsteps as she heads toward her clothes. I sneak a quick glance a few seconds later. Her back is to me, clad only in high-cut underwear. I begin to salivate as I take in her round ass, her strong thighs...

My lips part as she slides the tank top over her head and down her torso. As she busies herself fixing the fabric, I have time to take in the backs of her thighs, her hourglass shape, and the way her wet hair sticks to her straight spine. I look away again.

"Thank you for being a gentleman," she says a minute later, and I snap my eyes up to hers. She's grinning as she slides her feet into the sandals laying by the edge of the fountain, fully clothed in pink sweatpants.

"A warning would've been nice," I grit out. *But I don't regret it.*

"And miss seeing that expression on your face?" she teases, tying a matching pink zip up sweatshirt around her waist. Her hair is still dripping, creating wet spots on her white tank top. The water makes the material transparent, and I get a brief glimpse of pert, little nipples before she crosses her arms over her chest.

Well, fuck me.

"What expression?" I ask, keeping my tone serious.

She giggles. "That one."

I frown. "I have no idea what you're talking about."

This makes her laugh more. "God, you really are anal-retentive, aren't you?"

Letting out a frustrated breath, I shake my head before rubbing the back of my neck. "Compared to what? You? I'm sorry but I'm not about to strip down and show off my cock to random strangers."

I'd never let random strangers ogle me.

That same flurry of resentment twists through me at the thought. Even if I wanted to be carefree, I couldn't.

She grabs her purse and walks over to me. I take a step back as she approaches, but then I stop moving as she gets closer. When she's a few feet away, my eyes rove over her face, spying a small beauty mark on her left cheek. Her high cheekbones are glowing in the light of the Eiffel Tower, and the corners of her mouth are turned upward. I try not to notice her delicious, peach-shaped ass and the way her sweatpants cinch at her waist, accentuating her curves. Her wet hair is curling around her hairline, the color so blonde it's nearly white.

"You didn't answer my question," she asks, her eyes studying my face. I'm not sure I like being scrutinized by her. "*Do* you have any tattoos?"

I shake my head. "No."

"Not surprising," she breathes, almost wistfully. "Why mar that perfect body with ink," she adds, teasing.

How ironic. I'm already marred.

My jaw ticks. I should just walk away. She's a nobody. Just a random stranger.

I cock my head. "You're a hypocrite, you know."

Something defiant sparks behind her eyes. "Oh really? How so?"

I don't particularly enjoy the fact that I always have to be right. I've learned to read people over the years. In my line of work, I need to be able to sense when someone is uncomfortable. I'm not proud of the fact that I use it to my advantage. I am cunning, and I know exactly what to say and how to word it. Others might see me as manipulative. But I consider myself *driven*.

And in this case, it's clear that this woman is hiding something. I'm not sure what, but I intend to find out.

"You're here at three in the morning when the Jardin is empty. If you really wanted to make an impact, you'd be here at noon on a Saturday," I finish smugly.

"I'm not here to make a statement," she retorts. "I'm here for me."

I step closer, and I see the way she inhales sharply at my close proximity. The ball is in my court again, where it belongs.

"And what reason could you possibly have?"

She swallows, and I watch the way her throat bobs. I probably shouldn't be scrutinizing her so harshly. But her words got under my skin. I like to think I'm above the bullshit of stereotypes. That I'm *different*. That I don't care about inferior things.

But she's catalogued me so easily.

"Go on, then," I say, my jaw tight.

Her shoulders lower slightly. "It's just something I wanted to check off of a list," she says simply.

The zest is gone, and suddenly, her body language is all different than before. Physically deflated.

And *fuck*. It makes me feel... guilty. Like I owe her an apology.

But I don't owe her a damn thing.

"Well, I should go," she says quickly, looking at me. "Enjoy the rest of your stay in Paris. Hopefully it will be less eventful for your buttoned-up persona. Wouldn't want you to spontaneously combust, after all."

I open and close my mouth. *The audacity—*

"Doubtful," I retort. "I loathe Paris."

Now she's looking at me like I murdered a brood of puppies.

"Bloody hell. Are you telling me there's a person in existence who loathes *Paris*? How is that possible?" she asks, astonished.

I let out a cruel laugh. "Bad memories. It was my mother's favorite city, but my mother isn't alive anymore, so it's not like I can share it with her. And my father..." I snap my mouth shut. *Why the hell am I telling her all of this?*

She's quiet, and when I look back at her, she's still staring at me like she's trying to figure me out. Her nose is slightly wrinkled, and her eyes are narrowed and disbelieving as they search my face.

"I can't believe you just said you hate Paris," she mutters.

My lips twitch. "Yes, well, we can't all be romantics."

She scoffs. "I'm far from a romantic. But the culture, the history, the people..."

"The culture is a marketing tactic by the French tourism board, the history is appealing, sure—but so is most of Europe—and the people are, as a whole, very rude," I conclude, watching her face fall even further.

"Bollocks," she utters, shaking her head. "Are you always so surly?"

I scowl down at her. "I'm not surly."

She hollows her cheeks. "Whatever you say."

"You don't know me."

Walk away, Miles. The bright, shiny toy is not worth it.

Crossing her arms, she arches a brow. "You're wearing a Prada suit, Dior loafers, and your Cartier watch is obnoxiously expensive. I may not know you, but I know your type."

I bite my tongue as I look down at my cufflinks, adjusting them to give myself a chance to retort. It takes a lot to ruffle my feathers, but when they're ruffled ...

"Do you often make assumptions about people you've just met?" I ask, my voice frosty.

She doesn't cower or falter. Instead, she stands up straighter and glares right at me.

"Was I wrong?" she counters, glancing down at her painted nails as if she's bored. *Jesus, even her nails are bright fucking pink.* "I happen to know a lot of blokes like you. London is full of them."

I huff a laugh and shake my head. "You're ridiculous." Rubbing my neck, I glower down at her. "I hate to break it to you, but I'm probably worse than the men you know." Her eyes widen slightly, and I enjoy the way she physically shrinks a bit at my words. "You seem to have me all figured out. So, tell me, who are you?" I ask, tilting my head.

She gives me that unsure look again. The one that makes me feel irrationally angry at myself for making her uncomfortable.

Fuck, what am I doing? Starting a fight with some woman in the middle of the night?

Just as I open my mouth to apologize, an older man walks up to us with an armful of bracelets to sell.

"No, thank you," I tell him, grabbing the blonde's arm and dragging her to the other side of the fountain.

"He probably saw your fancy watch from a mile away," she says, laughing once we stop walking.

I clench my jaw when I stare down at her. "Right. And I'm sure he hardly noticed the naked woman," I deadpan.

That shuts her up.

"When do you leave Paris?" she asks. Her wide, curious blue eyes find mine. There's something hopeful in them. And *fuck me,* the irritation melts away.

"Tomorrow. Or, later today, I suppose. I've been here two days too many."

Her lips press together into a playful pout. "No wonder you don't like Paris. You've hardly been here long enough to appreciate it."

"I've been to Paris plenty of times, and I always prefer to leave as soon as possible."

She makes a noise that sounds halfway between indignance and annoyance. "Well, it seems I can't convince you otherwise." Her eyes are twinkling as she looks back up at me. "Have a safe flight home."

I bite the inside of my cheek as she turns and walks away. But some small, dead part of me wishes to continue arguing with her. My trips to Paris are depressing and uneventful, and for whatever reason, I've enjoyed the banter between us.

Fuck, maybe I need more friends.

I speak before I can think. "Convince me? You

haven't convinced me of anything except how *not* to engage with the naked woman in the fountain."

I see her stiffen a few feet away. She spins around, smiling.

It's like she smiles with her whole body. Open, accessible, lively.

She's the complete opposite of me—but for some reason, I can't ignore the magnetic pull between us.

"Oh, look who's being cheeky," she says, crossing her arms. "Truthfully, I didn't think you had it in you with that stick shoved so far up your arse."

I chuckle, feeling the tension of my whole body relax at her words. At our stupid argument. That familiar, hungry tug in my navel makes me take a step forward. And then another. I take in her posture—her narrow waist and wide hips. Her slender neck. Her pillowy lips. Her hair that's starting to dry in loose ringlets and how her curls are twisted and crinkled across her forehead. She is delicate and ethereal. *Something* about her plucks some chord inside of me, and I scrutinize her face harder.

I don't know her, but I can't stop the curiosity eating at me. I can't stop engaging. It's like Icarus and the sun.

Maybe this could be a fun fling.

One night of revelry before I go home.

Like I said before, she's not my type, but a small part of me wants to prove her wrong.

I can be fun. I *know* how to have fun.

I just don't have time for fun. But here? Now?

Why not?

I can show her a good time.

If she'll have me, that is.

My lips tug into the cocky smirk—the same one I can weaponize so easily when I want to—and I take a step closer.

"Convince me, then," I murmur, holding my hands out in front of me as a show of my surrender. "If you had half a day in Paris, what would you do?"

She seems a bit unsure as I move closer—so close that I could reach out and touch her face. But instead of retreating, she takes a tiny step into me.

"I'd spend the day wandering around Île Saint-Louis. It's a neighborhood on a small island in the middle of the Seine. I'd grab some ice cream at Berthillon, and I would just sit on a bench and soak it all up." She has a far off look on her face as she spouts off her favorite things to do.

"You'd sit and eat ice cream?" I ask skeptically. "You wouldn't go anywhere else?"

She shrugs, and her face loses its brightness for a second as she pulls her lower lip between her teeth.

"I don't *go* places in Paris. I let Paris come to me."

I roll my eyes. "Really? Ice cream?"

She arches a blonde brow. "Have you tried it?"

"No, but—"

"Then you can't form a proper opinion, can you?"

Being this close to her, I can smell her perfume. It's light. Classic. A hint of jasmine.

I'm surprised she doesn't smell like a swamp monster.

Still, if I'm going to win her over, I need to be nicer.

Cocking my head slightly, I let my eyes bore into hers. I'm not as cocky as Chase, but I've also never been rejected. I know that objectively, I am good looking, and I can smooth-talk my way into and out of any situation. I'm particular about my sexual partners and the things I like to do in bed, which means I don't sleep around much. But, when I decide I want someone—for whatever purpose—I make it happen with whatever I have at my disposal.

Which is why I take a small step forward. Her chest rises and falls rapidly, and a lovely scarlet flush spreads across her cheeks and chest. Licking her lips, her eyes grow slightly darker when I look down at her.

"If wandering around Île Saint-Louis is your favorite thing to do, will I be seeing you there later today?" I ask, smirking. "Or, perhaps, you'd like to come back to my apartment to dry off?" I add boldly.

Her pupils darken. "I'd like that," she says slowly, tilting her head slightly as she smiles up at me.

And fuck me, because that smile might be the death of me.

I reach out for her elbow and pull her to the street. "My driver is off tonight, but I can call us a taxi," I tell her, feeling impatient and frenzied.

Arguing with her was ... exhilarating.

I can only imagine what she's like in bed, and my cock throbs when I think about bending her over and showing her just how *spontaneous* I can be.

We both walk to the avenue in silence, but every time I look over at her, her bottom lip is between her teeth, and her eyes are bright with anticipation, like we're both being driven by the same sense of urgency. And every time our eyes meet, the pull becomes stronger.

This is either the dumbest or best thing I've ever done.

When we get to Av. des Nations Unies, I flag down the first taxi that I see. As soon as it pulls to the curb, I open the door and gesture for her to climb inside first.

Brushing against the side of my body as she gets in, her eyes meet mine for a split second. My cock stirs at her hooded eyelids and those red lips. Everything inside of me pulsates, and there's something undeniably alluring about the way she's watching me.

I tell the driver the address of my apartment quickly as I climb in behind her. I'm barely seated before she climbs on top of me, wrapping her legs around my hips and straddling me. My arms encircle her automatically, and before I can speak, she kisses me.

I groan as I buck up into her, my hands squeezing her thighs and moving her against me. Her soft curves mold to the contours of my body, and I reach up into her damp curls, fisting a handful. She's kissing me with a hunger I can't quite place. Not that I care. I move my mouth against hers, tongue searching as I devour her soft lips.

"Pas dans le taxi!" the driver says loudly.

We both ignore him as her hands come to the placket of my suit pants, bypassing my shirt and jacket completely.

Good girl.

I let her unbuckle my belt, thrusting against her

small hands. My cock is straining against my boxers, and the only thing I care about right now is tasting her, feeling her, driving her onto my shaft—

"Ceci est votre dernier avertissement!" the driver warns.

She sighs with pleasure, and I wonder if the driver is going to physically kick us out, or if he's spewing empty threats. Because I can't seem to tear my lips away from hers—can't seem to find any fucks left to give.

I let out a low chuckle when I think of how I've never been in the position of *being watched.*

Normally, I'm the one watching.

"Fuck," she whispers, her breath shaky. Her hands fumble with the zipper of my pants. "I can't wait," she says breathlessly.

Lightning bolts of excitement flash through me. I don't think I've ever had someone so enthusiastic to be with me, and it turns me the fuck on.

"You want me to fuck you here?" I mumble, my lips wandering to her jaw and sucking the soft flesh into my mouth, tasting her.

"Yes," she whispers.

She tastes like heaven and hell, a nectar all my own, like it was made for me.

A soft whimper escapes her lips as her hands pull at my zipper.

I throw my head back in ecstasy, but she grabs me and pulls me to her lips for another kiss. My hands find the band of her sweatpants at the same time her hand reaches into my suit pants. Breathing heavily, I wait for her to pull my cock out, not caring that we're in public.

Not caring about anything but being inside of her.

But instead of tugging my cock free, she pulls away from my lips as her eyes flick between mine, as if asking permission.

"Yes, fuck yes," I tell her impatiently.

Giving me a sly smile, her hand comes to my chest, and I go still under her touch. I don't realize her intentions until it's too late—until her little fingers are unbuttoning the collar of my shirt.

No, no, no.

My hand flies up to grab her wrist, intending to wrench it away, but at that exact moment, the taxi lurches to a stop.

"Sortez! Sortez!" the taxi driver yells, and the lights come on inside the cab.

In slow motion, her bright eyes rove over my face, and then, to my horror, they land on the bit of scar tissue visible above my shirt collar, trailing the thick, jagged line to my jaw. It probably wasn't visible by the fountain, but in the stark, artificial light, I'm sure it stands out.

Shock—or probably revulsion, more likely—is evident in her delicate features.

I reach over for the handle of the door, wrenching the door open and pushing her off me a little too roughly. She stumbles out of the cab before me. I throw forty euros at the driver, and he looks up at me in surprise just before I slam the door.

When I stand up and the taxi speeds off, my eyes

find hers. In the darkness of the street, she looks so small and vulnerable. Gone is the playful, bright light behind them. Her arms are crossed, and she's looking down at her feet.

Like she's *ashamed.*

"I'll hail you another taxi," I say gruffly, my eyes flicking up to the street.

"Okay, thanks." She clears her throat and takes a step back, some kind of unreadable expression passing over her face. Bowing her head, she keeps her eyes on the ground as shame fills me, turning my skin hot and fiery with humiliation. "I'm sorry if I came on too strong," she adds. "I'm not far from here. I don't mind walking."

When she looks up at me, her expression is ... different. Closed off. *Sad.* With furrowed brows, she takes another step back, her eyes glancing once again at my scars. That tug gets stronger the further away she gets —like I'm being pulled by some invisible string—and *fuck*, it's a shitty feeling knowing that she's repulsed by me.

She wouldn't be the first.

I'm just about to snap back with something cruel and rude—something about how stupid it would be to walk home alone this late—when she takes another step away and opens her mouth.

"If you do go to Berthillon, get the caramel-ginger."

And with that, she turns around and walks away, leaving me feeling wholly unsatisfied and entirely dejected for the first time in my life.

CHAPTER ONE
THE RUNAWAY

STELLA

Present – One Year Later

I straighten my royal blue blazer over my baby blue dress, running my fingers through my curls before entering the restaurant. I feel sweaty and gross thanks to the humidity, and I'm regretting my choice of heeled footwear as I pull the gold door open. The restaurant's name is Papillon, which means butterfly in French, and I can't help but wrinkle my nose as I walk inside. Why had my father chosen this place? It's full of arseholes with too much money. Still, I'll be glad to see him. It's been months since I've been back to Paris, and though he's only a train ride away from London, I don't see him nearly enough.

I glance around the crowded restaurant as I approach the hostess stand.

"Can I help you?" the employee asks politely, and I give her my best smile.

"Je rencontre mon père. Il s'appelle Prescott Deveraux," I tell her in perfect French, wondering if my father is already seated.

"Ah, right this way," she responds in accented English.

I follow her through the bright and airy dining room, feeling completely out of place in my bright ensemble. Everyone here—every single person—is wearing a business suit. Even the women. Grays, dark browns, and black ... My tall heels are causing my feet to ache, and I can't wait to sit down. The hostess stops in front of a table with four chairs, and my eyes flick up to the single man already seated. I stare at him in confusion.

"Non, ce n'est pas la bonne table," I tell her quickly, explaining that this isn't my table.

"Stella Deveraux?" the man asks, standing up. "Your father invited us to lunch today. I hope that's all right."

I glance at the man in surprise. Something about him is vaguely familiar, like I've seen his face somewhere before. His black hair is tied back into a low ponytail, and despite being older, he's very handsome. His accent is American.

"I'm Charles Ravage. Your father and I have become friends over the last couple of years," he adds, holding his hand out.

I shake it firmly as I plaster on a smile. "Nice to meet you, Charles," I say politely, tamping down the disappointment swirling in my gut. I'd been looking forward to a long lunch with my father, catching up, telling him about my business plans ...

Another man comes to stand next to him, and my eyes dart over to the stranger.

Except ... he's not a stranger. Not at all.

A low, pleasant hum works through me as I make eye contact with the man from the fountain last year. The aggravatingly good-looking one with a piss poor personality.

The one I—*unfortunately for me*—haven't stopped thinking about since we snogged like crazy in the taxi.

He looks exactly the same. Tall, with broad shoulders. A square jaw accented with day-old stubble, a long, straight nose, and the most intense green eyes I've ever seen. His dark brown hair is short on the sides, but the top is neatly styled to be modern and sophisticated. There's not a strand out of place, in fact, and his straight, intense brows only pull closer together as he scrutinizes me. He's wearing a double-breasted Gucci suit with a subtle checkered pattern, and my eyes catch on that same Cartier watch he was wearing last year. I can't deny that the man has good style.

He notices me watching him, and he raises one brow conspiratorially.

God. It should really be illegal for a person to look this good.

Out of the corner of my eye, I see Charles mutter something to him, and it takes me a second to realize that Fountain Man will be joining us for lunch. I turn to face him fully just as Charles introduces us.

"Stella, this is my son, Miles Ravage," he says smoothly. "Miles, this is Estelle Deveraux. Her father, Prescott Deveraux, has become a dear friend and client of mine."

My eyes flick to Miles again, and I hate that my stomach does a little flip as we make eye contact. He holds his hand out, and I take it. His skin is warm, the pads of his fingers rough for someone who probably spends all day behind a desk.

God, I remember how those hands felt on my back, my thighs, running against my lower stomach before diving below the band of my joggers—

He grips my hand tightly, so I do the same. Something akin to surprise flashes across his features at my firm handshake. *Ha.*

"So nice to meet you," I say sweetly.

"The pleasure is all mine, Estelle," he replies smoothly, not mentioning that we've met before.

Thank god.

"It's Stella."

"Of course," he says, tipping his head in apology before gesturing that I sit down beside him.

Fucking great.

I smooth my dress, cross my ankles, and place my hands in my lap. *Someone needs to swoop in and unalive me.* Not only did I humiliate myself last year by jumping his bones like a mad woman, but now I'm sitting here with his father. I close my eyes when I think of the way he murmured dirty things into my ear in the back of that taxi. The hard, thick length I wrapped my fingers around briefly over his pants.

Fuck.

I never expected to see him again. And by the way he's looking at me with a glowering, accusatory stare ... I'm guessing he never expected to see me again, either.

"So, Stella," Charles starts, sitting across from me. "Your father says you are starting your own fashion line?"

The busser walks over and pours us all some water. I take a sip before setting the glass on the table.

"Yes. Well, in a few years, that is. It's quite an endeavor, and requires a fair bit of startup money," I explain.

"I see." Something about the way he says those two words makes me uncomfortable, but I brush it off. Just as I'm about to ask him what he's doing for my father, he lights up as his eyes catch on something across the restaurant. "Ah, here's the man of the hour."

I follow his gaze to see my father strutting through the restaurant. He's dressed in a white button-down and dark jeans. His silver hair is slicked back, and his face seems slightly more weathered than the last time I saw him. When I stand, he walks straight to me and kisses me on both cheeks.

"Darling, I'm sorry I was late," he tells me, his half-British, half-French accent low and deep. "You look beautiful. Is this one of your pieces?" he asks, touching the sleeve of my blazer.

"It is. Thank you for noticing." He beams down at

me before greeting Charles and Miles with a friendly hello. I take note that he addresses Miles with some familiarity. They must've met before.

"Ma chérie, Charles Ravage has been helping me with my investments," he says brightly.

"Well, your portfolio is certainly impressive," Charles says.

When I look over at Miles, he's glaring at his father. "Is that so?" he asks, his voice hard and icy.

My brows knit together as I observe the three men and their dynamics. It almost seems like Miles is angry about his father helping mine. But why?

"Yes," Charles says, sipping his water and giving Miles a hard look. Before the two of them can say another word, my father interjects.

"I'm so glad we could all have lunch today," he says jovially. But then again, my father is always jovial.

As the founder of one of the biggest charities in Europe, he's had his fair share of hardships. After my mother died giving birth to me, he made a name for himself as a philanthropist. We weren't rich—in fact, until a few years ago, we had almost no money. My father had insisted we didn't need much to live on. I grew up working in soup kitchens all over Europe, residing in London and going to a normal school. No nannies, no household help. Just a two-bedroom flat and lots of beans on toast.

But because of his work, *Deveraux* became something of a household name. He was featured in all the big publications as someone who would change the world for the better—which of course, led to more notoriety and more introductions to people like Charles Ravage, apparently. My father believed these connections would bring more money to his charities, which is exactly what happened. Once big names got to know him—once he got into the same room with some of the most powerful people in the world—he began receiving large donations simply due to his wit and charm.

Most of that money was tied up in the charity, but my father gave himself a bigger salary—for the first time—as well as the rest of his employees. Instead of giving most of his salary away to the charity, like he'd done for decades, he was finally able to set some aside for himself.

So while we didn't have a ton of money to our name, we had enough to be comfortable. I'm not surprised that Charles is helping him manage his newfound success. After all, my father doesn't even know how to write a check, and all the charities had massive influxes of donations over the last couple of years. His net worth is sizable now, and I'm glad he has someone helping him with everything.

After another tense look from Miles, the conversation flows easily. Every couple of minutes, I sneak a glance at the man to my right, and every time, his eyes are on me.

Accusatory, stormy, dark.

I caught a glimpse of his surliness last year, but right now, he looks as though he's about to shatter the glass in his hand.

I order a goat cheese salad, and Miles orders a

medium rare steak. Our fathers get the lobster. I eat quickly, and the tension grows thicker with each minute as our fathers chat about their recent holidays. My father now resides in Paris, where he was born, though I grew up in London, where my mother was from. I like having that connection to her. And I know my father enjoyed it when I was young, too. It's what she would've wanted.

They were married for ten years before having me, and after her death, he never remarried, despite my encouragement.

She was the love of his life.

Maybe I'll be lucky enough to find that kind of love someday.

A couple of minutes later, Miles leans in a couple of inches and begins to speak.

"Go skinny dipping in any fountains lately?" he asks, wiping his mouth and frowning over at me.

"Not lately, no. I'm too afraid of being hassled by grumpy businessmen."

"Ah. Well, if it makes you feel any better, I haven't been wandering around Paris in the middle of the night. Too afraid of being affronted by exasperating naked women."

Is he insulting me? Or flirting with me?

With him, it's hard to tell.

"Well, it's a good thing you left when you did, then. I've heard Paris is full of women like me. I wouldn't want you to get your knickers in a twist and grow to hate this city more than you already do."

Something akin to surprise flashes across his

features. His eyes glitter as he assesses me. "You know, you have to be one of the most interesting women I've ever met, Estelle."

"Stella," I remind him. "And thank you. I abhor boring people. Case in point," I add, glaring at him.

"I never said *interesting* was a compliment," he murmurs.

I shrug. "Better to be *interesting* than boring, in my eyes."

He laughs quickly, but then his mouth closes tightly. He looks almost vulnerable when he utters his next sentence.

"I suppose being interesting is a privilege. Some of us must fly under the radar however we can."

"Well, maybe it'll make you feel better if I tell you that I don't actually think you're boring. You just want people to think you are."

He arches a brow as he stabs a piece of steak, chewing it slowly as he digests my words. I study the way his jaw muscles ripple when he chews. The way his mouth moves. The way his long fingers grip the fork and knife firmly. The image of Miles Ravage eating is highly erotic.

Oh, for fuck's sake. What is wrong with me?

I wait for him to respond. I don't like this game of mental football we've been playing. It makes me feel ill at ease. I pride myself on knowing *who* I am and what I stand for, and most certainly how to deal with men. I had to learn at a young age how to brush off snarky comments, how to deal with a male-centered world, and how to find my own unique strengths. I'm no stranger to men taunting me, and most of the time, I'm able to remain clear-headed.

Quick-witted.

That's what my father liked to call me. Being a curvy, plus-size woman meant I'd spent my twenties learning how to gain people's respect. Since most people didn't respect young, ambitious women—especially women with bodies that didn't fit into society's idea of acceptable—I had to teach myself ways to even the playing field. That meant learning how to call people out on their bullshit.

It was especially important lately, with people so interested in our family and what we were doing. I couldn't take anything personally, so I'd built up a thick skin.

But for whatever reason, being around Miles feels sort of like my head is buried in sand. All the witty remarks I'm normally so good at get lost somewhere between my brain and my tongue. The barbs and jabs that usually come easily fall to the wayside the second I stare into his bright, green eyes.

Why is that?

My whole body tingles when I think of how it felt to be pressed against his body in that taxi. How his hands ran down my thighs, reaching under my shirt and brushing my skin with his fingers. How it felt like my spine was being electrocuted. How *hard* he was underneath my hand, like he wanted me just as much as I wanted him.

I close my eyes briefly, thinking of the harsh way he

pushed me off of him—the stoic look on his face when the taxi sped off.

It was a total brush off.

When Miles is done chewing, he hums. "I see. It seems you've spent some time condensing me into a perfect, little box. What else have you observed about me?" he murmurs, his voice gravelly.

My cheeks heat. *So. Many. Things.*

"I can read people easily, that's all," I explain, dabbing my lips with my serviette.

His eyes narrow slightly as he stares at me. "And I can read people easily as well, Estelle."

"Please, call me Stella."

Cocking his head, he places his fork and knife on his plate as he looks me over. My skin erupts in goosebumps as they peruse over my neck, chest, down to my lap, and back up to my face.

"Why does your real name bother you so much?" I open my mouth to retort, suddenly feeling hot and flushed. *It's not the name. It's who used to call me that name.* But before I can reply, he lets out a low laugh. "It's a beautiful name. Did you know it means 'star' in Latin?"

Something dark and dangerous swoops low in my stomach at his words, and I can't look away from him.

He stares right back at me, daring me to look away with his cocky smirk. He knows he's unnerved me, and I take a slow, steady breath to orient myself. I've never met anyone like him—witty, quick, able to match my banter. I never get what I put out, but somehow, I suspect I've met my match in Miles Ravage.

His eyes darken slightly as they rove down to my mouth, and before I can register what he's doing, he's leaning forward and gripping my chin with his hand. I suck in a sharp breath as his thumb comes to rest on my lower lip.

"You have something on your lip ..." he trails off, and my eyes flutter as he swipes the rough pad of his thumb against the corner of my mouth.

Everything feels hot—and my whole body goes taut as his eyes flick between mine, as he stays there for just a second too long.

You want me to fuck you here?

My eyes briefly close when I remember what he said to me last year—how *hot* I'd gotten imagining myself riding him in the back of a taxi where anyone could see us.

It isn't until my father brings up my grandmother that I snap out of my haze. I'd completely forgotten that my father and Charles were having their own conversation on the other side of the table. I pull away from Miles and take a steadying breath.

"My mother passed away last year. My poor Stella took a lot of time to recover after her death. They were very close, you see. But now she's starting her own fashion line," he says proudly.

I smile as I lift a piece of cheese to my mouth, feeling flustered at my father's outright praise. Out of the corner of my eye, I see Miles watching me. Before I can respond, Charles laughs.

"And that's why we're having lunch today. To propose a solution to your unusual financial situation."

The table goes quiet, and I look over at my father. He's always so forthcoming. While I know he's working with Charles, I don't need Miles to know all about the struggles I've been facing as an up-and-coming fashion designer—namely, that I'm broke. And, that I'm barely surviving thanks to the very small amount of orders I get every month.

God, how humiliating.

"Father," Miles says, his tone a low warning. I can almost feel the fury radiating off him. "Please tell me this isn't what I think it is."

I glance between the Ravage men, confused. "And what exactly do you think this is?" I ask carefully.

Miles doesn't look at me. Instead, he's glaring at his father—his jaw tight, and his eyes bright with fury. My eyes flick down to the silvery, jagged lines on his skin underneath the collar of his buttoned shirt. The uneven scar runs up to nearly the left side of his jaw, giving him a distinguished look. They make me want to know *more* about him. Just before I turn away, he snaps his reptilian green eyes to mine, widening when they realize I'm staring at his neck.

If I'm not mistaken, something akin to shame passes over his features as his long fingers tug his collar up and over his scars.

"I'm not doing this," he says quickly, shooting a death glare at his father before glowering at me next.

"Will someone please explain what's going on?" I ask, my voice a little bit too loud. A few people turn to face us, and my cheeks heat.

Miles closes his eyes briefly. He places his palms flat on the table and he cocks his head at me.

Before he can speak, my father takes my hand from across from me. "Stella, darling," he says gently. "I'm only trying to help you."

I swallow. "Help me with what?"

He looks at Charles before continuing. "A couple of months ago, I'd mentioned your clothing line to Charles during a business meeting," he starts. "And I told him all about how you're struggling to make it happen financially," he says slowly.

God, kill me now.

A sinking feeling settles in my stomach and my brows pull together. "And?"

"Stella," Charles interjects, leaning forward.

"Father," Miles warns.

"Miles is a prominent businessman in California," Charles starts. "He is ... currently in need of a public relations miracle."

"Apologies for being daft, but I'm not quite sure what this has to do with me," I say.

My father clears his throat. "You need money. Miles needs someone to repair his public image. I wasn't sure at first, but I've met Miles a few times, and he's a perfect gentleman. I couldn't think of anyone better to help you." He must notice my confused expression, because he leans closer. "You know if my money wasn't tied up in the charity, I'd help you in a heartbeat, ma chérie."

I look between the three of them. "Someone to repair his public image? And how would I do that?"

"By marrying Miles, of course," Charles finishes, a pleased expression written all over his face.

The room spins before me and I grip the table firmly, turning to Miles. He's rubbing his chin and watching me—like he already knows.

Like he already suspected.

"Did you know?" I ask him.

He sighs and shrugs once. "I suspected. My father has been pressuring me to find someone to marry for months."

"I'm sorry," I say slowly, trying to come to terms with it all. "Which century are we living in again?"

"Darling," my father coos. "Think about it. It's just one year. Charles has agreed to front you the liquid cash in exchange for a few public outings with Miles as his wife—on paper only, of course. A million dollars, ma chérie. Think of what you could do with that money? Think of how quickly you could get your brand up and running?"

I open and close my mouth. A *million* dollars?

It certainly would change my career. I could start my clothing line with little to no risk. I could hire the expensive, ethical manufacturers. I could import the most eco-friendly textiles. I could source local artisans and make the brand everything I ever dreamed it would be.

While I may not have an MBA, I know that kind of money would solve a lot of my problems. I've ran the numbers. I have a ten-year plan but it's a plan that only exists *if and when* I'm able to save enough money to get to that point. However, with a million dollars in liquid cash I wouldn't need to wait ten years.

With my current plan, I'd need the money *before* I began production to safeguard from going under. I'd need employees and marketing campaigns before I had money from sales. None of that is cheap. And, it just so happens to be something I care deeply about. Something I am *itching* to do now. Not in ten years. I have a fresh take on affordable and accessible clothing that's good for the environment—something people can use *now*. I have so many aspirations, and all of them cost money. A *lot* of money.

It's something my grandmother *begged* me to do. The one dream she wanted me to follow. With Charles's money, I could do it. Her death sent me into a tailspin of darkness I'm only just now recovering from. Imagine how great it would feel to be able to *follow* through with it? To be able to live my dream, doing what I loved, *for her?*

To help people now instead of in ten or more years?

My eyes rove over to Miles. Who *is* the Ravage family? The name is familiar, but they must be extremely wealthy to be able to lend a client's daughter a million dollars.

And for what ... a fake wife? Miles is certainly attractive. Surely, he could find someone better suited to him.

Why me?

Sitting up straighter, I look between the three men.

Of course. Leave it to them to decide my future.

"No," I say simply. "I'm sorry, but I refuse to marry

a complete stranger for money, even if the money would be nice."

"Ma chérie," my father murmurs. "Please, think about it—"

"What can I do to get you to accept the terms?" Charles asks gently.

I see Miles go still in my peripheral vision. I look back at my father and put on my business hat.

"And what, exactly, are the terms?"

Charles clears his throat. "One year. You will live with Miles in his home, and you will accompany him to all events for the year. At the end of it all, you will divorce amicably, and you will both be better for it. You will have the money for your clothing line, and Miles will benefit from your family's superior reputation. You can't deny that everyone loves the Deveraux family."

He's right.

I hate that he's right.

People have been fascinated with us ever since my father hit the *Forbes* "Top 100 Most Philanthropic People" list. Not a celebrity, but someone that the public admired. With that admiration came a sort of fascination with *me*. I'd never seen a paparazzi camera until last year. While there were some hurtful and unflattering articles published about me, for the most part, people were curious about me. Not curious enough to buy the clothes I had up for sale, but ... with the Ravage name behind me, maybe I could get enough of a backing. Surely, he had connections.

But no.

Fuck no.

This is crazy.

"Your name would give the Ravage family legitimacy," Charles says, his voice tinged with sadness.

"Which is funny, considering you're the reason we need legitimacy," Miles growls from next to me.

"Do we have a say in this?" I ask, my voice wobbling a bit. "I already said no, and yet we're still talking about it." My father opens his mouth to speak, but I continue. "I can't believe I have to defend myself on this, papa."

"I'm sorry, ma chérie. Of course Charles and I aren't going to force anything. This isn't an arranged marriage. We're simply ... nudging you together. Conveniently. It's just an idea."

Miles scoffs from next to me. "It's not an arranged marriage?" he asks my father. "Except that you're dangling a million dollars in front of her." My heart skips a beat at the way he's defending me. He looks at me, his expression hard. Resolute. His hand comes to his collar again as he pulls it up over his scars.

He quickly turns to face Charles. "I don't want to marry her," he hisses.

I know I feel the same way, but ouch.

"I gave you time to find someone on your own, and you failed," Charles says to Miles, his voice even but menacing. "This is a pressing matter. Your business depends on it. I know people have been turning down the opportunity to meet with you. And not to mention the article in the *LA Weekly*—"

"I know," Miles says, voice strong. "And I asked for

more time to secure someone. I did not ask to be pressured into something neither of us wants," he adds.

"We don't have all the time in the world, Miles. Every weekend, another article is printed about our family. Between you, Chase, and Orion, I'm turning down calls from reporters every single day."

"Yes, well, Chase is spoken for," he says quickly. "He has Juliet now."

"Not until there are wedding bells." He gives Miles a withering look. "Orion is a lost cause. He's young. Maybe he'll come around, maybe he won't. Liam and Malakai are smart enough to stay hidden away—"

"Sort of like you?" Miles interjects.

"What's the big deal?" Charles asks. "A year is nothing."

"Actually, it is a big deal." Miles sighs and crosses his arms, looking at me again. There's something so heated and fractured in his expression. It makes the contents of my stomach turn to lead.

I sit up straight and my face flushes with embarrassment. Miles isn't just mad—he's *furious* at the prospect of marrying me. I mean, of course it's a completely silly idea, but he's acting as if this is the worst thing that could ever happen to him.

I've had enough. I'll let them fight amongst themselves, because I refuse to be a bargaining chip. And I refuse to watch Miles and his father dangle my clothing line on a string. It's the one thing I have—the *one* dream I refuse to ever give up on.

"Excuse me," I say quickly before grabbing my purse.

But just as I move to stand, Miles pushes up from his chair and walks away, muttering something about using the restroom.

Good. The last thing I need is for him to see the way my face is beginning to crumple, the way my chest aches when I think of my father marrying me off like a lamb sent to slaughter. I don't know whether to laugh or cry —it feels like a joke. This is the twenty-first century.

"Ma chérie," my father mutters.

I glare at him. "Give me a moment, papa," I say quickly, closing my eyes and trying to recalibrate my breathing as I sit back down.

Inhale, exhale, inhale, exhale ...

I hear Charles and my father talk softly amongst themselves, but the only thing going through my mind is what Miles said just a moment ago, repeating in a loop.

I don't want to marry her.

I don't want to marry her.

I don't want to marry her.

Though the money would be nice, I can't, in good conscience, agree to an *arranged* marriage. *God, how embarrassing.* This is all so fucked up. I know my father is only doing this because he wants me to pursue my dreams. I know he's not made of money, either. It's very kind of Charles to offer, but I can't possibly take the money.

Or can I?

No.

The money is a whole other thing. But I'm not sure

I can face the rejection of Miles Ravage. I can't hear him try to argue his way out of this, even if I agree with him.

I'm not paying attention to anything until my father places a hand on mine.

"Stella," he says gently. "Charles went to go check on Miles. Are you alright?"

I snap my head to look at my father. "Of course I'm not okay. I can't believe ..." I trail off when I see Charles walking back to our table. *Alone.*

"Well, he's not in the bathroom," Charles says, shrugging.

Oh god. Did he climb out of the fucking window or something?

My face flames.

He left.

Charles and my father resume speaking, but my food is threatening to come up my throat as I press the heels of my hands against my eyes.

Inhale, exhale ...

He left me to pick up the pieces.

Fucking bastard.

Charles says something to me about him coming around, about being patient, but I can't be here for another second. I can't listen to my father and Charles Ravage make excuses for what they did—for what *Miles* did.

This is the single most humiliating thing that's ever happened to me.

A burning anger begins to radiate from my chest

outward, so I clutch my purse and stand. I don't hear what my father says, what Charles says.

This whole lunch was completely preposterous, and if I had my say, I'd never have to see Miles Ravage again.

Lifting one foot in front of the other, I make it outside and quickly walk away from Papillon.

CHAPTER TWO
THE LIE

Miles

Setting the paper down, I give Luna a polite smile as she walks over to me holding her iPad. If it weren't for her, I'd never get anything done. I make a mental note to give her another raise soon. She stops in front of me and glances down at the device, looking like she means business. I take a sip of my coffee just as she begins her usual morning debriefing.

"Good morning, Mr. Ravage," she chirps, taking the seat next to me. "You have quite a full day today," she adds, grabbing a piece of melon and popping it into her mouth. "Your nine o'clock cancelled, so I've pushed your ten o'clock to nine-thirty. You and Chase have a meeting with Blue Light at two o'clock. Your three o'clock cancelled, so I can always push your two o'clock back if you'd like."

"Sorry to interrupt," I grumble, sitting up straighter. "*Two* clients cancelled today?"

She presses her lips together. "Well," she says, looking down at her screen. "Technically three of them did. Your five o'clock also cancelled."

I blow a heavy breath out of my lips. "Fuck."

"I've reached out to all three of them but haven't heard back," she offers.

That *fucking LA Weekly* article ...

I nod as my jaw tenses. "It's fine. Thank you, Luna."

"I'm not finished," she adds, arching a brow. "You have a six o'clock with Entice, but I can move it earlier if you'd like."

I wave her off. "No. Keep it. The last thing I want is to scare a fourth person away." She nods and gives me a pitying look. "Don't look at me like that, Luna," I growl, taking another bite of my toast.

"They don't know what they're missing, Miles," she says kindly. "It's their loss."

My toast turns to sawdust in my mouth, and I wipe my lips with my napkin once before standing.

"I appreciate that. Anything else?"

She's looking up at me with her brown eyes as I adjust my tie. "Yes. Your father sent over a flight itinerary for"—she glances down at the clipboard—"Estelle Deveraux?"

I go still, and Luna must take my silence as acceptance, because she clears her throat.

"Shall I send a car to the airport for her?"

Fuck.

"Did he give any indication about why she's visiting Los Angeles?" I ask carefully.

She shakes her head. "No. Just that she's here for business."

Business? What business?

I nod once. "Okay. Please send the car." I may have run out of our lunch last week, but I'm not a complete asshole. Especially when it's *my* father who coordinated the entire lunch last week. Prescott might've thought he was in on it, too, but I know how conniving my father is. "Where is she staying?"

Luna glances down, shuffling through several papers. "It doesn't say."

"Fine. Tell Louis to take her wherever she needs to go. I'm headed into the office. See you later tonight," I tell Luna quickly before I overthink anything.

I catch a mischievous smile sliding across her face as I walk away and out the front door. Knowing I still have plenty of meetings to prepare for, I waste no time in climbing into the black Escalade waiting for me by the gate. It's a twenty minute drive to downtown Crestwood, where the office for Ravage Consulting Firm is located. Niro, my driver, waves once before we head out.

I organize my thoughts for my nine-thirty meeting, ignoring the sense of doom when I think about why I had three cancelled meetings today. I shouldn't be shocked, and yet I am. I'm thirty-six and nowhere near naive enough to think that first impressions don't matter. Rumor mills persist, and unfortunately, they still control public opinion more than anything else.

And yet ... I really wish that weren't the case. It's the twenty-first century. Chase and I have turned RCF into a massively successful business, all on our own. *Despite* our last name.

However, we still hit walls with new companies constantly. The hesitant emails. The last minute cancellations. The wary glances and nervous smiles, like they're waiting for either Chase or I to turn into a viper and steal all their money. No matter how many success stories we have, there are still people who associate RCF with the Ravage family, and everything that happened with our father.

To this day, my father's *one* day in jail before he was bailed out—and the subsequent press coverage of his trials—follows all five of us around like the plague. It clings to the air whenever we introduce ourselves, and it has tarnished a lot of relationships. It also made for great tabloid fodder, as well as harsh opinion pieces, such as the most recent one in *LA Weekly*.

I close my eyes as I recall the scathing article and the headline shared over fifty-thousand times.

"Business Versus Bullying: How Far Is Too Far for Ravage Consulting Firm?"

While my father was formally and legally acquitted of his supposed crimes, no one could ignore all the people —and corporations—that he fucked over with his bad financial advice. Everyone assumed he went into hiding because he was guilty, which only intensified the hatred for the rest of us.

I mean, it's been years, and people are still publishing garbage about us.

Quickly dismissing my thoughts, I focus on my meeting.

Once I'm inside the building, Chase debriefs me as we walk into the main meeting room together. It's a large nonprofit based in Los Angeles. They are growing rapidly after utilizing social media influencers to push their product, which is a secondhand clothing store specializing in plus-size clothing. It's a great concept, and I am confident when I walk into the room to start our spiel.

I'm very apt at sizing people up, and I know almost immediately that these three potential clients aren't going to be signing any sort of contract today. I play with my pen as Chase takes the lead, explaining what we can do for them if they decide to work with us.

What's the fucking point?

I swear, meetings like this are like an adult version of choosing teams in school.

When he's done, one of the women clasps her hands together and sighs. "Thank you both for meeting with us," she says, looking between me and Chase. "Obviously, you've both done your research and your client list is impressive. But I must be honest and tell you that I wasn't sure about having this meeting today."

The two men shuffle uncomfortably, and all three of them murmur quietly amongst themselves.

Chase nods and I stiffen in my seat.

Here we fucking go again.

"I understand your concern," he says calmly, leaning forward in his chair. There's a reason he's usually the one to speak during the meetings. One, because he's the President, but most importantly, he can fake it like no other. Plus, he's charming as fuck. Something I've never been able to perfect.

"But I can assure you that we are very good at what we do. We have the funding sources and the clout—"

The man across from us clears his throat. "I think what Wendy is trying to say is we're meeting with other businesses to secure the funding, and we want to ensure that we have a solid team behind us. To be honest, we were more curious about you than anything, and while your presentation today has been impressive, I don't think we can risk working with you. I'm sorry for wasting your time."

Tale as old as fucking time.

"We've had several offers already, and we're still sorting through everything," the third man says, humoring us a bit more than the others. "If it weren't for the history behind your name, it might be something we'd consider more readily."

I sit up, jaw tight, and Chase gives me a warning look.

"Of course. And may I ask what kind of reputation you *are* looking for? I know what you don't want, but it may be easier to present our case if I know what you are looking for. Maybe we can surprise you."

Wendy gives me a gentle smile. "Well, we'd love to work with someone who has notoriety in the nonprofit sector. A philanthropist. Someone with the backing of Barbara Streisand or Lance Armstrong. Estelle Deveraux is on our board, for example, and she's wonderful," she finishes. "But everyone knows that."

The pen I was fumbling with drops with a heavy thud on the legal pad in front of me.

"Estelle Deveraux?" I ask tentatively.

The man—I believe his name is Garret—nods. "Yes. She's in California this week helping us with a few press events."

Wheels begin to spin in my mind. Wheels that *should not* be spinning. And maybe it's because we've had three cancellations today, or perhaps it's the insinuation that, yet again, our family name is fucked, but an idea forms in my mind.

What-if I can kill two birds with one stone?

The idea is insane. I can't believe I'm about to lie to this extent. I know I can be deceptive and cynical, but this is an entirely different ball game.

However ... I have no other choice. We need these clients. I need for people to start taking me seriously, and working with a non-profit of this size would be huge for our image.

It could make or break the next couple of months for us.

The scheming part of my brain has already made up his mind by the time I open my mouth.

"I see. Well, Estelle Deveraux can be quite captivating," I add, keeping my expression neutral.

Garret narrows his eyes. "You know her personally?"

Chase's eyes are on me when I nod, not bothering to hide the genuine smile that breaks out on my face. "I do. She's my fiancée."

I can practically see the realization hit them. Garret looks over at the other man before turning to Wendy, who is watching me with something akin to admiration.

Their countenance changes completely. Before, their expressions were closed off. But right now, I can practically *feel* their new opinions clicking into place. The looks they share—what it would mean to do business with Estelle's future husband ...

I should hate myself for lying. Really, I should. And I already know Chase is going to reprimand me like no other. But, I don't care.

It feels *fucking* incredible to be wanted.

"I had no idea Stella was engaged," she says slowly, her smile growing. "How wonderful. It seems I owe you a belated congratulations."

I smile and nod my head. "Thank you. It's a very recent development, and we're excited."

When I lean back in my chair, I once again feel the weight of Chase's stare.

"I know I may be out of line speaking for all of us, but ..." Wendy trails off. "We absolutely adore Stella, and anyone associated with the Deveraux family is practically family to us."

That's all it takes.

After a few minutes of pleasantries, they sign the contract. Wendy asks about Estelle, the wedding, the proposal ... it's scary how easily the lies keep coming to me.

Maybe I'm more like my father than I think.

That thought makes my stomach churn.

"It was spur-of-the-moment," I tell them as I walk them to the elevators. "We had lunch in Paris last week, and the next thing I knew, I was down on one knee."

Wendy swoons. "Paris! How romantic. Have you set a date yet?"

I shake my head. "No, but I do know we both want something quick and small. She keeps talking about the courthouse in Crestwood—the building is beautiful, after all—but we'll see what happens," I add, grinning. "I know we're both eager to get married soon."

"Oh, how charming," Wendy coos. She places a hand on my arm as the other men clamber inside of the elevator. I internally cringe at her intimate touch. "You know, I think I was entirely wrong about you, Mr. Ravage. I think we're going to be very happy working with Ravage Consulting Firm. Please give Stella my love," she says, walking into the elevator with the others.

As soon as the doors shut, I hear Chase clear his throat.

I twist around and walk away. "Not now," I growl, suddenly feeling like I'm going to suffocate under the self-made mountain of deception. I loosen my tie, feeling claustrophobic as my skin burns with the massive lie I just told to our new clients.

What the fuck did I just do?

"I suppose congratulations are in order," Chase says, chuckling as he follows me into my office and closes the door.

I quickly remove my tie, discarding it to the floor. Standing behind my desk, I place both hands on top of the cherry wood as I hang my head.

"Fuck," I mutter. "What just happened?"

"I believe you just got engaged to a woman named Estelle Deveraux and planned a courthouse wedding, all without her knowledge," Chase offers brightly.

"Fuck off and stop being facetious," I growl.

"Look, I assume you know this Stella woman, right?"

I sigh. "It's a long story."

I hadn't told Chase about what happened last week. Truth be told, I'm not proud of my actions. Leaving her there to contend with our fathers while I ran away like a coward ... and now I'm spreading rumors that we're engaged ...

I'm a fucking asshole.

Chase sits down on the couch across from my desk as I bask in my self-loathing. "Well, it's a good thing our next meeting is cancelled," he says, smirking. "You have time to tell me what happened."

I sigh and run a hand over my face before I explain the fountain last year—skipping over the part in the taxi—and then the lunch with our father and Prescott Deveraux last week. When I get to the part about walking out of the lunch, Chase chuckles and shakes his head.

I glare at him. "Is something funny?" I ask, frowning.

"Sorry, it's just … you have a lot of groveling to do."

"What do you mean?"

Chase shrugs. "Estelle is likely to find out about your fib soon. And then what? You better be prepared to intercept the news. And, because we want to please our newest clients, you should be willing to make sure she agrees to marry you."

I groan and close my eyes as I lean back in my seat. "Yeah. You're right."

"Oooh, say it again," Chase teases.

"I thought I told you to fuck off?"

He laughs and then stands up. "I never thought I'd see you get married before me," he says wistfully. "I'm a little bit jealous, to be honest."

I grunt. "You can thank my big fucking mouth for that."

"Juliet is going to lose it when I tell her," he adds, laughing. "We've taken bets on when you'll find someone."

I look up and send the most hateful glare I can muster toward my brother. "You're joking."

He opens my office door and shrugs. "Looks like she's going to win this bet. She'll never let me hear the end of it, so thanks for that. Why couldn't you have waited two weeks? I put money on November."

"Leave," I grit out. "Now."

He's still laughing when he walks out of my office.

CHAPTER THREE
THE SURPRISE

Miles

On my way home from work later that day, and after asking my father's assistant for Estelle's contact information, I draft a text to her. It all sounds so trivial. Truth be told, I'm not quite sure what to say, and as I mull over my words, I think of how I can entice her to make this work for one year. Because yeah, I sort of dug myself into a hole, and the only thing that makes sense is moving forward with what our fathers suggested. I owe her big time, and I know she's not going to like it. Especially because of how I acted last week in Paris. But I've given us no choice. If our new client learns that I lied, it will only fuel the fire for everyone to hate us *more* than they already do.

I need her to agree. Even if it means I need to grovel, as Chase suggested.

Even if I need to *beg*.

And I really fucking hate begging anyone for anything.

I run my hand through my hair for the hundredth time as I walk into the castle. I've already coordinated my evening entertainment with Luna, and the couple I've hired is awaiting my presence in the basement. Anticipation swoops low inside of me as I think about releasing all the tension from my workday—the meetings, everything with Estelle, my life in general. Just as I set my keys inside the abalone bowl in the foyer, I hear Luna's heels clacking against the marble.

I can always tell when she's in a rush to greet me— usually when things are amiss. Her tiny stature means she has to take quick, tiny steps. And tonight, she's practically jogging over to me.

Swallowing, I watch as she approaches.

"I'm sorry," she whispers when she's a few feet away. "I tried to stop her, and I tried to call you, but your phone must be on *Do Not Disturb*," she adds, looking behind her.

My brows shoot up. "Tried to stop who?"

Luna sighs and points at her iPad, as if I can read it from where I'm standing. "Estelle Deveraux. I sent the car to pick her up, and Louis said she appeared quite angry. Once she knew it was *your* car, she climbed in and demanded he take her to you," Luna explains. "I've managed to calm her down somewhat. She's currently in the kitchen with a drink."

I nod once.

Fuck.

"Thank you, Luna. I'll go talk to her."

"I'm not sure why she's so upset. I tried asking, but—"

"I think I know why," I admit, my voice exasperated.

Walking toward the kitchen, I glance back at Luna once, only to see her make the sign of a cross on her chest and shake her head. *Double fuck.* If Estelle is mad enough to unnerve Luna ...

I am in for it.

I take my time walking to the kitchen, and when I quietly turn the corner, Estelle is seated at the bar—staring right at me.

Her bright purple luggage is sitting next to her stool, and her clothes are bright green. Or, are they pajamas? She's wearing a green, short-sleeved blouse with the tiniest crop top underneath and matching green shorts that are entirely too short. Her hair is down and wild like it was at the restaurant, and I see her shoes—white sneakers—sitting by the back door.

"Estelle," I mutter, trying to keep my eyes off her toned thighs and light, honey-colored skin. "To what do I owe the pleasure?"

She narrows her eyes as she sips her martini. Dirty, if the cloudy liquid is any indication. As she audibly swallows, she sets her glass down and swivels to face me fully.

"I could ask you the same question," she murmurs, her voice low. *With anger,* I realize. "Imagine my surprise at having come off an eleven-hour flight to find out—from a fellow board member, mind you—that I'm engaged to a man I've met twice. Especially when that man made it very clear that he didn't want to marry me a week ago. *So much so*"—she snarls, glaring at me—"that you, what? Crawled out of the window? Ducked down behind a table as you walked out? Tell me, how *exactly* did you manage to sneak out of that lunch?"

I loosen my tie slowly. "It wasn't my finest moment."

She scoffs and takes another sip of her martini. "No kidding." After she swallows, she pins me with another icy glare. "And today? Why is Wendy Hannigan congratulating me on my upcoming nuptials to Miles Ravage? And asking me why I *haven't told anyone about our courthouse wedding?*" She lifts her glass and downs the rest of her drink in one go.

I must admit, seeing Estelle all riled up has me wanting to smile. She's cute when she's mad. Still, I keep my expression neutral. I don't want to show my hand too quickly. If I'm going to convince her to give this a try, I'm going to need to approach her like I'd approach an angry, feral cat.

"I panicked. I'm sorry," I tell her. *Apologizing is the first step of groveling, right?* "My father wasn't wrong last week. Clients are canceling on Ravage Consulting Firm left and right. I had a meeting with the charity earlier today, and they kept going on about our reputation," I explain. "Then they mentioned you were on the board, and I seized an opportunity. They signed a contract with us on the spot. I know it was wrong, and I promise to make it up to you."

She scoffs. "Yes you fucking will. You can start by making me another drink."

My lips twitch as I walk over to her, taking her glass from her and setting it inside of the sink. Procuring a fresh martini glass, I can feel her eyes on me as I walk over to the bar near the back door and measure out the gin, tipping it into the shaker. After I'm done, I portion out the olive juice, finally adding a splash of vermouth and a metal toothpick with three olives.

She takes it from me as soon as I set it down, and her eyes roll back as she moans.

"Fuck," she groans. "That's really good."

I ignore the way my cock stiffens at the sight of her throat swallowing the salty liquid, remembering her warm hands on me in the taxi, remembering how they reached into my pants for—

Fuck.

Leaning against the island, I shake the arousing thoughts away, watching as she takes a second sip of the martini. Pinning me with a calculating stare, she sits up straighter and clears her throat.

"I find it interesting that, one week ago, you were vehemently opposed to the prospect of marrying me. And now, when it benefits you, you're all for it."

"You're right," I tell her. She furrows her brows when I continue. "Also, as I recall, we were *both* vehemently opposed to the idea of marriage."

She considers me for a few minutes as her fingers play with the condensation on her martini glass.

"You're right. Except, I was willing to talk it out like an adult."

Fuck.

I don't know what I expected when Luna told me Estelle was sitting in my kitchen. However, when I think back to the first time we met, it doesn't surprise me that she's calling me out on my bullshit.

"If you agree to marriage, I promise to make it up to you."

"And how will you make it up to me?" she asks, her voice a soft purr.

God.

My mind spins with all kinds of ideas—ideas that I have no right to consider. Things like pushing her up against this counter and making her come so hard that she forgets her own name.

Finishing off what we never got to that night in Paris.

Kneeling before her and worshiping her dripping cunt.

Watching her play with herself before I make her scream my name—

I close my eyes and take a deep breath.

"You need my father's money, right?" I ask her.

She shrugs. "I guess. But I've gone twenty-eight years without money. I can make do without it."

I see an opening and I grab it, the scheming wheels turning in my head. She doesn't want my empty words. She wants assurance that I will make this arrangement worth her while. And, she hardly knows me. If nothing else, I am fantastic at the art of seduction.

"Let me rephrase that. You need money to start your own clothing line." I watch the way her hands grip the stem of her glass a little tighter at my words.

"I—yes. That's always been my dream," she adds, looking wistful.

Smirking, I nod once. "And a million dollars would help you?"

She nods. "Yes. Without a doubt."

I've got her right where I need her.

The instant the thought enters my mind, I push it out. I sound just like my father. And I know that when it comes to my father, he doesn't do anything for free.

But I'll have to worry about what my father wants from her *after* Estelle agrees to marry me.

"What-if I said I could get you in front of anyone you wanted?" She opens and closes her mouth, so I keep pushing. "And what-if I told you that I know of several ethical manufacturing companies who are booked up for years? Perhaps I could make a call for you when you're ready. You'll also need to think about publicity—and if we get married, the press will be hot on our tails. I could help you financially—"

"No," she says quickly. "I don't want your money."

But you'll take money from my father?

"All right." I lean in a bit so that we're only inches apart. "No money. But I can help you in other ways. For starters, you can live here for the year and utilize anything you need to get your clothing line up and running."

My eyes flick up to hers, and I stare into her dark blue irises.

"We both know what we get out of this, Estelle," I say slowly, my eyes dipping down to her cherry red lips before coming back up to her eyes. Her cheeks flush from the alcohol, though perhaps my slow perusal of her soft, moist lips have more of an effect on her than she wants to admit. "By ourselves, we'll flounder. But together?" I murmur, my eyes flicking between hers. "We could be formidable together. A power couple. We could both take what we want by the goddamn balls."

I can smell her perfume that I now recognize as Chanel No. 5. She doesn't seem like a Chanel No. 5 kind of woman, which only piques my interest further. Why is she wearing it? And why is she so unpredictable?

She huffs a laugh. "Fuck. You make a good argument."

"Is that a yes?" I ask, not moving from my spot right next to her.

"Are you asking me to marry you?"

"I'm asking you to consider it."

"Only if you promise me one thing," she counters, finishing her second drink in one large gulp.

"Anything."

"You have to let me redecorate the castle," she says, looking at me with a sly smile.

Her request takes me by surprise. "Which part?"

"All of it."

She sits up straighter and gives me her signature smile—the same one that makes everyone glance her way. The one that makes me grip the island a little too hard. I don't think she realizes just how fucking bright her energy is—how she's like the sun, in a way. Beaming. radiant.

She's impossible to look away from.

"No offense, but it looks like an assisted living center." My eyebrows shoot up as she continues. "Don't get me wrong—the building is stunning. But I think you need some color in your life, Miles."

My lips twitch with the threat of a smile. "Oh?"

"That ceiling in the foyer? It's gorgeous. It should be enhanced with some oranges, royal blues, a nice Persian rug—some throw pillows, perhaps. I mean, there are other colors other than beige and gray."

The audacity ...

"Fine. You can redecorate."

She grins, and *fuck me* she's gorgeous when she smiles like that.

"Wonderful. It's a deal." Before I can ask if she means it, she claps her hands and looks over at her luggage. "We should also set some ground rules—"

I hear the clacking of heels coming from behind Estelle, and I internally groan.

"Ms. Deveraux, so lovely to meet you," Luna says, walking over to us and pulling Estelle into a tight hug. I glare at Luna as she pulls away, but she just winks at me before turning back to Estelle. "I hope Mr. Ravage hasn't been too grouchy with you. I'll have Louis bring your things up to the North Wing?" It's a question, and I realize all too quickly that she's waiting for me to confirm.

I shake my head. "No. Please bring them to the

South Executive Suite." Her eyes go wide, so I clarify. "Ms. Deveraux and I are engaged," I explain. "It only makes sense for my *fiancée* to stay with me."

Luna looks between us with wide eyes. "Engaged?"

I nod, clenching my jaw and pleading with Luna to go along with it. "Yes. Very recently. It happened quickly," I explain.

Just. Go. With. It. I do my best to persuade Luna with my signature glare.

Luna must sense the urgency, because she slowly turns to my bride-to-be. "Of course," she says quickly. She gives me a look that says *we are talking about this later* before she taps something into the iPad she's always holding. "Right. I'll go let Louis know to bring your things up, Ms. Deveraux." She walks off.

Now it's Estelle's turn to look at me with wide eyes. I resist the urge to laugh, grabbing her arm and pulling her close to my side.

"Don't worry. Separate bedrooms," I growl, my voice low enough for only the two of us to hear.

She looks up at me with those blue eyes, and something settles low in my gut when I think of her so close.

Estelle pulls out of my grip and turns to face me. "Why is it necessary to share the same quarters as you?"

I huff a laugh as I pull my tie loose. I don't miss the way Estelle's eyes travel over my throat, landing on my scars before they dart up to my lips. I'm both hot and cold at once—uncomfortable at the notion of her fascination with my scars, but also so curious about the way she watches me.

Usually, I'm the one watching.

A flash of defensiveness washes over me as I'm assaulted by an unwanted memory of another woman being repulsed by me and my scars.

Why the fuck did I just coerce her into a marriage with me? And why am I flirting with her?

She made it very clear the first time we met that she didn't want me.

If I'm going to make this work, I need to stay professional. She may be beautiful, but she's off-limits.

"Because we're engaged," I say, frowning. "My employees might ask a lot of questions if we're living separately. *Especially* since they know I'm not a prude."

She gives me a rueful smile. "I see. I suppose that makes sense," she adds, quirking a blonde brow. "You don't expect me to …" she trails off, looking somewhat uncomfortable.

I clench my jaw. "Of course not. Besides, once you see my quarters, I don't think you'll have any complaints."

I turn and walk to the elevator. She follows me, leaving her bags for Louis. Once inside, she crosses her arms and eyes me suspiciously. The doors close us inside together.

"As I was saying earlier, if we're going to do this, we need to set some ground rules."

I press my lips together. "All right."

"One, we should remain monogamous throughout the entirety of this year—"

I snap my eyes to her. "Seriously?"

She shrugs as the elevator chimes loudly, following

me out and down a long hallway to the southern part of the castle.

"Well, I've already been humiliated once," she mumbles. "When you ditched me last week." I glare at her as she continues. "Plus, you seem like the kind of guy who sleeps around."

Oh, how wrong you are, Estelle.

"The kind of guy who sleeps around?" I ask. I have to actively stop the anger from tinging my voice.

"Multiple partners. Unsure of what he wants. Afraid of commitment," she adds, glancing at me with narrowed eyes. "Am I wrong? Need I mention the taxi ride?" I keep my mouth closed. "Plus, there are all the articles I scoured last week."

"Those magazine stories about me are trash. They're almost never telling the truth. Just because I have a woman on my arm or lipstick on my cheek doesn't mean I'm fucking them, Estelle."

She snorts. "Oh, so the articles about Chase and Miles Ravage breaking hearts all over Crestwood are total rubbish? Highly doubtful."

I look over at her, watching her smooth movements as she jogs to keep up with my long strides. "Chase is spoken for. He recently started dating someone."

"Okay, fine. But that doesn't negate the countless models hanging off your arms just in the last year—" She snaps her mouth closed.

"Jealous, Estelle?" I growl.

She scoffs. "No, but I don't want to be humiliated if

you're seen sneaking around with tall, brunette models."

I stop walking and grab her arm, tugging her close to me. *God, she's infuriating.*

"I can assure you, there will be no one else for the entirety of our fake marriage."

Her throat bobs. "Good."

"While we're at it," I purr, loving the way her neck and cheeks turn pink when I lower my voice, "I have some ground rules of my own."

"Go on."

"You will live in my quarters. We don't need to share a bed, but for appearances sake, you will play the part."

Her pupils darken slightly at my words, and she nods.

"You will take my last name, and you will attend events by my side. I'm happy to do the same for you."

"Fine. And I'll gladly take your father's money and pretend to talk you up to everyone I know."

"It's a deal," I murmur.

"It's a deal," she repeats, her eyes searching mine. "For one year, at least."

I walk over to the door of my living quarters and throw it open, gesturing for her to go inside.

"God, this place really needs some color," she muses.

I walk away in the opposite direction, ignoring my growing irritation: both at her for being so incessantly *there* and stirring the pot, and at myself for wanting to engage with her.

I need to keep it professional.

"Do your worst, Estelle."

She leans against the door frame. "Oh, and please, call me Stella."

"Why? Why do you hate your real name so much?"

Something intense flashes in her expression, but it's gone in an instant. "My grandmother used to call me Estelle. She's the only one who ever did."

And *fuck.*

I know I should call her by the name she wants me to call her, but I also can't help but *want* to call her something that no one else does—something that irritates her just a little bit.

"Please call me Stella," she says slowly.

I smirk as I turn and walk away. "Not going to happen," I call out over my shoulder, heading to the cellar.

CHAPTER FOUR
THE COUCH

STELLA

By the time Louis brings my luggage to Miles's living quarters, it's half-seven, and I'm knackered. Instead of unpacking, I drag my bags into the second bedroom, climbing onto the mattress fully clothed before falling asleep almost instantly. I suppose I can thank the two gin-heavy martinis for that. Jet lag kicks in around four in the morning, however, so I change into sweatpants and a sweatshirt. I glance around the fancy bathroom as I relieve myself. It's nice—white marble with thick, black veins, white cabinetry, brass fixtures. There's a large shower with sparkling glass walls that could fit a double bed, as well as a standing, clawfoot tub next to the large window overlooking the grounds.

There are also two sinks, and one of them has an electric toothbrush as well as a fancy shaving kit.

Lovely.

Not only am I stuck in this ostentatious castle for a year, but I also have to navigate sharing a bathroom with Miles.

I push the thought away for now.

When I'm done getting ready, I grab my water bottle before heading into the living area. Later today, I have a couple of meetings with Threads, the charity that Miles met with yesterday. But I have the morning free, which means I have time for my morning walk. Just as I glance at my phone, a note on the dining table catches my attention.

> Estelle,
>   Had to go out of town for a last-minute business meeting.
>   See you Thursday.
>   Miles

It's the least personable note ever, and I crumple it up and throw it into the bin before departing the living quarters. I was two sheets to the wind last night between the cocktails and jet lag, so I hardly had time to take in my new surroundings. I assumed the Ravage family was wealthy last week during lunch, but after a bit of research, I learned that Miles isn't just rich. He's *rich* rich.

As in, my future husband is a billionaire.

When I touched down in Los Angeles yesterday, I'd been too angry after Wendy's message to see straight —especially because of how Miles acted last week.

How dare he? I'd spent the forty minute drive positively fuming. And it felt good to hear him grovel. He'd messed up, after all.

Still, I can't believe I agreed to marry him.

I told myself I never wanted to see him again. I told myself that I'd get the last word in, that I'd tell him how messed up his lie was, and then maybe I'd throw a drink in his face for good measure. Except, he walked into that kitchen acting cool as a cucumber. And those eyes ... they turned me into a bumbling idiot again.

I have to admit, he has a way with words.

And, most importantly ...

A million dollars could change everything.

I keep coming back to that cold, hard truth. I don't have money. I can use this to my advantage. He needs me, and I hate to admit that perhaps I need him, too. The right connections, the right introductions ... I know that's how the world works. My father might be a bit more naive, but I know the top one percent are a well-connected bunch.

My fingers brush against the textured, beige wallpaper as I walk toward the elevator.

Of course he'd live in a fucking castle.

Maybe this won't be so bad. It's a literal castle, so coming from my tiny flat in North London is a welcome change. I can use the year getting everything up and running for my clothing brand, and by the time we amicably divorce, I'll be well on my way to living my dream.

What's one year, anyway?

Maybe getting out of the routine of my life in

London would be good. Maybe it would help me clear the cobwebs in my head ... the same ones that threaten to ruin my day.

Maybe the incessant, California sunshine will push all my dark thoughts away.

I quietly pad into the kitchen, admiring the shiny, modern fixtures, pale wood, and state-of-the-art cabinetry. My eyes rove over the fancy espresso machine, smirking as I go digging through the pantry for some proper tea. I find a sad-looking box of Lady Grey tea in the back, and I quickly go about preparing my morning ritual. It's barely half-four, and I scrounge around the pantry until I find a box of stale oats, moving into making a bowl of oatmeal with chocolate chips and peanut butter for myself. It's a strange combination, but one I've done for years. I find a pad of paper and pen and write out a list of things I'll need to get in the next food shop. First and foremost, there are zero biscuits.

I need to remedy that.

After I finish my oatmeal, I place my dishes in the dishwasher and head out to the back for a morning walk. It's just starting to get light out, so I walk slowly, enjoying the cool morning air on my skin. If I were in London, I'd be freezing my arse off. It's not warm, per se. But it's lacking the sharp, cold bite of autumn that England is famous for. I have a feeling that once the sun is out fully, everything will warm up. And I am here for it.

I walk the perimeter of the castle first, taking note of the four stories, the stone walls, the arched windows. There's also a massive pool in the back garden, a gate leading to the woods that surround the castle, and a fancy, circular driveway. It's *massive*. The fact that this might very well be my new home is mind-boggling.

Around six, I head back inside, showering quickly and changing into my favorite bright yellow romper. When I go downstairs to make another cup of mediocre tea, there's a man in the kitchen.

I stop walking as he looks up and notices me. He's holding a newspaper in both hands, and as his expression goes from curious to amused, he folds the paper and sets it on the island.

"Well, well, well," he drawls, smirking. "You must be my brother's new fiancée."

How the hell does he know? Did Miles tell him?

"Unfortunately," I bite back, walking over to him and holding my hand out. "Stella Deveraux."

"Liam Ravage," he says gruffly.

He's handsome—older than Miles if his silver-speckled scruff is any indication. He's wearing a red flannel and an old pair of jeans.

"Miles's *oldest* brother," he clarifies. "I live about twenty minutes from here, and I came to have breakfast with my brother, only to find that he's off on some highly suspect business meeting."

I huff a laugh as I make my way around the kitchen. "Running away from me is more like it," I mutter. "I sort of chewed him out last night."

Liam chuckles. "Good for you. He needs a good chewing out sometimes."

I grin as I look over at Liam. He's drinking black coffee, and his blue eyes bore into mine playfully. I make a sound of indignation when I pull a tea bag out.

"Your brother needs to get some proper tea," I explain, grimacing. "I'm not fancy, but I need something a bit more sturdy than Lady Grey."

"Ah. That's why there's a list in the corner with *proper tea* circled three times?"

I laugh. "Exactly."

"Give Luna a list. She normally orders groceries a couple of times a week. I'm sure she'd be more than happy to add anything that would make you feel more at home."

"I'm perfectly capable of doing my own shopping."

Liam lets out a low laugh. "I'm sure you are. But Luna is also happy to help. Anything you need. Or maybe I can help? I'd be happy to take you."

I look at him skeptically. "You're not busy?" I ask.

"I don't have classes today." When I don't respond, he continues. "I'm a creative writing professor."

I hum in acknowledgment. "I see." Suddenly, an idea forms. I wasn't really looking forward to lazing about the castle until my meetings later, and if Liam is willing to drive me around ... "Perhaps while we're at it, we can pick up a few things for around the house?" I suggest.

He stands up and gives me a friendly smile. Something about him is comforting—like the older brother I never had.

"I'd be happy to help. What did you have in mind?"

I shrug as I take a sip of my god-awful tea. "Some

color, perhaps? If I'm going to live here for a year, I need to liven the place up a bit."

Liam cocks his head as he crosses his arms. "Does Miles know about this?"

I grin. "I may have undersold my penchant for color."

This makes him smile more. "Let's go, then."

Following him out of the kitchen, we walk side by side toward the front of the castle.

"Are you and Miles close?" I ask.

He shrugs. "Yeah. I mean, all five of us are close, but Miles and I are the two oldest. We spent our childhood looking after the others, you know? But he works with Chase, the second youngest, so the two of them have a close working relationship."

"What made you choose creative writing?" I ask, grabbing my purse from the table foyer and following him out to the driveway.

"I've always enjoyed writing. Something about giving into my muse sets my soul on fire," he says slowly, opening the passenger door of a black Jeep Wrangler and gesturing for me to climb inside. It's covered in dirt, and I wonder briefly what Liam does during his free time. Once he's inside, he turns to me. "And what about you? What sets your soul on fire, Stella?"

I smile as we drive away, knowing that Liam and I are going to get along swimmingly.

———

The next three days follow the same sort of pattern. Liam and I ended up spending all morning together on my first day at Ravage Castle, and then he drove me to the fanciest supermarket I've ever seen, where I picked out all the fancy black tea my heart could ever desire.

And biscuits. *So* many posh biscuits.

Of course, I refused to let him pay for any of it.

I enjoy Liam's company. He's casual, kind, and yet, there's something deep about him. He quotes Shakespeare on the regular, wears glasses to read, and though he's never listened to a Taylor Swift song—a tragedy, to be sure—we still settle into a lovely camaraderie.

It's nice to know that I've made a friend in California so quickly. But ... it's sad to think that I know Liam and Luna better than I know Miles.

The second and third day, it's Luna who drives me to consignment shops and discount stores to purchase new things for the castle. Keeping busy helps me, and this is the perfect project to help me settle in. I learn that she and her partner, Emma, have been living at and running the castle for over ten years. She left her job as a project manager at a Fortune 500 company to work for Miles.

Apparently, he can be very persuasive.

In the afternoons, Niro drives me to my meetings with Thread. It's invigorating to be part of their board meetings, and I tamp down my excitement at being able to make important decisions. *Soon, I will have my own company to run.* I spend my evenings re-decorating, listening to my audiobooks, and exploring more of the castle. I'm able to map out the entire layout, aside from the cellar, which—according to Luna—is off limits to everyone but the main occupant of the castle.

My very own fake fiancé.

Speaking of which ...

Perhaps I'm still bitter about Miles deciding we had to get married without consulting me, or perhaps I'm just annoyed that I haven't heard from him at all, but I find myself growing more and more aggravated with him as the days wear on. I start doing things that I know will get a reaction out of him when he gets home. Things I know he'll hate.

Things such as the brand new, fuchsia-colored sofa, and the other touches of color I've placed throughout the living quarters. Luna arranged to have my things flown from my London flat to the castle, and it's nice to have some familiarity. Of course, my meager possessions look *tiny* in comparison to the enormous living room, but the new things I'd purchased have made all the difference.

On the evening of my third day at Ravage Castle, I'm lying down on the new couch with my Bluetooth earphones in, listening to my audiobook, when Miles enters the living quarters. He stops moving when he sees me, his eyes slowly registering the new look of *our* home.

A small part of me feels victorious.

He's the one who got us into this predicament by lying to the owners of Thread, after all.

I pop my earphones out and into their case, setting my phone down next to me.

"What the hell is *that*?" he asks, pointing to the new pink couch. He sets his small suitcase by the door as he eyes me suspiciously.

I laugh. "You don't like it? I think it livens the place up a bit."

His eyes catch on the fresh tulips sitting in my bright yellow vases on either side of the front door.

"Luna heard about my love of tulips, so she offered to stock the living area with them. Isn't that sweet? She's lovely, by the way. I think you should give her a raise."

He turns in a slow circle as he takes in my decorations. "I can assure you that Luna is very fairly compensated, but I'm glad you've taken it upon yourself to interfere in household matters only three days in," he drawls. "Should I have the household budget drawn up and sent for your approval? If you want to go all out, I can buy you one of those *Mrs.* monogrammed aprons ...?"

I snort. "Don't get ahead of yourself, Miles. I don't cook."

He smirks as he walks over to where I'm sitting on the couch and picks up one of the Emma Shipley cushions I brought from home. It's light pink velvet with bright pink leopards who happen to have teal wings and peacock feathers for tails.

Sighing, he sets it down, looking resigned.

"It's a lot, I know. You've probably never seen a non-beige wall."

He scowls as his eyes track over the orange lamp, the round, pink rug underneath the dining table, and the eccentric vases all over the place—all holding fresh tulips.

"For the sake of transparency, I had Luna order some curtains to match the pillows, which is very British, by the way," I add, smirking. "I got them for a bargain, so I couldn't resist."

Though, now that I think about it, I doubt Miles ever has to worry about bargains.

"Where are the old pillows? The old couch?" he asks, and he's giving nothing away about how he feels.

"Luna has them in storage. Don't worry, once I'm gone, you can have your boring gray pillows and furniture back."

"Anything else I should know? Any other insulting colors you'd like to show me?"

I grin. "You're going to hate the bedroom."

His eyes widen slightly as he stalks toward his bedroom, throwing the door open. I stand up and follow him inside, watching as he takes in the bright orange duvet cover. It's velvet, but the middle is bright orange faux fur. I'd snooped around a bit earlier but found nothing incriminating other than a mirror above his bed.

I don't want to think about what *that's* for.

He heads into the bathroom and glances down at the tufted butterfly rug that, in my opinion, gives the bathroom an entirely new feel.

Spinning on his heels, he crosses his arms as he turns to face me. "You have ... interesting taste," is all he says.

"Thank you. I like it," I tell him, though I know he

meant it as an insult. I lean against the door frame as Miles walks around the bathroom once. "Besides, marriage is about compromise." I mock.

"You call that pumpkin-colored bed a compromise?" he growls.

I smile. "You're really going to hate the refrigerator I ordered for the living quarters, then," I tell him.

His nostrils flare as walks over to me. Placing a hand on the door frame, he's close enough to touch. "You should have asked me for money."

I roll my eyes. "I told you. I don't want your money."

"Yes, but I also don't want you to go into debt," he says, his voice almost soft. Almost like he's concerned. "What's mine is yours."

I swallow thickly. "But we're not married yet. Plus, a lot of it came from my flat in London."

"Which is surely just dazzling and filled with pink puppies and singing, yellow flowers."

I look up at him. "No pink puppies, unfortunately. Don't worry. I'll be taking everything with me in a year."

"Damn straight you will. I've lived here for thirty-six years, and I like it how it is."

He's so fucking hot and cold. One minute, I think he might be concerned about me. And in the next breath, he's insulting me.

"Wonderful, we're in agreement then. Don't worry, you'll have your boring appliances back when we get divorced."

"How much did you spend?" he asks.

I shrug. "Not very much."

"I'll have Luna reimburse you."

"I told you I won't be taking a cent of your money. Not now and not ever. I've done perfectly fine for myself for twenty-eight years—"

"Aren't you, though? Maybe you're not taking my money, but you certainly have no qualms about taking my father's money."

Hurt lances through me. Despite everything that's happened to me in the last year, I've had one thing to cling to.

My integrity.

But he's right.

I have no qualms about taking his father's money.

I'm just about to tell him that he can take his father's money and shove it up his arse when he says something that makes zero sense.

"Don't take his money. Let *me* help you instead."

I bark out a laugh. "Like that's any better. At least there are no strings attached with your father. I can only imagine the things you'll put me through to earn that money."

His lips twitch, and he bends down slightly so that we're inches apart. "Trust me, Estelle. There are always strings attached when it comes to my father."

His words suck the oxygen out of my lungs. "My father trusts him," I retort, standing up straight. "So I do, too."

Miles tilts his head. "I'll give you two million."

I scoff. "You're ruthlessly Machiavellian. It's a little terrifying."

He smiles at this, and I think it's the first time I've seen a real smile grace his features. It catches me off guard, and I'm momentarily stunned.

"I'm adding another ground rule," he says, staring down at me once the smile leaves his face. "From this moment until we separate, you will use my money as if it is yours."

"No, I don't need—"

"Estelle."

His voice is low. Commanding. My eyes dip to the jagged lines on his neck, and I'm tempted to pull his shirt down so I can see just how far those scars run.

"You need money to survive. You need money for living expenses. So unless you expect it to magically appear at the bottom of a fountain, you will take my money and you will utilize it. I'll have Luna add you to my accounts and get you a copy of my credit card. You can also expect reimbursement for all of this imminently. If you don't want to take the two million I just offered you, that's fine. I will arrange for you to receive my father's money."

I open my mouth to protest, and he places a hand over my lips. His skin is salty, and I want to lick him.

What. Is. Wrong. With. Me.

"If you don't comply, I *will* make sure your year here is as unbearable as humanly possible."

I swallow as my eyes search his. He removes his hand, and I lick my lips as my cheeks flush.

"Blackmail? I didn't think you'd stoop so low, Miles," I murmur, narrowing my eyes.

He takes a step back, shrugging. "I am my father's son, after all."

With that, he turns and walks out of the bathroom. I take a few steadying breaths, replaying his words over and over in my mind.

I am my father's son, after all.

What the hell have I gotten myself into?

CHAPTER FIVE
THE PROPOSAL

MILES

I groan when I wake up sweating, shoving the duvet off as I climb out of bed. Whatever fabric this orange monstrosity is made of kept me up most of the night in a hot, itchy mess. I quickly climb out and exit my bedroom, glancing into Estelle's empty bedroom on my way to the kitchen.

"You've got to be fucking kidding," I grumble, my eyes skirting over the matching duvet cover in her room.

The rational part of me is telling me to just get rid of both heinous duvets, but fuck, she seemed so happy yesterday amongst her Crayola-themed decorations. And ... *comfortable.* Lounging on that eyesore of a couch. Looking content. Smiling as she clutched one of those god-awful pillows to her chest as she listened to something on her phone. She'd been wearing an oversized T-shirt and tight bicycle shorts that highlighted her toned legs, and I had to actively keep my eyes on her face.

The duvet cover will stay, as will the couch.

For her, I think reluctantly.

Besides—and it makes me feel like a horrible person to think this—I still need her.

I still need her to go through with this fake marriage.

Throwing out her brand new matching duvet set might not be the best way to go about that.

I quickly shower and change into a dark grey, two-piece Prada suit, glancing at myself in the mirror as I change. My eyes automatically fall to the misshapen skin around my neck and chest. I've reluctantly memorized the pattern of it. My eyes fall closed briefly as I think back to when I was eighteen.

"What's wrong with your neck?"

I try to pull my hoodie higher, but she reaches out and her mouth falls open before her face contorts with disgust.

"Is that why you kept your clothes on, you freak?"

I take a few steadying breaths before walking out of the bedroom. I can't help but glance over at Estelle's open door again as I clasp my watch around my wrist.

Someone who rises earlier than me?

I never thought I'd see the day.

When I get to the downstairs kitchen, I see her leaning against the island, a huge grin on her face as she sips her tea. I go still, not wanting to disturb her. Instead, I take in her small, tight, high-rise shorts and sports bra, leaving a sliver of her upper abdomen exposed. Her hair is piled up high on her head, and she has a sweatshirt wrapped around her waist. Glancing down at my watch, I note that it's only six in the morning. How long has she been awake, and why is she smiling maniacally? I clear my throat and she jumps, sending tea sloshing to the floor.

"Fucking hell, Miles," she breathes, grabbing the kitchen towel and using it to blot up her mess.

"Sorry," I mutter, scowling.

I walk over to the espresso machine and prepare my double macchiato. My eyes skirt over the expansive countertops, and that's when I notice the bright blue tins labeled *Coffee, Tea, Sugar,* and *Biscuits.* Narrowing my eyes, I walk to the tin labeled *biscuits* and pull the airtight lid off before peering inside.

"Cookies?" I ask.

"Biscuits," she corrects. "I also got you some proper breakfast tea."

"Wonderful," I deadpan. "Just what I need. Hot leaf water." When I look over at her, she's watching me with charged amusement.

"How dare you insult your soon-to-be English wife."

I furrow my brows as I pack the coffee grounds and press the *start* button on my espresso machine.

"Aren't you half-French?"

She rolls her eyes. "Sémantique, Miles. I was born and raised in London."

"You speak French?"

"Oui," she answers, her accent perfect.

"Super. On peut s'insulter en deux langues," I reply

in perfect French, watching as her brows shoot up in surprise as she considers me with wide eyes. "What other British-isms do I need to be aware of, then?" I ask in English, counting to twenty before I turn the machine off. My mouth waters. The crema is *perfect* on my double espresso. I grab some milk from the refrigerator, pouring a small amount into my steamer.

"Well, you already saw the biscuits. There are also proper crisps in the pantry."

"Crisps?"

"You lot call them potato chips."

I frown. "I don't eat potato chips."

She hums in response, and when I look over at her, she's eyeing me skeptically.

"Yeah, no surprise there. Well, if you'd prefer something a bit more nourishing, you could try Flapjacks."

"Pancakes?"

She huffs a laugh. "No. They're oat bars. And did you know the fancy supermarket in town has hot cross buns?"

"Okay," I reply skeptically, foaming the milk before adding it to the espresso.

"You should try one. Liam enjoyed them. He took a few home with him the other day."

I nearly drop my freshly made macchiato. "You met Liam?"

She nods, finishing her tea. "I did. He's very kind. Seems you did not inherit those genes."

I grind my jaw as I sip my drink. "Mmm. I suppose not. Speaking of snacks, I'd prefer you keep those new containers in the pantry. I like my counters sparse."

She turns to face me. "Fine."

Placing her mug in the dishwasher, I scowl when she picks up the tea towel and starts to clean the counter with it.

"We have paper towels, you know."

She shrugs. "It's wasteful. I can wash and reuse this."

Glaring at her, I lean against the counter. "Trust me, I'm all for being eco-friendly. But we are also in a drought here in California."

She spins to face me. "Are you going to cross-examine everything I do?" I can't help but admire the way her skin is practically glowing. She must've worked out earlier. My eyes rove to her neck briefly, where her skin still has a thin sheen of sweat. "Because if you are, we should get it all out in the open now."

I sip my macchiato to hide my smile. "We should probably discuss the wedding," I say, changing the subject.

Her eyes go wide. "That's one hell of a proposal, Miles."

I rub the back of my neck, realizing that I enjoy riling her up way too much. "I suppose we should make an appointment at the courthouse."

She blows out a slow, steady breath. "I suppose so, since you left us no choice."

"The good news is, I know the mayor of Crestwood, so I can get us an appointment for this weekend."

"How romantic."

"I know it's not ideal," I say, scowling. "But I think

the sooner this year is over, the better. For both of us. So, the courthouse it is."

I know I'm being curt and rude, but I need to get my point across.

She shrivels at my words as she swallows, giving me a resigned shrug. "Okay. You plan it," she says indifferently. "Just tell me when and where."

"Estelle," I growl as she begins to walk away.

Fuck.

"It appears that I have absolutely no say in any of this, do I?" she asks quietly from her place by the back door. Spinning around, I'm surprised to see that her eyes are sparkling with something resembling tears.

Now I really feel like an asshole …

"First, I'm bombarded with texts about being engaged to a man I'd only met twice, and then I get here, where I'm pressured into marrying you—"

"Pressured?" I ask, my voice hard.

"Yes. You plied me with martinis—"

"It was *two* martinis," I growl.

"And I believe your exact words were, 'we could both take what we want by the goddamn balls.'"

I wince. "I did say that." Setting my coffee down, I walk over to where she's standing. She sniffs once and gives me a resolute look, as if she's determined not to cry in front of me.

"I'm not very good at this," I tell her honestly as I rub my face with my hand. I almost reach for her hands, but then her eyes dart to my neck.

I pull the collar of my dress shirt farther up to hide as much of my scarring as possible.

Fuck.

Not only did I force her into this marriage and *pressure* her into it, but I also made sure she was legally bound to someone as deformed as me.

A sharp pang of self-loathing rolls through me.

She deserves better, but I need her.

And yeah, that makes me a gigantic asshole, but I need to look out for myself and my family. Besides, it's not like she'll be miserable here. She will have access to the castle, my connections, and eventually, a lot of money to start her clothing line.

It isn't like she's being sentenced to a year in Alcatraz.

Taking a step back, I hold my hands up. "What can I say to get you to marry me, Estelle?"

With furrowed brows, she tilts her head slightly as she studies me. "You can call me Stella, for starters," she murmurs under her breath. "Even if I did agree, how do you know I wouldn't crawl out of the bathroom window on the big day?"

My lips twitch, but I don't give her the satisfaction of knowing I find her amusing. She'd gloat about it and never let me live it down.

"I suppose I'll have to trust you."

I reach behind her, grabbing a green apple and bringing it to my mouth. My abdomen grazes her chest as I do, and her eyes track my movements, dark blue irises roaming over my face and neck unabashedly. If it wasn't for the way her eyes keep darting down to my scars, I might say that Estelle Deveraux is attracted to me.

"You should try a biscuit," she says, placing her hands on the counter behind her.

I cock my head. "Is that your way of saying yes?"

She shrugs. "It depends which biscuit you choose. I have to make sure we're truly compatible."

I smile as I chew. Everything that comes out of her mouth is surprising. Taking another bite of my apple, I walk over to the tin and open it, peeking inside. A rectangular one catches my eye—shortbread, I think. I hold it up and take a bite.

"Delicious," I say, shoving the rest in my mouth. "Did I pass?"

She smirks as she walks over to where I'm standing. Reaching into the tin, she grabs the same kind of shortbread cookie I just devoured.

"For now. I'm still waiting for you to make this all worth my while, Miles," she says, her voice low.

And fuck me, because that voice goes straight to my cock.

Taking a slow bite, she smiles as she walks away. "This weekend, then. Make it happen. I'll see you at the altar."

After she's gone, I rub my face with my hand.

I'd been attracted to many women in my lifetime. And though I didn't sleep around that much, I still enjoyed the eccentricities of each of those relationships.

But with Estelle? There's something different about her. Something resilient and vulnerable at the same time. I've never had a near stranger call me out like she does. Sure, my brothers do it, but they're family.

I look at the blue tins full of her things, unlatching the biscuit tin and quickly swiping another rectangle into my mouth.

For the sake of both of our sanities, keeping our distance would be best.

No taunting, no arguing, no flirting ... it's safer if I keep away from her for the entirety of the year.

It'll be better for both of us.

I need to think of this for what it is: a business transaction and nothing more.

I throw my apple core in the trash and grab one more biscuit.

Fuck, these are good.

CHAPTER SIX
THE NUPTIALS

Stella

I take a deep breath, adjusting a hair pin as I pull up to the courthouse in downtown Crestwood. My hands are shaking slightly as my father gets out of the Escalade and opens my door. It's warm today, and I relish in the way the sun heats my skin. I will never get tired of the sunshine here, and for a second, I'm sad I will have to go back to gray, drizzly London in a year.

"You look beautiful, ma chérie."

I grin. "Thanks, papa."

Taking my hand, he leads me up the grand staircase and into one of the most beautiful buildings I've ever seen. There are tall, stone columns, black and gold marble floors, and a majestic fountain in the center of the grand foyer. I clutch my bright yellow tulips tightly and smooth my silk dress as my father lets go of my hand. I catch a glimpse of my blonde curls in the mirror—something I hardly ever bother to tame anymore—as well as the form-fitting dress. I'd chosen to keep it simple and *me* today, which means no white. Just an elegant, lavender dress with thin straps, a wrap style bodice and waist, and a long thigh slit. I have on bright purple strappy heels, and I've kept my makeup minimal thanks to the heat. The last thing I need is to sweat it all off.

"Are you okay?" he asks me, linking his arm with mine again and leading us to one of the back rooms. I'm intentionally ten minutes late. I wanted to make Miles sweat a bit—just a little revenge for the day he abandoned me in Paris. This morning, I heard him showering in our joint bathroom, but I haven't spoken to him for the past two days, when he suggested we get married this weekend.

I was met with the thirty-page, prenuptial agreement this morning, though. In a nutshell, I am not entitled to any of the Ravage money after we divorce, aside from the million dollars promised to me, but I am free to use all of it during the year we're married. It all feels so ... clinical. Formal. The opposite of romantic.

Happy wedding day to me.

A small part of me was disappointed not to see him before today. I hung around the kitchen like a sad puppy dog yesterday morning but he never showed up. I didn't even get a reaction to the bread and pasta jars that now accompany the original tea, sugar, coffee, and biscuit jars in the kitchen.

It felt a bit cheeky to add them, but I wanted a reaction from him.

I can't help but think that he's avoiding me.

As my father and I round the corner, I nod once. "Yes. I'm fine. Just nervous."

"It's normal to be nervous on your wedding day," he says, his voice low and comforting.

Yes, it is. But this isn't a normal wedding day.

"I know. I'm still trying to wrap my head around all of it."

My father pauses, pulling me with him when he stops. "Stella, I know you're determined to go through with this, but I want you to know that I support you no matter what you decide."

"Thank you, papa," I tell him, kissing him on the cheek. "I'll be okay. After a year, I can pretend none of this ever happened."

My father's blue eyes search mine warily. "I hope so."

Before I can ask what he means by that, the door down the hall opens, and I turn my head to see a room full of people I don't know.

And of course, the instrumental music I chose plays through the speakers. I am now realizing what a terrible idea that was. "Love Story" by Taylor Swift is the song I always wanted to use when I walked down the aisle, but today, it just heightens how much of a sham this whole thing is.

Oh god, oh god, oh god.

Taking a steadying breath, I pull my face into a serene smile as we walk forward and into the ceremony.

Upward and onward.

My heart is hammering against my ribs, and I clutch my tulips tightly, suddenly feeling very silly for dressing so informally. A cold sweat breaks out on my skin when I see Miles at the other side of the room, waiting with two people. One of them appears to be the marriage commissioner for the civil ceremony, and the other one is Liam. *Thank fuck I have an ally here.* He's in a white button-down shirt and dark gray pants —which seems so informal next to Miles, who is wearing a classic navy suit.

Miles looks ... *god.* My palms begin to sweat more when I think of calling him my *husband.* How would I last the year with him? Watching him eat the way he does, feeling so alive when I quarrel with him, the way he looks in those bloody suits ... ugh.

I am doomed.

He looks the same as he always does, but there's something about his energy that's different today. It's almost like nervousness, or perhaps reverence. He watches me walk down the aisle, and I see two different emotions playing across his features, fighting for dominance.

My father guides me to Miles, and I quickly realize that I have no one to hand my flowers to.

I should've thought this through, but of course, it was so last minute—

"I'll take those," a woman behind me says. I spin around and hand the tulips to her, and she gives me a warm, encouraging smile. She has long, light brown hair and the most gorgeous set of green eyes I've ever seen. "I'm Juliet. I'm Chase's girlfriend," she explains quickly, pointing to the beguiling man next to her.

Chase gives me a knowing, cocky smile as he tips his head. "Nice to meet you, Stella," he practically purrs, blue eyes twinkling with mischief.

Do they all look like this? My god, the world is not safe from the Ravage brothers.

Before I can introduce myself, Miles tugs on my elbow and pulls me back to where he's standing.

"You look beautiful," he murmurs into my ear before taking my hands.

It's so intimate. *Too* intimate.

I close my eyes briefly to tamp down the panic crawling up my esophagus. *He's being nice. Get it together.* Still, I can't help but grieve the wedding I always wanted—a white dress, outdoors, with fairy lights and everyone I love gathered together. I suppose there's still time for that after this year is over, but still. My chest aches a bit when I think of the fact that *this* is the first time I'll ever be married.

In a courthouse.

Wearing a purple dress.

Reciting vows to a man I barely know.

The commissioner drones on about marriage—it's all very unemotional—and my eyes wander to the crowd. I don't recognize anyone aside from Luna and my father. Charles isn't here, which doesn't surprise me. Standing next to Chase and Juliet are two other men I can only presume are the other Ravage brothers. They both give me reassuring smiles.

As if they all know this is a ruse.

My heart is galloping inside of my chest, and I inhale for three seconds, exhale for three seconds ...

"You okay?" Miles asks me, his green eyes scanning my face. "Please don't tell me you're getting cold feet."

I manage a small smile.

Get. It. Together.

"I'm fine," I tell him quietly.

His eyes flash with something—alarm, maybe—and his thumb brushes the top of my palm briefly. My skin pebbles at the soft touch, and though I'm nervous, his eyes somehow ground me.

"Deep breaths, Estelle," he says, too low for anyone else to hear. He doesn't seem nervous at all. His brows are slightly pinched as he studies my face, but otherwise, his hands aren't shaking and sweaty like mine.

My chest rises and falls, stuttering when the commissioner says something about rings. It catches me off guard. *Rings?* Of course we'd need rings. *Shite.* Miles holds his palm out and hands me a plain, gold band. I take it as the commissioner talks about the significance of the rings. My pulse is whooshing too loudly through my eardrums for me to hear him. I slide the band over Miles's ring finger as my knees turn to jelly from sheer nervousness.

"Here," Miles says, sliding a gorgeous vintage platinum and amethyst ring on my ring finger.

It takes me a second to recognize it, and when I do, I pull my hand away, startled.

"That's my grandmother's ring," I whisper as the panic builds.

No, no, no.

This is all wrong.

"Estelle," Miles warns, taking my hand again. "Let's discuss this later, yeah?"

I nod once as he slides the familiar ring onto my shaking ring finger. A few seconds later, the commissioner declares us married, and the room tilts as I look up at Miles. There's something about a kiss—

I'm going to be sick. This is all wrong. This isn't how I'm supposed to feel on my wedding day.

I close my eyes and take a deep breath, calming myself.

I can do this. I *have* to do this. There are people here who are expecting us to be in love. Stupid and reckless, sure, but in love nonetheless. When I snap my eyes open, Miles is watching me with that pinched expression again, so I do the only thing I can think of. Wrapping my arms around his neck, I stand on my tip toes and press my lips against his.

He doesn't react at first, and while I can't be sure because my eyes are closed, I imagine his are open in surprise. I'm just about to pull away and call it a chaste kiss when his arms reach up and pull my waist into his body, deepening the kiss and reclaiming my lips as he crushes me against him. His tongue traces my lips, sending a smattering of sparks through me as a wild swirl of desire ignites in every nerve ending.

Just like the first time we kissed.

My skin is suddenly tingling and warm, and all I can smell and taste is green apples. Sweet, ripe, surprising ... His hand dips lower, ever so slowly, a searing sensation working through me as his fingers squeeze my arse once.

As he does, we both groan.

Audibly.

I push myself closer as my hands run up his neck and into his hair, grazing over his puckered skin. He groans again, his tongue wild against mine, and every single movement sends something white hot through me. His racing heart beats against my chest, so I know it's not just me. He runs his free hand around my waist, exploring the soft lines of my back, my hips ... before running the other one to my arse. I let out a low, whimpering sound. The intoxicating scent of green apples overwhelms me.

I've only ever been kissed like this once before.

In a taxi.

A tautness in my core grows tighter with each swoop of his tongue, and a hot ache grows between my thighs.

My god ...

Someone from the crowd audibly whoops and Miles pulls away quickly, as if he's been burned. Instead of pulling away completely, he takes my left hand in his, pulling me behind him as we walk toward the door. A few people cheer. I'm too stunned to do anything.

What the hell was that kiss? Not that I didn't expect it, but still ...

My heels clack against the black marble as we make our way to the front of the courthouse. Once outside, he waves at the small crowd of reporters and photographers.

Before I can process anything, he pulls my body close to his again, this time side by side. "Smile for the cameras, Estelle," Miles commands, his voice a low murmur in my ear. Placing a kiss on my cheek, one of his hands snakes around my waist, and his long fingers grip my hip firmly.

It sends a surge of electricity through me, and I smile through my stunned gasp.

He chuckles as we walk toward a black SUV limousine. Once I'm inside, he closes my door and walks to the other side, climbing in.

After he shuts the door, we're encased in silence. I look up at him as he stares at me from the other side of the SUV, several feet away. Neither of us says anything —he only just watches me as I catch my breath.

I ask the first thing I can think of—the one thing that's been at the forefront of my mind, even more so than that amazing kiss.

"How did you get her ring?" My voice is tinged with anger. I hardly ever get angry, but for some reason, the fact that he used my grandmother's ring makes me furious.

"Your father gave it to me this morning." At his response, I cross my arms and look out of the window as we make our way through downtown Crestwood. Surely, his scheming is behind this. "Care to explain *why* you're throwing a hissy fit over your wedding ring?"

"A hissy fit? I think not." I lean forward. "You had *no* right to use her ring."

He looks stunned. It should be amusing, but instead, that same concerned expression passes over his features. My eyes rove down to his neck, where that same shiny scar is peaking through. He notices, because he adjusts his collar and covers it up.

I laugh and shake my head. "It doesn't matter anyway."

"What doesn't matter?"

"This. All of it. In a year, I'll have my money, and you'll have your reputation. I was just surprised to see it, because—" I close my mouth. "Just forget it."

Why should I tell him? Spilling my guts to him would only result in him using it against me. I need to keep some sort of wall between him and the things that matter the most to me. I've tried to break through his barrier several times, and each time, he's shot me down.

Why should I let him inside of mine?

I grab a champagne flute and hold it out. "We should toast."

He looks at me like I'm speaking another language. "I want to know why you're so upset about the ring."

There it is. That same humbled expression he wore when I walked down the aisle.

I press my lips together. "I'll tell you if you tell me about that scar on your neck."

His eyes narrow ever so slightly. Without another word, he reaches over to where a bottle of Dom is sitting on ice. Uncorking it, he pours it for us both, and we toast.

"To marriage," he says, his voice somber.

"To marriage," I repeat, clinking my glass a little too hard against his.

Neither of us look away as we drink, and I down my flute in one go, as does he.

He refills both, but before he drinks, he clears his throat. "You really do look beautiful. That, at least, wasn't fake."

I give him a genuine smile. "Thank you. You don't look terrible yourself."

"Why purple?" he asks, taking a sip.

"Did you expect a white dress?" I counter, feeling a bit snarky from the alcohol.

He huffs out a laugh. "No, I suppose not."

We both look away and drink our champagne slowly in silence. *I should ask him about the kiss. Or his brothers. Or about just what my father said to him about the ring—*

"I had your things moved to my bedroom during the ceremony," he tells me, keeping his gaze on the view from the window. "I hope you don't mind. You don't actually have to sleep in bed with me, but we should appear to be sharing a bed. Your clothes will remain in your room as I assume you will need your own closet."

"Several closets, probably," I reply.

He smirks as he sips his champagne, and after that, an awkward silence fills the air. I pour myself a third glass of champagne. Miles does the same, and by the time we pull up to the castle, I'm already tipsy. Miles opens my door for me, and I nearly fall over as the champagne hits me quickly. He grabs my elbow and steadies me.

"Careful," he warns, green eyes twinkling. His expression is warmer now. More relaxed.

Ply him with alcohol. Good to know.

"I'm fine," I assure him, following him up the drive.

As we reach the front door, he turns to face me and holds out his arms. "Shall I?"

I stiffen. "What? No. I'm not—" I shake my head. "No."

He chuckles. "Let me carry you over the threshold, Estelle."

I take a step back. "No," I repeat, cheeks flaming. "I'm not the same size as your model ex-girlfriends —" I squeak as he leans down and picks me up, placing one arm under my knees and another one under my arms. I'm quiet as he carries me through the front door and sets me down gently on the other side.

"Come on," he directs, taking my hand and leading us to the elevator.

"Why are we rushing?" I ask, nearly jogging to keep up with him. Granted, he is almost a foot taller than me.

"Because I want everyone to think I can't wait to defile the new Mrs. Ravage."

"No one is here," I retort, looking around.

"The extra security is here," he replies. "For the reception later. And you can be damn sure they're watching our every move on the security cameras, Estelle."

The door closes us inside the elevator just as he finishes speaking, and when he looks down at me, his eyes are dark as they search mine. I'm suddenly reminded of our earlier kiss, and I pull my lower lip between my teeth as he watches me. For a second, it seems like he might kiss me again, and I'm instantly horrified with myself that I actually want it. I mean … I shouldn't be *entirely* horrified. My new beau is a catch. Our chemistry is off the charts. I'm not an idiot. I know we're both aware of it.

And it's like he bloody *knows* the navy blue of his suit is a stark contrast against his chartreuse eyes. But still.

No.

Agreeing to marry him is one thing.

But kissing him, or better yet, wanting him to kiss *me*, is more trouble than I bargained for.

Taking a step away from him, I look down at my shoes until the door opens. I push all thoughts of Miles *defiling me* out of my head as he grabs my hand and leads us to our living quarters.

CHAPTER SEVEN

THE RECEPTION

MILES

A few hours later, I'm adjusting my tie in front of my mirror when I hear someone knock softly on the door connecting my bedroom to the joint bathroom.

"Come in," I grumble.

Estelle walks into my bedroom, and I swear my heart skips a fucking beat.

I need to get myself fucking together.

"That's ... is that what you're wearing?" I ask, eyeing the way the short, white dress clings to her curves.

She's also wearing white strappy heels that make her legs look a mile long, and as my eyes wander up, I notice a gold necklace with a large, gold *R* smack dab between her glorious tits.

How in the world am I supposed to pretend I don't find her attractive for an entire year? Because right now, with her wild curls grazing her bare shoulders, her smooth curves, and my *fucking* initial dangling between her perky breasts ... she's sex personified. It's more than that, though. Her smile—the same one tilting her lips right this very instant—is contagious. Infectious. Everything about her is so ... lovely.

When she's not irritating the ever living shit out of me, that is.

"I figured I would lean into the whole virginal bride thing," she says, stepping farther into my bedroom. "Even though people will think you just spent three hours defiling me. The irony is appealing to me."

Fuck ...

My ...

Life.

I chuckle as I finish fixing my tie. "I'm surprised it's not fuchsia or lime green," I reply sarcastically.

"Well, I figured you only get fake married once, so ..." she trails off and comes to stand next to me.

I swallow as I see her dark blue eyes scanning our reflection—studying how we fit as a couple. And, as an unbiased observer, I can see the appeal. I *get* why people might consider us a good match. For one, Estelle is drop dead gorgeous. That was established the first time I laid eyes on her. But it's not just her looks. It's how she makes people *feel*. She radiates sunshine, which poses a juxtaposition to me. A solid foot taller than her—nine inches when she's in heels—I am no-nonsense. The lines of my suits are always crisp. My hair is always perfectly in place, and everything about me is exact.

Where she is soft, I'm firm.

Where she exudes light, I pull in the dark.

It's like she's Beauty, and I'm the Beast.

Thinking of the scar peeking out of my collar, I realize that analogy is not far off at all. Taken from her life to live in a strange castle with a beast ...

"Ready?" I ask her, my eyes darting down to the gold *R*.

Fuck. Why does seeing the initial of my last name across her chest make me feel frenzied and desperate for her? Wasn't this the deal? She's changing her name officially. Legally, she will be Estelle Ravage in three to five business days. She signed the contract, and I filed it with our lawyers *knowing* it was going to happen.

But I wasn't supposed to love it this fucking much, or even at all.

"Always," she says, smirking at me before walking out of the bedroom.

We head downstairs together, where a small crowd of friends and family is waiting for us. As soon as we round the corner, they all break out into applause, and Chase—*fuck him*—shouts at us to kiss.

Estelle looks up at me with wide eyes, and this time, it's my turn to surprise her. Snaking an arm around her waist, I pull her close to my body.

"Put your other arm around my neck," I murmur.

Licking her lips, she does as I say—and as soon as I feel her hand on my hot skin, I place my other hand on her upper back and dip her. Her hair is flowing down to the floor, and she looks not only surprised, but intrigued. Smirking, I lower my lips to hers as the crowd goes crazy.

And like last time, everything inside of me pulls taut. My hands burn where they're touching her cool skin. Her lips are *so fucking soft*, and I have to steel myself to keep from thinking about how they'd feel wrapped around my heavy cock.

I press my tongue between her lips and squeeze her waist with my fingers. She emits a moan—just like before—and for a second, I want to lower her to the ground and fuck her senseless. Estelle's fingers curl into my hair, and she pulls it ever so gently. Still, the feel of her fingers in my hair, the feel of her soft body against mine ...

If I wasn't worried about the year ahead before this kiss, I sure am now.

Pulling away, I lift her back up so she's standing, taking in a ragged breath. She seems just as dazed, stumbling slightly as people clap and holler. I wipe my mouth and give the room a tight smile as I walk her over to where Chase and Juliet are standing with Liam by the wet bar.

"Congratulations," Chase says, pulling me into a quick hug. His eyes roam to Estelle, and much to my amusement, her neck and chest are flushed pink. "Stella," he says, pulling her into a hug. "Nice to officially meet you," he says, giving me a look that screams *what the fuck, man?*

I hug Liam and Juliet before standing next to Estelle. She stiffens, and when I look over at her, I can see that she's crossing her arms and looking away.

Before I can ask her what's wrong, Juliet pulls her away.

"So," Liam says, holding a glass of whiskey and passing another glass full of the amber liquid to Chase and me next. "Stella Deveraux?"

I shrug. "Technically it's Estelle Ravage now."

They both stare at me with wide eyes, so I keep talking.

"It makes sense," I tell them with a low voice. "For all intents and purposes, and to the public, we are truly, madly in love."

"Of course," Chase quips, taking a sip of his drink. "That kiss certainly highlighted your amorous feelings."

"Fuck off," I bite back. Liam and Chase share a look. "What?"

"I wasn't being facetious. Look at her. She can barely pay attention to Juliet right now," Chase murmurs.

All three of us look over, and I realize with a start that he's right. Estelle is smiling, but her eyes have that foggy, faraway look. One hand is on her neck, and she's rubbing her skin softly. Her other hand is touching her swollen lips. A second later, she looks over at me, and I can see the flush visibly creep up to her cheeks.

"*What* are you saying?" I ask.

Liam snorts and places a hand on my shoulder, leaning down. "We're trying to say that we think she liked the kiss, little brother."

I scowl at Chase, who is smirking triumphantly, before my eyes flit back to Estelle. Except ... she's gone.

"Juliet is probably off showing her the library," Chase explains.

"I like her," Liam offers, pouring us all some more whiskey. "If that matters. We spent some time together earlier this week. She feels like a kindred spirit."

Something hot and jealous works through me suddenly, and I take a deep breath before pushing those unwanted feelings back down to where they belong—in the recesses of my mind, never to be seen again.

I have no right to be jealous, especially of my own brother.

However, I can't help but wish *I'd* been able to spend more unguarded time with Estelle.

I'm just about to respond when Chase claps me on the back. "I give it a few weeks before the two of you are in love. Five, to be exact," he adds, winking at Liam.

Liam chuckles, and the blood drains from my face.

Looking back over at where Stella was standing earlier, I think about how she was looking at me. How maybe she got the wrong idea with that kiss.

And worst of all, how she seems to be infiltrating every cell of my body. How I can't stop thinking about her. How I'm beginning to feel *obsessed*.

Like *she's* the shiny, new toy.

I have to put a stop to this, because I can't fall in love with my new wife.

It would only complicate everything.

"It won't happen," I tell my brothers as I sip my whiskey.

"And why not? What's the worst case scenario?

This starts as a fake marriage but turns into a real one?"

My head is spinning, and I set my glass down too roughly. "Just drop it."

I walk away before they can poison me with more of their optimistic nonsense. If there's one thing I've learned, it's that people like Estelle Deveraux were wholly good. And people like me? And my family? I would only taint her. I coerced her into this—more than she knows. If things were to progress with us, I'd never know if my coercion was the reason.

And what I haven't said to my brothers is that I *did* give her a chance once, and she took one look at my scars and rejected me. Sure, maybe she doesn't feel the same way anymore now that she knows me a little better, but pity can seem a lot like interest. I'm good at deciphering the difference, unfortunately.

It's easier to distance myself.

It's easier to fuck around when and only when I needed to get off.

I'd already gotten used to the idea of being alone forever.

It wouldn't be hard to continue down the solo path.

I need to put a stop to this. I had to drive a wedge between whatever it was that existed between us. If that meant turning off my charm and being the asshole everyone saw me as, then so be it.

The rest of the evening passes slowly. I hop from one person to the next, thanking them for coming. Luna went above and beyond, inviting many of my acquaintances and clients. She also invited a curated list of media outlets in hopes of getting the word out about our marriage. I roam around the castle thanking people for coming, hardly having time to eat the delicious food everyone else is eating.

I only catch glimpses of Estelle. Juliet hasn't left her side. *I should be the one by her side.* Pushing the thought away, I suppose I should be grateful that Juliet has taken my new bride under her wing. By the time people begin to leave, Luna comes to find me.

"Miles," she says, looking guilty. "Your father has promised *US Weekly* a front page exclusive," she starts.

I glare down at her. "He knows how much I hate that particular editor," I growl.

"I know. But—"

"It's fine. We'll do it. I presume they want a photoshoot?"

"Yes. Just the two of you around the castle. Thirty minutes, tops. We can do it now."

I nod. I know Luna technically works for the estate —which means she works for my father, too. Because I reside here full-time, I sometimes forget that her allegiance lies with the family and not just me. Though I know if it came down to it, she'd take my side. Not just because I'm the one who found her and brought her on, but because we've grown close over the last ten years. She's sort of become one of my only non-familial allies.

"I'll go let Estelle know."

The party is winding down, and as I walk from room to room in search of my newly appointed spouse,

I say goodbye to people as they leave. After a few minutes, I find her on the patio overlooking all of Crestwood. It's cold, and I instinctively take my coat off and place it around her shoulders. She tenses when she realizes it's me.

"Hello," she says softly. "Lovely party, don't you think?"

She's staring out at the city below. Her expression has that same tug of sadness that I saw last year by the fountain. Like the smile she usually wears is just a mask to hide the real turmoil. All of my earlier resoluteness about driving a wedge between us gets harder to come to terms with. A stray curl breaks free from behind her ear, and I resist the urge to tuck it away.

I can't get close to her.

I have to keep that distance between us.

"Estelle ..." I trail off, looking out over the city. "I think it was irresponsible of me to kiss you like that earlier."

She turns to face me, and I'm surprised to see an angry glare settle across her expression. "And why do you say that?"

I shrug. "I got carried away. I'm sorry. It won't happen again."

Polite and to the point.

Her jaw clenches. "Fine."

Just as she turns her head away, I hear a click followed quickly by a flash. Estelle jumps with surprise.

"Beautiful," the photographer says from behind us. "Pretend like I'm not here," he says, his voice nasally.

Estelle glances up at me. "Who is that?" she asks.

My lips tug down into a deeper frown. "Sorry," I tell her, my voice low, so only she can hear. "I was just coming to warn you that my father booked a quick photoshoot for *US Weekly*."

She drops her lashes quickly and looks down at the ground. "Of course. How do you want me?"

I furrow my brows at her. In place of her usual sunny personality is a monotone voice and restrained body language. *Did I do that to her by apologizing for the kiss?*

She steps closer. "Like this?" she asks, looking up at me with those large, indigo eyes.

It feels like a test. Something sparks behind her eyes, and I can't tell if she's angry or disappointed.

Probably both.

I place my hands on her shoulders. "Perfect."

I don't break eye contact, but before I can pull away, the camera flashes.

"Amazing," the photographer says. "Miles, can you kiss her?"

I swallow. *Fuck.*

"Don't get carried away this time," she whispers so only I can hear her. When my eyes flash to hers, she only glares right back at me.

Of course, I do the exact opposite of what she asks. Gripping the back of her neck, I pull her to my lips for the third time today, thrusting my tongue inside of her mouth and pressing her against the railing a little too roughly. My other hand moves down to her hip, and I tug her pelvis into mine just as she moans.

Fuck ...

I pull away—no, I nearly *push* her away as I take a few steadying breaths. My eyes dart across her face, and she gives me a feline smile.

She knew what she was doing when she warned me not to get carried away.

"Excellent," the photographer says, clicking away. "Miles, can you have a seat on one of those chairs?" he asks, gesturing to the iron patio furniture.

I twist away from Estelle, jaw ticking, as I take a seat.

Estelle saunters over, sitting on my lap without taking any direction from him whatsoever. She's a natural. Her ass is warm and soft, and I get a whiff of Chanel No. 5 as she slides one arm around the back of my shoulders, leaning into me.

"You look like you're being tortured," she says, her voice a low growl into my ear.

"This is worse than torture," I snap back quietly, nostrils flaring.

She rears her head and looks down at me with surprise. "You're an arsehole. Has anyone ever told you that?"

I bark a laugh. "I told you to stay away from me."

She scoffs. The photographer snaps more pictures, and she leans down toward my ear as if she's about to whisper sweet nothings. But I know better.

"Well, I'm stuck with you now, so let's try to make the best of it."

"Estelle, can you kiss his neck?" the photographer asks.

Estelle stiffens on top of me, and it only further fuels the fire inside of me. Of course she doesn't want to go anywhere near my scars. Why would she?

"Don't you dare," I growl.

"Don't make a scene," she grits out, her lips moving down to my jaw.

My eyes flutter closed as her warm breath makes my cock twitch. Her mouth inches lower, and I feel the first brush of her lips against the gnarled skin of my neck. Sucking in a ragged breath, I grind my jaw and fist the fabric of her dress.

No.

Too much.

I pull away and shove her off me. She stumbles slightly as I storm toward the photographer.

"You got your pictures. You can leave now," I tell him, breathing heavily.

I don't dare to look back at Estelle as I follow him inside and away from my new bride.

CHAPTER EIGHT
THE DINNER

STELLA

I don't see Miles at all the day after our wedding. *Honeymoon, my arse.* I spend the day sketching and dreaming up exactly what my clothing line will look like to distract myself. Around five, Luna informs me that dinner is at seven, and that Miles is expecting me to join him. I grumble the entire time I get ready, showering slowly and taking my time diffusing my hair. When I'm done, I pull on one of my favorite colorful blouses with a crazy, bright pattern, as well as cut-off denims. Slipping into sandals, I dab some of my grandmother's perfume behind my ear, and then I make my way to the formal dining room fifteen minutes late.

I'm not sure what happened yesterday, but after our kiss at the reception, he pulled away. Not that he was a warm, friendly person to begin with. I knew that going into the marriage. But for some reason, Miles Ravage was shielding his true emotions. He *was* concerned for me at the ceremony. I could see it. And the way he kissed me at the reception ... no one is that good of an actor. Also, I felt his *excitement* against my hip when he kissed me on the balcony. I know he's attracted to me.

There was a point last night that I thought maybe his walls were crumbling down, but for whatever reason, he built it back up higher and stronger than before. He apologized for kissing me and promised me it would never happen again.

And I want to know why.

Walking into the dining room, I see Miles seated at the head of the table, frowning at something on his phone. His icy gaze flicks up to my legs, roaming up to my face slowly. His slow perusal of my bare legs makes something flutter inside of me, but I ignore it, biting my tongue as I sit down at the seat to his left.

I can be cordial.

It's only a year.

He's my fake husband, not my friend. There was nothing in the prenuptial agreement that said we had to be friends.

"Do you own any clothing that doesn't resemble a highlighter?" he grumbles, taking a sip of his red wine.

Okay, then. Starting the evening off with his arse-holery. Lovely.

I pick up my glass, sipping my wine slowly before

answering. My new ring clinks against the glass, and I can feel his eyes on my throat as I swallow.

"Do you own any clothing that isn't a suit?" I ask, my eyes traveling down to his *R* cufflinks.

He presses his lips together as he steeples his hands. "You're late."

"It takes a long time to dry my hair," I explain, taking another large gulp of wine. I'm going to need the entire bottle if he continues to be a prat.

His eyes drag over my hair slowly, and then they narrow with distaste. He nods once, swallowing his words with his wine.

I know whatever response he swallowed was not a nice one.

"My father sent over the contract for our financial agreement this morning," he says smoothly as the chef walks into the dining room with two plates. "Did you receive it?"

I shrug as he sets the watermelon and feta salad in front of me. My mouth waters. I'm a horrible cook, and my diet usually consists of biscuits, oatmeal with chocolate chips, peanut butter, and plain pasta cooked in the microwave. Luna offered to have the chef cook me dinner while Miles was away last week, but I refused.

It's silly to cook for one person.

"I haven't checked my email today," I respond.

"Very well. Once you sign the contract, we will schedule a monthly bank transfer." I nod without answering. Miles looks at me as he chews. When he's done, he swallows slowly. "Monthly installments are all right?"

"That's fine."

The hand holding the fork stills. "Are you sure? We can work out a weekly arrangement instead, if you'd like—"

"I said it's fine, Miles. To be honest, I assumed you would lord the money over me for the entire year."

Something flashes in his eyes when I say that. Almost ... surprise. Possibly guilt.

The expression is gone in an instant.

Interesting.

Why would he feel guilty?

I wasn't sure of the logistics of Charles Ravage's money, but I assumed I wouldn't receive it until the end of the year. That was the verbal agreement, after all.

"Well, this way you can utilize the money for the startup of your clothing line. And of course, what's mine is yours for the duration of the year," he adds, referring to the clause I knew he added to the prenuptial agreement.

"Thank you."

His eyes slide to mine briefly before he swallows the rest of his wine. I do the same, and he refills both of our glasses. We eat and drink in silence, though I can feel his eyes on me throughout the meal. Every time I look up, he's already turning away, but the hairs on the back of my neck continue to stand up under his intense gaze.

I have to actively keep quiet when the infusion of

flavors in the watermelon, feta, and mint create the perfect combination in my mouth. I love food—if someone else cooks it. When we finish, the next course arrives. I do a double take when the chef sets the plate down in front of me.

"Is this …" I look down at what can't possibly be my favorite meal from home.

"I spoke to your father this morning, and he mentioned you love cottage pie. So we researched the ingredients," he says matter-of-factly. "Voila, ma femme."

I look down at the perfectly browned mash, swallowing the emotion clawing up my throat.

Get a grip, Estelle. He's still an arse, whether or not he has your favorite meal cooked. I've never been won over that easily before. If I keep swooning at every morsel of attention and kindness he throws my way, this is going to be a remarkably unbearable year.

I clear my throat. "Thank you," I tell him, taking a steadying breath. He doesn't look at me as he tucks into his dish—he just hums in acknowledgement without saying anything else.

Fine, we'll just spend the year eating in awkward silence, no big deal.

When we're both finished, the chef clears the table before bringing in the pudding course—which is decadent chocolate cake. I nearly moan when I take a bite.

As awkward as these dinners might become, I could get used to the idea of three-course dinners every evening.

"This is delicious," I say to no one in particular.

"I'm glad you're enjoying it," Miles says, his voice controlled. "I'd like for you to dine with me every night."

His lack of enthusiasm makes it sound like he's asking me if I'd like to get a nightly colonoscopy.

"Sure."

"And I'll let the chef know you liked his cottage pie. He can make it for you anytime you want."

I nod. "Thanks. My grandmother used to make it for me."

Miles is quiet for a few minutes, and at first I think he's choosing to ignore my olive branch.

"The one who passed away last year?"

"Yes. In fact, that night in the fountain? That was the day of her funeral."

Miles watches me quietly as I take a bite of cake. "You did it for her," he states.

I nod. "She had this list of things she wanted to do before she died. It was the last thing on her list."

Miles stops chewing, his eyes studying me as he contemplates what to say next. Maybe he feels like a right arse now that he knows how important that whole night was to me.

"What other things were on your grandmother's list?"

"Well, aside from skinny dipping in a public fountain, she wanted to get a tattoo, run a marathon, go snorkeling, and go to Oktoberfest. She was an adventurous woman despite being wheelchair bound, so she got to most of the other things on her list." I swallow once. "I can only hope that when my time comes, my list will be just as short or shorter than hers."

Miles watches me with curiosity. "We can all hope, I suppose." He takes a sip of wine. "So did you do all of those things? The ones left on her list?"

"I did."

He nods once before he resumes eating his cake.

I suddenly remember the question I'd wanted to ask Miles a few days ago. "Why is the cellar door locked?"

He coughs on his cake, covering his mouth with his napkin. A few seconds later, he holds my gaze with a stormy expression before turning away.

"Don't go near the cellar, Estelle."

I'm taken aback. I mean, sure, he's entitled to his privacy. But I also find it wildly bizarre to have a place that's off limits.

"Why?" I narrow my eyes as I take another bite of the delicious cake. "Are you hiding dead bodies down there or something?"

He looks up at me with a hardened expression. "It's a personal matter," he says quickly, wiping his mouth as he stands abruptly. "And I'm asking you to stay away from that area of the castle. Am I making myself clear?"

I stand up too, glaring at him. "Crystal," I bite back. "However, as your *wife*, I have a right to know if you're hiding something illegal, or—"

"Did you not read the prenup? You relinquished your rights the minute you walked down the aisle."

The air gets sucked out of my lungs. "Charming,

Miles," I sneer. "You've outdone yourself. Forcing me to marry you, threatening to blackmail me, telling me that I've relinquished my rights ..." I laugh harshly. "You know, up until last night, I was actually starting to enjoy your company." I swallow as I think of the way he apologized for kissing me at the reception. How it felt disingenuous. How it felt like he was *lying*. "Why are you acting like you can't stand me all of a sudden?" I ask quietly.

He turns his icy gaze to me, his eyes boring into mine. "Because I can't."

"I don't believe you," I tell him honestly, stepping closer.

He huffs a cruel laugh. "Fine. Don't believe me," he growls. I take a step closer to him, and I swear I see him flinch slightly. As if he's *afraid* of me.

"Fine," I bite back and jab a finger into his chest once I'm close enough, but a second later, he grabs my hand and pushes it off him.

"Do not touch me," he adds, eyes blazing.

I search his face for something—*anything*. Some sort of clue as to why he's being so callous, so hot and cold.

It suddenly all feels like too much, too soon. All of it. The lunch in Paris. The texts from Wendy. The lies. The wedding. The kiss. And now, learning that my husband is a rude prick capable of blackmail, superiority, and coercion.

I miss my father.

I miss London, even if it is rainy and foggy right now.

I miss my flat. Sure, it wasn't a castle, but it was home.

I left *everything* behind. And for what?

My eyes prick with tears, but I take a deep breath, pushing them away. "All I'm asking is for you to be *nice*," I tell him, my voice thick with emotion.

His expression oscillates between contempt and concern as his eyes flick over mine. I see his hand twitch at his side, like he's about to touch me, but he must think better of it.

"I'm not sure I know how to play nice," he admits, his answer surprisingly honest. His expression slides into a frown as he studies me closely.

I'm just about to respond when his phone chimes loudly. He looks away from me, glancing down at his screen. Picking it up, he turns the screen to face me.

"It's the *US Weekly* article," he tells me, unlocking his phone as he clicks on the text from Luna.

Despite wanting to throttle him, I scoot closer, looking down at his phone as my eyes rove over the exclusive photoshoot from last night. The pictures are exquisite, and my heart skips a beat at the cover photo —the image of Miles kissing me on the balcony. My hand is around his neck, and his hand is gripping the fabric at my hip tightly while his other is fisting the back of my hair.

It's sexy and passionate, and my chest flushes as Miles continues to scroll.

The kissing picture was chosen as the main image for a reason. Every other image looks ... stilted. Posed. There's one of us on the chair, and Miles is looking away from the camera, almost scowling. I just look sad.

You look like you're being tortured.

This is worse than torture.

The words he spoke just before that picture was taken roll around my mind as he closes his phone and pockets it.

"We need to work on our physical chemistry," I tell him bluntly. "You look like you have an actual stick up your—"

"Enough, Estelle."

Anger blooms through me. "Look at us! We look truly miserable. No one is ever going to believe that we're in love if we continue to look like we hate each other. *Both* of our reputations are on the line here."

His eyebrows knit together as his nostrils flare. "We can come up with a solution tomorrow."

He moves past me to the door, and I follow him out of the dining room. "That's it?" I ask, feeling frustrated.

He continues walking past the kitchen. "I said we'd talk tomorrow," he grits out, not bothering to turn around.

I watch as he walks away, heading down the hallway I know goes down to the cellar.

What the hell is Miles Ravage hiding down there?

I wait a few minutes to give him time. But by the time I get to the iron door, it's closed and locked.

When I get back to my bedroom, I'm fuming. And sometimes, there's only one thing to do when you're angry and dealing with pent up tension. Grabbing my handy little vibrator, I lie down and rub one out under my orange duvet.

I come with a cry thinking about those *R* cufflinks pressed against the inside of my thigh.

Worst of all, after I finish, I'm still sexually frustrated.

CHAPTER NINE
THE WAND

MILES

Without intending for it to happen, Estelle has become more than just someone I'm physically attracted to. It's bordering on *obsession*. The way she speaks. The way she uses a knife and fork—her fingers curling around the silverware delicately. The way her plush lips move as she chews. She doesn't shy away from me, and that makes me covet her. It makes me *desperate* for her.

I can feel my controlled facade beginning to crack.

What the hell is she doing to me?

Before dinner, I told myself that I could be professional. Instead of focusing on Estelle and the way her legs looked in those denim cut-offs, I focused on her incessant need to be right and the way she loved to push my buttons. The additional containers now adorning my kitchen counter proved that. If I said not to do something, she would do it, and that pissed me the fuck off.

Instead of admiring the way her ass and thighs filled those shorts out, I focused on pushing her away by being an asshole. It's better this way, anyway. Better to push her away before she gets attached. Better to keep her questions about the cellar at bay. Better to fight her every step of the way so she learns Miles Ravage is *not* redeemable.

Everyone else already suspects as much.

Why not add her to the bunch?

I'm such a self-deprecating asshole, I think, watching the couple before me.

As I sit on the couch in the cellar, all I can concentrate on is the way Estelle's blouse was unbuttoned slightly, exposing the golden skin of her décolletage. I close my eyes and pinch the bridge of my nose, ignoring the sounds emitting from my state-of-the-art glass room. Normally, watching people is enough to get me out of my funk. One hour in the cellar, one couple who is paid handsomely to perform together, one room with two-way mirrors. They can't see me, but I can see them.

It's always enough to loosen me up.

It *used to be* enough.

Unbuckling my pants, I urge my cock to wake the fuck up. Nothing happens. I can't stop thinking about the woman upstairs.

Walking out of the cellar feeling frustrated and pissed off, I take the stairs to the ground floor two at a time. *How is it that she's been able to affect me like this?*

Usually, I can count on this one thing.

This *one* penchant for watching other people.

It's always been my weakness.

But I suppose Estelle has now taken first place.

Once in the kitchen, I pour myself more wine. Luna is seated at the island, tapping away on her iPad.

"You aren't downstairs?" she asks carefully, watching me as I take a slow, steady sip of the red liquid.

I shake my head, not ready to explain myself.

Only Luna and Chase know about my proclivities.

Voyeurism—meaning I am sexually aroused by watching others when they are naked or fucking.

It started young. Being naturally observant, I enjoy watching people. And it wasn't until I was eighteen and watching two strangers getting their rocks off that I realized I got aroused by watching other people get off. As a young eighteen-year-old, it was a safe haven for me. I didn't actually have to fuck anyone—I didn't have to show anyone my scars. It was the best of both worlds in my eyes. When I moved to the castle officially after we started Ravage Consulting Firm, I had the glass room in the cellar built. A couple of times a week, I hire couples to fuck, or sometimes, only solo women. It depends on my mood. They know they are being watched, but they don't know by whom. Thanks to the NDA, even if they suspect who's behind those mirrored walls, they are legally bound to stay quiet.

I still sleep around—still find ways to satisfy my carnal urges. But all the women I sleep with know that I keep my clothes on, that they can't touch my scars, and that it's for one night only. I never join the people I hire to perform. All I need is to watch them. That's the beauty of it.

I can watch from afar and still have an orgasm.

I know Chase is into the dominant primal stuff, but that's not really my cup of tea. Voyeurism gets a lot of bad press. Peeping Tom's, people taking upskirt pictures ... I don't do that shit. Consent is still important, and I keep my kink locked up in the cellar downstairs, only engaging with the people I pay and get consent from.

I keep it very controlled—like every other aspect of my life.

Estelle is the first person to try and shatter those glass walls, and it terrifies me.

"Do you want me to send them home?" Luna asks carefully.

I nod. "Thank you, Luna. Did Estelle go to bed?"

Luna's red-tinted lips twitch with the hint of a smile. "I believe so."

Finishing my glass of wine, I lay the glass down in the dishwasher before walking toward the exit of the kitchen.

"She's lovely," Luna says just as I'm nearing the door. "Estelle, I mean. Does she know about the cellar?"

I stiffen, my jaw grinding. "No. And I'd prefer to keep it that way."

I take one more step out of the kitchen when Luna speaks again. "Forgive me for meddling, but as someone who has been married for nearly a decade, this might be something you'd like to share with her."

My mind is screaming.

It's not real. None of this is real.

"Maybe," I answer, appeasing her.

"I don't know her very well, but I can see that she adores you," Luna adds. "I wonder if she'd be interested in joining you downstairs one night?"

I thumb my nose and give Luna a kind smile. I know she means well, but I can't help but feel sad that the scenario she's talking about will never happen because Estelle is my wife by name only.

We will never have that sort of intimacy.

She would never want to be with me in that way.

"I'll think about it," I lie, walking away.

Once inside the living quarters, I glance at Estelle's bedroom door, only to see that it's closed. Removing my tie, I grab a bottle of water from the fridge and walk into my bedroom. I'm not tired yet, but perhaps a long shower is in order. Discarding my suit to be dry cleaned, I walk into the bathroom in only my boxer briefs.

And the first thing I see is the vibrator sitting next to Estelle's sink.

I don't move for a solid minute, letting it register in that my *wife* pleasured herself tonight. And then had the cojones to leave it sitting out for me to see.

Almost like she wanted *me to see it—like she wanted me to imagine her using it.*

She knows we share this bathroom, after all.

My cock throbs with need as I walk over to her side,

picking the wand up and gripping it in my hand as I stare at it. There's some toy cleansing spray nearby, so she must've left it out to dry.

A flash of jealousy works through me, and my cock hardens completely when I think about her running this toy down to her aching, wet cunt. I palm my erection when I think about her coming in the bed just one room away, back arching, little whimpers escaping those pouty lips. I set the vibrator down on my side of the bathroom, staring at her door.

Did she think of me? Or someone else?

Fuck.

I couldn't even get hard down in the cellar as I watched the couple I'd paid to be there, and here I am imagining Estelle playing with herself, hard as steel.

Glancing at the vibrator again, I walk over to the shower and turn it on, discarding my boxers and climbing into the large, waterfall encasement with glass paneling.

It only takes me three seconds to grab some of Estelle's jasmine-scented conditioner, rub it all over my aching cock, and fuck my hand. It smells like her, and that only enhances everything. I stroke myself faster, squeezing the head of my cock and rubbing the conditioner all around.

I think of Estelle as I cup my balls with my other hand, think of the sounds she might've made while pleasuring herself. I can almost *see* it in my mind. Those perky tits pointing up as she lays across that atrocious orange duvet cover, her pebbled, dusty pink nipples, toned legs spread wide and bent at the knees...

Is she bare? Or does she have blonde curls above her cunt?

And why do I want to know so badly?

I fuck my hand harder, tightening my grip. The hand that was playing with my balls comes up to the wall of the shower, and I lean against it as I work my other hand faster. My balls pull up as the telltale tingling starts at the base of my spine. I imagine hovering over Estelle and fucking her instead of my hand, and that sets me off completely. I feel wholly unhinged—I can't remember the last time I had to get myself off like this. I can't remember the last time I felt this turned on.

She does this to me.

I let out a low moan as pleasure courses through me.

Keeping my mouth closed and ensuring I stay quiet, I speed up my pace and begin to relentlessly stroke myself, using the conditioner to graze the head of my aching cock with my thumb. Squeezing tighter, my whole cock goes completely rigid, and my balls pull up as my toes curl against the marble floor of the shower.

"Estelle—"

I come. Hard. My cock arches up, bobbing and pulsing in my hand as large, thick ropes of cum paint the shower wall. Hissing audibly, my whole body quivers as I continue to erupt for several seconds, coming harder than I have in years. Gasping for breath, I lean both hands on the wall, placing my forehead against the cool marble.

The warm water hits my back as I stay there for a minute, closing my eyes and grinding my jaw.

I can't believe I lost control like that.

Fuck.

What did I just do?

I promised myself yesterday that I would try to stay away from her—try to stay professional.

But this? This is the opposite of professional.

If I'm already acting like a horny teenager around her on the first day of our fake marriage, there's no telling what the next 364 days will bring.

I am so completely fucked.

CHAPTER TEN
THE PRACTICE

Stella

After changing into pajamas, I realize with a start that I left my vibrator out in the open for all of Ravage Castle to see, or more importantly, my crabby husband. *God, imagine if he saw it just sitting next to my sink!*

Talk about embarrassing.

I pull the bathroom door open, and a few things become very, very clear in rapid succession.

One, the lights are dimmed.

Two, the shower is on, and there's a pile of dark clothes in front of it.

Three, my vibrator is now on *Miles's* side of the bathroom.

I'm just about to ask if my arsehole husband messed with my sex toy when he lets out a low, heady groan from inside of the shower.

My lips part as I glance at the shower. The lights

are too low to see anything in graphic detail, but I can make out the general outline of Miles.

And what he's doing.

I can't move.

I know I should leave him to wank in peace, I really do.

But ... something about the way the water is splashing against his hand, the wet sound as he strokes himself, the echo of the moan he let out a second ago ...

My heart pounds against my chest.

He groans again and I watch with wide eyes as he braces himself against the shower wall. He's facing away from me, and the shower must be cool because there's hardly any steam.

My eyes adjust as my eyes work down his muscled back to his arse, to the muscles as they contract.

As he moves his hips up and into his hand.

I should look away, but I can't.

I want—*need*—to watch this.

To watch as he brings himself over the edge ...

He's breathing heavily now, letting out breathy puffs of air.

This is wrong.

Walk away, Estelle.

Just as I get my feet to move, he makes some sort of animalistic, rumbling roar that has my whole body tingling, has my skin pebbling with arousal. I watch his hips stutter, the way they jerk as he throws his head back, almost like he's being electrocuted.

"Estelle," he rasps.

Fuck.

Then he drops his hand and leans his forehead against the wall, catching his breath.

My heart is still racing as I turn around and walk out of the bathroom, making sure my bedroom door is closed.

Fuck, my wand...

No time.

I can't risk him stepping out of the shower and realizing that I *watched* him like a stalker.

I climb into my bed and sink my hand underneath the band of my pajama bottoms, two fingers against my wet clit. *Why am I so wet?* A fierce orgasm rips through me thirty seconds later, and I suddenly realize that it's because of him.

It turned me on to watch him.

And the worst thing? It turned me on *more* that he had no idea I was privy to his shower wank.

I fall asleep feeling satisfied ... with a tinge of guilt wearing on me.

Even still ... he said my name.

That has to mean something.

————

I wake up before the sun is up, so after brushing my teeth, I gather my sketching supplies and head downstairs in my pajamas. It's barely five in the morning, and Miles's door is closed, so I am hoping for some alone time to work on my drawings before I go on my daily walk. Quietly treading down the carpeted stairs, I regret not putting on my slippers as my feet meet the cool tile of the ground floor. The kitchen is still dark, and I turn the light on so I can prepare my cup of tea—and my oats with chocolate chips and peanut butter.

I learned, over the last year, that routines are pivotal to my mental health. I tried to keep as much as possible of my home routine when I moved here—namely, my tea and oats, a long morning walk, twenty minutes sunbathing for natural vitamin D, and a long, luxurious shower. The rest of the day could go to shite, but if I had those four things, it was bound to be an okay day.

After sitting on one of the stools at the island, I start sketching ideas for my clothing line, ignoring the newly bare countertops in the kitchen. Miles had obviously seen the additional containers and placed them in the pantry.

Prat.

This was going to be an obscenely long year of tug of war.

I shake all thoughts of my new husband out of my mind, leaning back as I stare at the sketch I'm in the middle of.

I've already done the legwork on the marketing side of VeRue—the tentative name of my clothing line. It's a play on my last name. I like how simple it sounds. First and foremost, as with any new business venture, I've identified the niche market. I already know the basics. I want to design and manufacture fashionable, trendy accessible clothing—shirts, trousers, jumpers, and lingerie for those with disabilities. I'm also very adamant about having inclusive sizing.

I swallow when I look down at the ripped denim jeans that are cut higher in the back and lower in the front. My grandmother was wheelchair bound most of her adult life, and I remember her telling me that she was always on the hunt for jeans that would be comfortable for individuals who sat for most of the day.

In a way, this clothing line is all for her, and for people like her.

Beloved individuals who want—and deserve—to look and *feel* beautiful.

I crunched some numbers last night in bed, and it's a good thing I'll be receiving the first installment of Charles's money today. I need to hit the ground running if I want to get this line up and running within the next year. I need a ton of money for advertising to start out, so I'm glad to have a decent reservoir of funds to utilize. I also reached out to a website designer about building a website and designing a logo —my current website is a sad, sad affair, and it needs a major revamping.

I'll need a sewing machine, too—something to start playing around with patterns and designs. In London, I borrowed a friend's machine.

Currently, I have a few ethically sourced things on my website: blazers, dresses, and shirts, mostly. I like to get a feel for the fabrics, and a handful of people have been supporting my tiny independent shop. The VeRue social media accounts are small, but I'm hoping to ramp them all up before launching. Everything is starting to fall into place, and I'm tentatively hopeful that maybe, just maybe, VeRue will be up and running full steam ahead by this time next year.

I'm concentrating on finishing the sketch of the jeans as Miles saunters into the kitchen, looking alert.

"Morning," he says gruffly.

He's already dressed in a white button-down, sleeves adorned with those gold *R* cufflinks. The black trousers hug his waist and hips perfectly, and I quickly glance at his black belt with the gold Cartier buckle, admiring how the gold of his cufflinks complement his entire outfit.

How is it that he always looks so put together?

I'm staring at him and wondering if he sleeps in his suit—standing up, like a vampiric bat—when he clears his throat and wakes me from my stupor.

"Estelle?"

I jump at his use of my name, and I'm suddenly reminded of last night. Of my secret wank. Of *his*.

Fuck.

"Sorry, yes, good morning."

He smirks as he grinds his espresso, but he doesn't say anything. I suddenly realize I'm still in my silk turquoise pajama set and *not* wearing a bra.

I don't even want to know what my hair looks like …

I smooth it down with my hands before clearing

my throat. "So, I was thinking …" I start, clasping my hands together on the island. "We should probably practice."

My cheeks flame, and when I look up at Miles, he's leaning his hip against the counter, watching me with a confounded expression.

"Practice what?" he asks carefully.

I sigh. "Those pictures from the wedding reception were truly atrocious. Anyone with half a mind will see through our ruse if it happens again. We might be able to play those pictures off by saying it was nerves, but if it happens again? The media will see right through us. Not to mention, they won't want to give us publicity if they think we're always miserable together."

"And what, exactly, are you proposing?" he asks.

Shrugging, I tuck a stray curl behind my left ear. His eyes track my movements as I swallow nervously.

"On a scale of one to ten, how comfortable are you with me? Physically?" I add, hating myself for having to ask him such an audacious question.

"Zero."

I press my lips together. "Charming," I mutter, irritated. "I figured as much, and that's why we should practice."

"Estelle, what are you asking me?"

My nostrils flare at his use of my full name. I know he's doing it to piss me off, and it's working. Suddenly, an idea comes to me.

"I know you're probably used to women falling at your feet, but you're going to need to work a little harder with me," I tell him. "For starters, we should have nicknames. What do you think of sweetheart?"

His hands stop fidgeting with his cufflinks at the pet name. "Don't call me that."

"Pookie?" I try.

He scoffs. "I'm going to vomit."

I laugh. "I'll keep trying out different names until you like one, *love*," I offer, crossing my arms.

"Or we could just call each other by our first names," he mutters, pressing the start button for his espresso.

"We could, but you seem to have a problem with calling me Stella."

His jaw tenses as he watches the coffee drip into his porcelain cappuccino mug. "I'm not a nickname person."

I purse my lips and lower my voice. "Aw, is my big, surly husband always such a grump?" I taunt.

He flicks his green irises to my face, glaring at me. "Do you expect me to interact with you when you're being such a nuisance?"

"Oh, come on," I tease, smiling widely.

He walks to the refrigerator and pulls some milk out, adding it to his stainless steel frother.

"All right, I'll humor you. We can *practice*, Estelle," he says slowly, his eyes on the machine as he expertly foams his milk.

For the first time, I think I enjoy the fact that he refuses to call me Stella. That he's the only one who hasn't gotten the hint. Like it's a name only he can use.

Why does your real name bother you so much? It's a beautiful name. Did you know it means star *in Latin?*

"But I have three questions for you before we begin."

I swallow. "Okay."

He adds the foam to his espresso, the veins in his hands prominent with each flick of his wrist. When he's done, he places everything into the dishwasher. I've noticed that he does this a lot. Instead of leaving things on the counter, he instantly cleans it up. Turning to face me, he raises his mug and takes a deep sip before speaking.

"On a scale of one to ten, how comfortable are you with me? Physically," he adds, arching a brow.

"Zero," I tell him honestly.

It's not entirely true. We've had ... practice.

"How is it that I knew you'd make this difficult?" He grunts. "And your goal is to ... what? Get to ten?"

I shrug. "Yeah. But that will involve you not being a prat. Are you sure you're up for that?"

He nods once, not allowing my teasing to affect him. Outwardly, at least.

"I can try."

Smirking, I cock my head. "Thank you."

"Second question," he says slowly, his eyes tracking over my face. "Why Chanel No. 5?"

"It was my grandmother's perfume. It reminds me of her," I tell him honestly.

He looks down at his coffee. "She meant a lot to you? That's not my third question, by the way."

Pressing my lips together, I think about how much

I should tell him. However, unlike him, I have no reason to keep things hidden, so I take a shaky breath before answering.

"Yes. I didn't know my mother, so what I lacked in maternal warmth, I got from her," I explain, feeling my throat tighten like it does every time I talk about my grandmother. "She lived in Paris when I was growing up in London, but we saw each other all the time. And I used to spend summers in her flat in the Île Saint-Louis."

His head snaps up to mine. "Île Saint-Louis? Where you told me to go ..." he trails off as realization hits. "That's your favorite part of Paris because that's where she lived," he concludes.

I don't say anything as I nod once in affirmation.

"Okay, third question. What tattoo did you get to honor your grandmother?"

Of all the questions he could have asked, I was *not* expecting that one. Looking down at the island, I answer quietly, thinking back to the late night in a dingy Paris tattoo parlor.

"A butterfly," I answer, looking up at him.

His lips twitch, but he doesn't smile. "Where?"

Without answering, I sit up straight and unbutton my pajama shirt without thinking, lowering it just enough to show off the butterfly on my sternum. It's right in the middle of my chest—just underneath my breasts. I don't let him see anything he shouldn't, but the way Miles sets his mug down heavily on the marble counter and takes several steps forward, eyes locked on my chest ...

My skin burns under his perusal.

"I wanted some place that I could hide away under a shirt. This way, it's close to my heart," I explain, swallowing thickly.

"That night," he murmurs. "When you asked me if I had a tattoo. Did you have this?"

I nod. "I did. You might've seen it if you weren't being such a gentleman."

His green eyes bore down into mine, a look of determination on his face as he reaches a hand forward.

"May I?" he asks.

His surly mask is gone, replaced yet again with *that look*. The one that makes me swoon. The one that makes me think Miles Ravage is very, very good at burying his true feelings. He looks almost in a daze.

"Go ahead," I tell him.

Reaching down, he uses his thumb to trace the outline of the small butterfly—about two inches wide. His fingers are curled, and they graze against my bare skin. My pajama shirt is mere inches from falling open completely, exposing myself. With each sweep of his thumb, I try not to gasp out loud. My skin pebbles, and Miles hums low in his throat.

Fuck.

Why is that noise so sexy?

"I think we're at least a one out of ten now, don't you think, butterfly?" he asks, his voice almost gentle.

"I–what–yeah," I answer dumbly, processing his words.

And that nickname …

A heavy, aching stone settles between my legs at the way his gravelly voice enunciates each syllable.

Butterfly.

He pulls away, and when I look back up into his eyes, his pupils are slightly blown out. Licking his lips, he shakes his head as he takes a step back.

I can practically see the bricks he's placing up, building a wall too tall for anyone to possibly scale.

Clearing his throat, he walks back over to his macchiato, and I pull my shirt together, buttoning it quickly.

"I'm going for a walk in a few minutes if you'd like to join me," I offer. "Maybe we can have breakfast together. The more time we spend together, the more comfortable we will be in public."

He scowls as he watches me, sipping his coffee. "A walk?"

I nod. "I go on a walk every morning. It helps me ..." I trail off, biting my lower lip. "It keeps me feeling even keeled."

Cocking his head, he doesn't say anything, so I continue talking nervously.

"I'll just go up and change out of my pajamas," I tell him.

He frowns. "I don't have time to *walk*, Estelle."

My brows furrow. "How do you expect to get to a ten if we never spend time together?"

"What are you talking about? I told you we can have dinner together every night—"

"It's not enough!" I blurt, cheeks flaming. "And even if it were, surely berating me over cottage pie and spending most of the evening in awkward silence is not the way to befriend me."

His jaw ticks as he studies me with a scowl. "Fine. Let's go on a walk, then." He stalks out of the kitchen, and I swear I hear him mutter *insufferable wench* as he turns the corner.

CHAPTER ELEVEN
THE WALK

MILES

A few minutes later, I'm pacing by the back door as I wait for Estelle to meet me for a walk. The sun is beginning to peak over the hills of Crestwood, bathing the back of the castle in golden, peach-colored light. I place my hands in the pocket of my pants as I gaze out over the horizon, wondering why I agreed to a *walk* with her. I wasn't lying when I said I don't have time for a walk. I have an eight o'clock meeting in the office, and it's now nearing six. I have to leave in the next hour if I'm going to make it on time. Grumbling to myself about Estelle's perkiness, I'm just about to march upstairs and demand to know what's taking so long when I hear her tromp into the room, her sneakers squeaking against the marble.

"You know, most people set their feet down when they walk," I muse, turning around and arching a brow as she saunters over. "You stomp everywhere you go, and it's incredibly loud."

She cocks her head and smiles up at me. Her curly hair is pulled up into a high ponytail, and she's wearing—what the *hell* is she wearing? It's like a leotard but for her whole body. It's black, skintight, and she has a bright pink sweatshirt in her hands. On her feet are highlighter yellow sneakers. The black fabric clings to every curve of her body, and my mouth fills with saliva as my eyes do a slow perusal of her outfit.

She must not be wearing a bra, because I can see her tight, little nipples poking through the fabric just before she pulls her sweatshirt on. I feel my cock twitch when I think of how soft her skin was earlier. How I could see the swell of both of her breasts, so close to being exposed, only inches from my finger. I imagine they're buoyant and soft, a perfect handful. And *that* thought leads me to thinking about how I jerked off to thoughts of her last night. How it would feel to slide my cock between those supple mounds, how it would feel to squeeze them together around my cock, the doughy, velvet feel of her skin enveloping me as I come all over her chest ...

These kinds of outfits are not helping me to stay away from her.

And I really, *really* need to stay away from her.

"Shall we?" she asks brightly, oblivious to my lewd, obscene thoughts.

"If we must," I answer, keeping my voice hard.

"Oh, please. You'll probably really enjoy it. I find

that exercising first thing in the morning helps my mood all day long. Maybe if you exercised regularly, you wouldn't be so bad-tempered."

I scowl down at her as she opens the back door and leads us out and to the spacious back garden of the castle.

"I do exercise. I have weights and a treadmill in my office at work," I answer, almost petulantly. Frowning, I try not to stare at her voluptuous ass when she walks ahead of me. "Is that why you're so upbeat all the time?"

She doesn't say anything as we set out around the pool. She leads me to the side of the garden, opening a gate on the left of the castle grounds and walking toward the path I'd completely forgotten about since I was a kid. My mother used to walk here sometimes. It's a dirt path that circles the entirety of the property, and then it snakes up the mountain a bit above the castle. As I recall, it's a couple miles long.

I'd have to push my meeting back if we did the whole loop, and knowing her, she wants to do the whole damn loop.

Scowling at the thought of Estelle upending my morning, I stop walking.

"I have another idea," I say loudly.

She's a few feet ahead of me, and she turns around to face me. "You're actually going to show me what you're hiding in your cellar?" she asks, quirking a brow.

This woman ...

"No. But do you want to meet Lucifer?"

She tilts her head as she watches me skeptically. "I feel like that's a trick question."

I laugh despite my irritation. "Come on."

"I know you loathe me, Miles, but bringing your wife to meet the devil is probably frowned upon," she adds, her voice low and throaty as she comes to stand next to me.

The way her lips casually roll over *your wife* ...

I shake my head to clear my thoughts, walking in the opposite direction toward the right side of the castle where Lucifer's paddock is located. It's hidden behind a hedge, and only a few people, including Louis, who cares for Lucifer on a day-to-day basis, know it's back here. Estelle follows me warily when I walk up to the gate and enter the code. Swinging the gate open, I gesture for her to go before me.

"After you," I tell her.

She eyes me with caution before walking through the gate first.

And then, before I understand what's happening, she mutters something under her breath and twists around, colliding with my body and wrapping her arms around me.

"Oh no, oh no, oh no," she murmurs.

I'm too surprised to do anything, and before I can ask her what's wrong, Lucifer bleats and hops over to us.

"Oh my God, Miles. You've got to be kidding me."

She sounds terrified, and as I wrap my arms around her, I glance over her shoulder to check for a bear or something else just as terrifying. There's nothing—only Lucifer.

My pygmy goat.

"Um," I murmur, not wanting to let her go. Her body is warm, and soft, and she feels fucking amazing against me. "Is something wrong?" I ask slowly.

"I am terrified of goats," she says, her voice breaking. "Utterly, terribly, insanely afraid of them."

I press my lips together to keep from laughing out loud. "You're ... scared ... of ... goats?" I ask tentatively.

She huffs indignantly. "Yes, Miles. I know it doesn't make any sense, but it's something about their beady, little eyes—"

My laugh interrupts her, and she pushes away from me quickly, anger flooding her expression. Her features pinch together as she shoves my chest.

"It's not funny!" she yells.

Lucifer is standing behind her, and he bleats loudly.

Perfect timing, little buddy.

Estelle screams and jumps, scurrying away and back through the gate behind me.

"Not today, Satan," she says before closing the gate.

Lucifer looks at the gate she left through, and I can't help but grin as I bend down, patting the top of his head.

"Don't worry, Luc. We'll work on her, okay? She obviously doesn't know how cute and innocent you are."

Lucifer lets out a small bleat, and I walk over to the little house Liam built for him last year. I check his water and food, ensuring he has enough, and then I tell him I'll be back later to check on him.

As I walk off toward the gate, I hear him hop over to his play area. Because, yes, goats apparently need enriching toys and a stimulating environment. And, since the chances of actually reproducing with someone and creating another human are very, very low, I've gone out of my way to make this place as state-of-the-art as possible. Boulders, tree trunks of varying sizes, platforms, tunnels, a seesaw, and a field of overgrown grass ...

He's the most spoiled goat I've ever met.

I'm still grinning when I close the gate behind me. Estelle is leaning against the nearby side of the castle, glaring angrily at me.

"You could have warned me," she accuses.

As much as I want to apologize for laughing, I also can't help but find her fear of Lucifer fucking adorable.

I hold my hands up in mock surrender. "I promise he won't chase after you with his beady, little eyes," I tease. "Though I suppose if you really piss me off, I won't hesitate to let him loose in our quarters."

She growls as she charges forward, pushing me roughly. "That's not funny," she says indignantly. "You wouldn't dare," she says, narrowing her eyes.

And—*fuck*.

I smile down at her as my hands grab her wrists of their own volition. The sun is now peeking over the horizon, making her skin glow golden. Her blue eyes, normally so dark, look almost icy, and her cheeks are flushed from the foggy, cool morning and probably a little bit from being angry with me.

"I find it disturbing that terrifying me with your goat is what gets you to actually smile at me," she says dryly.

I huff a laugh. I suppose she's not wrong, but *fuck. Why do I enjoy riling her up so much?*

And why do I really want to fucking kiss her right now?

I step away quickly as the thought enters my mind. Sometimes I admire my brother, Chase, for going after Juliet so ruthlessly once she got through to him. She had to push him to get to that place, sure, but once she did, their relationship was explosive and fiery—a maelstrom of angst and years of pent-up longing. I'm sure if he were in my shoes, he'd have her on her knees, begging for more. I swallow as I look away, trying to keep my expression neutral and unaffected.

That's not me.

I'm not as confident as my other brothers, even if I want people to think I am.

It's why I keep my scars covered—because it's easier to step into the role I've created if people don't stare at the one thing I can't stand about myself.

Despite that, though ... Estelle *is* starting to affect me. Slowly—like smelling a wildfire from far off. Little hints of a scent at first. Not enough to make you pause. Nothing to worry about. But the closer it gets, the more it begins to permeate my senses. And like a wildfire, it burns slowly at first. Small embers catching on a nearby tree, which lead to more embers, more flames.

Until it's too late, and you're engulfed in flames you never saw coming.

I don't give myself easily—to anyone. I've never been in love. I never saw myself in a serious relationship, and until a few months ago, I sure as hell never saw myself getting married. It only became an option recently, and only to smooth over the defective Ravage reputation.

Why would I have ever considered marriage outside of those terms? Who could love me when I'm defective? A workaholic. Scheming, lying, and probably a little bit corrupt. Quiet. *Scarred.*

Cautious.

I am cautious.

Estelle looks up at me with wide eyes, as if she can read my mind.

"Well, I suppose we should head back," she says quietly, giving me a soft smile.

I nod once. "Sure. I have to get to work anyway."

She crosses her arms. "I swear to God, if you even think about pranking me with that goat—"

"His name is Lucifer. You're going to have to befriend him at some point, you know."

"Why?" she asks, her voice incredulous.

"Because what's mine is yours," I concede.

"Really?"

She looks like she wants to say something, but she must change her mind because she doesn't respond.

I don't say anything as we start our trek back because I know what she's thinking.

What's mine is yours ... *except when it comes to my secrets.*

"Now that I know he's here, I'm not going to be able to sleep," she adds.

I chuckle. "Why goats? He's a *pygmy* goat. He weighs like twenty pounds."

"I don't know. When I was little, my grandmother would put on the television to distract me while she went out onto her patio to smoke. One time, there was this weird French children's show with an evil cartoon goat." Shrugging, she smiles. "I guess it had an effect on me."

I laugh again. "I promise Lucifer is not evil."

"Why did you name him Lucifer?"

"His eyes turn red when it's dark."

She stops walking and stares at me with horror.

I can't help but laugh. "Fuck, you're gullible."

"You're a bastard," she mutters, marching ahead of me and pushing the back door open.

I follow her into the kitchen. "I couldn't help it. I'm sorry."

She walks over to the kettle, and flips it on, turning around as she leans her hip against the counter.

"Isn't there anything you're scared of?"

I shrug. "Not really. I've already lived through my worst nightmare," I add without thinking.

Her lips part slightly as her eyes wander over my neck—right over my scar.

Fuck.

I adjust my collar, clearing my throat.

"How did it happen?" she asks gently.

I press my lips together. "I don't like talking about it."

She frowns. "Wonderful. We can add it to the list of secrets you're keeping from me."

If you only knew ...

Anger flares through me as I stand up straighter. Clenching my jaw, I walk toward the door of the kitchen.

"I'm happy to talk about anything you'd like, but that is one topic that's off-limits. Is that understood?"

She doesn't back down. Instead, she just stares at me.

I don't like it when she looks at me like that—like she can read my thoughts.

It feels like she's examining me under a microscope.

"Have a good day, Estelle," I grit out, intending to leave her there so I don't say anything hurtful.

She follows me out of the kitchen, and I sigh as I turn around near the main library.

"You can't keep pushing me away, you know. We'll never get to ten if you refuse to let me in on your secrets. I don't need to know everything, but I should probably know how my husband got that scar on his neck, or, while we're on the subject of secrets, if my husband is hiding dead bodies in that bloody cellar—"

I stalk to where she's standing and grab her elbow, seething. She's so fucking infuriating. Pushing, pushing, pushing. Always *pushing*. And she's so goddamn gorgeous doing it that I forget to be irritated half the time.

My lips curl back as I glare at her. "Like I said, I have been very generous thus far in this marriage of convenience we seem to have gotten ourselves into," I growl. "But I promise you, keep pushing me and I dare you to see what happens, Estelle."

"You mean the marriage *you* got us into by lying to a person I work with," she bites back, nostrils flaring.

I take an intimidating step closer. "I didn't force you to agree," I grit out.

She considers me for a minute. "Didn't you, though?" she asks softly. Her expression crumples slightly before she takes a step back and looks down at the floor. "Have a good day at work, Miles."

I watch her walk away, unsure if I should say anything—apologize, tell her everything I'm hiding from her, kiss her ...

The guilt might eat me alive before I have the chance.

Sighing, I run a hand over my face before stalking to the front door.

It's not like anyone will think it's weird that I'm in the office before seven.

It just opens my eyes further to the fact that I can't have meaningful relationships in life, even if I want to.

And not just because of my physical scars.

But because of my psychological ones, too.

CHAPTER TWELVE
THE CLAIMING

The next week passes the same way. I wake up early and spend my mornings in the kitchen, sketching and building out my business plan for VeRue. With wide, disbelieving eyes, I remembered to check my bank account balance last night. Sure enough, I'm now almost six figures richer, so I spend the first two mornings of the week sending out emails to website designers and wholesalers to get fabric samples. Later on in the week, I work on more sketches so I have everything prepared for when the website goes live.

Every morning, at six on the dot, Miles saunters into the kitchen. We're cordial, though I jokingly use the term *frenemy,* since we're sort of friends, sort of enemies, due to the constant bickering. Whether it be bickering over the jars that magically appear on the counters every morning—and disappear every night—

or bickering over whether tea or coffee is better. By Wednesday, I've figured out that he's less grumpy *after* coffee, so I let him stew until he's done with his first cup. He refuses to join me for my morning walks despite my asking him every morning, but he does allow me to play around with nicknames. So far, he's hated all of them, but I persist.

Usually after more bickering about our plan to work on our physical chemistry, he leaves for work. I spend my mornings working as well, and when I need a break, I wander around the castle alone. On Thursday afternoon, I decide to try the cellar door again—to no avail.

I join Miles for dinner every evening, and so far, it's more cordial pleasantries mixed with, you guessed it, more bickering. The food is delicious, so I focus on that instead of the way his eyes sometimes linger on mine for a second too long. Or the way his long fingers grip his cutlery with a delicacy that has me wondering just how formal his upbringing was. I don't push him to be physical or to *practice*, because I don't want to be on the receiving end of his coldness. It's better if we stay neutral, and though I joke about his demeanor, I can sense him relaxing around me by Thursday evening— just barely. No matter what I do, I can't seem to bring the Miles I first met back to the surface.

I'm not sure where he spends his free time, as it's sure as fuck not in our shared living quarters. I suspect he spends most of his time at his office, or possibly down in his mystery cellar. It's like he's pushing me away on purpose to keep his distance.

But why?

By Friday, I am absolutely going stir crazy. I nearly cry with relief when Juliet texts me, inviting Miles and I out for drinks with her and Chase in Crestwood that evening. It's a welcome surprise, and though I suppose it's technically a double date, at least I'll have someone there to buffer the tension with Miles.

So, with something exciting on the horizon, I spend my afternoon getting ready to go out to a bar instead of having dinner with my crotchety husband. Instead of texting me directly, he sends Luna to inform me that he will be late tonight, and he'll meet us all at the pub when he finishes working. I grumble to myself at that after Luna leaves me to continue getting ready.

Deciding to screw with his head, I decide on a dark brown leather mini skirt with a snakeskin pattern. Normally, I'd pair it with a colorful top, but instead, I decide on a cream-colored sweater with a low neckline and bell sleeves. It's early November, and it's significantly cooler out now, so I also pull on sheer tights. I straighten my hair for the first time in years, and then I step into a pair of strappy, gold stiletto heels.

Assessing myself, I smile as I clasp the gold *R* necklace around my neck before grabbing my clutch and making my way downstairs for Niro. Chase and Juliet offered to pick me up, but I declined. There's no point in coming all the way to the castle only to drive back into Crestwood, where they live.

My husband could have offered. Should *have offered. But I digress.*

I grind my jaw when I think of how Miles couldn't

bother to text me. I was restricted to information he filtered down to the people he employed. Like I didn't matter enough to get a direct text. I distract myself on the drive to the bar by FaceTiming with my father. It's past midnight in London, but he's usually up late. I update him on everything, leaving out the bickering and general sense of discontent with Miles. If I tell him how lonely the last week has been, he might worry—given my past—so I don't bring it up. I end the video call just as we pull up to the low-key pub in downtown Crestwood.

Thanking Niro, I walk into the establishment, noting the quaint British touches. My gaze lingers over the horrid and outdated curtains, the old rugs that have seen better days, a pool table, and lots of sticky tables. I smile as I walk inside, suddenly reminiscing about home. It even *smells* like a British pub—stale beer and fried food.

"Stella!" Juliet comes barreling toward me, enveloping me in a tight hug. When she pulls away, she gives me a sly smile. "You look incredible."

I laugh. "Thank you." She takes my hand and leads me to the table she's secured with Chase. She's wearing a short, dark red dress with black boots. Her hair is pulled back into a loose ponytail. "You look beautiful as well." My eyes skirt to Chase, who stands to hug me.

"Stella," he murmurs, pulling away. "So glad you could make it."

"Thanks for inviting me. To be honest, I am starting to feel a bit like Beauty in that castle."

"I'll get you a drink," Chase offers. "What's your poison?"

I look up at him, startled to see a familiar smirk on his face. But instead of being accompanied by cold indifference, Chase is all warm energy. Large smiles. Ease of movements versus the jerky, stilted movements of his older brother. He's wearing jeans and a flannel button-down. I would bet a hundred pounds that Miles doesn't own jeans.

The realization of that has me reeling.

Who the hell did I marry? He's so *different from me. From them.*

"Uh, anything. I like lagers," I offer, giving him a small smile.

After he walks away, Juliet leans forward on the table. "How has it been?" she asks, sipping a beer. "Living in that massive castle with Miles ... I'm sure you have *sooo* many stories."

I open and close my mouth.

"It's been ..." Swallowing once, I shake my head. Why bother lying? I've never been a closed off person, and Juliet seems nice. "It's been a bit lonely. I don't see him much."

Her eyebrows furrow. "Really? Oh. I guess I just thought ..." she trails off. "I mean, I know the circumstances. Chase told me. But you guys seemed happy at the wedding."

I shrug. "Something changed the night of the reception."

Her face pinches with pity, but before she can

respond, Chase returns with three beers, setting one down in front of each of us. Juliet looks at her boyfriend with pure adoration. She wrinkles her nose at him and he smiles, kissing the tip of it before turning back to me.

"So, how long have you guys been dating?" I ask, suddenly feeling like I'm intruding on a private date. Their chemistry is palpable.

"Three months and a few weeks," Chase answers, his lips twitching up into a smile. "And ..." he looks at Juliet. "We're not dating anymore."

"What?" I start, confused.

"We're married," Juliet answers, cheeks flushing. My eyes immediately go down to Juliet's ring finger, where I see a gold signet ring with an engraved *R* set with tiny diamonds.

"That's so exciting! When?"

"The same day you and Miles got married," Chase says, grimacing. "I hope you don't mind sharing an anniversary with us."

I bark a laugh. "I hardly think Miles and I will be celebrating anniversaries," I tell them.

Juliet tilts her head. "Are you sure about that?"

I take a long, long sip of my beer to avoid her question. I'm grateful when the server comes to our table to take our food order. His British accent catches me off guard, and we all agree on the bottomless basket of chicken wings.

"A fellow Brit," I tell him after Juliet is done ordering.

He's young—mid-twenties, probably, with shaggy

blond hair. Attractive. He gives me a genuine smile before answering.

"Where are you from?" he asks, his northern accent prominent.

"London."

He nods. "I can see that," he says, unabashedly letting his eyes wander down my body. I realize that because my hands are clasped in my lap, he can't see my wedding ring. "I'm from Yorkshire. What brings you to California?"

I'm too surprised to hear a familiar accent to think straight, which is why I say, "Oh, lots of reasons."

He smiles wider. "Same here. It's so different from England."

"In so many ways," I agree.

He smiles down at me. "Listen, I'm off at nine if you'd like to grab a drink."

"I can't. But thank you for offering," I answer, giving him a gentle smile.

He looks disappointed, but he soon recovers. "No problem."

After he takes our orders, Juliet starts to laugh. "If Miles had been here ..." she trails off. Chase watches me with something bordering on amusement and maybe a bit of surprise.

Can they blame me? It's the first time *anyone* has looked right at me since I married his brother.

I don't say anything, because truthfully, I'm not sure what Miles would have done seeing someone hit on me. I haven't seen one iota of jealousy from him, or even a sliver of interest in me.

Chase, Juliet, and I slide into a comfortable conversation after that. One large sharing basket of chicken wings and two beers later, I'm feeling much better about my situation. The more I drink, the less my eyes flick to the front door every time someone comes through. Chase and Juliet are doing their best to keep me distracted. I know their choice of establishment tonight was for me, too. I appreciate it. Between Liam, Luna, Juliet, and Chase, I'm starting to feel close to all of the important people in Miles's life.

Everyone except him.

When I finish my second beer, I get up to use the bathroom. As I make my way down the darkened hallway, I run smack into the server. He ducks his head to let me pass.

"I'm sorry if I made you uncomfortable back there," he says when I'm a few feet away.

I turn to face him, ignoring my nearly-bursting bladder. "No, you didn't," I tell him. "The truth is, you seem really nice. But I'm married," I tell him, holding up my left hand.

Even as it leaves my mouth, it feels fake. The words taste like ash on my tongue. Because what Miles and I have is not a marriage.

It's hardly a friendship most days.

He cocks his head. "Where's your husband, then?" he asks. I can tell he means well, and I give him a small smile.

"He's working late," I answer.

The server presses his lips together as he shakes his

head. "His loss. If I were the one married to you, I wouldn't—"

"Is there a reason you're still flirting with my wife?"

I spin around to face a seething Miles. His jaw is clenched, and his hands are in his pockets. He doesn't look at me—he just continues staring at the server.

"Miles, he was just being nice," I explain.

His eyes flick over to my face, and I can see the unmitigated fury in his flared nostrils and flushed cheeks. He turns to face the server again.

"I suggest you leave," Miles grits out.

The server holds his hands up. "I was just speaking the truth, mate. You have a beautiful wife."

"Get. Out."

The server chuckles. "All I'm saying is I'm a nice bloke, but the next guy might not be. I'm just a fellow Brit watching out for her."

I hear a deep, low growl emitting from Miles's chest. He steps forward. "If I see you speak another word to her, I will ensure you're unemployable for the rest of your life." The server's eyes widen, but there's a hint of skepticism. Miles must see it too, because he takes another step closer. "Go ahead and underestimate me. I'd love to prove you wrong," he snarls.

The server must realize he's in a losing battle, because he gives me a small nod before turning and leaving Miles and I alone in the dark hallway.

"That was unnecessary," I tell him, crossing my arms.

Miles slowly turns to face me. His darkened eyes skirt from my feet to my face slowly, like he's drinking me in. His expression softens slightly when he meets my gaze, and he rubs his mouth with his hand.

"You look lovely," he says curtly. *Formally.*

I roll my eyes. "So nice of you to grace us with your presence," I retort, suddenly feeling angry at his jealous antics. He has *no right* to stake a claim over me like that. Not when he doesn't seem to give a single fuck about me.

"I'm sorry I'm late," he offers, walking closer. And despite really needing a wee, I can't help but be transfixed by him. His crisp suit. His intense scowl. His light green eyes. I go still until he's right in front of me. Reaching out, his hand comes to my straightened hair. "I like it better when it's curly," he says, his voice husky.

I get a whiff of green apples, and I fight the urge to kick him in the bollocks. "I'll take your *preferences* into consideration next time." *Next time.* As if getting drinks with his brother and new sister-in-law will become a regular occurrence. Which means more days of solitude and solo drives into Crestwood. More being the third wheel until Miles deigns us with his presence. Wondering if he even *sees* me most days, or if there's ever a time he doesn't act like a robot.

A new rush of anger floods me. "You know, if you'd heard the conversation I was having with that man, you might've heard me tell him that I was married," I tell him. "I promised you monogamy and I intend to keep my word."

Something akin to surprise flashes over his expression. "You think I'm worried about *you*, butterfly?"

His nickname for me turns my knees to jelly. He's *almost* close enough to brush the front of his body with mine, but not quite.

I shrug. "It sure seems like you don't trust me."

He laughs at that, and I'm thrown off by the way it floods me with warmth, and the way the sound is almost light—like a purr. I haven't really heard it before.

He should laugh more.

"You think I don't know that you're mine?" My breathing hitches as his hand brushes against my hip, gripping it firmly. "You're lucky he didn't touch you, Estelle."

"And why's that?" I whisper, my breath shaky. *Damn him. Damn him for always being able to pull me back into his strong, gravitational pull.*

Giving me a cruel, lopsided smile, he leans down until he's inches away from my face.

"Because I don't like it when people touch my things."

He turns and leaves before I can process his words. Stepping into the bathroom, I have to take a few steadying breaths at the sink before I'm able to relieve myself.

Because I don't like it when people touch my things.

When I'm finished, I'm oscillating between begrudging him for his audacity and calming the flutters in my core.

You think I don't know that you're mine?

I take some more deep breaths as I exit the bathroom, staring at my reflection in the full-length mirror leaning against the darkened hallway. I start to wonder why I thought the pink lip gloss was a good idea. Why I pulled the tight skirt on. Why I went through the effort of straightening my hair, making it fall to my waist in thick, straight lines.

Why am I doing all of this for him?

Marriage is about compromises, but it sure seems like I'm doing a hell of a lot of the compromising lately. And yet, when *one* person talks to me—respectfully, I might add—Miles acts jealous?

Fuck. That.

Walking out of the bathroom, I make my way back to the table slowly. My eyes catch on the server as I move, and I glance over at our table to see Miles watching me. Smirking, I change directions and head for the server. He's walking away from a table, so I jog to catch up with him.

"Hey," I tell him, tapping his shoulder.

He turns to face me, eyes wary. "Hey, look. I'm sorry about earlier. I didn't mean to cause trouble."

"No, you don't have to apologize. My husband, he's ..." I trail off. "Anyway, I'm sorry. He shouldn't have threatened you."

The server gives me a warm smile as he flips his blonde hair. "Thanks. He seems to love you a lot."

I scoff. "Yes, well ... thank you for understanding. Have a good night, okay?"

He gives me a warm smile. "You too. If you're ever in the mood for a proper chippy, feel free to come back any time." He glances over my shoulder. "As a friend," he clarifies. "You may want to tell your jealous husband that last bit, yeah?"

Without another word, he turns and walks away.

I spin around with a large grin. *Ha, take that, you jealous arsehole.* My eyes catch on Miles instantly. A shadowed, dark look flits across his face—almost like he's in pain. I go still and the smile drops off my face when he locks eyes with me—and not because he's angry, like I expected.

No, what makes me stop in my tracks is the turbulent expression marring his features.

CHAPTER THIRTEEN
THE REALIZATION

MILES

I nurse my beer, sipping slowly as Estelle laughs with Chase and Juliet. I want to join in, but all I can think about is what she said to the *fucking* server. I refused to ask, internally citing my pride. They didn't talk for long, but I can't stop the possibilities running through my mind. He's English, so obviously she has that in common with him. He's young, like her. Even though she's only eight years younger than me, it's still significant enough for me to wonder if she would have more in common with someone closer to her age.

And, unlike me, he didn't seem to be scarred beyond recognition.

Perhaps Estelle deserves to be with someone more like him. A friendly server at a pub instead of a damaged CEO. Someone who would understand her damn cookie and tea obsession. Someone who doesn't work eighteen hour days.

Someone who doesn't hole themselves in their office to avoid her.

And, most importantly, someone who doesn't lie to her.

"Miles."

I snap my head up as Juliet watches me with concern. "Sorry," I tell her. "Long day at the office."

My eyes flick to Chase. He watches me with narrowed eyes but doesn't say anything.

"I don't know anyone who works as much as you," Estelle chimes in, sipping her cider.

"Chase used to be like that," Juliet offers her. "But I made him start working normal hours. Which is still sixty hours a week," she adds, smirking.

"What's the secret?" Estelle asks, winking at me. "I'd like to see my husband more."

I don't deserve her.

"I swear, he must sleep in his office some nights," she adds, patting my thigh in a teasing manner.

I do.

"I wouldn't be surprised," Chase adds, looking at me with an arched brow. "Though I'm not sure why he would when he has a lovely, orange duvet to curl up with."

Estelle cackles.

I love it when she laughs like that.

I can't help but smile at Chase's joke. "Yes, well, some of us prefer the cold, hard leather to polyester," I retort, hollowing my cheeks as I look down at my wife.

"Though, the sentiment is much appreciated," I add for her sake.

"Okay, well now I have to see what all the fuss is about," Juliet answers. "Chase told me that Stella has livened the place up a bit, but I haven't had a chance to look around since before your wedding day."

"You mean *your* wedding day?" I ask her, and she throws her head back as she laughs. I turn to Estelle. "Did they tell you about that?"

Estelle nods. "They did." Something sad crosses her features. "It'll be fun for them to remember when they celebrate their anniversary."

Theirs.

Not *ours.*

Because she doesn't see us celebrating any anniversaries.

I take another sip of my beer as the three of them get back to their conversation, unaware of my self-flagellating inner monologue. Chase and Juliet are talking about their upcoming honeymoon when I see Estelle look up at me out of the corner of my eye.

She's seated next to me, nearly thigh to thigh. Leaning back, I place my arm around the back of the booth, and to my surprise, she scoots slightly closer to me. I get a whiff of her perfume, and I have to close my eyes briefly to keep from actively sniffing the top of her scalp. Her warm body presses against me as Juliet and Chase continue talking about the Maldives. I'm not paying attention. All I can think about is how my wife fits so perfectly against me. How soft her thighs feel against mine, even through the thick fabric of my trousers.

How she always smells like jasmine.

How she's constantly smiling—except when she talks to me.

Her hand roves over to my thigh, and I have to clench my teeth so that I don't moan out loud.

Why is she doing this to me?

More importantly ... why am I letting her?

Before I can put distance between us once again, Estelle leans in close enough to whisper in my ear.

"It was nothing, you know."

Chase and Juliet are talking to only each other now —something about the logistics of their overwater cabana. I tilt my face slightly so that my lips are closer to her ear.

"What was nothing?" I ask, though I know exactly what she's referring to.

"The server. When I went back over to him. I just apologized. Like I said, it was nothing."

"Thanks for letting me know," I murmur, pulling away slightly.

Her grip tightens on my thigh, and *fuck me* if my cock doesn't twitch against the placket of my pants.

"I didn't realize you were so jealous," she says slowly.

My jaw feathers as I consider her words. "I'm not jealous."

"Then what would you call that whole stunt earlier?" she asks, her voice low.

I chuckle. "Like I said, I'm not jealous. I'm territorial. Jealousy implies wanting something that's not yours. Territorial is protecting what's already yours."

She stiffens next to me. "You sure have a funny way of showing me that I'm yours," she murmurs. "Try harder, Miles."

Before I can respond, she pulls out from under my arms, excusing herself to use the restroom.

After she's gone, Juliet and Chase return their attention to me.

"I really like her," Juliet squeaks, her cheeks flushed from the alcohol. "I think you should marry her."

"Too late," I answer, deadpan.

She scoffs impatiently. "You know what I mean. Marry her *for real*," she slurs, her eyes slitted.

I arch a brow at my brother, who just watches his new wife with a soft, enamored look.

God, they're nauseating.

"Yes, well, I doubt she'll want to continue for the year with the way I've been acting."

Especially when she finds out what I've done.

"It couldn't hurt to tell her how you feel," Chase says smugly, sipping his whiskey.

I glare at him, frowning. "Juliet, it's time to take your drunken husband home."

She laughs. "I don't think so. I'm on Chase's side this time. I've never seen you like this with anyone."

I grind my jaw before taking another sip of my beer. "I think you're misinterpreting things," I tell her slowly.

She shakes her head. "No. I'm not. And I think she feels the same way about you."

"Can you believe this is the same guy who was giving *me* advice about *you* only three months ago?" Chase asks Juliet, obviously goading me. "My, how times have changed. He can dish it out, but he can't take it."

"Fuck off," I mutter, though I can't help the small smile playing at my lips. I finish off the rest of my drink.

Chase slides the rest of his double whiskey over to me. "Drink this and go give your wife a real kiss, Miles."

I stare at him. "You can't be serious."

He raises his brows in a silent challenge. "I *dare* you."

"Fuck you," I grunt, shooting the rest of his whiskey and wishing I'd eaten dinner. It instantly makes me feel courageous and *way* too brave for my own good.

"Go, Miles, go!" Juliet cheers, giggling.

I flip them off before walking off to find my wife.

She's just coming out of the bathroom when I see her, and I step to the side, into the shadows of the hallway, so that she doesn't see me right away. I watch her as she glances at herself in the full-size mirror, pulling on her skirt slightly and rolling one of her ankles. She runs a hand through her hair, and my eyes flick over to her reflection. My heart pounds when she places a hand against her chest, closing her eyes and muttering something I can't hear.

Like she's gearing up to see me again.

Like she has to work herself up to be near me.

Fuck.

I can't move. I *won't* move.

Because I'm just now realizing that my feelings for Estelle go way deeper than physical lust. I want to make her happy. I want her to *want* me. But I don't think she does—not in the way I need her to. In fact, looking at the way she seems to be giving herself a pep talk, it almost seems like she's dreading it.

Even though I tried so hard to avoid it, to avoid her, she's become the shiny new toy I can't stop thinking about.

And I've become the six-year-old version of myself who would do anything for that toy. Who loved that toy *too* much. Who *suffocated* that toy to death, until my mother had to throw it away, tattered and torn.

Because, more than anything, I am afraid of suffocating her.

That's just who I am—my father's son.

Conniving. Scheming. *Selfish.*

My scars are only the physical manifestations of my brokenness.

What's behind those scars runs so, so much deeper.

I lied to her.

The money didn't come from my father. I knew before she agreed to marry me that he wouldn't keep his end of the deal. It's what he's famous for, after all— losing someone else's money and making it look like an accident. Making it look like *their* fault.

He would probably blame her father, too, to keep his hands clean.

So, I deposited my money into her account. And I'll continue to do so every month, under the guise of my father. There was never a monthly installment agreement. I made that up to keep her *here* with me. So yes, I'm a selfish motherfucker. A lying, scheming Ravage.

If she knew...

I close my eyes with a quiet sigh.

The worst thing is, I don't want to tell her. Because once I do, there will be nothing keeping her here. She'd realize my image isn't worth salvaging. She'd realize the extent of my dishonesty—and how tainted the Ravage name really is.

She wouldn't want anything to do with us.

I promised her no more secrets, and then I went and hid the biggest one from her.

So, no. I can't kiss her. *Won't* kiss her.

The best thing I can do is save her from myself.

Taking a step back from the dark hallway, I walk out of the restaurant without another word to anyone.

CHAPTER FOURTEEN
THE KEY

Stella

When I was in primary school, I used to get in trouble for sneaking around. I've always been a curious person, and very good at smelling bullshit. Perhaps it's because I was raised by my father and grandmother, the latter of whom was the epitome of badass, but I've questioned authority since I could talk. Being able to tell when someone is lying is one of my best traits. It's kept me safe thus far, and my intuition is strong around other people. It's never led me astray.

Which is why, the next day, I find myself distracted, pacing our living quarters, and trying to sniff out what Miles is hiding.

After last night, I am especially curious.

And pissed.

It was the second time he's ditched me, and though

Chase and Juliet had no idea where he went, they did share a look that said perhaps there was a reason he left.

Niro was waiting for me outside the pub to take me home, of course. But I haven't seen or spoken to Miles since last night.

I had *too* much time to think about how he acted last night. Which led to me theorizing about his secrets. Which led to me going down to the cellar and grumbling when I found it locked *again*.

I was getting tired of feeling like Beauty—locked up in the castle, forbidden to go to certain areas of the house.

So, instead of responding to emails or drawing more sketches, I spend the morning Googling everything I can about the Ravage family. I read all about Charles Ravage's trial—how he lost a lot of people's money in bad business deals, was formally charged in court, but was then acquitted.

I find out that their mother, Felicity, died nearly five years ago. There's no cause of death, but apparently she was only in her late fifties. There's a picture of her, and she had long, brown hair and sparkling blue eyes. Tall, lithe, and stunning. It's no wonder all the Ravage brothers look like models. Even Charles is handsome now in his seventies. Pulling up an older picture of him, it nearly takes my breath away to see how much Miles resembles a young Charles.

Felicity remarried when Miles was in his early twenties, but Orion, the youngest, was only fourteen.

I bookmark my research on him, noting that he and I are the same age.

Chase and Miles are discussed the most online, since their company is public facing. Tabloids, gossip articles ... the gossip is endless.

Juliet briefly told me about how she'd known Chase Ravage most of her life because he was best friends with her brother, but that she didn't know Miles or the other brothers very well. I keep digging, pulling up some poetry books that Liam has published and ordering them.

Moving onto the other brothers, I'm surprised to find that Malakai, the middle brother, works as the headmaster of Saint Helena Academy—a Catholic private school here in Crestwood. He's an ordained pastor, unmarried, and there's almost nothing about him online.

Finally ... Orion.

There are a few articles about him, and in every one of them, he appears drunken or otherwise involved in some sort of misconduct. Apparently, Felicity remarried a man who had a daughter a little bit younger than Orion, so there are a few pictures of the brothers out and about with their stepsister, Layla.

There's not much on her, either.

After an hour of digging, I do find a mention of an accident that happened over twenty years ago—something for which Miles was hospitalized. Again, it doesn't go into details, but he was in the hospital for months.

Months.

What happened to him? Is it the cause of his scars? If he was in the hospital for months, surely that means the injury was way more extensive than he's letting on.

I ruminate on the information, sitting on the pink couch as I listen to one of my favorite smutty audiobooks.

But getting all worked up by listening to the audiobook is the wrong thing to do, because by the time dinner rolls around, I'm thoroughly turned on. Debating if I have time to use my vibrator, I quickly decide not to. I'm sure Miles will disappear into the cellar after dinner—or wherever else he goes—and I will have the living quarters to myself. *Again.*

I'd changed into faded jeans and a cropped yellow jumper, leaving my hair in a top knot. I glance at myself in the mirror quickly before heading down, realizing that my chest is all splotchy from my smutty book.

Wonderful.

I take the stairs the three flights down, opting not to take the elevator. When I get to the ground floor, I walk slowly past the various living and sitting rooms. Farther back, toward the kitchen, are a few rooms with doors. One of them has a sign that indicates it's an office, so I look both ways to ensure the coast is clear before I push the door open.

It's a generic office that's full of beiges and light wood. The plaque on the desk reads *Luna Hernandez*, and for a second, I feel guilty for snooping through

Luna's office ... but my curiosity about the cellar is burning a hole through my brain.

I quickly walk over to the desk, pulling the first drawer open and gasping when I see an assortment of things such as paper clips, pens, Post-its, and ... keys.

Not all of them are labeled, though, and I quickly filter through them.

Front gate. Back gate 1. Back gate 2. Garage—Spare. East Wing. Executive Suite. Office 1.

"Come on," I mutter, glancing up at the door before pilfering through the rest of the keys.

My eyes widen when they snag on a brass key with the label, *Cellar—Spare.*

Bingo.

I pocket it and leave the office quickly, feeling both elated and nervous for what I'll discover.

Better to suss out anything untoward now, anyway. Knowing Miles, it's something completely boring like a gym or man cave.

But ... what-if it's not?

There's something about him that he keeps hidden away from everyone. I can tell he keeps something—or a few things—hidden close to his heart. He's closed off, but there's a reason.

And I want to know why.

Especially if I have to spend the next year with him.

Miles is already seated when I walk into the dining room.

His eyes track across my face before quickly darting down to my still-flushed chest.

"Are you feeling alright?" he asks, brows furrowed.

I swear my cheeks must be bright red right now. "I'm fine," I say quickly, sitting down next to him and taking a sip of my white wine. Hopefully it'll cool me down. It's delicious—lightly sweet and tart. My favorite mix of flavors.

And it hits me then—that it reminds me of Miles and those damn green apples he's always eating.

Pressing my lips together, I set the wine down as my whole body heats even more—as I think of his breath fanning across my face, the scent of those apples on his breath ...

"Apologies for bowing out last night," he says coolly.

I shrug. "I'm used to it by now," I snark, referring to the time he left me in the restaurant with our fathers.

He pins me with a dark glare, but before he can respond, the chef comes in and serves us a bowl of soup. It's bright green, and I eye it suspiciously as the familiar, grassy scent permeates the air.

There's no way ...

Suddenly, the anger and annoyance I was feeling dissipates.

"Is this celeriac soup?" I ask, my voice small.

"It is."

I sit back and stare down at the bowl. He asked the chef to make my favorite foods, and I realize suddenly, after going through the past week of meals in my head, that he's been ensuring every dinner has some remnants of home.

For me.

The gravity of that makes me feel emotional. *Why*

does he have to be such an arse most of the time? When he's being decent, he's actually very kind and thoughtful.

I don't say anything as I slowly eat the soup. It's quite good, and Miles seems to agree because he finishes the whole bowl and makes a low humming sound in the back of his throat.

"Did you like it?" I ask.

"I did. It's very flavorful. I've never had it before." Leaning forward with clasped hands, he gives me a pointed look. "I meant to tell you earlier, but I asked the chef to prepare some of your favorite foods, at least for the first couple of weeks."

"Why?"

He tilts his head and smirks. "Because my wife is British."

I nearly roll my eyes, but I stop myself. It's a sweet gesture. I swallow the knot in my throat when I think of the key sitting in my front pocket.

He's trying.

I have to give him some credit for that.

"Thank you," I tell him genuinely.

"How was your day?" he asks, his eyes meeting mine.

"Good. And yours?" I ask politely.

He shrugs as he takes a sip of his wine, so I do the same.

"It was ..." he trails off. "Well, a potential client cancelled our meeting on Monday," he tells me.

I arch a brow. *Why is he telling me this?*

"I'm sorry. Maybe you should start wearing a

badge that says, *Estelle Deveraux's husband* so people stop canceling on you."

It takes him a second for my words to sink in. And then ... he smiles.

Genuinely.

"You know, that's not a terrible idea. I only have you for a year. Might as well maximize the exposure and good reputation."

I only have you for a year.

Something about the solemn way he says that mixed with his smile makes my heart pound against my ribs and my stomach drop with anticipatory excitement.

"Maybe we need to start making more appearances in public together. But that would entail spending *more time* together, buttercup," I warn.

"Don't call me that."

I smirk as the chef brings the next course: chicken marsala. My stomach grumbles with appreciation as I dig in, cutting the succulent meat and quietly moaning with pleasure when the creamy, earthy sauce hits my tongue.

When I look up at Miles, he's watching me with a rapt expression. For the second time in under a minute, my stomach swoops low at the way his eyes watch my lips as I chew.

"I'm glad you're enjoying the food," he says quickly, slicing through the tender chicken. "And I agree. Maybe we should go out to dinner next Saturday evening."

I nod. "We should. We could make a few calls to make sure we're photographed."

His fork stills and he stares at me. "You know, that's not a terrible idea."

Shrugging, I set my cutlery on the side of my plate as I use the serviette to wipe my mouth.

"I could talk you up, and the paparazzi could take some more pictures where you *don't* look like you're receiving a fucking enema—"

"On second thought, with that language, I'm not sure I could win them over," he teases.

I bat my lashes and give him a sultry smile. "I can win anyone over, Miles," I tell him, twisting my lips to the side.

He clears his throat and sets his cutlery down, and I swear I see a faint blush painting his sharp cheekbones. *Hmm.* "Very well. Saturday evening then."

We eat in silence after that. I'm just about to bring up the notion that we need to practice our physical chemistry beforehand when he steeples his hands and pins me with a serious gaze.

"I've been thinking ..." he says slowly. He looks almost uncomfortable as he clears his throat one more time before continuing. "You were right earlier. I shouldn't be so secretive. So I wanted to offer an olive branch."

I stare at him in surprise. "Okay."

He sets his serviette down on the side of his plate. "When I was thirteen, my brothers and I were camping. One of the nights we were out there, we left our campfire burning, and it was a particularly windy night." He swallows and I sit up straighter, listening. "We were sharing a tent—all sort of cuddled up under one blanket to stay warm. I'm a heavy sleeper, so I didn't smell the smoke until it was too late." He pauses and closes his eyes briefly. "Orion was closest to the flames. He was only five at the time. He started screaming, and Liam woke Chase and Malakai up. The zipper got caught, and I saw a spark land on the blanket near Orion."

I study the way his expression is closed off—like he's shuttering his mind against the memory of that night.

"Anyway, I threw myself on top of him to staunch the flames. I ended up with third degree burns over sixty percent of my body. I spent almost three months in the hospital, but even now, most of my torso, arms, and thighs are riddled with burn marks," he finishes.

There's a pensive shimmer in the shadow of his eyes, and my heart clenches at his story.

"I'm so sorry," I whisper.

"It's quite ... gruesome," he adds. "The first woman I was with made a comment about it, and ..." he trails off, clearing his throat. "Anyway, I just wanted you to know."

"That's horrible. I can't believe someone would say that." I place my hand on top of his. It twitches, almost like he's unsure—like he wants to pull away.

"Is this for telling you one of my truths, or is it a part of your physical chemistry game?" he asks, his voice tentative—as if he's testing me.

"Maybe a little bit of both," I tease, smiling. "But really, thank you for telling me. It means a lot to me."

To my surprise, he brushes a thumb along the underside of my palm, and the feel of his calloused skin against mine makes my skin break out in gooseflesh.

His eyes look down at my hand over his, and then he gives me a small, lopsided smile. "I have an idea for our little game."

I open my mouth to ask what he means when he turns his hand over and holds mine against his, tugging it slightly.

"Come here."

I don't let go of his hand as I stand, and before I know what's happening, he's tugging me onto his lap. Just as I'm about to protest, the chef comes back in with pudding.

And it's eclairs.

Oh, fuck me.

It's almost unfair—like he's slowly seducing me with food.

"I believe these are your favorite?" he asks smugly.

"They are," I grumble. I'm sitting stiffly on his thighs, and I go still as he reaches to the plate, holding an eclair in his hand, offering it up to me.

"Take a bite, butterfly," he murmurs.

That nickname is going to be the death of me.

I lean forward, my skin buzzing where we're in contact—namely, my back and arse against his warm thighs. I suck in a breath as he wraps an arm around my middle, pulling me closer as I open my mouth and take a small bite of the eclair.

"Oh my god," I mutter, chewing as my eyes roll to the back of my head.

And then I feel something underneath me. Something long, hard, and thick ...

My eyes widen. I adjust myself slightly so I don't feel it—all the while hoping he doesn't realize I can feel it.

I move again, this time trying to get closer to the edge of his knees. He sets the eclair down with his other hand, and the next thing I know, he grips my hip and holds me still. His lips come to my ear without being able to see him, and his low voice sends shivers down my spine.

"Stop moving," he commands.

A small smile plays on my lips. "Why?"

"Either stop moving like that or be ready to go ten out of ten tonight, wife," he growls.

I stop moving. Stop *existing* at his words. I am deceased. My eyes flutter closed as he squeezes my hip once more in warning. Everything is hot–from my hair to the tips of my toes.

Did he just insinuate ...

No.

An idea forms in my mind, and it's mean and wrong, but I can't help myself. Rolling my hips slightly, I lean back and push my chest out so that my arse grinds right against his erection.

Something low and angry rumbles in his chest. He pushes me off him, throwing his serviette down on the table and giving me a chagrined look before walking toward the door.

"Goodnight, Estelle. I'd say that was a three out of ten, yes?"

And then he's gone.

I reach into my front pocket and grab the key to the cellar.

Time to find out what you're hiding, husband.

CHAPTER FIFTEEN
THE CELLAR

STELLA

I scour the castle to quell my nerves, ensuring that Miles is most likely down in the cellar before heading down there. My nerves are raw, both from the intense dinner we had and the adrenaline at possibly finding out what he could be hiding from me. I'd rather be disappointed than surprised. To do that, I am imagining the worst possible outcomes. A dungeon full of women. A secret family. A bomb shelter. A room full of pictures of me. Sex dolls. My mind runs wild with possibilities, though it could also be something entirely innocent, like restoring old cars.

Whatever it is, I have a right to know as his wife.

That's what I tell myself when I quietly and quickly slip the brass key into the lock, turning it and pulling the door open. It's a dark stairwell leading down into the unknown, and my hands shake nervously as I begin my descent. To calm myself, I count each stair as I pad downward, grateful that I'm barefoot and can be as quiet as possible. Also, the stairs are made of stone—no creaking or loose floorboards to give me away.

The farther down I go, the more I hear.

It starts as a light, rustling sound. I slowly go down the last few stairs, and when I meet the cellar ground, I go still as I take in my surroundings.

To my right is an ordinary cellar, filled with cooking essentials, wine, and a large shelf full of tools and gadgets. Presumably, this is the makeshift garage. The lighting is low, and I'm thankful for that as I tiptoe to my right, where a white door awaits me.

The rustling sound is coming from there.

God, what-if it's more goats?

I briefly close my eyes and take a deep breath. There's no backing out now. I'm already down here, so I may as well see what he's keeping locked away—possibly literally.

I pause.

This could change everything. He opened up to me tonight, and right now, I sort of feel like I'm betraying the trust he so carefully placed in me. It could destroy the headway we're just starting to make. That thought gives me pause, and I stare at the door for several seconds.

I need to know what he's hiding.

I *deserve* to know, as someone bound to him in holy matrimony.

After one more steadying breath, I reach out and turn the handle.

As I push the door inward a crack, I lean forward to peek inside. Obviously, Miles is inside—I can hear what sounds like ... slapping?

Oh god, what-if he's having sex? What-if this is his sex room?

As my eyes adjust to the darkened room, I nearly gasp out loud at what I see.

The first thing that becomes very evident is the size of this room. It must be double the size of our living quarters—almost the size of a gymnasium. In the center, there's a glass room about the size of my bedroom. It's lit from within, giving the rest of the cellar room a soft glow. And inside the glass encasement is ...

My other hand comes to my mouth as I see two people having sex.

Very, very rough sex.

What ... the ... fuck.

The man—a blond—is bent over a small, curvy redhead. He has her pushed against the bed, his hand on the base of her neck as he pounds into her.

She groans, and I realize with a start that though the room looks soundproof, every sound is broadcast all over the cellar room. I can even hear the way the woman grips the sheets, the rustling of the fabric against her long nails evident all around me.

"That's it," the man growls, his voice a low, pleasurable purr.

I squeeze my thighs together at the very arousing scene before me.

What the hell is this?

Why does Miles have a glass room, and why are there people having sex here? I swallow the hurt that works up my esophagus, trying to justify it.

Maybe he rents the room out to friends?

Maybe he has secret roommates?

Maybe he owns a porn studio?

I look around for cameras, and I nearly fall over when I spot Miles.

I hadn't seen him before, as the light of the glass room created a shadow off to the right of the encasement. He's sitting—leaning forward on a large, sectional sofa, legs spread wide.

Watching.

My eyes flick between Miles and the couple. What is going on? Is he going to join? As my eyes rove back to the glass room, I realize that they haven't once looked at Miles.

Because they can't see him.

Something hot and sharp lances through me at the thought of this couple having sex and Miles just ... *watching them quietly.*

I'd considered the possibility that the cellar might house something kinky, and to my delight, this is certainly *that.* I suppress a smile as I open the door a bit wider and lean against the door frame.

Just as my eyes flick back to Miles, he leans back and unzips his trousers.

Oh.

Oh.

I swallow as I watch him, and from this angle, I can hardly see a thing thanks to the arms of the sofa, but from the way his face hardens, the way his wrists move ... I know exactly what he's doing.

Because I've seen him do it before.

Okay, this isn't so bad. I mean, he gets his rocks off to watching someone else have sex ... that's normal, right? It's like a live porn show. I cross my legs the other way, begrudging the feel of my damp knickers, squeezing my thighs slightly to get a bit of relief.

The couple gets more vocal as the seconds wear on, and I hear a few loud slaps and smacks. I almost look over at them, but I can't take my eyes off Miles.

He's leaning back fully now, and his hand is moving over what appears to be a long, thick shaft. My mouth waters as his jaw slackens slightly before tensing again. Watching his face makes me feel like I'm riding the waves of pleasure with him. My breathing hitches at the thought, and one of my hands comes to my throat as I do a slow perusal of his body—of the way his dress shirt is buttoned all the way, how his sleeves are still fastened together with cufflinks. Like even in the height of wanton desire, he still manages to seem conservative and buttoned-up.

And then my traitorous mind imagines the most inconvenient thing.

Miles bending *me* over a bed, fully dressed, as my naked body trembles beneath him.

While someone watches.

I pull away from the door frame, suddenly stunned at the audacity of my mind to concoct such an illicit scene, and three things happen at once.

The woman appears to climax, screaming as her

partner slams into her rough and wild, so hard that the bed is moving with each thrust.

The door creaks slightly as I move away.

And, at the noise, Miles snaps his eyes to me.

Fuck.

My eyes widen as he holds eye contact, locking his gaze on me. Mouth dry, I watch with wanton interest as he strokes himself, as he doesn't turn away or stop. My lips part as he throws his head back, hollowing his cheeks as his arms shake and his body twitches. He's looking at me, but he seems unable to stop whatever he's doing.

He's coming.

God, this is so—

I can't look away.

Watching his body convulse, watching the way his hips snap up and into his hand, watching as his darkened eyes pierce mine during such an intimate moment ...

I take one step backward, and in the next instant, Miles is jumping up, cleaning himself off, and tucking himself away.

Turning, I walk quickly back to the stairs, and I hear Miles's dress shoes slapping against the stone floor behind me.

"Estelle," he says loudly, his voice a thunderous growl. I'm just about to ascend the stairs when his hand wraps around my wrist, pushing me back against the wall and caging me with both arms. "What the *fuck*," he snarls.

I attempt to get out from under him, but he lowers

himself so I can't move. "I could say the same thing," I retort, my voice shaking.

He sighs and runs a hand over his mouth. "How the hell did you get down here?" I hold his stare as I pull the spare key from my front pocket. He snatches it out of my hand. "Happy now?"

I shrug. "It depends. What was that?"

He spreads his legs slightly, almost looking surprised that I'm not recoiling in horror. "What?" he asks.

I narrow my eyes. "Don't be coy. You know what. The glass room. The couple. Do you know them?"

His jaw flexes a couple of times before he looks away. "I'm a voyeur," he says simply. "I find pleasure in watching others engage in sexual acts."

I scoff. "I got that part."

Rolling his jaw, he rubs the back of his neck, looking almost uncomfortable. "I don't know them. I pay couples to fuck so that I can watch them. They know they are being watched, but they don't know by whom—the room is a two-way mirror, so they only see themselves. It's all consensual. They sign an NDA and get two-thousand dollars, and I get to come."

I cross my arms as I consider his words. "Do you ever join them?"

"No."

"How come?" I ask, curious.

He takes half a step closer to me. "Because, despite what you originally thought of my playboy tendencies, I don't like to fuck in person unless I'm fully clothed. It can be cumbersome to explain to people, so it's easier if I don't."

Those magazine stories about me are trash. They're almost never telling the truth. Just because I have a woman on my arm or lipstick on my cheek doesn't mean I'm fucking them, Estelle.

"Because of your scars?" I ask quietly. His expression hardens slightly, and he only nods. I look down at the floor, feeling silly. This, while unusual, is not something that would ever scare me away. I'm sure we've all had the fantasy of being watched–or watching. The latter sends a shiver down my spine.

"If you'd like me to stop for the duration of our marriage, I will," he says slowly.

I snap my eyes to his. "No, it's fine. It's not like you're sleeping with them." Expecting him to look relieved that I'm not reprimanding him, I'm a bit thrown off when he moves closer still—so close that his abdomen brushes against mine.

"And what did you think of it?" he asks, his voice low. His lips are so close to my neck that I can feel his breath feather against my skin. I nearly stop breathing as he reaches up to tuck a stray curl behind my ear. Realizing what his hand was doing not even a minute ago, I stiffen.

"It was interesting," I tell him honestly.

His eyes are glittering with something I can't decipher. The hardness is gone, replaced by something tender.

This means a lot to him, I realize. Me accepting this part of him. I continue to speak.

"Tell me more," I ask him. *Beg* him.

His lips brush against my neck and I close my eyes. "How about I tell you everything tomorrow?" He takes a step back, and the room is spinning slightly, making me dizzy from being so close to him. "I should make sure they know they can leave."

It takes me a minute to process his words. "Tomorrow," I repeat.

Not tonight?

He nods. "Yes." Gesturing to the door we came through, he gives me a soft smile. "I'll be up a little later."

He turns around and walks away, leaving me feeling confused, breathless, and extremely turned on. I quickly jog up the stairs, feeling the telltale sign of tingling and need between my legs. Rushing into the suite, I hardly have time to second guess myself as I pull my vibrator out of my bedside table. Walking over to my bedroom door, I shut it.

And then, the most inconvenient thought enters my mind.

I walk to the door leading to the joint bathroom, opening it a crack.

Because...

I want him to watch me.

I tug my jeans off in a frenzy. My back arches when I power on my vibrator and press the thick head against my clit, moaning uncontrollably.

Pretending it's his tongue. Thinking about his long fingers pushing into me, thinking about his warm skin against mine. I squeeze my eyes shut and pull up the image of him wanking—of the way he watched me, unable to stop. The way his hips snapped up into his hand.

I spread my legs and pretend he's on the other side of the door, already hard.

Already *needing* to be inside of me despite just finishing moments ago.

Thinking of how his thick shaft would stretch me deliciously.

I angle the vibrator and press it down harder as I whimper out his name.

"Miles."

And then I come—*hard.*

It barely takes the edge off, so after a moment to rest, I do it all over again.

All the while imagining him watching me from the dark bathroom.

All the while ... watching *me.*

CHAPTER SIXTEEN
THE CREEP

Miles

I make my way up to the suite quickly, hoping to catch Estelle before she goes to sleep. Remorse and embarrassment work through me at the same time, and despite the thrill of knowing she finds my proclivities *interesting,* I still didn't want her to find out that way.

In fact, I didn't want her to find out *at all.*

I should've known she'd go searching for a spare key. It doesn't surprise me—she's a wily, unpredictable person who, like me, is naturally curious.

If I were in her shoes, I would've done the same thing.

The problem is, now that I know she knows ...

I clench my jaw. The distance I'd so painstakingly placed between us felt like a taut thread ready to snap.

How much longer could I stay away from her?

Once the elevator doors open, I half-jog to the door

of our suite, wondering if she's going to be sitting on that atrocious couch, or if I'm going to have to buck up and knock on her bedroom door. Either way, she deserves a formal apology—for keeping this from her, for acting inappropriately during dinner, for everything.

She's not in the suite, which means she's probably in her room.

I pause before walking to her door. Closing my eyes briefly, I think of the way my heart leapt into my throat when I saw Estelle standing in the doorway of the cellar—how fucking hard I came because of the surprise, anger, and excitement swirling around inside of me.

I think of the way her skin smelled sweet with arousal, and how her hair was so fucking soft. I think of how she filled out the jeans she was wearing—how they cut off around her tapered waist, but filled out her sculpted ass and thighs.

How her small, yellow sweater was *just* short enough to expose the golden skin of her abdomen.

How her full, pink lips were always tilted up into a mischievous smile.

How she seemed to be able to read my moods, and how fucking happy she looked when I had the chef make her celeriac soup earlier tonight.

And ... how fucking happy that made *me*.

I want her to feel at home.

My chest nearly tore in half every time I thought about her.

And worst of all, I am dreading the day she realizes

our sham marriage isn't worth it anymore—the day another man can have her the way I've wanted to since the night of the fountain in Paris.

Just the idea of her being with anyone else makes me feel sick.

Once she finds out about the money, she'll want to be as far away from me as possible.

And it will ruin me.

I pinch the bridge of my nose as I exhale slowly.

Fuck.

I am so fucked.

With a determined pep in my step, I walk over to Estelle's door, raising my arm to knock once, but a noise stops me. I lean closer, and then—

"Oh, god."

I stare at the wood grain. Is she ...

"Oh, fuck," she whimpers, clear as day.

Everything inside of me heats, and my cock pulses inside of my trousers. I take a step back, wondering what to do.

I know what I *should* do.

I *should* go back to my room and lie down on my bed, pretending my wife isn't pleasuring herself on the other side of this door.

I *should* leave this entire suite and distract myself with a cold dip in the pool.

It's what a gentleman would do.

"Please, Miles."

My cock is fully hard now, and I palm it once as I walk to the joint bathroom.

Because as much as I want to be the gentleman, the voyeuristic side of me wants to watch her.

I never said I was a good person. In fact, I make terrible decisions a lot of the time. If given the choice between being a good boy and walking away, or possibly watching my wife bring herself to the brink of an orgasm saying *my* name? I'd purchase my one-way ticket to hell if I could watch her for just a second.

There was never a choice with Estelle.

She already had me wrapped about her little finger.

To my surprise, the door leading to her bedroom is open just a crack, and since the light is off in the bathroom, I can stay hidden in the shadows. Her bedside table lamp is on low, casting a soft, warm light over Estelle as she's ...

Fuck.

She's lying down on her bed, legs spread, facing the door of the bathroom. Facing *me*. I can't see anything indecent, since she's still wearing black underwear, but I can't look away from her writhing body.

She groans again as the white, magic wand slides up and down her slit, pausing as she presses it harder against her clit. Slowly, I begin to unzip my pants— which are still damp from cleaning myself off. I lick my palm, take my aching length in my hand, and fuck up into it. I meet her tempo as she bucks her hips, suppressing the moan that threatens to escape my clenched jaw.

Why would I ever need to hire a couple again when I'm married to Estelle? This is a thousand times better than a stranger ...

"Fuck," she whimpers, squeezing her eyes shut as her legs snap together. "Miles ..."

Spread those legs, Estelle. Let me see how wet you get when you think of me.

Let me see what you like so I can *take notes* for the future.

I shouldn't think it, but I can't help but wonder if I'll ever get the chance to learn her tells, to see what gets her off.

Her body twitches a few times as she throws her head back, and I realize with a start that she's close. Working my hand faster and tighter, I imagine pushing the door open.

I imagine standing next to the bed and locking eyes with her as she gasps my name, as she trembles on her orange duvet cover.

I imagine lifting her sweater and coming all over those soft tits, painting her butterfly tattoo with my cum.

Rubbing the head of my cock a few times to spread the precum, my orgasm builds. Estelle is circling her hips, gyrating against the wand instead of moving her hand, and it's the most erotic thing I've ever seen in my entire life. I haven't gotten myself off twice in a row like this in a long time, but watching her?

I don't think I'll ever get sick of watching my wife come.

The flushed chest.

The eyes she insists on squeezing shut.

The trembling hands and curled toes.

She spreads her legs again, this time bringing her knees up a bit. Her ass lifts off the duvet as she cries out, and I watch in rapture as she climaxes mere feet away from me.

It pushes me over the edge—and I grip onto the door frame with my free hand as my spend streaks all over the bathroom floor, creating a mess. I'm breathing heavily as her cries echo through the suite, feeling my cock pulse out the last of my depleted balls.

When I'm finished, I look down as panic begins to set in.

Quickly glancing up, I see Estelle lying on her back with her arm over her eyes, chest rising and falling rapidly.

I tuck myself away, walking over to my sink and grabbing the hand towel. Cleaning up the floor as quietly as I can, I quickly walk back into my room where I sit on my bed with my head in my hands.

What the fuck did I just do?

That was, hands down, the creepiest thing I've ever done.

I watched her in a private moment, but not only that, I couldn't stop myself from doing it.

The notion of watching her has become so compulsive, I'm not sure if I'll ever be able to stop. Now that I know how she looks ...

How she sounds ...

I'll never be able to stay away.

My mind races with thoughts of sneaking into the bathroom when she's showering, of watching her sleep, of glancing out of the window while she's on her morning walk.

God, I've opened Pandora's Box.

I'm thoroughly and inconveniently *obsessed* with her.

I have to actively tamp down the guilt that threatens to derail me. I must ignore it in favor of giving myself distance—giving myself the night to wallow. To think. If I talk to her now, there's no telling what I'll do.

Because now that I've watched her like that, my obsession will only grow.

I need time to come to terms with the idea that I physically crave my wife.

But not only that ...

I crave her in *all* ways, mind, body, and soul.

And perhaps tomorrow, I'll have to tell her.

I wake up at five, take a quick shower, and change into a black Tom Ford suit. I go slower than usual as I exit my bedroom around six, hoping to run into Estelle. However, her door is still closed. A small, niggling feeling is telling me to check on her, but I leave her be. I go downstairs to make coffee, not thinking twice when I set the kettle to boil for her tea. I've watched her as she prepares it, so I decide to go ahead and make it for her—adding a splash of milk and two sugars.

I bring both mugs back to our living quarters and

take a seat on the sofa with a nonfiction paperback I've been trying to read for months. That way, once she wakes up, we can discuss what happened. After last night, I want her to feel like she can come to me and ask me questions.

Sometime between watching her climax on her bed and waking up this morning, I'd decided to lay it all out on the table for her—the voyeurism, the money transfers, everything. No secrets. Maybe she'll leave, but she deserves to have the choice.

And I can't keep ignoring my feelings for her.

I must doze off on the atrocious pink sofa, because I wake up a couple of hours later with the sun streaming through the living room window. I jump up and look around, glancing down at my phone.

9:58

Fuck.

It's nearly ten, and I can't remember the last time I slept this late.

Yawning, I glance at Estelle's door, and it's still closed. Her tea is untouched on the coffee table.

With furrowed brows, I walk around the suite, wondering if she saw me and left a note. But, nothing.

I pull the suite door open and walk through the castle, hoping I find her sketching or sitting in one of the living rooms, perhaps listening to one of her audio-books. But the castle is empty—aside from Luna, who is working at her computer. I knock on her open door twice to alert her of my presence, and she smiles up at me.

"Well, good morning, sunshine," she chirps.

"It's nearly afternoon," I grumble, sitting down in the chair opposite of her desk and crossing my legs, realizing how rumpled my suit is.

She gives me a coy smile. "Sleep well?"

"Yes," I concede, rubbing my face. "Surprisingly. Is Estelle around?"

Luna shakes her head. "No, I haven't seen her. I assumed she was with you?"

Alarm bells are going off in my mind. I uncross my legs and lean forward. "But it's after ten."

Her brows pull together. "Maybe she's not feeling well?"

I stand quickly. "Maybe. Thanks Luna. I'll go check on her."

"Let me know if you need anything," Luna says softly as I rush out of her office.

I avoid the elevator and take the staircase two at a time. Panic shudders through me, and I curl my fists as I round the corner of our living quarters.

Is she sick?

Did something happen?

Maybe she saw me watching her last night.

I shove the thoughts away as I walk up to her door and knock twice.

"Estelle," I say, my voice a bit too hard and firm. "Open up."

Nothing.

Silence.

"I'm coming in."

I push the door open, and my eyes fall on her—

awake, eyes open and vacant, body curled up in a fetal position.

"Estelle?" I ask, trying to keep my voice from shaking.

Her eyes find mine, and goosebumps erupt along my skin, because I don't see my wife in her eyes. The light is gone, and behind her normally bright, blue eyes is ... nothing. Like she's shuttered behind her irises, somehow.

"Go away," she says, her voice monotone.

"What's wrong?" I ask, trying to keep my voice even.

She turns and faces the other wall, her back to me. She's in an oversized T-shirt, her legs pulled tightly to her chest.

"I said go away, Miles."

I take a tentative step forward, reaching the edge of her bed. "Is this about last night?" I ask softly.

She twists around to look at me over her shoulder. "You really are so conceited," she answers, her voice low and monotone. "No, this is not about last night."

I look around her room for a clue, wondering if she's sick, or just missing home ...

"Estelle, you need to tell me what's wrong so I can help you."

"I don't want your help." I walk the perimeter of her room, arms crossed, watching as my wife pulls the covers over herself slowly. Fidgeting with my watch, I begin to pace.

"Just one of the bad days," she explains a few

minutes later. "I promise I'm not about to off myself, so you can leave now."

One of the bad days.

Off myself.

My.

Wife.

It's like someone pours cold water over me. "Estelle," I growl.

She sits up and glares at me. "It's called depression, you arsehole. I just so happen to have the kind that's resistant to treatment, so when I have these kinds of days ... or weeks ... I sort of just have to weather it." Her eyes are still closed off, but at least she's sitting up now. Though, now that she's facing the light of the window, I can see the purple bags underneath her eyes.

The sight of her looking so wearied and desolate ...

I already know I'm not leaving her here like this.

"How can I help you?" I ask, removing my jacket and placing it on the sitting chair next to her window. My whole body is frantic and electric with worry, and I remove my tie in one quick motion, needing something to do with my hands.

She rolls her eyes, pulling her knees to her chest as she watches me. "Nothing. There's nothing you can do. Because despite ensuring I had a routine, despite my life changing so drastically, I'd stupidly hoped these days were over."

I step out of my shoes. "This has happened before?" She nods. "How many times?" Shrugging, she rests her cheek on her knees as she looks at me with those haunted, hollow eyes. I don't know what comes over me, because suddenly, I want to curl my body against her.

"After my grandmother died ... I didn't get out of bed for weeks. Since then, it happens every couple of months."

I nod once. "Scoot over."

She straightens up. "What?"

"Scoot over," I tell her, removing my belt.

"Miles ..."

She looks so unsure, pulling her lower lip between her teeth.

Broken.

My.

Wife.

"Estelle, scoot over or I'll move you myself."

She doesn't respond as she moves to one side of the bed, her eyes not daring to leave mine. When she gets to the other side, she turns so that her back is to me.

I climb into her bed, noting the floral, jasmine scent permeating the soft sheets. *God, I could sleep here every night.*

Even *with* the damned orange duvet cover.

I shuffle myself closer until I can wrap an arm around her, tugging her close to my chest. She stiffens at first, but as the seconds wear on, she slowly starts to relax. I suppose this is very different from our previous interactions. Her breathing is so steady, so constant, that I find my eyes drooping a few minutes later.

"Why?" she whispers, her voice far away.

"Because you're my wife," I tell her truthfully. "And that means for better or for worse."

"It's not real," she answers, her voice so, *so* faint.

"I think we both know that's not true," I murmur, feeling the lull of sleep pulling me under a few seconds later, curled around Estelle's warm body.

CHAPTER SEVENTEEN
THE GLOOM

STELLA

I wake up in a panic. That same, familiar darkness surrounds me. It's suffocating, and yet, it's as if I'm floating with nothing to anchor me.

It's strange to feel like I'm being strangled by the air.

Like the room is pressing down on me.

Like my heart might shatter from the ache.

A masculine grunt from behind me startles me, and when I slowly turn around, I see Miles stirring next to me.

"You okay?" he asks, voice groggy.

It's dark out now. The last thing I remember is him cuddling up behind me, and subsequently falling into one of the deepest sleeps I've ever experienced in a depressive state.

I'm used to the bone deep, exhausted ache that makes crawling out of bed physically painful.

Normally, the cruel insomnia that doesn't relent is just a bonus, but I slept well with him here.

"What time is it?" I ask.

"No idea," he says gruffly.

The adrenaline from his presence is gone now, and all I feel is that deep, hollow pain as I turn over and pull my body back into fetal position.

"Go back to sleep, butterfly," he murmurs.

The mattress shift as he scoots closer. I squeeze my eyes shut, feeling nothing but wanting to feel everything. The numbness is so isolating. It's like I'm dreaming and can't wake up. His hand comes to the hem of my oversized shirt, which trails along the back of my thigh, covering my knickers. I stare at the wall opposite of me as Miles's fingers hike my shirt up. I can tell by the way his calloused fingers work the fabric up that he's not looking to do anything untoward. Once my back is exposed, his fingers start to trail along my spine in a slow, circular motion. It's ... nice.

If I weren't so desensitized, I might find this more exciting, but right now, it does a good job of taking the edge off the darkness.

"Thank you," I whisper.

"Sleep now," he says softly.

I fall asleep to the feel of his knuckles grazing the sensitive skin of my lower back.

———

I wake up in a room filled with sunshine. The first thing I notice is that Miles is gone. That makes sense.

It's Monday, and he has work. I take a deep breath, and though it still hurts to inhale, the pain has lessened significantly. I once asked my General Practitioner about the pain I experienced during my episodes, and we could never figure out the cause. Upon further research, I'd concluded that I must carry tension in the muscles between my breast bones. It always goes away when I start to feel better, but every time, I use it as a gauge to see how I'm feeling.

Right now, it's better than yesterday, and that's all I can hope for.

I spend several minutes staring at the bedroom wall, thinking and yet not thinking. Breathing and yet seemingly needing to gasp for air periodically. With my knees curled up to my chest, I breathe in and out, closing my eyes and willing the shadows of the room to leave.

I must fall back to sleep briefly, because I'm startled awake by a knocking on my bedroom door. I sit up, glancing around.

"One second," I tell my guest, pulling an oversized jumper over my days-old pajamas. I quickly run my fingers through my knotted curls, pulling it all up into a messy bun. I haven't showered in two days, and I desperately need to brush my teeth.

Would Miles knock? Probably not.

Walking to the door, I pull it open.

"Liam?"

He's wearing a gray T-shirt and jeans that look like they've never been washed. He has more scruff than normal, and I notice that most of it is tinged with silver. His eyes find mine, and he gives me a soft smile. It's only then that I notice the greasy bag and drinks he's holding.

"Hungry?" he asks, gesturing for me to come out of my room.

"What are you doing here?" I ask carefully, moving out of my bedroom and closing the door quickly so that he doesn't see the messy bed I just climbed out of.

"Figured you'd want some company. It's lunchtime, and I know Miles is at work."

I swallow. "Oh, um, thanks," I offer, wrapping my arms around myself. "I was just reading," I explain, hoping he buys it.

Smirking, he turns and walks to the pink couch. "Sit."

I follow him and sit down, acutely aware of how I must look. "Did Miles put you up to this?" I ask, pulling my legs into my chest and wrapping my arms around my knees.

He shrugs. "He might've said something." I arch a brow, and he chuckles, holding his hands up in surrender. "Fine. He demanded I come and check on you. He made me cut class early," he explains. "He has a meeting he can't miss, otherwise, I'm sure he'd be here." I swallow the ache in my throat. *So different from the grump I've grown used to.* "Even still, I wanted to make sure you were okay."

"Thank you," I tell him quietly. "That's nice of him. And you."

"I like taking care of people," he adds gruffly, setting the bag down and taking out two cheeseburgers wrapped in brown paper. "My brothers, and the people close to them. Since you're married to my brother, that includes you."

I don't answer as a wave of homesickness washes through me.

Somehow, despite everything, I'm starting to consider these people friends. And one day ... possibly family.

Handing me a burger, he leans back and eats. I clutch mine, unable to stomach the smell of the greasy meat. During my episodes, it's hard to enjoy the simple things I normally love, like food, audiobooks, music ... it's all just sort of *there*, existing. I bring it closer to my face, but the melted, yellow cheese is the last thing I want. Politely setting it back down on the coffee table, I rest my cheek on my knees as my eyes prick with tears.

God, this is embarrassing.

I'm just about to excuse myself when Liam sets his cheeseburger down and begins to speak.

"You know, three years ago, my best friend died." He pauses, grabbing his drink and taking a sip before setting it back down. "His name was Elias. I met him in university. I was the best man at his wedding. I was there for the birth of his daughter, Zoe. We grew apart a bit as Zoe grew up, especially during the first few years of her life, but I was at every birthday party. I was there for every holiday and special occasion."

I pull my knees closer to my chest as he continues. "Three years ago, Elias and his wife, Brooke, were hiking. They'd left Zoe at home—she was fifteen at the time. You know how it is with teenage girls. Anyway, they didn't come back that night. The next morning, Zoe and I went to the police station to report them missing. We searched for them for days—and about a week later, we learned they'd gotten swept up in a freak flash flood accident. It had been raining, and the river where they were hiking was swollen and dangerous."

I swallow. "I'm so sorry," I tell him. "What happened to Zoe?"

At that, Liam smiles. "Zoe was distraught. We both were. Especially when we found out that they'd appointed me as her guardian."

I sit up a bit straighter. "I didn't know that."

He shrugs. "In name only. She wants nothing to do with me. She'd been attending boarding school since she was eleven, so aside from taking time off for the funeral, she wanted to go back to her friends. She was fifteen ... I don't blame her. She's fiercely independent, and the strongest person I know. I hardly see her, and when I do call her, I get one-word answers. Typical almost eighteen-year-old."

"Is she graduating soon?" I ask.

He nods. "Yeah. She's applying to the local University, where I work. She wants to save money, so she'll be living with me." He rubs his mouth. "I anticipate it'll be an adjustment for both of us. Anyway, the point of my story is, after Elias died, I was diagnosed with depression and anxiety."

I go still, not saying anything. I've met a few people

who had depression, but I never would've guessed Liam suffered from it, too.

He takes another bite of his cheeseburger. "It took a few months to adjust to my meds, and sometimes I still have my bad days, but ..." He trails off, giving me a pointed look. "If you ever need to talk about it with someone other than my sourpuss brother, give me a call."

"How did you know?" I ask carefully.

"I sort of deduced it when we spent some time together last week. And then Miles told me this morning when I called him. He told me about your grandmother. I'm sorry for your loss, Stella."

My response catches in my throat. "Thanks." Clearing my throat, I straighten my legs and grab the drink. I may not be hungry, but the taste of the cold soda is very refreshing. "I've always had bad days," I start. "Ups and downs, like any normal person. But the grief from losing my grandmother was unlike anything I've ever experienced. She was my *person*. It felt like someone ripped the carpet out from under me. In the days after she died, I hardly got out of bed. Apparently, grief can trigger a plethora of mental health issues that are lying dormant. By the time her funeral rolled around, I was on autopilot."

I think of Miles and the fountain. That had been one of the only good nights in a year of bad nights.

"I tried medication, but nothing worked. My doctors officially diagnosed me with treatment-resistant depression four months ago."

"Fuck," Liam utters, blowing out a breath of air. "That must've been really hard."

I nod, swallowing again. "It was. But, we implemented a plan of action. And until this week, it had been working. I started exercising every morning. Waking up at the same time, doing the same things, seeing the same people. Routine helps me. But of course, my life was sort of thrown for a loop when ..." I trail off.

When I fake-married your brother.

"You know, I might've encouraged him *not* to go through with the fake marriage if I'd known the whole story. But our father can be very convincing. Miles has always felt the need to be the martyr of the family. He'd take a bullet for any of us in an instant, and I think doing this is his way of protecting us. His way of diverting the attention away from us. To ensure that our father feels as if he's in control of one of his children's lives."

And Miles hates every second of that control, I think glumly.

He's doing it for his brothers, in the only way he can, so Charles will leave the rest of them alone.

"I understand," I say slowly.

"He cares about you," Liam adds, his voice softer than before. "I can tell by the way he talks about you."

Doubtful, I want to say. But I stay quiet as Liam continues, soaking up his words.

"I'm not sure if he told you about what happened to him," Liam says, eyeing me with his pine-green eyes.

I nod. "He told me. About the accident."

"He saved our lives. Despite me telling him to get himself out. Despite knowing he could die. Imagine being a kid and being that courageous?"

Tears prick at the corners of my eyes, but I hold myself back from crying. "I can't imagine," I whisper.

"He sort of withdrew into himself after that. Developed a very dry sense of humor to go along with it, too. He can be an ass, but he has a big heart."

I smile. "I know." Looking down at the ground again, I think back to the night we met. How he seemed ... *different.* More brusque and guarded, sure. But also ... kind. Maybe a little bit fun. "I just don't know how to get him to open up to me. It's like pulling teeth."

Liam laughs. "My advice?" I nod, and he continues. "Don't force it. Just continue being around him. Talk to him. Get to know him. Once you're in, you're in for life. It's laughable to think that in a year—" He shakes his head. "I don't foresee him letting you go. That's all."

I only have you for a year.

Miles's words from two nights ago reverberate in my mind.

"Thanks, Liam. We'll see what happens."

Chase and Juliet both said the same thing, but so far, I haven't seen that side of my husband.

"You're doing great, Stella. Just take care of yourself, okay?"

I nod and smile. "I will. Thank you for the food. I don't normally have an appetite during these episodes, but the soda is delicious," I offer, giving him a small smile.

"Anytime."

Standing up, he gestures to my uneaten cheese-burger. "I'll put this in the fridge for you in case you get hungry later."

I nod. "Perfect."

He cleans up the bag and his food, looking down at me. "I find that baby steps help. One foot in front of the other. Maybe today, it's a shower. Tomorrow, it's going downstairs."

I laugh. "Do I smell that bad?"

He chuckles. "No. I just mean, focusing on one thing helps me. Don't worry about anything else. Just get in that shower. I think you'll find that autopilot can sometimes lead your mind and body taking over again. Just give yourself grace, okay?"

"Okay. Thank you."

He smiles and walks out, leaving me to contemplate the enormous task of standing up, walking to the bathroom, and turning the water on.

By the time I'm done and my body is clean, I am exhausted, so I crawl back into bed before falling into a deep, restorative sleep.

One foot in front of the other.

CHAPTER EIGHTEEN
THE AUDIOBOOK

Stella

It takes me a couple of days, but by Wednesday, I'm feeling back to myself. Waking up to Miles's warm, heavy arm around me certainly helps—though neither of us acknowledge his presence in my bed *at all*. I don't think we manage to utter a single word to each other all of Monday and Tuesday. He just shows up after work and crawls into bed with me. In the mornings, he leaves to get ready for work, and we don't talk about it.

My memories of the last few days are haze–filled with bright light, a cool breeze, warmth, and knuckles brushing across my spine.

I wake up late on Wednesday, and take the longest shower I've ever taken, making sure to brush my hair, shave my legs, and really scrub my face. It feels good to have energy again. To *want* to do things again. I change into a mustard yellow sweater dress, quickly drying my hair with a diffuser. I know Miles is at work, so I head downstairs and make myself a double portion of oats. I haven't had an appetite for days, subsisting on only water, but now?

I'm ravenous.

Instead of forcing myself to walk today, I decide to take it easy. Over the last year, I've discovered that slowly easing back into my routine is the best course of action. Today, showering and getting dressed will have to be my only accomplishments—and that's fine with me. I'm taking Liam's advice and giving myself grace. Placing my headphones in, I turn on a raunchy book about a pleasure Dom, smiling when I realize lounging around and listening to smut is exactly what the doctor ordered.

As I sip my tea and eat my large bowl of oats, I lean against the kitchen counter as I listen, grinning at a particularly spicy part.

It's nice to feel back to normal.

As horrible as my episodes are, the days after an episode always seem to be my best days. I know, physically, it's because my serotonin is out of whack, but still. My emotions may be see-sawing, but I'd be damned if I didn't enjoy the good days as best as I can. Especially when I never know when a bad day will hit.

As I set my phone down to wash my bowl, the Bluetooth cuts out, and I realize with a start that the audiobook is playing out loud on my phone at full volume. Because my hands are wet, I let it run.

I'm alone down here anyway.

"That's it. You're such a good girl, taking my cock so well," Ryder growls.

"Yes, god, yes! Harder, please."

"You want Daddy to fuck you harder, Belle? How do you ask?"

"Please, Daddy. Please give it to me harder," I beg.

I blush as I load my bowl in the dishwasher, biting my lower lip as it continues to play.

"Are you going to come for Daddy, angel?"

"Yes, Daddy. I'm so close."

"That's it," he growls. *"Your cunt is milking my cock, sweet girl."* Wrapping his hands around my neck, he continues to pound into me. My knees shake beneath me as he thrusts up into me and—

Someone clears their throat behind me, and I jump about twenty feet into the air, spinning around and swiping my phone, pressing pause quickly.

Miles is leaning against the opposite wall of the kitchen, smirking.

"Morning, Estelle."

My heart is in my throat, and I take a steadying breath before glaring at him. "Jesus, Miles. You scared me."

His eyebrows quirk up as he glances down at my phone quickly. "Now I know why you always have those earbuds in. You're listening to porn."

I scowl. "It's not *porn*, you heathen. It's romance." I close the dishwasher and turn to face him, arms crossed. "I'll have you know I read, like, three books a week," I add, defending my addiction.

His lips twitch as he pushes off the wall. "I probably would, too, if my books had scenes like that in them. So, Daddy kink?" he asks, his lips curving ever so slightly. Not quite a smile, but close.

I glare at him. "How long were you listening?"

"Long enough," he adds, walking to the fridge. "Feeling better?" he asks, eyes scanning my face.

I shuffle my feet a bit, looking down at the floor for a second before meeting his gaze once more. "I am."

Is he going to bring up the fact that we cuddled every night?

Something unsure flashes across his features. "Good. I'm happy to hear that."

Something about the way he says that last part makes my heart flutter lightly in my chest, and I can't help but smile wider.

It sounds almost like *concern*.

Before I can contemplate his words further, he takes a step closer, hands in the pockets of his pants. He has more scruff than normal, he's not wearing a tie, and his white button-up is unbuttoned by one button– the furthest I've ever seen his throat exposed. A mix of intrigue and guilt swirl in my gut when I realize he likely didn't have time to shave the last few mornings. My eyes flick to the shiny scar right under his jaw before coming back to his face.

"What was that book called, anyway?" he asks, his voice a low murmur.

Relief washes through me. I'm glad he's not talking about it. It helps me to move on—to forget about it until the next episode happens.

It helps me when I get back to my normal life.

I swallow as he stops a foot away. "I can't remember."

At this, he smiles. And ... *god*. His smile could win entire wars.

Before I can stop him, he reaches behind me and swipes my phone from the counter. I try to grab it from him, but he's quicker. I see his eyes widen as he takes in the screen—a cover of the scantily-clad, older man.

"*His Virgin Bride?*" Miles says slowly, his eyes glittering with mirth.

I purse my lips as I snatch the phone out of his hand. "Excuse me," I say quickly, swiping out of my audio app. "You can't just take my phone like that—"

"Is that the kind of thing that turns you on?"

His eyes haven't left mine since before I grabbed my phone, and he seems genuinely curious.

I shrug. "I like all kinds of romance. I don't have a favorite trope. I couldn't say if that sort of thing turned me on in real life. It's just a fantasy."

Rolling his tongue along his cheek, he cocks his head slightly. Taking a step forward, he places his hands on either side of me, boxing me in. Leaning down, his breath makes me tremble.

"And if real life could be better than your fantasy? What would you say then?"

Good lord.

I place my hands on his chest as I look up into his face. "I guess I'll never know," I reply, knowing my cheekiness might push him away again. "I'm married to this grump who works all the time."

His eyes bore into mine with ... something. It's

heated and intense, but I'm not sure if it's lust or hatred.

"Well, this *grump* decided to cancel all of his meetings today," he says, his green eyes sparkling. And then he bends down, brushing his lips over my cheek ever so gently. "I missed my wife," he adds, his voice soft.

My heart races inside of my chest as I pull away slightly. "Miles—"

"Have a good breakfast," he says slowly, pulling away and walking out of the kitchen.

———

I spend the day finishing *His Virgin Bride* in the castle library—which is fitting, I think. I'm not ashamed of my book choice. The writing is amazing, and the smut is top-tier. Miles can kiss my arse. Around two, Miles saunters into the library with a paperback book about investing money and a plate of sandwiches for us to share. I watch as he takes a seat across from me, chewing quietly, but other than a polite smile when I thank him for feeding me, he doesn't say a word.

At six, he excuses himself, and I wander around the stacks of books, having just finished my book. I try to make notes about the kinds of things I still need to do for VeRue, but as my fingers graze the book spines, my mind continues to wander to the scene where the main male character pressed the main female character against a library shelf just like these.

By the time I'm walking into the dining room for dinner, my skin is flushed and my palms are sweaty.

Miles is already seated, and he nods once as I take my usual seat.

We haven't discussed practicing our physical chemistry in days, and while I appreciate the fact that he's not walking on eggshells around me, I also want to ask him why he stayed with me every night.

Why he continues to flirt with me as if he can't resist me.

Why he told me he came home from work today because he *missed* me.

The chef brings in a salad, and I sip my wine as I watch Miles eat. He brings the food on his fork up to his mouth slowly, chewing with a closed mouth. My lips part as I watch the way his long fingers grip the cutlery—*God, why is it so erotic to watch him eating?*

"Are you going to eat your salad, or are you going to continue drooling?" he asks, flicking his green eyes to mine.

Instead of coldness, there's only warmth.

My stomach does a little flip as his lips tilt up into a smile.

"I'm just enjoying my wine," I tell him, grateful that my turtleneck sweater hides my splotchy chest.

We eat our salads in relatively comfortable silence, and then the chef brings in a steak with potatoes.

My mouth waters.

"If you don't want to talk about it, I'd understand," he says after taking his first bite. "But I'd like to know more about your condition."

I stop eating and briefly close my eyes. I didn't want him to ask. I didn't want him to *see* me like that.

And while I was grateful for his help and his constant company, I feel better today. I want to move on. I know ignoring it probably isn't a healthy coping mechanism, but still. I don't enjoy dwelling on it.

Before I can tell him this, he clears his throat and wipes his mouth with his serviette.

"I did some research," he says, placing his hands flat on the table. "Since your depression is treatment-resistant, there's likely nothing chemical we can do. But it seems like therapy might help, if you're okay to see my therapist?"

My head is swimming with so many emotions. "I—um—"

"Or there's cognitive behavioral therapy, which looks promising. Ketamine is also supposed to help some types of treatment-resistant depression, but before delving into that, we might want to look at how to manage your stress," he finishes.

I'm speechless.

Just the fact that my stoic husband took the time to research—to lay out some of my options ...

Like he cares about me.

I stay quiet as I swallow the emotion clogging my throat.

Miles squeezes his eyes shut as he pinches the bridge of his nose. "Sorry, you've probably done your own research. I don't mean to meddle. I just ..." he trails off, looking away briefly. My breath catches when I see the pain flicker across his expression. "I want to help you," he finishes, sighing heavily.

The anguish in his voice is palpable.

"Thank you," I tell him, my voice breaking. I stare down at my wine glass, willing myself not to cry.

"You just seemed so broken."

When I look back up at him, he's watching me with worry. "It's not a fun experience, that's for sure," I tell him quietly.

He takes a sip of his wine. "You're very strong. To be able to weather that. You're so happy all the time, and I just thought ..." he trails off.

I swipe at my cheeks, sniffing once. "I suppose you can have the brightest smile in the room and still have the darkest shadows to battle."

He doesn't drop his eyes from mine as we stare at each other. My heart turns over with every breath, every second that passes between us. It's like something changed—the air, the energy ... it's suddenly wild and frenetic. The smoldering flame I see in his eyes nearly startles me. His hands curl briefly on top of the table, and his jaw hardens, almost like he can sense it, too.

"I want to show you something," he says softly. Before I can respond, he stands up and unbuttons his collar. I stare at him in raptured silence as he unbuttons the first few buttons at his neck. I press my lips together—afraid I'll say something that will make him change his mind. He doesn't look at me. My heart is pounding against my ribs as I watch my husband slowly unbutton his shirt, tugging it out of where it's tucked into his pants. Then, he pulls it open.

Most of his abdomen is covered in large, coiling burn marks. Some areas are thicker, with shiny skin, and others are smaller—almost like pockmarks. The burns branch upward, across his taut muscles, twisting around his neck and down his corded, muscular arms.

"Beautiful," I murmur, standing and walking over before I realize I'm doing it. "May I?" I ask, holding my hand up.

He's gritting his jaw, but he doesn't speak. Instead, he just nods once.

I place my hand in the center of his chest before I run it up to his pectoral, over his shoulder, and down the back of his arm.

When I look up at him, his eyes are closed, and his nostrils are flared—like he's in pain.

"Sorry, does it hurt?" I ask, starting to pull my hand away.

His eyes snap open and he grabs my wrist to keep it on his skin, and I nearly gasp at the sight of his blown out pupils.

"No, butterfly. It doesn't hurt."

Even if I wanted to look away from him, I'm not sure that I could. His eyes slide down to my lips, expression softening. Excitement flares through me at his entrancement, and all too suddenly I realize he wants to *kiss* me.

Not for the cameras, but because he wants to.

My skin tingles as his eyes crinkle slightly. "Estelle," he says, voice low and hesitant.

"No more secrets," I whisper, wanting to kiss him. *Needing* to kiss him.

That same anguished expression passes over his features, and his jaw tightens. Before he can change his mind, I run my hand up to his neck, fingers catching in his hair.

Something flashes in his eyes. In the next second, he pulls me roughly against his body and crushes his lips against mine.

I moan when his tongue presses into my mouth, and my other hand reaches for his hair. His arms wrap around my waist and his hands fist the material of my sweater dress, sending shimmers of pleasure through me. My heart thunders inside of my chest as he groans, pulling away.

"Tell me to stop," he murmurs.

"Don't stop."

The words are barely out of my mouth when he kisses me again, twisting us around so that my back is to the wall of the dining room. He presses me firmly against the damask wallpaper, rucking his hips up against me. I gasp as he lifts me up, hands splayed under my thighs as my legs wrap around his hips.

"Tell me to stop," he repeats, lips brushing against mine.

"Never, *darling*."

He pulls away, eyes blazing. He doesn't need to say anything. I can tell by the way he's smirking—by the way his hand comes up to my face—that he likes this nickname.

Lowering his head, he places another gentle kiss against my lips, and then my jaw, my neck ...

I let my head fall back against the wall as he trails kisses down my neck, pushing my turtleneck down slightly. The hem of my dress inches up. His breath is warm against my skin, and my eyes roll back when he thrusts into me once again.

"Fuck," I whisper, tingling and trembling all over.

I gasp in shallow breaths as he drives into me, his length hard and firm against my knickers. The friction makes me whimper, pleasure radiating outward and down to my fingers and toes. He licks and sucks at the junction between my neck and shoulder, and my eyes roll back as he rocks into my core again.

"I want you to come for me like this, butterfly," Miles mumbles against my skin. "I want to feel how wet you are through my pants. Do you understand?"

Where did this dirty mouth come from?

I whimper again, clenching my thighs tighter against him. My hands come down to his chest, trailing over his scars.

He presses against me harder, directly over my clit. I'm so worked up from my book earlier that I know it won't take me long.

Not when he keeps pressing himself against me the way he is—hips rolling, pressure firm but not too hard.

Miles rests his forehead against mine as his hands come to my hips, squeezing my bare flesh as he fucks me with clothes on.

God, this is so hot.

My legs shake as he thrusts up against me. "Miles," I moan.

"You have no idea how badly I want to sink into your sweet pussy, Estelle," he growls. "How much I want to watch you fall apart underneath me. And on top of me. And bent over our bed. God, I've imagined this for so long," he adds.

"Me too," I whisper.

"Fuck." His voice is hoarse, and his heart is beating erratically under my hand.

Closing my eyes, I circle my hips, chasing my orgasm.

"Eyes open," he commands. "I want to watch you as you fall apart."

"God, Miles," I groan. "I'm close."

He starts to move my hips over his cock roughly, breathing heavily as he jerks into me at the same time.

"Yes you are," he growls. "And you're going to come all over my cock, aren't you?"

"Y-yes," I mewl, feeling the telltale signs of my impending climax.

"You like the way our dinner is growing cold on the table, wife?"

"Yes," I gasp out.

"Mmm, I'm sure you do. What about the fact that anyone could walk in and see us?"

I can hardly see straight. Stars begin to dance in my vision, and each thrust against my clit threatens to send me over the edge.

"My wife is so needy," he murmurs. "I fucking love it."

A whole body shiver works through me at his words. If I'd known how much of a dirty talker he was—

"There are so many ways I want to paint you with

my cum," he says, hips jerking erratically. "So many things I can do to you," he adds.

"Miles, I'm coming."

He lets out a low groan just as my orgasm slices through me quickly. Gripping onto his shoulders, I let it roll through me as my toes curl, as my thighs clench.

"That's it, butterfly," he growls. "Fuck, I'm going to come."

He stills, but his cock pulses against me from inside of his pants. Wetness seeps between us, and I'm still panting as he finishes.

I lower myself carefully, even though my legs are jelly. When I look up at Miles, he's watching me with a heated expression. A smile tugs at his lips, and then he's reaching over to the table for a serviette to clean us up. Without a second thought, his arm comes underneath my dress, wiping up the mess he created against my knickers. Quickly grabbing his shirt, he buttons himself back up.

"You should finish your dinner, Estelle," he says, discarding the napkin and placing his hands in the pockets of his suit pants as he watches me.

I don't know what else to do, so I walk back around to my seat at the table, feeling disoriented. Miles takes his usual seat, too, and when I look up at him, he's watching me with fire behind his eyes.

"I'd say that was a six out of ten, yeah?"

I'm still laughing when the chef comes in to clear our plates a minute later, looking thoroughly confused as to why our food seems completely untouched.

CHAPTER NINETEEN
THE EDUCATION

MILES

After finishing the dessert course, Estelle and I walk back to our living quarters side by side. A small part of me is proud at the way her cheeks are still flushed—at how wild her hair looks. When I close the door behind us, she turns to face me.

"Thank you. For showing me your scars," she clarifies, cheeks reddening to an even deeper shade.

I take a step forward so we're only inches apart. Placing a hand on her cheek, something inside of me stirs at the way she seems to nuzzle into my touch.

"It's only fair." I smile as I step away, letting my hand fall. "Goodnight, Estelle. I'll see you in the morning for our walk."

I barely catch the surprised expression on her face before I turn and walk to my bedroom, closing the door behind me as I lean against it.

She might think I'm finally conceding to her walks, but the truth is, I am terrified to see her sad again. And if walking helps her, I'd do it every goddamn day of the week. Though I know it's very likely she'll have more episodes over the course of the year, I can at least do my part to help her to avoid them however I can.

I pull off my clothes, smiling when I think of the way she writhed against me. The way she smelled. The noises she made. This had, somehow, become bigger than an obsession.

I am consumed. Tormented. *Possessed.*

After taking a quick shower, I sit down on my bed and check my phone, my towel still wrapped around my waist. There's a text from Chase, and I scowl when I see it's a link to Instagram. I don't have any social media accounts that I run personally, though our publicists run our RCF accounts.

When I open it up, I'm surprised to find that it's a link to a picture of Estelle and I on our wedding day. I'm not sure who took it because the image is slightly blurry, and I recognize it as our kiss at the altar.

Right after the commissioner had pronounced us husband and wife.

My eyes scan the account, and I realize with a start that it's Estelle's account. I scroll a bit to read the caption of the picture she posted.

My husband. Kind. Generous. Thoughtful. There for me during my darkest of days. Happy almost two weeks of marriage, darling.

My heart is hammering in my chest as I read it

twice. Three times. Just as I'm about to ask her why she posted it, my phone begins to vibrate.

"Yes?" I ask my brother.

"Have you checked your email?" Chase asks.

My brows furrow. "No. Why?"

"We'd had like fifteen inquiries from people asking to meet with us."

I rub the back of my neck. "Really?"

"Yeah," he laughs. "I could kiss your wife, Miles."

I ignore the spike of jealousy floating through me at his words. "Well, I'll have to thank her in the morning."

"She has a lot of followers. Have you seen some of these comments? People fucking love her. The picture of you guys already has twenty thousand likes. *Twenty thousand.* I guess a lot of people didn't realize you two were married. The power of social media," he adds, chuckling.

People fucking love her—of course they do. Who wouldn't?

I swallow, but before I can respond, Chase continues. "It's going to be a busy rest of the week. I'll have Shira book in as many people as we can."

I nod once. It's strange—suddenly feeling like maybe everything might be okay with RCF. *Fifteen inquiries over the course of half an hour.*

He's not wrong. This could be a turning point for us.

"Thanks for letting me know."

"Wow. She's really milking this whole fake marriage thing," he says.

"What do you mean?" I ask.

"Check her account. She posted a story."

I glance at my screen, tapping back to the picture of us, and clicking over to her profile. I tap on her profile picture, and it's a story of her lying in her bed, the orange duvet pulled up to her chin. She's smiling in the way that makes my heart gallop, and before I know what I'm doing, I screenshot the picture.

Goodnight from the Ravages. x

My pulse is whooshing in my ears. "Look, I should go," I tell Chase.

"Go thank your wife for saving our asses," he murmurs. "Have a good night, brother," he adds before ending the call.

Before I know what I'm doing, I lean back against my headboard and start to scroll through my wife's Instagram account. It's a mix of travel photos, pictures of her designs, outfits, and then I stop when I see a picture of her with an older woman. It's obviously her grandmother, and it looks as though they're in Paris.

My whole heart.

Her caption makes me pause, and I reframe everything I know about Estelle. She's obviously still grieving—I can sense it in the way her face softens anytime someone mentions her grandmother. The night of the fountain, the taxi ... *she was grieving.* My hand comes up to my neck, and I suddenly feel like such an asshole about everything. I assumed she got turned off by my scars, when in reality, she was probably dealing with her own demons.

And I was too self-absorbed to realize it.

The more I scroll, the more I realize how much I don't know about my wife. There are pictures of her in Los Angeles two years ago. Pictures of her with her arm around another man, which makes me irrationally jealous. Pictures of what I can only assume was her apartment in London, because I recognize the horrid, crazy patterns of that designer she loves—the same one who is now all over our living quarters.

Glancing at the wall separating our bedrooms, I make an executive decision. Two decisions, actually— to wear the one pair of sweatpants that I own, and to go knock on her bedroom door to ask her about her life.

She was right last week. We need to be friends if we're going to convince people that we're in love. That doesn't just include the physicality of being with someone. It's knowing their favorite color, food, place. It's knowing their dating history. It's knowing more about the person she loved more than anyone in the world.

And I don't really know my wife at all.

Maybe offering to learn more, while wearing *fucking sweatpants*, will help her realize that I'm serious about making this marriage succeed.

The light is on under her door, so I rap my knuckles against the wood twice.

"Come in," she says, and I push the door open.

She's sitting cross-legged on her bed, wearing nothing but a small tank top and underwear. As soon as she realizes it's me, she pulls the duvet over herself.

I hold a hand up. "I think we're past that," I

murmur, hoping she understands what a big deal it is for me to show up in her bedroom without a shirt.

Her throat bobs. "Everything okay?"

I hold up my phone. "I liked your post."

She grins as she leans back in bed, and *fuck* if she isn't the most gorgeous woman I've ever seen. *Her*. Just her. With wild curls, and soft, golden skin. No makeup. No fancy dresses. Just ... *her*.

She's radiant.

"I wasn't sure if you would see it. I tried searching for you, but it appears my husband doesn't have an account."

I smirk as I walk over to the other side of her bed. "Chase showed me," I tell her, climbing under the covers with her. My eyes rake over the way her chest flushes at my close proximity. At the way she pulls her lower lip between her teeth as her eyes scan my scars with mild interest. "And I realized, during my light stalking, that I know almost nothing about you."

She gives me a sheepish smile as she pulls her knees up to her chest and rests her chin on top of it as she looks at me. Her hair is pulled up into a messy bun, and a blonde curl falls free over her cheek. Without thinking, I reach over and tuck it behind her ear.

"What do you want to know? I bet you know more than you think you do," she adds.

"What's your favorite color?"

She wrinkles her nose. "I don't have one. If you haven't noticed, I like them all."

Huffing a laugh, I shake my head. "I should've known. Favorite travel destination?"

She considers this for a few seconds, looking over my shoulder as her brows furrow. "Probably Fiji. I went with my father during one of his philanthropic trips, and the people were so nice. It flies under the radar a bit compared to the other infamous islands, but everything about it was a dream."

"Maybe we can go one day," I tell her, my voice low.

Her cheeks go pink, and *fuck*, she's adorable. "I'd like that."

I look down at the orange duvet, considering my next question. "Why did you post about us? It isn't a requirement of our deal."

She shrugs. "I don't know. I think I was just feeling appreciative," she teases. I arch a brow as she continues. "I guess I just wanted everyone to know the Miles Ravage I've gotten to know over the last few weeks. And since I have a decent following, I thought getting a head start on repairing your image couldn't hurt."

"Well, you seem to have made us irresistible. Chase told me we've received fifteen inquiries since you posted it."

Her mouth drops open, and her eyes shine with pride.

For me.

She's proud of me. The idea hits me so suddenly, and with such force, that it's as if someone is driving a stake through my heart.

"Miles, that's amazing! Seriously? I'll post everyday if that's what it takes."

I grab her shirt and tug her over to me. "I don't deserve you."

And then I kiss her, fully, with zero abandon and no qualms. Because *fuck* if I can go another second without her pouty lips against mine. I need her. Everything. Her soft body. Her moans. Her goodness. Her heart. The way everything about her is romantic and sunny. Like she's my sunshine, and I'm the dark planet orbiting her.

I hoist her up so her knees are straddling my hips. Guiding her over my length, she looks down at me with a wicked smile. Reaching up, I remove the hair band from her hair slowly, letting her soft curls tumble down her shoulders and chest.

"Miles," she whispers, looking almost nervous.

I open my mouth to tell her we can go however far she feels comfortable going when my phone pings loudly. I plan on ignoring it, but then it happens again a few seconds later.

"Let me just turn it on silent," I tell her, feeling irritated with whoever is trying to get ahold of me.

My eyes catch on the two text messages that flash across my screen.

LUNA

They're waiting

I'm happy to send them home, if you'd prefer. :)

I set my phone down and place my hands on Estelle's hips. My usual evening activities were forgotten when I was pressing my wife against the wall of our dining room. Suddenly, an idea occurs to me.

"It's just Luna. It appears we have company."

Estelle gives me a confused smile. "We do?"

Running a hand up under her shirt, I give her a knowing smirk. "In the cellar." I pause, wondering her answer to my next question. "Would you like to join me?"

"Yes, please."

That's all the answer I need.

CHAPTER TWENTY
THE VOYEUR

STELLA

Miles leaves me to change, and adrenaline rushes through me at the prospect of joining him in the cellar this evening. I'd planned on listening to one of my audiobooks since the night was still young, but this was way more enticing than one of my smutty books. He told me to wear something comfortable, so I decide on a simple short green dress with puff sleeves. I keep my hair down and slip into sandals before heading out of the bedroom.

Miles is leaning against the pink couch, arms crossed, wearing a fitted white button-down with his signature gold cufflinks, Cartier watch and belt, and navy trousers. My heart hammers in my chest as he pushes off the couch, walking over to me.

Stopping right in front of me, he places a hand on my cheek. "Gorgeous. As always." His fingers trail down to the sweetheart neckline, playing with the ruffles for a second before he steps back. "Shall we?" he asks, offering his hand.

"Yes," I answer a little breathlessly, taking it.

He doesn't let go of my hand until we get to the cellar door, and the hair on the back of my neck continues to stand on end due to the electricity thrumming between us.

"Are you ready?" he asks, reaching into his pocket for a key. I nod, and he gives me a sidelong smile. "The viewing room is mirrored on their side, so they won't be able to see us. While I've had the cellar outfitted with speakers, their room is soundproof—so they won't be able to hear us, either."

"I'm ready," I tell him a little too eagerly.

He pushes the door open and helps me down the dark staircase. I follow him to the door that I now know leads to the glass room, or the *viewing room*, as he called it. He opens the door, and my breath catches when I see a new couple kissing on the bed. The woman has long, dark hair and golden skin. She's wearing black lingerie, and her partner is a muscled man with a beard. She's sitting on the bed, and he's leaning down to kiss her, still fully clothed in dark jeans and a gray T-shirt.

"Come here," Miles murmurs, leading me to the couch. He turns me around so that I'm facing away from him.

To sit on his lap, I realize.

He tugs at my hips, pulling me down.

His firm thighs are warm underneath me, and

every inch of my skin is hot and needy. My eyes flutter closed as he moves my hair away from my neck and presses a kiss to sensitive skin there just as his hands rove to my hips, squeezing once.

"What do we do?" I whisper, though I know the couple can't hear me.

"Just watch, butterfly," he murmurs, his voice vibrating down my spine.

My eyes snap open as I watch the couple before me. The man pulls away and removes his shirt, showcasing a muscled, taut abdomen. The woman watches him with hooded eyes, and I notice for the first time that her lingerie is sheer. Her hands come to her nipples, and she massages them as she watches her partner undress.

It feels wrong to watch them during such a private moment, but I can't help the thrill that works down my spine at the thought of watching these two beautiful people come together.

"Turn around." The man's voice booms through the speakers. I jump, hearing Miles chuckle from behind me as he tugs me closer.

The woman smiles at her partner before standing up and turning to face the bed. The man pulls a scarf out of his back pocket, and then he walks up to the woman, wrapping the silk around her wrists. She arches her back away from him, and I can see the pink flush appearing along her neck and jaw as he steps away, leaving her bound.

They both stay still, and I realize with a start that the woman is breathing heavily. Her body starts to tremble, and the man steps out of his jeans, show-casing a large erection bulging out of his boxers.

My heart pounds harder, faster, building me into a frenzy. The area between my legs is already slick with need; the anticipation already swirling in my gut. Just at that moment, one of Miles's hands comes to my bare thigh.

I nearly jump at the unexpected contact. Scooting back slightly, I'm pleased to find him hard beneath me.

"Does my wife like to watch?" he purrs against the base of my neck.

"Yes," I answer.

His hand moves in circles on my thigh, his index finger brushing the most sensitive part of my inner thigh. I squirm as I continue watching the couple before us.

"Aren't you worried they'll know it's you who's watching? That they'll put two and two together?" I ask.

He shrugs underneath me. "Luna ensures their NDA is signed before we disclose the location. If they suspect, they are legally obligated to stay quiet."

"But—"

His hand comes to my mouth as he leans forward, brushing more of my hair away from my neck.

"I assure you, Estelle. They want to be here. Almost all of these couples do it for the high they get from others watching them. The money, and the voyeur's identity, is an afterthought."

"Exhibitionists, you mean."

His lips graze my ear lobe, and my eyes fall closed at the same time my thighs open a tiny bit wider.

"Precisely."

"I took a quiz once," I whisper. "It said I was ... that I *liked* that," I finish, stumbling over my words. "To be watched."

He pauses his ministrations on my thighs, and I feel a quick, hot exhale against the base of my spine.

"Well, I suppose that's good news for me. Because I like to watch," he adds, his voice a low, seductive purr. If I'm not soaking through my knickers to his trousers already, it's only a matter of time.

"I like to watch, too," I murmur, barely able to concentrate on the words I'm saying. I'm just about to confess to watching him in the shower that night when he hums against the back of my neck.

"I've always liked to watch people, and as I got older and more curious about my sexuality, I craved something I could do without participating. I like observing people—and voyeurism was a natural progression for me. It's never felt malicious because I always obtain consent. It never feels shameful. Chase helped me embrace my kink."

"Chase?" I ask, suddenly curious.

"Let's talk about my brother another time, yeah?" he says, gently nibbling my neck.

My back arches as my half-hooded eyes flick back up to the stage. Miles's hands begin to circle my bare thighs again, but this time, he moves them up slightly, a few inches underneath the hem of my dress.

I watch as the man slowly walks over to the

woman. She's fully trembling now, her hands tied up behind her. He grabs her hair, fisting it as he walks up behind her and pulling her neck back.

"When they sign their contract, they are told they're free to do whatever they please. Whatever brings them pleasure. Sometimes they are tied up, like she is," he adds, his voice soft. "Other times, it's a little bit rougher."

I stiffen. *Rougher.* A spike of heat flares through me. I'm not the most experienced woman; I've had a handful of sexual partners, and I know now that they have all been vanilla. Still, with my last partner, I remember the feeling of him pounding into me. I remember asking him to go harder. He hadn't wanted to—but when I think of asking Miles to fuck me roughly ...

Something deep inside of me stirs, because I know he'd do it.

I can see it clear as day as I remember the way his hands gripped my hips in the dining room earlier. How they drove me against his erection with zero abandon ...

I squeeze my thighs together.

"Do you like it rough?" I ask, my voice trembling slightly.

His index finger slips higher, grazing the outside of my knickers. He lets out a low chuckle.

"I do, and I think you do too," he says, running his finger along my slit.

I can feel how wet I am by the way he's pressing against my skin. The way my knickers are sticking to the space between my thighs, the way his heart is pounding behind me ...

The way he's breathing heavily underneath me, like he can't get himself under control.

I don't want him to control himself.

The man pushes the woman against the bed, her thighs hitting the edge, and then he takes her hips and lifts her onto the mattress gently, stomach down. Stepping out of his boxers, he strokes himself several times as the woman lifts her arse up for him to admire. Letting out a pleased grunt, he crawls on top of her, a large, anticipatory smile on his face as he murmurs into her ear, his hand sliding up between her legs. They're comfortable with each other; I can tell by the way his hands peruse her skin like he's done it a thousand times before. She moans when he pushes her thighs apart.

I squirm on Miles's lap when I see him insert his middle finger inside of her.

"Like what you see?" he asks, his hand brushing gently against my clit.

My skin flushes, and everything feels hot and heavy. My head drops back as I lean into Miles, spreading my legs wider so that he has better access.

"That's it," he purrs. "Spread your legs like the good little wife I know you are."

I squeeze my eyes shut. Even though I don't want to miss watching the couple in front of us, his words send a flash of electricity through me that renders me completely boneless. My legs are quivering slightly, and my pussy clenches around nothing as one of his fingers hooks underneath my knickers, moving them to the side.

I gasp as he slides two fingers up and down my soaking core, and without warning, he plunges them deep inside of me. I moan as my hands fly out, gripping the material clinging to his thighs for purchase so I don't fly off him.

"Miles," I whimper.

"You're so wet for me, butterfly." He groans against the back of my neck. "Do you know what you're going to do for me?" he asks, his voice dipping an octave. He continues before I can answer, curling his fingers slightly as he slowly massages my inner walls, removing them almost all the way. "You're going to pull your dress down and play with your nipples while I fuck you with my hand."

I jerk as he pushes back inside of me. "Yes—"

"I'm not done," he murmurs. "Keep those pretty lips closed unless you're screaming and coming all over my cufflinks, Estelle."

I nod but don't say anything. My breathing stutters as he slowly curves his fingers and pulls them out of me.

"I want you to play with your tits while I make you come, okay?"

I nod, my eyes fluttering open and closed as I watch the man in the glass room pull back and admire his partner's arse. He spreads her wider, and she moans when he enters her, holding onto her hips and pulling them up slightly so that she's propped up on his thighs. He's truly and properly fucking her—the way her hands are tied behind her back and her legs are around his thighs as she rests on her stomach ... she's completely and totally unable to move. He pulls her harder, the smacking of their skin permeating the air around us.

The woman moans again, and I let out a low moan of my own as Miles's other hand comes to my chest, undoing the little tie to loosen my neckline. My nipples tighten in anticipation. He nudges it down so the top falls off my shoulders, falling past my breasts and exposing them to the cold air.

I hadn't worn a bra, and I feel the deep vibration of Miles's groan as he realizes.

He presses a kiss to my shoulder. "You're so fucking perfect, do you know that?" His praise makes me keen as I writhe against his wrist. "Play with those flawless nipples. I want to feel you squeeze my fingers before you squeeze my cock," he adds.

I circle my hips at his words. Such filthy, dirty words. I've never been spoken to like this—and certainly not in bed.

"You like the thought of fucking your husband, don't you?" he asks, moving his fingers deeper.

"Yes," I gasp out, my hips rocking against his arm. I spread my legs as wide as they'll go, and Miles growls in approval.

"There you go."

I watch the couple on the bed in front of me as Miles works his hand faster. My hands come up to my nipples, twisting and pulling at them as shockwaves of pleasure sear through me. I moan again when Miles' teeth sink into the area between my neck and shoulder, arching my back. My core flutters around Miles' fingers.

He adds a thumb to my clit, pressing directly down, and I cry out loudly.

"Louder," Miles commands. "Scream for me, butterfly."

"God, Miles." My head falls back against him as I buck my hips wildly on top of him. I've never been this brazen before, but something about experiencing this with *him*, perhaps because, despite everything, I trust him, heightens everything.

"I need to feel your cunt squeeze me, wife," he growls. "I want you to come for me."

"I'm close—"

He massages my clit with his thumb, and it makes all the difference. I begin to convulse as he curls his fingers deeper inside of me, and then he uses his left hand to squeeze my left nipple.

I shatter on top of him, screaming as my hips jerk against his wrist. My legs lift off the floor slightly as my toes curl, and the feel of Miles grinding against me, the feel of him pulling me close into his body, twisting and tugging at my nipple with practiced ease—

"That's it, one more," he murmurs, his soft breath against my ear coaxing a second orgasm out of me.

My eyes roll to the back of my head, and it's suddenly too much–

"Miles," I gasp, chest heaving.

"Let go," he commands, his voice hot and direct in my right ear.

"No, I'm going to—"

"Estelle, *let go*."

I go taut as my legs shake, and then it happens. I eject his fingers as my body convulses on top of him. The most intense feeling of ... something ... overcomes me. I see white, stars begin to dance in my vision, and something is coming out of me ...

He moans and pulls me close just as I try to pull my legs closed.

I can't believe I just did that.

"Such a good fucking girl," he says, pulling me into his chest. "You came so hard for me, butterfly. I'm so proud of you."

I'm gasping for air when I open my eyes. It's too dark to see it, but I can feel how wet he is underneath me.

"Oh, god," I say, covering my mouth before I die of humiliation.. "I just peed on you."

Miles laughs, his hands finding my waist. "That's never happened to you before?"

I gawk even though he can't see me. I'm still shaking, and his hands come to my thighs to calm my nerves, rubbing small circles into my flesh.

"Did I ..." I trail off.

"Squirt all over my cufflinks? You really do follow directions well."

"You don't mind?" I ask, looking over my shoulder at him. "It's—that's never happened to me before."

"Mind?" he growls. "Stand up."

I stumble to my feet, knees shaky, and turn to face him. Silently, he leans forward and reaches between my thighs, pulling my knickers down my legs. Watching him with weak knees, he fumbles with his belt buckle, and I suck in a breath when he unsheathes his thick cock.

"Do you think I mind that my wife came all over my lap?" he asks incredulously, spreading his legs slightly. Stroking his cock slowly, my mouth goes dry when I see the way he works the tip of his shaft, swirling what I assume is precum before working down again. "My cock is weeping, butterfly. For you. That was, hands down, the hottest thing I've ever seen. And I've seen a lot." He chuckles lightly.

I nearly gasp at his words, but before I can answer him, he reaches out for me. Twisting me around, he tugs me closer so that I'm standing between his legs. I briefly glance at the couple who are still happily fucking in front of us.

"Since you're so good at following directions, I'm going to give you some more," he says, his calloused fingers tracing the outsides of my thighs. He lifts my dress up, and my cheeks heat when I realize my arse is right in his face. A second later, I feel a sharp pinch on my flesh, and he groans so low that I feel it travel from my feet up to my head. "Such a perfect ass," he adds, running a hand over my left cheek. "Sit on my cock, Estelle."

His words reverberate through me, and I suck in a sharp breath as I bend my knees, lowering myself over his lap. He moans when my aching center meets the tip of his hard length. He holds me there, palms on the undersides of my thighs just as we make contact.

"Fuck, I'm not even inside of you, and yet I could come just from the feel of you touching me. So fucking warm. So fucking soft. So *fucking* wet," he mutters.

"Miles," I whimper, needing him inside of me.

He starts to lower me, hissing as he presses inside of me. He's almost too large—long and thick. I squeeze my eyes shut at the intrusion and the feeling of being stretched. It stings at first, but he goes slow, setting me down on top of his cock inch by inch until he's fully seated inside of me.

He lets out a shaky breath when he removes his hands. His breath on the back of my neck, mixed with being so *full* of him, makes me shiver.

"Perfect," he murmurs, hands coming around my waist. He presses a kiss against the back of my neck. I contract my thighs to ready myself to ride him, but his hands press down on my hips. "Don't move. Just watch."

My mouth drops open as my eyes flick to the couple in front of me lazily.

Don't move. Just watch.

"But—"

"Do you know what cock warming is, Estelle?" he asks.

My head is spinning. "I have an idea, yes," I answer, my breathing ragged.

"Good," he murmurs warmly, caressing the back of my neck.

The couple is fucking harder now, and his hands are gripping her fleshy thighs so tightly that he's leaving marks. The woman's back is arched off the bed as she moans. A loud slap reverberates through the cellar as he smacks her ass. He grunts loudly and as his cock pulses inside of me.

I move the tiniest bit, but Miles keeps me planted where I am, not letting me move any more.

"Stop moving," he growls. "Just watch and enjoy the show," he adds, hands coming up to my breasts.

My core clenches, and Miles groans underneath me. *He felt that.* Shifting his position, his cock presses slightly deeper inside me, the tip hitting my cervix, making me gasp in surprise.

"It's hard to concentrate," I whisper, feeling impatient and frenzied. Just the thought of sitting here, full of his cock ...

"Trust me, Estelle. Just watch. When they're done, you'll get your turn."

I let out a disgruntled whimper but I do as he says, turning back to the couple. Even though I want to grind against his cock, I know he won't let me until they finish. I've never been in a situation like this before with past partners, and though I know certain terms from my books, I've never been commanded like this. What the hell do I do? Sit here until they finish?

Hurry up, I think crossly.

"Don't rush through it," Miles says against the back of my neck. "Enjoy the show."

How did he ...

Suddenly, the man unties the woman's hands, pulling out and flipping her onto her back. I think he's going to fuck her like that, but then she places two pillows under her head, tilts her chin down, and opens her mouth as he straddles her chest. He lets out a loud, low groan as he places his cock into her mouth, thrusting up and into the back of her throat.

My pussy contracts when I think of watching Miles do that to *me*.

"Do you like the idea of letting me fuck your mouth like that, butterfly?" Miles murmurs.

"Y-yes," I stutter, *needing* friction. Everything inside of me aches with wanting, and I swear he must feel my pulse fluttering around his cock, because it feels like all of my blood is flowing to the area between my legs.

"I thought so. Your cunt is squeezing me like a greedy, little harlot."

I let out a half-gasp, half-sigh. *The mouth on this man ...*

His fingers press into my hips as I snap my eyes back to the couple. His hot breath comes to my right shoulder, and the change in movement pulls his cock out the tiniest bit. Since I've been waiting for him to move, that tiny movement has me feeling needy and whimpering.

"There are so many things I want to do to you. *With you.* You have no idea, Estelle. I am a very patient man who has been waiting a long time for this."

I begin to tremble. "Me too," I whisper, my breathing uneven from watching the couple.

The man's arse muscles contract, and his move-ments get stilted as he throws his head back and groans. I realize with a heated flash that he's going to come soon.

Miles twists my nipples lightly. The rough pads of his fingers brush against my sensitive buds, and I let out a frustrated mewl. It feels amazing, but I need more.

Miles must read my mind, because one of his hands trails down to the area between my legs.

"You're soaking wet, wife," he says in a pleased groan. "It's running down your thighs. What I wouldn't give to push you down on the couch and taste you," he adds, his middle finger beginning to lightly circle my clit. I can feel how aroused I am—how with each circle, my pussy squeezes his cock.

"Please," I beg.

"Another day. Tonight, I want my cock inside of you when you come."

"Yes," I pant.

I try to shift my hips, but he holds me still. "Watch them," he orders.

My eyes dart to the couple. I watch as the man fists her hair roughly, watch as tears stream down her cheeks in black rivers. She doesn't look scared, though. Her eyes are hooded with lust, and I realize with a start that she's playing with herself—one finger inserted, and the other playing with her clit. *She likes this.* And she's watching her partner with love, adoration, and something else that makes my chest ache.

I can see the trust shining through the glass.

My hips tilt of their own accord, and Miles lets me. His finger works faster against my clit, and the sensation of his cock hitting my inner walls makes me want to scream out loud.

It's too much. I close my eyes, and somehow Miles notices. He removes his finger from my clit, and I whimper loudly.

"Please," I beg. "Please, don't stop."

"I thought I told you to watch them?" he asks, his voice hard.

The way he can be so gentle in one second, and yet so commanding the next second ... *I fucking love it.*

My eyes snap open just as the man roars, and I know instantly that he's coming. His motions still, and I can see the way his cock pulses into her mouth. The look on his face—the slackened jaw, the pure, unfiltered reverence toward his partner ...

"Fuck," I whisper, trembling, my pussy gripping Miles tightly. The hard ache between my legs physically hurts—the burning and stretching of his cock, the way my clit is swollen with need ...

My thighs contract, needing something. My hands move to his thighs, and I squeeze him. He moans, and his hips jerk slightly, moving his cock deeper.

I cry out, watching the couple in front of us with hooded eyes. The man is stroking the woman's hair, using his thumb to clean her lips and mascara marks. She's smiling up at him as he tucks his cock away.

"Are they ..." I trail off, unable to think clearly.

"No, they're not finished. I pay them for an hour," he adds. "I want you to keep watching as he makes her come."

"Okay," I answer, my voice hoarse. I'm not sure how much more I can take, but then the man works his way down her legs, spreading them wide before he buries his face in her dark curls and places one leg over his shoulder. Her back arches and she lets out a low, guttural moan that makes me contract around my husband's thick shaft again.

Miles continues his ministrations against my clit, and I groan, wanting nothing more than to move my hips in small, subtle circles.

"Fuck, Estelle," he rasps. "If you keep squeezing me like that, you just might make me come without moving," he utters. "You're such a little tease, aren't you?"

The idea of him unraveling underneath me is so hot. I feel out of control. It's almost like I'm being tortured with pleasure.

"Miles, I need more," I beg, my voice uneven, almost a sob. "Please."

"Not yet," he says, his voice low. He adds a finger to my clit, massaging either side of it, giving me some friction but not enough to push me over the edge. "This is just a taste of what's to come, Estelle."

"Stop edging me, please," I blurt.

He chuckles behind me. "Do you enjoy being edged?"

I whimper. "Yes, sometimes ... but this is torture."

The woman's legs shake as the man adds two fingers. He's laving his tongue up and down her slit, and with each sweep of his tongue, she jerks uncontrollably.

"What else was on that quiz you took?" he asks. "What kinds of things do you like?"

I can't think, but I answer as best as I can. "Exhibitionism, edging, public sex, being caught," I start, my voice shaking. He scissors his fingers, and I moan before he moves them away again. "Um ..." I close my eyes.

"Eyes open, butterfly." I do as he says. "What else?"

"Rough sex, nipple play, body modification ..."

Miles rocks up into me, and I groan. "What else?"

"D-dirty talk," I add, remembering being surprised at that result, because I'd never experienced it.

Until Miles.

He chuckles. "Good. Thank you for telling me," he says softly. As if to reward me, he circles my clit softly as he moves his hips *just* enough to press against the inner walls of my pussy. "Keep watching."

The man works his hand faster, and as he does, Miles moves his faster, too. I'm panting now, my whole body taut and on the precipice of a climax. I'm *so* close —each brush of his finger on my swollen nub has me careening closer and closer toward my orgasm. The woman writhes and undulates her hips, and then she cries out as he groans.

I watch the way her hips stutter—the way her hands fist his hair, the way her body shakes uncontrollably.

"Fuck," I whisper, thighs tensing as Miles works his fingers faster. Everything inside of me coils tightly, waiting and ready to break. I whimper again, hating how desperate I sound. "How are you okay right now? This is worse than torture," I huff out, skin hot and tingling. I don't think I've ever been this turned on in my life.

He laughs behind me, pausing his fingers. "You're assuming I'm okay," he starts, brushing the hair away from my sticky neck. "One should never assume, Estelle. I'm just better at controlling myself. I've had years—*decades*—of practice. They're leaving now. Their hour is up. You've been very patient."

Thank fuck.

The couple inside the glass room get dressed, and I watch the way the man caresses her skin, how he makes sure she's okay, murmuring something soft into her ear as he helps her into her heels. Something cracks inside of me. *I want that.* And not just in a general sense.

I want that with Miles.

They exit through a door I hadn't seen, leaving Miles and I alone in the cellar.

"Where does ... that door ... lead to?" I ask, not really caring about the answer.

Miles hums behind me, his hand slowly pressing down on my clit. My pussy flutters around his hard cock, and he hums again in satisfaction.

"To the parking lot."

"Miles, I—" My breathing hitches when he uses my wetness to begin rubbing against my engorged bud, swiping some with his other hand and rubbing it all over my left nipple.

"You know, you're beautiful when you lose control," he murmurs.

"It hurts," I whimper, thighs aching from squeezing them so hard. "I want it so bad that it hurts."

He laughs behind me. The arsehole *laughs*.

Shifting underneath me, sparks fly through me with every movement, making my toes curl. One hard thrust, and I'll come.

"I know, butterfly." His teeth graze the skin of my shoulder again, and *god*, is it possible to come like this? I think it might be. Surely, if he continued, one touch and I'd be gone. "Stand up."

What?!

Whimpering, I pull myself up as my legs shake, feeling my arousal slide down my thighs. Miles grabs at my dress, twisting me and tugging me around to face him.

"Now, sit back down on my cock so I can watch you unravel on top of me," he growls, tugging me down so that I'm straddling him. I place my knees on either side of his hips. "Arms up."

I raise them and he drags my dress up over my head, discarding it off to the side. I lay my palms flat against his chest as his cock presses against my core, not thrusting up into me yet. I nearly gasp at the way his eyes peruse me—realizing with a start that I'm straddling him completely naked whereas he's still fully-clothed. His gaze roves over me, lazily appraising me as his hands caress the bare flesh of my breasts, my stomach, my hips, my arse ...

Something intense flares through his entrancement, and his throat bobs as he guides my hips lower, lining himself up with my opening. My pulse pounds against my veins, and I sink down onto his hard cock.

He hisses as he exhales, and his heart hammers

underneath my hands as I get a subtle whiff of green apples.

"Fuck," he rasps. One of his hands comes to my butterfly tattoo, and he traces the outline, eyes blazing with need. "I hope you know that this tattoo is so fucking sexy."

I roll my hips on top of him, and he squeezes my arse appreciatively. It sends a wave of pleasure skittering down my spine.

"Yes," I cry out, not daring to take my eyes off him. There's a dark, smoldering flame in his eyes as he watches me, and it startles me for a second. He's so ... intense. *This* is intense. I take a deep breath and slow down, wanting to watch every emotion and reaction play across his features in real time. I reach down for his hands, lacing my fingers through his, gripping him tightly.

"Estelle," Miles says, his voice hoarse. His hands squeeze mine as his jaw tightens. "I want you to come for me."

I nod, working my hips in small circles to get the friction I need. Holding hands with him as I ride him feels so intimate.

This is *intimate. You're* married *to him.*

The thought makes me groan as I arch my back slightly. I am so full, so complete here with him. Like somehow, watching him unravel before me somehow ties us together officially. A delicate thread begins to form between us. Even though my instincts are telling me to close my eyes and throw my head back, I can't look away from him.

From the way his jaw feathers with each snap of my hips.

The way his hands squeeze mine, encouraging me to keep going. The darkened pupils of his green eyes. The way his nostrils are flaring—like he's holding back slightly.

Small whimpers escape my mouth. I'm on fire. The feel of him sliding in and out of me—it's glorious, sensual, and everything I never knew I needed.

"Estelle," he murmurs again, bending forward to kiss me. I stop moving to kiss him back, but he growls and bucks his hips up into me. "Don't you dare fucking stop."

I groan as I work my hips faster, harder, meeting every one of his thrusts. "I'm close," I tell him.

He moves my right hand, that's still laced with his, and presses it on my lower abdomen. "Play with yourself. Let me watch as you fall apart."

He doesn't have to ask me twice. As I grind against him, I use my hand to rub my clit.

"Fuck, Miles, I'm …"

Everything pulls tight, but I keep my eyes open, watching him as my orgasm crests. His mouth drops open, and the dark, fervent *need* written all over his face sends me over the edge. My whole body convulses on top of him, my thighs squeezing his hips as I scream his name over and over. A maelstrom of sensation explodes through me over and over. I stop moving, going boneless, and he drives up into me. My toes curl against the leather of the couch, and I have to actively work to keep my eyes open.

Watching him as he watches me.

"You're so fucking perfect," he mutters as my climax slows. His thrusts get harder, deeper. My forehead presses against his as his hips start to jerk erratically. "I could watch you forever." He pants against my face. "I fucking love—" A groan escapes his lips, coming from somewhere deep in his chest.

I bring my hands to the sides of his face, pulling back slightly and watching him as he breaks apart underneath me. Face slackening, his eyes cloud over as his hips still and he lets out a low, sensual moan as he comes, hands squeezing my hips tightly with each pulse of his cock inside of me. My eyes don't leave his face as he sighs contentedly, cheeks pink from the exertion.

"Fuck, wife," he growls, tugging my body into his as he holds me.

We stay that way for at least a minute, heaving chests, steadying breaths, coming down from something I never expected to be so intense. My cheek rests on his shoulder as his hands trail up my lower back, rubbing me there softly. It reminds me so much of the nights he spent in bed with me when I was having one of my episodes ...

I'm falling for him.

Throat constricting, I pull away and look down at him. "Miles ..."

One of his hands cups the side of my face. "I know." He swallows once. "Come on. Let's get you cleaned up."

He helps me off him, and I'm grateful for the low

lighting. I'm sure we both look a right mess—from earlier, when he fingered me, to now, with his seed dripping down my thighs. I'm just about to ignore it when Miles drops to his knees. I gasp when he knocks my knees apart.

"I need to memorize how my wife looks with my cum dripping out of her cunt," he says, looking up at me from his knees as his hands run up the inside of my thighs.

I smirk, running a hand through his hair. "Take a picture."

He pauses. "Can I?"

I laugh. "We're married, Miles. You'll hardly be the first husband to have a picture of his wife's fanny."

He chuckles. "Fine. Spread your legs wider." A heated thrill works through me as I give him a coy smile. He removes his phone and looks up at me, his expression pained. "Fuck, Estelle. You have the most gorgeous cunt I've ever seen," he growls. He unlocks his phone and aims it right at my fanny. "Are you sure?"

"Yes. Just do it before I change my mind."

He takes two pictures. Grunting, he pockets his phone and stands, grabbing my dress and handing it to me.

I slip it over my head, thinking of the fact that Miles now has a picture of something so lascivious. He can look at it anytime—at work, at dinner, when he's lying in bed ...

I smile as I reach for my knickers, but Miles is

quicker. He snatches them from the floor and pockets them.

"Excuse me," I chastise him. "I need those."

He laughs as he walks toward the door. "I need them more, butterfly." Holding the door open, he gestures for me to go ahead of him. "Would you like something to eat?"

I snort. "Is that your idea of aftercare?"

He grins, and I swear, I'll never get over the feel of Miles smiling because of something I said.

"Come on. Let me take care of you."

His words cause a dangerous flutter to erupt inside of my chest.

I am *so* fucked and head over heels for my husband.

CHAPTER TWENTY-ONE
THE ADVICE

MILES

I putz around the kitchen, making neat piles of ingredients on my chopping board as Estelle watches me from the island. Every time I look up at her, she's either sipping her wine and watching me with a smile, or leaning back on the stool and watching me with a smile. I have to fight the grin that threatens to twist my lips upward every time I do. Once I have everything ready, I grab a large pan and add some butter as it heats up.

"Thank god one of us can cook," she says mirthfully. "I can barely crack an egg. What are you making, anyway?"

My lips twist to the side. "You'll see."

I feel her eyes on me as I add the ingredients to the pan, unsure of if I'm doing it right. I've never made this, and it's been awhile since I've cooked for myself.

When I flick my eyes up to hers, I swallow before looking away. She's so fucking stunning, and she doesn't even realize it. That green dress hanging off one shoulder. Her wild, white-blonde curls parted over to one side. Her lips a shade of dark pink from kissing me a couple of minutes ago. After cleaning us both up in the guest bathroom, I'd kissed her against the wall of the kitchen before pouring her a glass of wine and ordering her to sit and relax. She doesn't know it yet, but tonight changed something inside of me.

I'd never watched a couple while being with a woman—*my* woman. I'd never fucked someone while I watched, either. I'd never told anyone aside from Chase about my kink—assuming I'd scare any potential dates away if I did. Voyeurs don't exactly have a good reputation.

But Estelle took everything in stride, not missing a beat by joining me in the cellar. Enjoying it as much as I did. Knowing *exactly* what I needed, and when. And everything that happened ... it makes me crazy for her. Unstable. Needy and possessive. Now that I'd had a taste, I wasn't sure I'd ever be able to walk away from her.

Not when she was the only person to see the real me. My scars. My kinks. My secrets.

Well, all but one of my secrets.

I clear my throat. "Fried eggs or scrambled?" I ask, trying to shake the negative thoughts from my mind.

"Surprise me," she says, smiling.

Her smile is fucking contagious.

I finish up with the sausages, plating everything

else while they cook. Estelle gives me space, watching me as I grab some juice from the refrigerator. A minute later, I place a glass of orange juice in front of each of us before I set our plates down.

She stares down at her plate without saying anything for several seconds, and at first, I assume I massively fucked up. But then she snaps her glassy eyes up to mine, and there's something open and warm as she laughs.

"You made us an English breakfast," she croaks, pressing her lips together.

"I did," I say slowly, trying to gauge how she's feeling. Before I can ask her if I did an okay job, she bursts into tears.

"You ... this ... I'm not ..." She sobs, tears streaming down her face.

I walk around the island and wrap my arms around her, trying not to laugh. She's so fucking lovely, and I can't help but smile as I lean down to kiss the top of her head.

"That bad?" I joke.

She laughs through her tears, swiping at her cheeks as I take a step back. "No, no, it's perfect. I'm just ... surprised. A *good* surprised."

Fuck.

I chew on the inside of my cheek as realization dawns. She's surprised because I'm normally a giant asshole. Because I'm normally bickering with her, giving her the cold shoulder, or ignoring her completely. She's surprised because I'm not normally this nice.

It feels like someone is stabbing me with ice as I take a step back, and I wince before I say what's on my mind. I'm not usually this forthcoming, but I want to prove to her that I'm worthy of whatever she's willing to give me.

"I'm sorry," I tell her gently.

"For what?" she asks, tilting her head slightly.

"You eat. I'll talk," I add, gesturing to her plate. She nods before she begins to cut the sausage with her knife. I rub my mouth and lean against the island. "Growing up, I hardly had any friends. I've always been skeptical of people. My brothers were my only friends, and then the accident happened, and that ensured no one wanted to spend time with the mangled brother."

She stops chewing. "Miles ..."

I hold a hand up. "Let me finish. I've—I've never told anyone any of this."

"Okay."

"When I was eighteen, I lost my virginity. I kept my hoodie on the entire time, and after, she made a comment about my scars. She called me a freak. It stuck in my mind. I walked away and never spoke to her again. It felt *uncomfortable* being vulnerable with people. So I just stopped. I didn't fuck anyone else until I was twenty-eight."

Estelle's eyes widen, but she doesn't say anything.

"In those ten years, I discovered voyeurism. I used to go to a kink club in Los Angeles, but the drive was sometimes over an hour. When Chase and I started Ravage Consulting Firm, I decided it would be easier to design my own space, so the cellar was born. I hired

Luna shortly after that, and she's been helping to coordinate along with her partner ever since—though she now does a lot more for me around the castle."

"Anyway, after the room was complete, I felt comfortable taking it a step further physically. I never brought them in there, of course, but knowing I had something *just for me* gave me the conviction to try again. And, when you watch how men act around women night after night, it sort of starts to become second nature. My confidence grew. I started dating casually, fucking women here and there, and I always came back to the room for months on end. It's safe. I don't have to make sure my collar is covering my scars. I don't have to undress. I don't have to answer questions about why I don't undress. It's easier," I add.

Estelle takes a sip of her orange juice, watching me with interest. "Have you ever been in love?"

I shrug. "Infatuation, maybe. But nothing like ..." I trail off and clear my throat. "What about you?"

She laughs at that. "At least a dozen times. Until last year, I dated around a lot. Fell in love easily. Live, love, laugh, and all of that. But then my grandmother died, and I didn't have that urge to date. Nothing sparked that flame, you know?" She takes another sip of juice. "Well, that's not true. There was this one man."

I stand up straighter as she grins at me.

"Tall, wickedly handsome, always wears suits ..." I smile before I can catch myself. "We met in Paris when I was swimming naked in a fountain, and then, using one of the *worst* pickup lines I've ever heard, invited me back to his flat to dry off."

"One of the worst pickup lines? Really?" I ask, feigning woundedness.

She laughs again. "It worked, so I guess it wasn't that bad." She sets her fork down and rests her head in her hand as she looks at me. "Why did you pull away from me that night in Paris?"

I shift uncomfortably. "I thought you saw my scars and got spooked. I overreacted and pushed you away before I got hurt."

"That makes sense. I thought I came on too strong and spooked you."

I smirk as we make eye contact. "I suppose it was a miscommunication all around."

She cocks her head as she assesses me. "I suppose so."

I walk over to my plate and spear a mushroom with my fork. "It feels silly now."

Before she can answer, her phone chimes. She reaches for where it's sitting a few feet away, glancing down at the screen.

I smile as her eyes widen. I've been wondering when she'd find out—before or after the cellar.

"Miles," she says, her voice shaky. "Why is the editor-in-chief of Cosmopolitan magazine emailing me about featuring VeRue in their next issue?"

"Because I emailed her just before we went down to the cellar."

She sets her phone down and pushes her plate away. "This is ... Miles, this is *huge*."

"I told you I'd make this marriage worth your while, didn't I?" I ask, chewing on a piece of sausage.

Her eyes glitter as she stares at me in awe, and *fuck* if it doesn't feel great to make her happy. I want this.

I want *her*.

Us.

Every single day.

She sits up straighter as she wipes her mouth with her napkin. "Oh my god. I have so much work to do."

"Makes two of us," I answer, smiling.

She gives me a warm smile as she stands. Walking over to me, she wraps her arms around me, and I'm suddenly filled with something warm. Something comforting. Having her here, with me, knowing she cares about me. Despite everything.

"Thank you," she murmurs, kissing my cheek. "I should go prepare everything. I need to make sure my sketches are done, my website, my social media ..." she trails off, a faraway, excited look on her face. "I'll see you in the morning, darling." With another quick peck to my lips, she walks out of the kitchen.

I realize I'm still smiling when Luna walks into the kitchen a minute later.

Arching a brow, she looks around at the food. "Can I join you?"

I nod once. "Of course."

Luna makes herself a plate, skipping the sausage because she and Emma are vegetarians. Sitting down across from me, she picks at her toast.

"I really like Stella," she says casually. "She seems good for you."

"It's why I married her," I say, smirking.

Luna narrows her eyes. "We haven't had that much time to talk since all of it happened, but I've known you for over a decade, Miles Ravage. I probably know you better than your brothers."

"Probably."

Looking down at her plate, she clears her throat before she continues to speak. "I don't know what kind of arrangement the two of you agreed on—"

"Luna, drop it," I tell her sternly. The last thing I need is for more people to know about this marriage of convenience. So far, only my brothers and Juliet know.

"Let me talk," she bites back, looking at me with a commanding expression.

I sit up straighter and try not to smile. Sometimes I forget what a bulldog Luna can be. She's feisty, and strong, and a hell of a good employee. *And a hell of a good friend.* At forty-three, she and her wife, Emma, have become the sisters I didn't know I needed. Not just because she knows about the cellar and my proclivities, but because I *trust* her. She's constantly looking out for me, defending me, supporting me, and making sure I'm okay.

"I'm going to give you some marriage advice from someone who has been married nearly twenty years," she says slowly, piercing me with her brown eyes. "No secrets."

"No secrets," I repeat.

She nods, taking a bite of mushrooms. "Exactly."

I look down at my plate as guilt swarms through me. "I'm working on it, Luna."

"Good. Secrets destroy marriages. Just ask Emma. We know everything about each other—the good, the bad, the ugly. She's seen me at my worst," she says slowly. "If you want this marriage with Stella to last, make sure all of your secrets are out in the open." I push the food around on my plate as I take in her words. "You do want this marriage to last, don't you?" she pushes.

I lean back and sigh, running a hand through my hair. "Yes."

Luna smiles. "You're different around her. Softer. Happier. She's good for you, Miles. She smoothes out all of your hard lines, and somehow, she's managed to crack through your hard exterior."

Rubbing the back of my neck, I sigh loudly. "I lied to her."

Luna shrugs, taking another bite of toast. "So fix it."

"It's not that easy," I mutter.

"I never said it would be easy," she deadpans. "She could very well walk out the front door and never return once you come clean. But it's better to tell her now. Lay it all out in the open in the beginning. Build that foundation of a marriage on truth and honesty. Don't start this journey on a house of cards. Don't let it collapse before it even begins."

My lips tug into a smile as I consider her words. "When did you become so wise?" I tease.

She laughs as she collects our plates, walking to the sink. "I've always been wise. You've just been too cranky to notice."

I huff a laugh. "I appreciate the advice. Thank you."

When she's done putting our dishes away, she places her hands on her hips and winks. "You should get some sleep. I've seen the emails come in; you have a busy day tomorrow."

Without another word, Luna walks out of the kitchen, and I stand up to begin the task of cleaning up the mess.

I have to tell Estelle about the money, and I have to do it soon.

Because if there's one thing tonight proved, it's that there's no way in hell I'm letting her go after the year is up.

I want her—*all* of her.

I want to make her happy, to cook her food, to kiss her, to spar with her, to wake up every morning to the feel of her curls suffocating me ...

To make sure she's taken care of when she's sad.

To *watch people* with her.

To watch *her*.

I want it all. Every second. The good, the bad, the ugly.

My heart hammers in my chest as realization dawns.

I'm in love with my wife.

CHAPTER TWENTY-TWO

THE INTERVIEW

Stella

The next two days are so busy that I hardly see Miles. I don't even have time for my daily walks. He's in the office by seven, and usually not home until dinner. Being that we're both working extremely hard, we catch up quickly over a home-cooked meal, and then we both go our separate ways after a quick kiss. It's oddly domestic, and while I wish I could spend some genuine time with him, I know it's only temporary for both of us.

Ravage Consulting Firm was inundated with over a hundred inquiries, and I know Miles and Chase are fielding potential clients all day long. It's exciting, but I can tell it's taking a toll on Miles. Every night during dinner, he seems distracted and physically exhausted.

Not that I'm doing any better.

After I'd received the email from the editor-in-chief of *Cosmopolitan* magazine, I'd gone into beast mode. The interview was scheduled for Saturday morning in Beverly Hills, and I wanted to be sure I had everything I needed before then. I decided to pay my web designer a rush fee, ensuring my website could handle any extra traffic in the coming weeks. I also added a countdown timer to the main page for the launch—which I was forced to schedule. If I'm going to be featured in Cosmo, I need to have a place to send people.

The website and logo is now done and ready to launch in six months.

That meant scheduling social media posts, a bit of advertising, and lots of coordinating with manufacturing facilities. Miles has a contact with one of my favorite places in downtown Los Angeles, meaning all my clothing would be made here in California. I spent all day Friday sourcing fabrics and materials, sending them all to the factory to get samples.

My sketches are done, the sewing patterns are cut, and I have everything prepped.

On Friday night, I spent an hour on the couch panicking about the magazine feature. It'll be my first, and though I have everything ready, I'm still a nervous wreck. Deciding on an early evening stroll, I make my way to the back garden. It's much cooler at night now, so I wrap my cardigan tightly around me as I make my way to Lucifer's pen.

I've been thinking of that damn goat ever since Miles introduced me. He was right. I need to get used to him. And I have to get over my irrational fear.

As I inch closer to the gate, I hear Lucifer let out a loud bleat, and I yelp with surprise, scurrying away.

Maybe another day.

That night, I toss and turn for hours. At some point, Miles crawls into bed with me, his body falling on top of the orange duvet in an exhausted heap. When my alarm goes off at five on Saturday morning, he's still asleep.

I sit up and stare at him for a minute—still clad in a white dress shirt and black slacks. Nudging him to the center of the mattress, I pull the duvet out from under him, tucking him in as I quietly get ready for the feature.

By the time seven rolls around, he's still asleep, and I don't wake him.

> *Be back around noon.*
> *Excited for our date later.*
> *Xo,*
> *Stella*

I leave the note on my bedside table before assessing my reflection in the mirror. I'm wearing one of my pieces—a bright yellow linen shirt that's cropped and knotted in the middle and matching wide leg yellow trousers. I tamed my curls slightly and pulled the outfit together with nude heels and a tan-colored, vintage Celine bag—a hand-me-down from my grandmother.

And of course, my *R* necklace.

I see Miles's watch on my dresser, and in a moment of spontaneity, I pull it over my wrist, securing it as tight as I can. *Perfect.*

It'll be nice to have a piece of him with me.

I'm too nervous to eat anything, so I have half a cup of tea and a biscuit before meeting Niro outside at ten past seven.

The stoic driver is quiet the entire drive into Beverly Hills, which I'm grateful for. There's hardly any traffic, but that doesn't stop my legs from bouncing on the carpeted floor the entire drive there. Once we arrive at the Beverly Hills hotel, I say a quick goodbye to Niro as I walk into the lobby, looking for the journalist who was sent to interview me.

"Estelle Ravage?" The name startles me, sending warmth through me. An older woman with graying hair smiles at me from a few feet away.

"Yes, hello!" I chirp, and she reaches a hand out to shake.

"I'm Annette. I'll grab us a table and we can begin the interview after we've had some coffee," she explains, her smile warm. "Sound good?"

I have to clamp my mouth closed so I don't laugh like a maniac. "Of course."

Be cool, I tell myself, using Miles's watch to center myself.

————

The interview goes amazingly. Annette and I talk for almost three hours, and though I know she's recording me, it doesn't feel like an interview. I tell her about growing up in London, living with my father, his charitable work, and then we get into my clothing line. I don't stop talking about VeRue for nearly thirty minutes, and I only cry once when talking about my grandmother.

All in all, a win for me.

Finally, at the end of the interview, she asks about my marriage to Miles. I tell her that it's been a crazy, wonderful couple of weeks. When she asks how we met, I don't have to lie. I realize we'd never discussed what we were going to say if anyone asked us about our dating life, so I give her all of the details—the fountain, the taxi, how we kept our budding relationship secret until he asked me to marry him in Paris.

"Sounds like a whirlwind engagement," she muses, smiling as she sips her coffee. "Almost like a fairytale."

"It was," I answer. "I couldn't be happier."

"How was it being folded into the Ravage family? That must've been interesting."

I nod as I sip my third cup of tea, feeling caffeinated and perky. "I don't understand the stigma," I tell her honestly. "I know I'm biased now that I bear their last name, but all of them—Charles included—have been absolutely lovely to be around."

Annette assesses me as she takes another sip of coffee, and I swallow nervously at her assessing gaze.

"Of course. But I think we're all curious how someone with such a good-natured and philanthropic family came to merge with a family notorious for stealing money."

I take a deep breath. "With all due respect, I'm not sure that's a fair comparison to make. People are a lot more than their name, or their history. Everyone deserves a second chance."

"I see where you're coming from," she says softly. "But Charles Ravage lost over thirty-four million dollars. That money belonged to hard-working families. He might've been acquitted legally and on paper, but his infamous trial—and the reaction to his verdict—just goes to show that a lot of people still don't trust the Ravage family. It's your word against everyone else's."

My palms curl in my lap as I take a steadying breath. I expected a question or two about Miles—but I didn't expect *Cosmo* to get into the trial and everything that Charles Ravage did.

What are her intentions by asking me about all of this?

"I knew what I was getting into when I married Miles," I tell her, my voice a tad icier than before. "And despite the horrible things his father did, Miles Ravage is a good man."

Annette eyes me skeptically, and I have to temper the unjust anger beginning to flood me.

"I have sources that say the opposite, Stella," she says gently. "In fact, is it true that he's the only one of his brothers who is still in contact with Charles?"

"No, I believe Orion still sees his father from time to time."

"And the article from *LA Weekly* a few weeks ago? What do you make of that?"

I remember the article down to the title.

"Business Versus Bullying: How Far Is Too Far for Ravage Consulting Firm?"

I read it. Of course I'd read it. My hands curl against my thighs. I want to tell her that she's wrong—that Miles is nothing like his father. That he's thoughtful, and funny, with a wicked, dry sense of humor. I want to tell her that the tabloids don't know my husband like I do.

"Quite honestly, it was a load of rubbish," I tell her, my voice firm.

Her brows furrow, and she leans forward. "Forgive me for the inquisition, Stella. A lot of people are concerned about you. They feel like you and your father have been taken advantage of by a very powerful, very manipulative family."

My heart clenches at her words. "I fell in love with Miles Ravage before I knew who he was. Before I knew the man attached to the name. He's funny, and kind, and he takes good care of me. He's the reason we're sitting here today—because he believes in this clothing line. Which, by the way, is what I thought we'd be talking about."

Annette looks somewhat surprised. "Very well. Back to VeRue then. When can we expect your website to go live?"

I sip my tea as I give her a polite smile. *That's more like it.* "I'm hoping by next Spring."

The interview ends shortly after that, and I walk out to Niro's car with shaky knees. The entire drive back to Ravage Castle, I go over what I said, how I said it, and if my words are going to make any difference in the Ravage family reputation. Miles especially deserves a second chance, and I'll do everything in my power to ensure people believed that by the time our year was over.

I rub my chest when I think of what that will look like. How am I supposed to walk away from him after everything that's already happened between us?

More importantly … what-if I don't want to walk away?

CHAPTER TWENTY-THREE
THE SHOWER

MILES

After waking up just before eight, practically the afternoon for me, I spend the morning working on my laptop with my feet propped up on the pink couch. Much to my chagrin, the color is growing on me. It's not as offensive as I'd once thought, and if it made Estelle happy, then it could stay as long as she did.

As long as she wants to stay.

After checking my email, I send a large batch of follow-up emails. RCF signed thirty new clients this week, which was a record for us. Shira was onboarding more employees as soon as we could get them in, and Chase was working on possibly expanding our office to the floor above us. Expansion was good. Being busy was good. I make a mental note to thank Estelle when she gets home.

I check my phone for the hundredth time. It's nearly noon, and I know she'll be home soon. I can't wait to see her—to spend more than a quick dinner with her. I want to see her laugh at something I say, nose crinkling in the cute way it usually does. I want to ask her about her first kiss. I want to feel her hand as I hold it on top of the table. I want to ask her about the interview.

I want to kiss her, touch her, *feel* her body against mine.

My days are empty without her, and though I know we're both still feeling this relationship out, I already know I want to be around her for longer than a dinner.

I quickly finish out my batched emails, hoping to be able to spend the afternoon with her before our date, and I suddenly remember something Juliet said about Chase last weekend.

Chase used to be like that. But I made him start working normal hours.

Just as I go to shut my laptop, Estelle opens the door to our suite. Her lips break into a wide smile as she walks over to me, and *fuck* ... my eyes slowly wander down her sleek curls, to her neck and cleavage, to the strip of bare skin on her stomach, to the way the band of her pants cinches her waist, and those heels ...

"You're drooling," she says, setting her purse down and stepping out of her shoes.

"I can't help it," I murmur as my eyes wander up to her face. "I have the most beautiful wife in the world." Her cheeks flush at my words. "So, how did it go?"

She shrugs. "It went well, I think. We'll see how well it went when the article comes out next month."

I furrow my brows. "Surely she must've loved the idea for VeRue," I say softly, feeling defensive.

Estelle pulls her lower lip between her teeth. "She did. But then she asked about you and insinuated that I was some naive girl being taken advantage of by 'a very powerful family,'" she finishes and lets out an angry huff. "Don't worry. I defended your honor. It was just frustrating because everyone has this preconceived notion of you, and it pisses me off."

My lips twitch with a smile as her chest flushes with anger and contempt. If she wasn't already my wife, her defending my honor like this might make me want to ask her to do so.

I open my mouth to speak, but Estelle continues as she takes a step closer. "No wonder you needed me. People have it all wrong. They have no idea what a great person you are," she says, her voice gentle.

I swallow and look down at the floor, the guilt making my throat clog up.

Do great people lie to their wife? The same wife they coerced into marriage?

"Well, thank you," I tell her. "I appreciate you defending my honor," I say, tugging on her pants and pulling her between my knees. "Really. It means a lot," I add, just as her hand comes to my neck.

I close my eyes, working past the urge to shove her hand away. Grinding my jaw, I take a deep breath.

"Do you want to go on a walk with me?" I ask, looking up at her.

"Sounds lovely. But first, I need to go take a shower. I was so nervous I think I sweat through my top," she answers, pulling away and walking to the bathroom door. When she gets to the frame, she turns to face me, arching a brow before continuing into the shared bathroom.

Did she just ...

I wait for her to close the door, but she makes no move to do so. Instead, I hear her turn the shower on, and my mouth goes dry when realization dawns.

She wants me to watch.

I'm already hard by the time I stand, so I adjust myself in my pants and walk over to the bathroom door. Estelle is already in the shower, and I can't see anything other than the outline of her hourglass-shaped body because of the steam against the glass. Does she know I'm here? Does she want me here? Or did I read the signs all wrong? Just as I consider leaving, she uses her hand to clear the steam, and my mouth drops open when I realize she's staring right at me on the other side of the glass.

Instead of acknowledging me, she just gives me a tiny smile and goes about her shower. She lathers shampoo into her hair, and when she's done, she tips her head back to rinse it out. As she does, her hands come to her heavy tits, massaging them in the soap of the shampoo. A low moan escapes her throat, and she stays under the stream of the shower for a few seconds, twisting her dusty pink nipples. The water runs down her golden skin, and my eyes track to the small patch of blonde curls between her legs.

It makes me think of the photo she let me take—the same photo that had gotten me off several times in the bathroom of RCF between meetings.

She'd somehow turned me into a horny teenager again—eager to watch, eager to play, always in the mood. Knowing I have a picture of her cunt dripping with my seed, knowing I always have that picture on me ... it's been my saving grace these last few days, especially being so busy and away from her.

But now I'm ready to be inside of her again.

I take a step closer as I palm my pulsing cock. She clears the steam away again as she pumps some conditioner into her hand before smoothing it over her hair. My cock twitches when I get a whiff of it—the reaction is totally psychosomatic now that I've used it to jerk off a few times. She turns away from me, taking the bar of soap and working a lather over her chest, moaning as she gets to her tits again.

Fuck.

Me.

I step closer so that I'm just on the other side of the glass.

She uses the soap to lather between her legs, turning so that she's facing me. "Are you just going to stand there?" she asks, smirking, rinsing herself off.

What I wouldn't give to wash her with my hands ...

I tilt my head as I unzip my pants, pulling my cock out. Her eyes roam down, widening slightly as I stroke myself.

"That's exactly what I'm going to do, butterfly," I tell her.

She pouts, and I can't help but laugh. "Really? You don't want to join me?"

I shrug. "I want to watch you."

Giving me a coy smile, she doesn't answer me as she trails a hand down to her clit, beginning to rub herself.

"What do you want me to do?" she asks, her voice breathy as her hand works faster.

"I want you to give me something to watch," I rasp, stroking myself in earnest now.

Her chest gets blotchy as she quickens her pace, using her free hand to clear the steam. I watch her hand rub her clit fervently, and I groan when I see her insert a finger inside of herself.

"That's it," I murmur. "Two," I command.

She tips her head back slightly as she inserts another finger. Her thumb works her clit now, and I can see the way her legs are shaking slightly.

I squeeze my cock, rolling my palm over the head to use my precum as lube, but it's not enough. With my free hand, I open the door to the shower.

"What are you—"

I pull on the hand that's inside of her, ignoring the way the water bounces off her body and onto mine. She removes her fingers, and I bring them to my cock, wrapping my hand around her tiny one, ensuring I'm all lubed with her arousal before stepping back.

Her blue eyes darken as she realizes what I've just done, and then she resumes her ministrations with more fervor.

"That was hot," she says through clenched teeth,

inserting two fingers inside of her cunt again. "I'm getting close."

"Play with your nipple," I command, stepping back but keeping the shower door open so I have a better view of her body, of the way her lips part slightly as she works her hand faster. Her other hand comes to her left nipple, and she tweaks it slightly.

I let out a low groan as my balls tighten, imagining standing above her and coming all over those gorgeous tits.

"Come for me, Estelle," I tell her.

She moans as her eyes flutter closed, and as she begins to shake, I stop stroking my cock. I'm seconds away from exploding, and I want her to come first.

I watch my wife shatter before me, her face scrunching up as she spasms uncontrollably. She whimpers as she slows her hand, and when her eyes open, she looks down at my cock that's still hard and seeping with precum.

"Did you—"

"On your knees," I tell her, stepping forward.

Her mouth drops open, but like a good little wife, she does as I ask.

She watches me with those large, denim blue eyes, and I groan as I slowly work my hand up and down my shaft. My eyes flick over her wet skin—the blotches all over her neck, her hair that's already curled at her hair-line, the way her full lips are curved into a small, coquettish smile, the way the rivulets of water streak down her full tits, down her stomach …

"Fuck," I rasp. "I'm going to come."

The base of my spine tingles, and my cock arches up fuller and harder as I moan, the first jet of cum hitting her chest. My knees almost give out as my orgasm slams through me, and I let out a few hard puffs of breath as rope after rope of cum paint my wife's tits. I'm still shaking after it ends, and I look down at her with a cocky smirk.

"Go ahead," she says, eyes dark. "Take your picture."

Fuck.

She's fucking perfect.

I reach into my pants and pull my phone out, taking one step away from the shower so it doesn't get wet. After snapping my photo, I set my phone down on the table next to the shower and help her up. Then, I begin to remove my shirt.

"What are you doing?" she asks, watching me.

Watching me with my cum dripping off her perfect tits.

"What kind of husband would I be if I didn't clean my wife?"

The smile she gives me makes my chest ache.

I love you, I think as I step out of my pants and boxers.

It takes me a second to realize this is the first time I've ever been naked in front of anyone other than my brothers and the doctors after my incident.

The first time anyone has ever seen all my scars like this.

The first time *she's* seen the warped skin on my hips and the tops of my thighs.

I go still with that realization, but Estelle's small,

warm hand takes mine, pulling me into the shower with her.

And I let her.

CHAPTER TWENTY-FOUR
THE DEFENSE

STELLA

After cleaning me up and drying me off, Miles follows me to my bedroom. I give him a cheeky smile as I shed my towel, a whole body shiver going through me when he lets out a low, primal growl. I quickly change into jeans, a white tube top, a bright pink blazer, and flat sandals. My husband watches me with darkened eyes the entire time, like he's ready to devour me at any moment.

It makes my stomach erupt with butterflies. I've never had anyone *crave* me the way he seems to. I've never had anyone appreciate the cellulite on the backs of my thighs, the stomach that's most definitely not flat, the stretch marks all over my hips and thighs. I'm a plus-size woman with curves and an arse, and while I've always been comfortable with the way that I look, I can't help the small insecurities that slip in from time to time. While society is getting better about accepting all types of bodies, certain things still penetrate my tough exterior. Sample sizing, models, the fashion industry as a whole ... it's a lot to wade through.

As I run my fingers through my wet curls, I look over my shoulder at Miles.

He's so ... *perfect.*

And even if I'm confident enough to know that I'm beautiful, a very, very small voice sometimes breaks through the noise.

You're too big for him.

He prefers women who are smaller.

Your curves are the exact opposite of the hard planes of his body.

It's enough to make me second guess everything for the first time since we got married. I know he finds me attractive—I'm not worried about that.

It's just that sometimes the intrusive thoughts, which are worse immediately after my episodes, make me feel insignificant and like I'm not enough.

After running some curl cream through my hair, I turn to face him with a bare face.

"Come here," Miles murmurs.

My eyes dart to the white towel around his waist. The muscles that sculpt his abdomen, his arms. The veins that run down to his fingers. Walking over to him, I come to stand between his legs as my fingers trace his scars. Tilting my head slightly, I let my nails lightly drag over the puckered skin. He closes his eyes as his nostrils flare. I know this is hard for him—letting someone *see* him.

Letting someone *touch* him.

I swallow the lump in my throat when I think about the fact that he's letting *me* do both.

That Miles Ravage, grump extraordinaire, has somehow, some way, let me in enough to allow me to do this.

That I'm the first.

"Miles," I whisper, my hands coming to the sides of his face, and when he looks up into my eyes, his expression nearly knocks me over.

Love.

Is it possible that he loves me? And, in that same vein, is it possible that I love him right back?

"Our reservation is at seven. What would you like to do until then?" he asks, his eyes soft.

I shrug. "I just want to spend time with you."

Brows furrowed, he leans forward and places a kiss on my bare abdomen. It's so reverent, so soft, that my hands fist his hair from the intensity of emotions flowing through me.

When did this happen?

How did this happen? A year ago, I considered him a different kind of one night stand. Not someone I could *love,* someone I would come to care about. He was too stuffy, too serious.

Too much of an arsehole.

But now?

I can't imagine my life without him.

"How about I make us some food and we have a picnic?"

I grin. "Sounds perfect."

He stands up and gives me a soft peck against my cheek before walking away, white towel slung over his hips. I admire his backside. His firm arse and muscled back. I'm staring when he gets to the door, turning around with that signature smirk twisting his lips.

"Aren't you coming?"

And for whatever reason, maybe I am a romantic, after all, those three words tug on my heartstrings more than I expect them to. Being here, being *present* with him, means a lot to me. The fact that he's inviting me into his personal space, to presumably watch him get dressed ...

I nod once before rubbing my chest.

Sometime between the cellar and now, Miles decided to let me in. He gave me a proverbial knife to chip away at his icy heart, and now that I'm in, I never want to leave.

I follow him into his bedroom, my eyes instantly roaming up to the mirror paneling adhered to the ceiling. Stepping into the large walk-in closet, Miles chuckles as he drops his towel, pulling a pair of black boxer briefs on.

"Like what you see?" he asks, his eyes meeting mine in the clear mirror.

My chest flushes as I think about Miles moving on top of me, watching as his arse muscles contract with every thrust ...

"It may have piqued my interest a couple of weeks ago when I was snooping," I admit, sitting down on his bed.

He gives me a rueful smile as he pulls dark gray

trousers on. "Is this before or after you happened upon the only spare key to the cellar?"

I laugh. "Before. You coerced me into marriage and then left me to my own devices for a few days afterward. What else was I supposed to do? I saw it when I swapped out the duvet covers." He pulls a silver button-down shirt on, deftly working his fingers to button it slowly as he watches me. "I suppose I should tell you that I also snooped through your bathroom drawers," I add, my lips twisting to the side. "I see you have a box of magnum johnnies."

He arches a brow. "Johnnies?"

"Condoms," I tell him.

After tucking his shirt in—which is highly erotic to watch—he slides a camel-colored Cartier belt through his belt loops. I walk out of his closet and lean back on his bed as I take in his long, lean body. The way his trousers hug his hips. The fitted way his shirt accentuates his muscles. I feel like I've gotten a behind the scenes look at how Miles gets dressed so impeccably every day.

He cocks his head as he sits down in the chair across from me, pulling on black socks.

"Speaking of ... we should probably figure out birth control."

"I have a coil," I tell him. "And I was recently tested by my gynecologist," I explain. "All good."

His green eyes pin me to the spot. "Good. I'm also regularly tested. That's sorted, then. I should've asked the other night. I apologize."

I cross my arms as I watch him slip his feet into

camel-colored dress shoes. "I would've said something if it was a problem."

His expression softens slightly, and I can tell he's working up the courage to ask me something. He must change his mind because he only gives me a small smile as he stands.

"Let's go."

———

"Well, the picnic is off," I tease, looking out of the kitchen window as the rain splatters against the concrete just outside the door.

"I should check on Lucifer," Miles murmurs, coming to stand behind me. "Would you like to come with me?"

"No," I grumble. Turning around, I wrap my arms around his waist. "But I will, because it's important to you."

He laughs as he walks to the back door, grabbing two rain jackets and handing one to me.

"You must feel right at home," he tells me, pulling the black rubber coat over himself.

Of fucking course Miles Ravage looks chic in wellies and a raincoat. I have to roll mine up because it's about five sizes too big. His eyes skate over my face as I step into the boots I pulled from the bench.

"I can't believe I'm going to say this, but a small part of me misses the drizzly, London rain," I tell him wryly. "Don't ever tell anyone I said that."

He laughs as we walk out to the back garden, and I follow him around the castle to Lucifer's paddock.

Opening the gate, he gestures for me to go first.

"Oh no, after you," I tell him, crossing my arms.

He chuckles as he goes ahead of me. I spot Lucifer bleating at the door of his little house, and for a second, my heart clenches because it's so pathetic to see.

"Did you get locked out of your house?" Miles coos, and I can't help the way my whole body warms at his tone. It's so... paternal. Unlatching the door, he pushes it open as Lucifer bleats again, nuzzling against Miles' thigh.

Fine, I guess he's kind of, sort of adorable.

To my horror, the little goat wanders over to me, and I stumble backward.

"No," I tell it. "No, stay away," I beg.

Miles is shaking with laughter as the rain pelts his coat, and I glare at him as I back up to the side of Lucifer's little house.

"This isn't funny," I growl.

"Actually, it's really funny."

The goat stops in front of me and tilts his head in question before nuzzling into my leg, and I screech as my heart hammers in my chest.

"Oh god," I say loudly, scrunching up my face in fear.

Miles is still laughing as he walks over and guides Lucifer into his house. I hear him use that same soft tone, and when I crane my neck around the side of the little house, I see Miles drying the goat off with a towel.

Once he's done, he walks out with a smug fucking smile.

"Shut up," I tell him, stomping away.

Before I get far, though, he grabs my wrist and pulls us together. The wet rubber of my coat slides against his, and his wet hand reaches up to my wet face.

"You," he murmurs, leaning down and planting a kiss on my forehead. "Are," he continues, using his other hand to pull my waist flush with his body. "Adorable."

And then he kisses me, pressing me against the cement of the little house, groaning when his tongue slips between my wet lips.

I pull away. "You have goat hands," I tease.

"I'm proud of you," he answers. "You're coming around. And I most certainly don't have goat hands."

"You do," I whine. "They smell like goat—"

He smashes his lips against mine again, and I can feel his smile against my lips as the rain pelts our faces. Pulling away, his chest presses against mine with every one of his inhales.

Something passes over his face then, and I swallow as his hand comes to my cheek.

"Estelle ..."

He looks conflicted. Like he's going to say something. But then he presses his lips together and shakes his head.

"We should get inside and dry off."

"Sure," I reply, smiling.

———

After drying ourselves off, Miles and I end up spending the afternoon together. I make us popcorn, and he agrees to watch the Taylor Swift documentary. He doesn't even complain. When it's over, I reach over to check his temperature—he just scowls at me and tells me it was okay. Which is better than I expected, anyway. Around five, I go upstairs to begin getting ready.

Smoothing out my curls, I pull on a black blouse— the only black item I own—as well as a pair of green trousers I designed—cinched at the waist with a thick belt and tapered at the ankle. I apply some light makeup and then I slip into vintage heeled python-print boots, as well as my vintage black Gucci bag with a black chain, finishing the look up with my *R* necklace.

Miles is waiting for me when I walk out of my bedroom. His head snaps up as his eyes peruse my outfit slowly—agonizingly.

"You look ..." He trails off, and my eyes track the way his throat bobs. "Gorgeous. As always.

He's in a black suit with a light green tie—the same color as his eyes— as well as his signature Cartier watch and Dior shoes. I can't help the butterflies that erupt inside of me when I take in his whole ensemble —especially since none of my ex's knew how to dress themselves quite like Miles Ravage.

"Oh, and I stole my watch back, by the way.

Though, the idea of my hot wife wearing it is appealing. Maybe I need to get you a matching one."

"I don't want my own. I like wearing yours," I tell him.

When I get close enough, I stand on my tiptoes to give him a kiss. Instead of complying, his hand flies to my throat, and he pushes me against the wall of the living quarters. My heart hammers in my chest as his tongue slips into my mouth. My moan vibrates against his hand, and he squeezes once, pressing his body against mine. An electric current passes from his mouth to my toes, and everything between my legs pulses with desire.

He pulls away.

"I couldn't help myself," he murmurs.

"I didn't mind," I tell him, pressing a palm to his chest. His heart beats erratically underneath my fingertips, matching my own sped-up pulse.

"I didn't think you would."

"You could do it again," I taunt, pressing my chest against his.

He groans, darkness blooming in his pupils. "If I did, we would most certainly miss dinner."

I shrug. "Fine with me."

He laughs, leaning down and pressing his forehead against mine. "As much as I'd love to fuck you senseless, it'll have to wait until later."

I pout as he pulls away. "You better make it up to me," I tease.

"For the rest of my life," he murmurs.

I can't help my sharp inhale at his words, and he pulls away quickly, shaking his head.

"We should go," he says quickly, his indifferent mask sliding into place.

I follow him out of the living quarters, and we silently walk to the elevator as I contemplate his words.

For the rest of my life.

Did that mean he was thinking about this marriage in a long-term sense? What about the contract we signed that said we would dissolve the marriage after a year? I don't recall there being a clause for what would happen if one of us didn't want the marriage to end.

I'm still thinking about it as we climb into the backseat of the black SUV, and I say a quick hello to Niro as we make our way to West Hollywood. I knew Miles had chosen a place that would likely be ripe with paparazzi. Soft music plays over the speakers, and I silently thank Niro for cutting the tension a bit. Even though I'm still thinking over what Miles said, I reach out for his hand, holding it tightly the entire drive to the restaurant.

And, as predicted, cameras flash as we pull up to the front.

"I might've made some calls," Miles says quickly. He turns to face me and gives me a tight smile. "Ready?"

I nod as realization dawns—as I think about how I'd be ready for anything with him by my side.

With him watching me shower, watching me get ready, as if I was *his person.*

With him stroking my back before settling into a numb, dreamless, fitful sleep.

With him cooking for me.

With him telling me *for the rest of my life.*

"Ready," I tell him, hoping he understands the double entendre of my words.

We exit the car, and people begin to shout at us. Miles' hand starts on my lower back, but by the time we step onto the curb, he tugs me into his body.

"Stella! Miles! How is married life?"

"Fan-fucking-tastic," Miles answers, smiling warmly. "Thanks for asking."

"Stella! How are you adjusting to living in California?"

I grin as I look up at Miles. "It's been incredible."

Miles smiles down at me, and then to my surprise, he pulls me in for a kiss.

It's not acting.

There's no pretending.

His low groan vibrating in the back of my throat is real.

This—*us*—is real.

"Lovebirds!" someone shouts.

"So romantic!"

"Young love!"

Miles pulls away and I can't wipe the smile off my face. As we get closer to the door, someone steps in front of me.

"How does it feel to be married to someone so distrustful?"

My head snaps to the photographer, and he's watching Miles with pure hatred.

"Excuse me?" I ask, my voice sharp as the smile drips off my face.

"Let's go," Miles murmurs in my ear. "Drop it, Estelle."

The photographer turns to look at me. "You heard me. How much is he paying you to play house?"

My cheeks heat as I pull away from Miles and walk right up to the photographer.

"You have no idea what you're talking about," I reply, feeling Miles tug on my hand. I ignore it. "My husband is one of the best people I've been lucky enough to know. You might know that if you spoke to him instead of dwelling on something his father did a decade ago."

"Isn't it exhausting to continue defending a man *LA Weekly* called a bully?"

My nostrils flare as my hands clench at my side.

"Estelle, he's not worth it," Miles growls from behind me.

"I love my husband. No amount of money or false reputation could change that."

With that, I spin away from both Miles and the photographer, heading inside the restaurant alone. It takes me a moment for me to realize what I've said, and as Miles walks inside, he looks a bit dazed.

"I don't want to talk about it," I tell him, crossing my arms.

His lips twitch. "I wasn't going to say anything."

"Good."

"Good," he repeats.

The hostess brings us to our table, and like the car ride over, we spend the next few minutes in a tense silence as we decide what to eat. Miles orders us some wine as I deliberate, still furious that the photographer would say such asinine things.

Still furious that I told the world I love Miles Ravage.

I mean, I'm sure the public assumes it—we're married, after all—but Miles doesn't.

God, I am such an idiot.

A minute later, before the wine arrives, Miles sets his menu down.

"Fuck this," he murmurs. "Let's get out of here."

When I look up at him, he has a mischievous smile on his face.

My heart pounds against my ribs as I answer. "Sounds fucking great."

We're still laughing as we duck out of the restaurant, ignoring everyone as we climb back into Niro's car.

CHAPTER TWENTY-FIVE
THE BEACH

MILES

If love is a tangible thing, I imagine it would look a lot like Estelle Deveraux eating a cheeseburger, barefoot on the beach, as she watches me with bright eyes and a large smile.

Every fucking time she smiles at me, my heart stutters. Like somehow, her mouth is tied to my heart muscles.

She has no idea how much fucking trouble I'm in now—how I'm at her mercy from this day forward.

"This has to be the best cheeseburger I've ever eaten," she says, a satisfied noise coming from her throat.

I ignore the way it makes my cock pulse with the incessant need to be inside of her again.

"I agree."

"Thanks," she says a second later, wiping her mouth before leaning back on the damp sand with her hands. "Tonight was ... perfect."

After we ditched the fancy restaurant, I had Niro drive us to my favorite burger place. Then we took the canyon to Santa Monica, and despite it being cold and stormy, we decided to eat on the beach. Estelle had never seen the Pacific Ocean and watching as her eyes lit up in the dark—as the Ferris wheel lights from the Santa Monica Pier danced in her pupils—I realized that tonight couldn't possibly be more perfect.

I finish my food and lean back next to her as my bare toes curl in the sand. Because it had been raining earlier, we're both slightly damp—not that Estelle seems to care at all. She plopped right down on the wet sand, kicked her boots off, and squealed with delight.

I haven't felt sand between my toes since I was a kid. Most definitely *before* the fire.

I hadn't bothered with the beach—or anything that would reveal any skin—since that fateful day.

"I'm sorry about that photographer," Estelle says quietly. She's facing forward, watching the waves break in front of us.

Sighing, I scoot closer to her so that our legs are touching. "Why are you apologizing? It's not your fault. Everything he said was true."

Estelle scowls, the frown lines around her mouth prominent. "It's not, though. That's what bloody pisses me off." She looks at me with furrowed brows. "Nothing he said was true. You're not distrustful."

"But I *did* pay you to marry me," I tell her, smirking.

She scoffs. "No, your father did. And that's beside the point."

Not quite.

"And anyway, it's none of his business."

I chuckle. She's cute when she's angry, and that's especially true when she's angry *on my behalf.*

I've never had anyone get so defensive over me. I swallow thickly as I look away, guilt wrapping around my lungs and squeezing me tightly.

I have to tell her.

I *should* tell her right now.

I *should* tell her about the call I had with my father earlier. About how he was already talking about reneging on his word to her.

How he was doing the same exact shit I knew he would.

The same exact shit that photographer was talking about.

There would be no money from my father, and while I still wasn't sure how he would manage to explain it away, at least she had my money.

If I told her now, she'd refuse to take it.

And her clothing line would be dead upon arrival.

No, I couldn't do that to her.

She'd also be on the first flight back to London, and I might not ever see her again.

She deserved the truth, but I was a selfish asshole.

I'll tell her eventually. One day, I'll explain everything to her. I'll eat the guilt. I'll suffer the consequences.

But that day is not today.

"I appreciate you defending me," I tell her, wrapping an arm around her shoulders.

"I'll always defend you," she answers.

I'm not so sure about that, butterfly.

"I have an idea," she says slowly. I narrow my eyes as she stands, giving me a coy smile. When she begins to unbutton her blouse, I look around frantically. We're mostly alone, but there are a few people close enough to witness the two of us fucking in the sand.

"Estelle—"

"Come on," she begs, pulling her blouse off, exposing her hot pink, lace bra.

I glare at her. "I know you said you were an exhibitionist, but this is not—"

Her throaty laugh makes me smile. "That's not what I meant, you prat. Let's go skinny dipping."

I tilt my head as I watch her pull her pants down, revealing matching pink underwear. *Fuck.*

"I should've known," I grumble, standing. "A germ-infested pool of water and my wife. Like a moth to a flame," I tease.

"Very funny," she chides, grinning as I cross my arms. "Come on then."

"Absolutely not," I tell her. Twisting her lips to one side, she reaches behind her. "Estelle, don't you dare."

She unclasps her bra, letting it drop onto the sand. I look around again, but no one is really paying attention. Dragging my eyes back to my wife, she steps out of her underwear, standing on a public beach completely fucking naked.

Fuuuuck.

"Come on," she begs, putting her hands on her hips.

I admire her body for a minute—the hourglass shape, the muscular thighs, the *bite-able* ass, and her tits—God. Her tits will be the death of me. Her nipples are hard from the cold, and in the dim light, I can just make out the golden skin on the rest of her body.

"Have fun," I tell her, frowning. "Try not to pick any strange men up this time."

She cackles. "I suppose it's a good thing you were the only one I ever wanted."

Her words rocket straight to my heart, and for a split second, I consider it.

Removing my clothes in public. Being naked—showing my scars off to the general public. Being *free* for the first time in my life.

Not giving a flying fuck if someone sees. If someone thinks my scars are ugly, or my skin marred and warped.

Not caring if I get a pitying, curious look.

"Take your clothes off, darling. Live a little." She turns around and walks to the water. "Let's make my grandmother proud," she adds over her shoulder.

And—fuck.

Those five words do something to me. Because I know how much Estelle cared about her grandmother. I know this is important to her, just as the night at the fountain was important to her. And I fucked up that night—I made fun of her by not being able to unclench for once.

Maybe I can do it right this time.

I can do the one thing I longed to do that night.

Have the freedom to do what I want.

Fuck it.

Sighing heavily, I curse under my breath as I undo my tie.

Estelle squeals as her feet hit the ice cold water.

"Fuck, it's cold!" she cries out, tiptoeing along the shore and screaming as the water chases her.

I laugh as I shuck my shirt off.

What am I doing? And do I even fucking care?

Stepping out of my pants, I look around once more. A few people are eyeing us curiously, and I start to panic. But as my eyes adjust to their faces, I can see that they're smiling.

So ... *fuck it.*

I laugh again as I get rid of my boxers, praying the cold water isn't too unforgiveable to my cock.

I walk over to my wife, who must've been too distracted by the cold water to notice my trek over to her, because her eyes widen.

"You did it! Miles, you're free," she tells me like I'm five. "And you're not spontaneously combusting like I thought you would," she adds, smirking as she refers to what she said to me that night at the fountain.

"Very funny," I growl, wrapping my arms around her. "And, as punishment for making me go skinny dipping ..." I pick her up and jog into the water.

Her piercing cry of surprise makes me cackle like a maniac as I dump her into the icy water.

She gasps and stands up, waist deep, her face contorting into fury. "You fucking arsehole—"

I grab her wrist and tug her into my body. She goes pliantly, molding her curves against me. She places her arms around my waist, I look down at her as I walk us deeper into the ocean, until her bits are covered. Then, I reach down and lift her so she's straddling me. I moan when her legs wrap around my hips.

"Miles," she whispers, looking at me with adoration. Like she wants to savor me.

I lean down and smash my lips against hers. "Thank you," I tell her, smiling. "For making me do this."

She swallows, and then I devour her—my hands finding the back of her neck and my right hand running through her wet hair.

"Please tell me you're not going to shag me in this filthy water," she jokes, and I laugh.

"Absolutely not. I just want to kiss my wife, because ..." I pull away, my eyes piercing into hers.

"Because what?" she asks, pulling her lower lip between her teeth.

Because I love you.

Because I could spend forever with you.

Because I can't imagine my life without you.

And one day, you're going to hate me.

I close my eyes as the last thought filters through my mind. I have to tell her. Tomorrow. I will tell her tomorrow. And tonight? It will be perfection before ruination.

"Because I want to shag my wife in a warm bed."

"Then do it," she counters, quirking a brow.

"Let's go, then."

I'm going to enjoy my few hours of heaven before I descend into hell.

CHAPTER TWENTY-SIX

THE MIRROR

Stella

The car ride home is quiet, and despite my eagerness for Miles to make good on his word, I find my eyes drooping from the full stomach and warm heated air blasting through the vents. It also doesn't help that the road leading up to Ravage Castle is long and winding, so all those things mixed together means that I'm jolted awake by my husband as we pull up to the front door.

"Did I fall asleep?" I ask.

"You did. Niro had to put up the barrier because you were snoring so loud."

"I don't snore!" I tell him, hitting his shoulder as he laughs and exits the car.

Walking around to my side, he opens my door and holds his hand out. "It's cute, butterfly."

I wince as he helps me out of the SUV. "I have sand in places I didn't think was possible."

Laughing, he pulls me into his body as Niro drives away, going off to park the car.

"I'd be happy to clean you up," he says seriously.

"I'm sure you would."

His lips twitch with the hint of a smile as he grabs my elbow, tugging me toward the front door. It's quite cold tonight, and I instantly relax once we get inside the warm castle.

Home, I think absentmindedly.

We walk to the elevators, and as soon as we're inside, Miles tugs me close. I vaguely register the ding of the doors closing, as well as Miles's shoulder muscles contracting as he presses the button for the third floor. As soon as we ascend, he leans down and kisses me, hoisting me up so that my legs are wrapped around his waist.

"This is my favorite," he murmurs against my lips. "My wife's legs wrapped around me."

"Oh yeah?" I tease.

"Like a little koala," he mutters.

I huff a laugh. "If you say so."

"I do say so," he answers.

His hands run along the curve of my arse, squeezing once.

I reach my hands up and run them through his hair. He lets out a low moan when I do, his head shifting into my touch as a shiver works through his whole body.

How long has he gone without someone touching him?

How long has he craved someone to do just this?

I swallow the emotion causing my chest to ache. Instead, I kiss him back as the elevator doors open. He doesn't set me down—instead, he marches to our living quarters with purpose. I whimper when his hands squeeze my arse again, and just as I reach down for his belt buckle, someone clears their throat.

"Sorry to interrupt," Luna says. Miles spins so that we can both look at her, and I blush as she gives us both a knowing smile. "Your curtains arrived, Stella," she tells me quickly. "I just finished installing them."

I nod awkwardly. "Amazing. Thank you, Luna."

"Thanks, Luna," Miles says, smirking.

She shoots Miles a knowing look before scurrying off. Once she's out of earshot, a low growl emits from his throat.

"Those fucking curtains," he mutters, irritated. "Elephant, leopard, and peacock feathers..."

I laugh. "Are you saying that flying lynxes and zebra unicorns aren't your thing?"

He grunts as he walks us to the door. "I mean, where do they draw the line?"

"You know you love it," I tease.

"I do. I love all your shit so fucking much."

My heart is hammering in my chest as he pushes the door open, his lips crashing down against mine again. He walks us to his bedroom, tongue darting into my mouth. I hear him kick the door closed as he deposits us both onto the bed and crawls on top of me.

"Shower," I say against his mouth.

"No time. I need you now," he growls, pulling my

lower lip between his teeth and then ripping my blouse off. I hear the buttons hit the floor.

I arch my back as he groans, reaching to take my belt off.

"Shoes."

"Fuck, you're wearing too many things, wife. I want you naked."

I laugh as he scoots down to the edge of the bed. Sitting on his heels, he gives me a rakish smile before reaching for my left foot, unzipping the boot, and discarding it onto the floor. He does the same with the other shoe.

Sliding his hands up my trousers, his fingers slowly pull the zipper down before he drags them down my legs. I expect him to climb on top of me again, but instead he hooks a finger along the seam of my knickers, tugging them down just as slowly. My bra is the next casualty.

"Miles—"

"Spread your legs," he commands, rocking back on his heels as his hands come to the inside of my thighs, pushing them apart.

"But, I'm going to taste like sea water—"

His pupils darken as he pushes my knees apart, eyes hungry and predatory before darting back to my face.

"Do you think I fucking care?"

My breathing hitches as he runs a hand along the inside of my thigh, and I tremble at his touch. I've never had anyone *this* close and personal with my fanny, but he seems to be enjoying it.

Which of course turns me the fuck on.

"Look up, butterfly. I want you to watch as your husband devours your perfect cunt."

I barely have time to register his words before he's tugging my bottom farther down the bed and draping one of my legs over his shoulders.

Holy shit.

I tilt my chin up and look up at the large mirror above his bed, nearly gasping at the image I see. I'm spread out on the orange duvet, and Miles's face dives between my legs, gently biting the inside of my thigh. I moan and arch my back, observing the way his hands dig into the flesh of my thighs.

"Miles," I whimper.

"Do you want me to fuck your cunt with my tongue, Estelle?"

"God, yes."

"Don't you dare close your eyes. Watch me. Watch *us.*"

Before I can agree, he laves his tongue down my slit, and the sound that escapes my throat is barely human. When I watch my reflection, I can see how my legs are trembling slightly. I hear Miles's belt clinking before the image registers in my mind, and my mouth drops open as he licks top to bottom again. He inserts one long, curved finger inside of me, and with his other hand, he pulls his erect cock free, stroking it slowly.

"See what you do to me?" he murmurs against my moans. "The sight, the taste, the scent of your perfect slit, so wet on my tongue ..."

"Fuck me," I rasp, a feeling of ecstasy flowing through me.

"Trust me, Estelle. I'm going to fuck you until you can barely walk tomorrow."

I arch my back and whimper at his words. Curling my toes, I reach out and run a hand through his hair, my eyes not leaving the mirror above us.

Watching as one of his hands pumps into me—watching as the other one runs up and down his cock with fervor. My chest is flushed, and my legs are still shaking. It's highly erotic—watching my husband pleasure himself while he pleasures me. I let out a low moan as he inserts another finger, curving them both inside of me so that they massage my inner walls, clawing pleasure from me. The feel of his flat tongue against my clit mixed with the way his hand drives into me, curling his finger when he pulls out and twisting slightly when he thrusts them into me ...

"Miles," I whimper.

"Your hot cunt is squeezing me, butterfly. Let go. I want all of you, every last drop. If my sleeves are dry when you're done screaming my name, I haven't done my job well enough."

Fucking hell ...

"Oh god," I cry out, feeling the way I'm fluttering against his fingers.

He dips his head and his teeth barely graze my clit before I shatter under him. My body convulses as wave after wave of my climax work through me, and then that unfamiliar sense of pressure begins to build, heightening everything.

"Miles—" I warn.

"That's it, Estelle. Relax," he murmurs, doing something inside of me with his fingers that sends my hips flying up against his mouth–almost like he's scissoring them inside of me. The sensation is ... *God*.

Closing my eyes, I scream as something unleashes, the dam breaking quickly and forcefully. My legs attempt to close on instinct. It's too much, too powerful. But Miles's elbow holds them open as a stronger orgasm works through me. I instantly feel wet all over, trembling as Miles slows his hand, drawing the last of it out of me.

"Fuck yes," Miles rasps. "This is so fucking hot. You're going to make me come—" He sits up and hovers over me a bit so that I can see him work himself to a climax. "Where do you want me, butterfly?"

On shaky elbows, I lift myself up and scoot back a bit, spreading my legs for him.

His eyes flash to mine, widening slightly. His neck is flushed with exertion, and I love the way he's still fully clothed as he hovers over my naked lower half.

"I don't think you could be any more perfect." He groans as hot jets of cum land between us on my exposed pussy. Some lands on my stomach, and I watch as he covers my body with his spend.

He twitches a few times before collapsing next to me.

I roll over to face him, breathing heavily. He's still panting as he tucks himself away, rolling to face me.

Without a word, he reaches out and rubs his cum into my skin.

"I think I have a new kink," he murmurs.

I grin. "Oh yeah?"

"You look so fucking good with my cum painted all over your body."

I pull my lower lip between my teeth. Truth be told, I always found spunk to be gross before Miles. It was always just a consequence of having a coil with past partners—I didn't enjoy johnnies so I always had to waddle to the bathroom after the act. But this? I'm finding that I don't mind Miles claiming me in this primitive way. It makes *me* happy when he's happy, and this seems to make him happy.

"I don't mind it," I tell him, leaning over to kiss him.

He kisses me back, pulling my face close as his fingers curl around my hair possessively.

"Let me clean you up," he says quickly, pulling away and rolling off the bed.

I watch as he walks to our shared bathroom, coming back out a moment later with a damp washcloth.

I swallow as he dips between my legs, lovingly cleaning me from my stomach and down to my slit. He lets out a barely audible moan as he does, moving me slightly.

"You ruined this bedspread," he says, his voice low and guttural. "We'll have to get a new one. That's too bad," he adds, a small smile playing on his lips as he discards the washcloth. The air is cold on my wet skin, and when I look down, I see what he's talking about.

"How is that possible?" I ask, slightly embarrassed.

He grunts as he begins to undress. "Consider yourself lucky, Estelle. Most women would kill to come as hard as you do." Sliding his belt through his belt loops, I watch as my husband starts to take his clothes off, studying his movements as he does.

I'm overcome with something oddly domestic.

I watched him dress, and now I'm watching him undress.

Like a real married couple.

I sit up as the realization hits, pulling my knees to my chest as Miles watches me with concern.

"You okay?" he asks gently, untucking his shirt from his pants.

Yep, untucking is just as erotic as tucking ...

"Well," I start, figuring honesty is the best course of action. "Normally when a couple starts fucking, they may go on dates, fall in love, become exclusive, and then a few years later, they get engaged and plan a wedding ..." I trail off, trying to put what I'm feeling into words. "But we're already there. We're already married."

He smiles as he unbuttons his shirt. Despite just finishing, something hot and heady works through me when he tugs his shirt off slowly, his eyes never leaving mine.

"And it scares you because we're doing everything backward?" he asks, taking a step closer. His long fingers deftly work the zipper of his trousers, and his lips form a lopsided smile as he tugs them down his muscled legs.

"A little," I tell him honestly. "I mean, I never would've guessed ..."

He walks up to me in only his black boxer briefs. I can see his erection bulging from the material, and I trail off as my cheeks heat.

"Really? Never would've guessed? Even after that taxi ride?" he murmurs, reaching a hand out to my chin. "I tried to stay away, Estelle. I tried to keep myself from you. But the more time I spend with you, the more I can't remember my life without you."

My throat sticks with emotion at his words. "And I was in denial."

He nods. "I'm sorry. For pushing you away after the wedding. Chase said something to me, and I got spooked."

I laugh. "You were a right arse."

"I was. How can I make it up to you?"

"Just ... be honest with me. Communicate with me. This is never going to work if we don't *talk* like an actual, married couple."

His brows furrow slightly as his throat bobs. "Okay."

"No more secrets?" I whisper, loving the feel of his rough thumb and index finger against the skin of my chin.

His happy facade falls for just a split second. "Okay," he answers.

He drops his hand, removes his boxers, and climbs into bed with me.

"Are we going to sleep?" I ask, hoping my voice

doesn't give me away. Instead of answering me, he pushes me onto my back and climbs on top of me.

"Do you want to go to sleep right now, butterfly?"

I shake my head.

"Good. Me either. In fact, I think I want to do this a few times before sleeping."

Every place he's touching me turns molten. "Yes," I agree.

He buries his face into my neck, sucking and nibbling my sensitive skin. I arch my back underneath him, realizing that, besides skinny dipping earlier, this is the first time we're naked together.

"May I?" he asks, his face inches from mine.

I don't say anything right away. I just stare up into his green eyes, our eyes meeting for a few heart-stopping seconds.

"May you what?" I ask, a smile playing on my lips.

"May I fuck my wife? Properly, I mean?"

I giggle. "Does the other night not count?"

His eyes dart between mine. "Is that a yes?"

"Yes," I whisper. "Please."

He kisses me as one hand comes to my curls, fingers tangling in my hair as his cock nudges at my entrance. I spread my legs a bit for him, giving him easier access, and he moans against my mouth in response.

In one swift movement, he pushes inside of me, stretching me deliciously.

"Fuck, Estelle," he whispers against my lips. "Being inside of your cunt is my favorite fucking place to be."

I rock my hips upward slightly, and he pushes in all the way—which makes me gasp.

"Miles," I whimper.

"You take my cock so well," he murmurs, pulling out slowly. Blinding pleasure flares through me when he pulls one of my legs up, thrusting back into me with force before he bottoms out. I let out a shaky breath, my nails coming to his shoulder as I drag them roughly down his back. He shudders on top of me as I do it. "You like that?" he asks, pulling out slowly.

"Yes, fuck yes," I tell him, rolling my hips.

He groans. "You're going to fucking kill me, wife. You feel too good," he adds, dropping onto his elbows so that he's directly on top of me as he moves.

"I love your cock," I tell him boldly.

"Yeah?" he asks, eyes flashing with amusement. "Does my wife like it when I fuck her like—" He drives into me so hard that the bed creaks loudly, making me cry out. "This?"

"Yes," I tell him, mewling as he does it again.

He takes one hand and presses my hip into the mattress, holding me in place as he continues to sink into me with force. His fingers dig into the flesh of my hip, and his other hand fists my curls, and just as he drives into me again, my eyes flick to the mirror above us.

The reflection of us is ... *too much.*

"Oh my god," I whimper, watching as his arse muscles work to fuck me properly. How the muscles of his back contract each time he pulls out. How he has one of my legs higher so that he can sink deeper into me.

"That's it," he murmurs against my throat. "Watch as I fuck you."

I nearly close my eyes; it's too much. The feel of him above me, his chest and abdomen pressing against mine. The sting of my thigh as he nudges it higher. The bite of his fingers gripping my hip and holding it down. The burn of his fingers tangling in my hair. The fullness of his cock inside of me. Each drive into me brings me closer. Each nip of teeth against my neck pulls me tighter, ready to release.

My pussy pulsates around his cock.

"Fucking come on my cock, butterfly. I want you to take all of my cum. I want to feel your cunt milk me dry."

The mouth on this man ...

I throw my head back against the mattress as he works my leg higher, fucking me harder and faster.

Each movement creates a maelstrom of electricity to surge through me. Each drag of his cock out, each thrust in—

"Miles, I'm going to—"

He groans against my lips, his breath shaky. "Come for me, Estelle. *Please.*"

The begging tone evident in his voice is what sends me over the edge. My orgasm rips through me, and every nerve ending is on fire as I convulse underneath him. His loud groan and stuttering hips tells me that he's coming too, which sends an additional shockwave of pleasure through me, heightening everything.

"Oh god, oh god," I whimper. "Miles," I warn, feeling the drawing up of pressure in my lower abdomen.

My hips jolt up as I release his cock, my eyes rolling to the back of my head. I vaguely register Miles letting out a string of strangled curses as he works his hand against my clit, extending everything as I shake and tremble for what feels like hours. His voice pulls me back to earth a few minutes later.

"So fucking beautiful when you come," he murmurs, kissing my neck, my chest, my stomach ... "I could watch you come forever," he says reverently.

I blink as he collapses onto the bed next to me, but I can't form words as his hand comes to my face, as his lips brush my forehead.

He tugs my back into his body, wrapping his arms around me. "You did so well," he adds, a contented hum working through his chest. I shiver when I feel it against my back. "We can stay here for a few minutes if you'd like, but we should also clean up."

I grimace when I realize the duvet underneath me is completely soaked. I try to twist out of his grip, but he tugs me tightly against his chest.

"In a few minutes," he says against the back of my neck. "Just a few more minutes."

I relax my body, letting my husband pull me tightly against his body, shivering every time his finger brushes my hip and completely unable to wipe the smile from my face.

CHAPTER TWENTY-SEVEN
THE CONFESSION

MILES

After cleaning Estelle up in the shower—and taking her against the marble wall one more time—she falls asleep in the fresh bedding I procured for us. I unwrap myself and watch her sleeping, feeling like my chest might very well crack in half with each soft, satisfied breath coming from her.

Just ... be honest with me. Communicate with me. This is never going to work if we don't talk *like an actual, married couple.*

No more secrets.

Sighing, I climb out of bed and grab some boxers. I step into them before pulling on sweatpants and a T-shirt. I hardly ever wear anything but a suit, however, right now I can't find it in me to give a fuck. Grabbing my phone, I exit the bedroom, shutting the door quietly behind me.

I have to fix this.

Peering into Estelle's bedroom, an open sketch-book on her desk catches my eye. I walk inside and glance over the sketches. I don't know what I expected, but as I flip through Estelle's drawings, the aching feeling in my chest begins to worsen. She's good. *Really* fucking good. She's also drafted a mission statement, and I read through it as pride swells within me.

VeRue is a high-quality, stylish, adaptive clothing line started by Estelle Ravage (née Deveraux). We will work to find clothes that fit you, whether that be inclusive sizing, clothing for those with restricted movement, or those with disabilities who want to look their best. Why adaptive clothing? Because Estelle's grandmother spent most of her adult life in a wheelchair. She loved fashion, but she was never able to find the kinds of clothes that she wanted to wear. The kinds of clothes that made her feel good. This clothing line is for her, and it's why we named it VeRue.

I flip through the whole sketchbook, from the specially designed jeans without buttons or zippers, to shirts that open at the sides with magnetic closures. There are shoes, sweaters for those who may have medical equipment to work around, sensory-friendly clothing, and in the margins of each design, the sizes: 00-32. I don't know a lot about women's fashion, I'll admit, but just the fact that Estelle is doing this for her grandmother, the fact that *this* is her passion ...

How the fuck did I get so lucky?

I'm both so fucking proud of her, but also so fucking furious at my father for betraying her and Prescott.

I'm dialing my father's number before I realize what I'm doing. It's early morning in Paris, so he's likely awake. He answers on the third ring.

"Miles, how are y—"

"Pay her," I growl, walking out of the living quarters. "Pay her all of the money now, in full."

My father sighs. "We still have a ways to go with Prescott's portfolio before the investment accrues enough to—"

"I don't fucking care. You have the money. Pay her now."

My father laughs on the other end. "And why would I do that when I promised her the money at the end of the year? Who's to say she won't run off before your year is up?"

Pinching the bridge of my nose, I lean against the wall and take a couple of steadying breaths.

"Please. I will pay you back instantly. But the money has to come from you. She doesn't want my money. I promise you, she won't be going anywhere."

The eerie silence on the other end is disheartening. Finally, he speaks.

"You fucked her," he says crassly. "Or worse, you're in love with her."

My lips tremble as I run my hand over my lips. "She can't know the money is mine."

"Oh, Miles. What did you do?"

"No, father. What did *you* do?" I growl.

"I lost it. Is that what you want to hear? Prescott was adamant about investing into a high-yield stock. He knew the risks."

I sink down onto the floor. "Have you told him?"

"Of course not," my father answers.

Conniving, manipulative, piece of shit.

"I don't understand why you can't just pay her and tell her it's coming from me?"

Because I already am.

Because I promised her that I wouldn't lie to her.

Because I'm a selfish fuck, and I want her to stay the full year.

"Because I'm not you. Because unlike you, I don't want to lie to my wife."

My father has the audacity to click his tongue in a condescending manner.

"I think it's a little too late for that, no?"

I look down at my phone screen and end the call before I hit someone.

I need to tell her. I need to lay it all out for her to decide, and I need to be okay with her leaving.

She needs the money.

She needs to bring VeRue to fruition.

I can't be the reason she isn't successful.

The first installment—a little less than one hundred thousand—isn't enough.

My father lost Prescott Deveraux's money. We're a month in, and we've already conned both of them out of a million dollars.

I pull my phone out and call my accountant.

I don't care if it's nearly midnight.

I don't care if I haven't thought this through.

I don't care if I'm acting impulsively.

He answers on the first ring. "Miles Ravage," he

drawls. "Calls this late are never a good thing, but I suppose that's why you pay me so well."

"Hello, Thomas. I need you to immediately wire a million dollars to Estelle Ravage. My wife."

"I know who Estelle is," he says, chuckling. "I've seen the headlines."

I grimace. *Just another reminder that all of this started as a sham.*

But it's not a sham anymore. Not to me.

I want her to stay.

Past the year.

Forever.

I want to propose to her *after* getting to know her.

I want to watch her fall in love with me, because I'm sure as fuck already in love with her.

I want to give her the biggest, most ostentatious wedding ever—something to make up for the courthouse wedding.

And I want to marry my wife *again*, this time when she's wearing her dream dress, listening to her favorite song, and walking down the aisle toward the person she wants to spend the rest of her life with.

Not the person who coerced her with money and connections.

"Right. Well, if possible, can you please transfer the money from my father's account? You can reimburse it with one of my accounts, and I'll even throw in a bit of hush money—"

"Miles, surely you know I can't do that. Your mother separated your accounts before her death on purpose. You can't touch your father's money, and vice versa."

I sigh, feeling defeated. I knew my mother went behind my father's back before her death, dividing our trust five ways and leaving the scraps for my father. Scraps being more than most people made in their life-times, but still.

And then another thought occurs to me. If I transfer the other nine hundred thousand, give or take, tonight, she will see it and wonder why we're not doing the installments.

This call is pointless. The best course of action is to continue the installments from me so she's not suspicious. I can tell her in eleven months when she has all of her money. But the real question is, can I lie to the woman I love for eleven months to ensure she's taken care of?

Yes.

I'll do anything to ensure she's taken care of.

I hate myself for it, though.

"I understand. Thank you."

"Is there anything else I can do for you?"

"Yes, actually. Can you please confirm that the transfers will be completed every month on the 15th, like we'd discussed?"

"Yes, sir. I can see here that the next one is sched-uled in two weeks."

"Wonderful. Thank you."

After hanging up, I pace the hall.

I knew this would happen, and it was at the expense of Estelle and Prescott. My father did what he always does, and I made it worse by trying to protect her.

Oscillating between telling her and not telling her, I decide to text the one person who always gives me the best advice.

ME

I need to talk to you

LIAM

Liam: Okay. Be right over.

———

I'm still pacing—this time in the kitchen as I panic eat Estelle's delicious fucking *biscuits*—when Liam walks in.

He takes one look at me and chuckles. "Well, now I understand the late night booty call."

I frown. "Very funny," I say between bites of the sugary cookie.

"I didn't know you owned a pair of sweatpants, truthfully. I thought you slept in your suit."

I throw a cookie at him, and he laughs and ducks. "Alright, alright. Let's call a truce." His eyes track over my face, landing on my hair. "I assume from the sex hair that this is about Stella?"

"That part is obvious," I answer petulantly, grabbing another biscuit.

"What's the problem, then? You're having sex with your wife. Isn't that a good thing?"

"That's just it. I've gone and fallen in love with her," I admit, voice hard.

Liam sighs, eyes wide. "Well, I think you've officially outmatched all of our bets."

"Your bets?" I growl, though I'm pretty sure I know what he's talking about.

He ignores me. "So, that's it? You're in love? That's the big emergency?"

I scoff. "Of course not. If that were the case, I'd be sleeping with my wife in our bed."

He cocks his head as he studies me. "Your wife?"

Shrugging, I walk over to the cabinet, pulling a water glass down. "Well, she *is* my wife."

Liam gives me a small smile as I fill my glass with water. "Very well. So, explain the issue, then."

"You know about the marriage of convenience," I tell him, my voice low. "How father promised Estelle a million dollars to salvage my reputation."

"Of course. Let me guess ..." he trails off, narrowing his eyes. "That money has mysteriously disappeared?"

I nod once.

Liam lets out a slow, steady breath. "That motherfucker."

"Trust me," I growl. "I could kill him."

"Okay, so just explain to Estelle what happened. If you love her, chances are she loves you too. It's not like you can't front her the money, right?"

I grind my jaw as I trail a finger along the rim of my water glass.

"It's not that easy. She doesn't want my money."

"Okay. Well, I still think you should tell her."

I look up at Liam. "I lied to her. I told her that father set up monthly transfers. I forged a contract that laid out the terms—how she would get that million equally dispersed over the course of the year."

Whistling, Liam leans back and rubs the back of his neck. "Okay, that's a bit more complicated. But again, just tell her the truth."

I hang my head. "If I don't tell her, she'll never know."

"I'll never know what, *husband?*"

Both Liam and I jump, spinning around to find Estelle standing in the door of the kitchen, looking ... *furious.*

Her eyes drag over my sweatpants and T-shirt before flicking to Liam.

"Hi, Liam," she says curtly.

Liam stands up and gives me an apologetic look. "You know where I stand." Ducking his head, he walks out of the kitchen, leaving Estelle and I alone.

Tilting her head and narrowing her eyes, she walks into the kitchen wearing nothing but an oversized T-shirt.

Fuuuuuck.

When she's a foot away, she looks up at me with an open expression. "I'll never know what, Miles?"

I am fucked.

So utterly, completely fucked.

I lean my elbows on the island, head still hanging between my shoulders. "There's something I need to tell you."

She stands up straighter, and I notice, for the first time, her ability to seem distant and cold.

Please don't hate me.

Please don't push me away after this.

"Go on, then," she says, jaw tight.

"My father is not a good man," I start, and her eyes widen in surprise. "Your father's money is gone. The million dollars? It's gone."

She just stares at me. "I'm confused. At what point in the last day, or the last week, even, made you think I was still doing this for the money?"

Her words are like a dagger to my heart.

"I'm trying to tell you that the money is gone," I try, hoping she lets me explain what an asshole I am. Hoping that she sees I'm not worth fighting for. Better to pull the Band-Aid off now than in eleven months.

"And I'm trying to tell you that I don't care," she hisses, shoving me. "Seriously? After everything tonight ... the beach, the restaurant ... I don't care about the money."

My brows furrow. "But what about VeRue—"

"I'll figure it out. I just don't want you to think that I'm not going to hold up my end of the deal just because the money is gone. And not because I have to." She takes a step closer, and I swallow thickly. "But because I *want* to."

"Estelle," I beg, holding a hand out.

"Wait," she says slowly, looking up at me. "I received the first payment."

Steepling my hands, I take a step back. "Because I

transferred the money. I forged my father's signature and presented you with a fake contract."

Her mouth drops open. "He was never going to pay me?"

"I tried warning you," I explain, reaching out for her.

She moves away from me. Now she's the one holding a hand out to stop me. "Were you ever going to tell me?" she whispers.

I hesitate, my mouth opening and closing.

A few seconds later, I answer her. "Trust me, it's been eating me alive for a long time. It's why I did the installments. I wanted to take care of you. I wanted you to use that money. Even if it didn't come from my father, I wanted to make sure you were financially secure. And I'll reimburse your father as soon as I talk to mine. As soon as I know what happened—"

"Did the two of you work together?" she asks, her jaw feathering as she crosses her arms.

"What? No, Estelle—"

"Charles sought my father out," she says slowly. "It was right after we met at the fountain."

I shake my head. "No. That was a coincidence."

Narrowing her eyes, I can see how the crease between her eyes deepens, how her eyes start to water.

"Are you sure? Because it sounds like too much of a coincidence to me. Like maybe you hatched a plan," she says, her voice wrought with emotion. "What, did you plan to take advantage of the philanthropist and his struggling daughter? Was it all a long con, Miles? Marry his son, get her to fall in love with him so she didn't notice the money went missing—" I rush forward, but she holds her hands out to stop me. "Don't touch me."

"I did the fucking installments so you would stay," I tell her, my voice breaking on the last word. "Because I was so fucking in love with you, and I didn't even realize it."

She lets out a small sob as one hand goes to cover her mouth. "Don't do that. Don't tell me you're in love with me right after I find out you've betrayed me."

"Why does it matter if the money comes from me instead? Nothing has to change! You'll get your money every month—"

"I don't care about the bloody money, Miles! How many times do I have to tell you that?" she cries out as a single tear slides down her right cheekbone. "You promised me no more secrets, and that didn't even last the night."

Fuck.

"I'm sorry," I say slowly.

Her nostrils flare as she studies me, and I know whatever she's about to say will ruin me.

"I should've known. You really are your father's son."

"Estelle, please. What can I do to get you to forgive me?"

She laughs, but it's not a kind laugh. "Have you tried a martini or two? Coercion and alcohol seem to work well for you, after all."

I step forward. "Estelle—"

"No. Don't *Estelle* me." She shakes her head. "You

know, it's not about the money. It's about the fact that you hesitated when I asked if you were ever going to tell me."

My jaw clicks with anger. "I did it to protect you!" I tell her, raising my voice. "I fucking did it all for you!"

"Yeah, to keep me here. In a cage of your own making," she adds, another tear falling down her cheek. "This castle is cursed. I'm leaving. You can take your money and shove it up your arse. I never wanted it in the first place."

She turns to walk out, and just then, Liam walks back into the kitchen.

"Estelle," I growl, walking toward her.

Liam shakes his head. "I'll take her to my place to cool off," he tells me.

I stare at Liam as Estelle mutters something about packing her things before leaving my brother and I alone.

"That went well," I grit out.

"Give her a few days. She'll come to her senses," he says gently.

I sigh and place my forehead against the cool wood of the cabinetry. "I don't know how this happened," I tell him honestly, my voice hoarse.

"How *what* happened?" Liam asks.

"How it went from not caring about anything to only caring about *her*. How it feels like someone reached into my chest and tore my heart out just now."

Liam rubs my back as I squeeze my eyes shut. "I'll take care of her. Zoe is coming home soon, so I have her room all ready and made up."

"Yeah, thanks," I answer absently. Pushing off the cabinet, I run a hand over my face. "I'm going downstairs. Drive safe," I tell him.

"You don't want to say goodbye?" he asks, concern marring his features.

I shake my head. "No. I can't watch her walk out of this place."

Without another word, I turn and walk out of the kitchen, heading down to the cellar even though it's empty.

I need a dark, quiet place to think.

I need about a thousand alcoholic drinks to numb the pain of my wife walking out on me.

I need to forget about the idea of her never coming back here.

By the time Liam texts me that they're about to drive away, I'm three sheets to the wind and nearly passed out on the cold leather couch.

CHAPTER TWENTY-EIGHT

THE PRESENT

Stella

I hardly register packing up my clothes as quickly as possible, or the way Liam lets me stew in silence the entire twenty-minute drive to his house. I vaguely take in the large cabin—only registering that everything inside looks like it belongs to a writer. There are no televisions or phones anywhere. There are papers with text scattered everywhere, and a typewriter on the dining room table. Despite being a bit messy, it's very peaceful.

He leads us both up the stairs, stopping in front of a guest bedroom that's decorated with white furniture, a lavender bedspread, and a bright pink neon sign on the wall that says *You've Got This.*

"You can stay as long as you need," Liam says gruffly, leaning against the door frame.

"Thank you," I answer, my voice quiet. My eyes flick up to the sign. "What does that even mean?"

He huffs a laugh. "Honestly, I don't know. I bought a bunch of shit for Zoe—she's coming back for Christmas break, and I wanted her room to feel cozy. It's the first time she'll be back for more than a couple of nights since everything happened."

My chest aches at the thought of Liam and Zoe spending Christmas without her parents. Without Liam's best friend.

"I appreciate you letting me stay in her room."

Liam just nods once in response before pushing off the door frame and looking around.

"Listen, my brother is an idiot for what he did, but he means well."

I sit down on Zoe's bed and pull one of her pillows to my chest, hugging it tightly. I'd pulled on a bra and leggings, and as the chilly air works through the house, I wish I'd thought to pack a jumper.

"I know. But, how can I trust him now? He lied to me."

Liam shrugs. "I think, in his mind, he thought he was doing the right thing. And ... he was afraid of losing you. By the time he realized there would be no money, he couldn't fathom the idea of letting you go."

I swallow as I stare down at the carpeted floor. "I'm not even angry. I'm just hurt. And disappointed. After everything..." I trail off, pressing my lips together so that I don't cry. "It all feels tainted now. Like he was just being nice to keep me there. Like he didn't actually care about me. He just wanted to keep me there so I'd hold up my end of the deal. Otherwise, he would've been honest with me when he found out your father lost the money."

Liam hangs his head and shoves his hands in the pockets of his pants. "Did Miles ever tell you why he's the only one, besides Orion, who still talks to our father?"

I shake my head as I squeeze the pillow tighter.

"After Miles's accident, the police came into the hospital room to ask about what happened. Miles was a minor, only thirteen, so of course they had questions. He was unconscious as Chase, Malakai, and I all lied to the authorities. Orion was too young to get involved."

"Why did you lie?" I ask, my voice tight.

Liam shrugs. "Because our father thought that sending us all out to go camping for a week would teach us to become men. He was drinking a lot, and our mother was gone at the time. I was only sixteen. I had to take care of my brothers for five days. I made sure they were fed and hydrated and that Orion didn't wet the blanket we all shared at night. And then the tent caught fire, and as you know, Miles made sure we all got out before him."

A single tear slips down my cheek, but I don't say anything as I continue listening.

"Anyway, it was gross negligence on my father's part. None of us wanted to be left out in the woods for days on end. So when we were asked, we told the authorities it was our idea. I took the blame because I was the oldest. I had a mark on my record until I turned eighteen. And the entire time, my father just sat there and let us lie. His children. While one of his sons sat unconscious mere feet away, and the other one slept soundly on my lap because he was *barely* out of fucking toddlerhood."

Liam sighs and runs a hand through his hair. "Anyway, after that, Chase, Malakai, and I all vowed to cut him out of our lives when we turned eighteen. And, in the end, we all did. Miles doesn't know, because he wasn't conscious for that conversation. I think he assumes we all cut him off because of the big money scandal. And Orion was too little to understand, and as his oldest brother, it's not my place to tell him, though he has an inkling of what happened."

I take a shaky breath as I digest all the information. It paints Charles Ravage in a whole new light.

"What do I tell my father?" I ask. "If Charles lost his investment ..."

Liam winces. "The truth. You tell him the truth, Stella."

I nod as I swallow again. "Thank you. For telling me. For letting me stay here."

"It's no problem. You're family, after all," he says, his voice warm. "Also, I'm afraid I don't have black tea for you," he says, holding his hands up.

I gasp in mock outrage. "How will I live?"

He chuckles. "Miles offered to drop your favorite tea off in the morning, and he gave me strict instructions to make you a fry up—whatever the hell that means."

"Okay, thank you," I tell him, trying to quell the sob that wants to escape my chest.

He must sense it, because he just nods once and then leaves, closing the door behind him.

I fall back onto the bed and curl up on my side as the dam breaks, and suddenly, I'm sobbing into one of Zoe's fuzzy pillows. Everything hurts—the sting in my throat from crying, the ache in my chest, the heaviness behind my eyes since it's so late ...

I fall asleep with the pink sign still shining between the lids of my closing eyes.

You've got this.

———

The next week passes slowly. Miles must drop my computer and sketchbook off at some point, because I wake up the first morning with both things sitting on the white desk in Zoe's room. At first I'm sad because of course I miss him, but the more I think about last night, the more I realize that I still need time.

I spend the whole day sketching, trying to heal the way my heart feels like it's cracked in half. Trying to salvage the flame inside of me that feels like it's growing smaller by the hour. I let myself stay in my room, but I refuse to stay in bed, even though I want to.

Liam brings me my meals, complete with my favorite breakfast tea. He even manages to get the milk to sugar ratio perfect—something I attribute to my vexing husband.

The fry up is delicious as well, damn him.

The second day, I go on a three-hour walk in the woods behind Liam's house. He lives thirty minutes away from the castle, snuggled in the vast woods east of Los Angeles and Crestwood. Since he teaches at Crestwood University, he's gone during the day with his classes and office hours, and that leaves me a lot of time to think. As I make my way back toward the house, knees and ankles aching from trekking through the uneven terrain for hours, I have a revelation.

I'm not mad about the money. I've already decided to talk to my father about everything. I don't blame Miles for doing what he did. I probably would've done the same thing.

I'm hurt that he lied to me.

I'm furious that he withheld his secrets from me and didn't treat me as the equals we're supposed to be.

The cellar, the money, the installments, the contract...

All lies.

And yes, he eventually told me about the cellar, but only because I found a spare key.

Only because he had to.

Same with the money; how long would he have gone without telling me about either thing if I hadn't walked in on him in the cellar?

If I hadn't overheard him talking to Liam the other night?

Would he have gone the entire year keeping those two things from me?

The third and fourth days are spent doing a mix of sketching, speaking to my website designer, and taking long walks. Every evening, Liam brings my dinner to my room without asking any intrusive questions. It's like he somehow understands that I need space and silence, which I appreciate.

The fifth day, I wake up to an email that my magazine feature is now live on the *Cosmopolitan* website, and that it will be live in all US magazines later this month. I click through the article, smiling when I see the picture of me that Annette had taken quickly at the very end. My eyes stop when I get to the end of the article.

Estelle: *I knew what I was getting into when I married Miles. And despite the horrible things his father did, Miles Ravage is a good man.*

Cosmo: *Forgive me for the inquisition, Stella. A lot of people are concerned about you. They feel like you and your father have been taken advantage of by a very powerful, very manipulative family.*

Estelle: *I fell in love with Miles Ravage before I knew who he was. Before I knew the man attached to the name. He's funny, and kind, and he takes good care of me. He's the reason we're sitting here today—because he believes in this clothing line ...*

I squeeze my eyes shut. I'd forgotten I'd added in that little tidbit.

I fell in love with Miles Ravage before I knew who he was.

And then I fell in love with him *despite* him being who he was.

I get ready for my day slowly, throwing on a yellow blouse with balloon sleeves. Then I step into my favorite pair of dark purple trousers. They are wide-legged and made up of a velvet material. After diffusing my hair, I head downstairs only to see Liam sitting at the kitchen table with Chase.

"Stella," Chase says, standing. He walks over and pulls me into a tight hug. "How are you?" he asks, pulling away.

I shrug. "I've been better. How's Miles?"

"He's miserable."

Good, I think, but of course I feel bad for thinking that.

"I wanted to invite you to our wedding reception tomorrow," he says with a smirk.

My brows shoot up. "Oh?"

"Juliet wanted to throw a little party at the castle," he adds, sounding resigned. "You know, to celebrate our one-month anniversary."

I catch the double entendre immediately. *Our* as in his and Juliet's, as well as my anniversary with Miles.

"Sure," I tell him, looking at Liam. "Are you going?"

He laughs. "Chase would murder me if I didn't go," he answers, taking his hand and running it through Chase's perfectly coiffed hair.

Chase grunts and takes a step back. "Hey man. Fuck right off with that," he says, laughing.

Liam just gives him an affectionate smile. "Sorry, can't help it. You'll always be my annoying little brother."

"I'm not the only one," Chase grumbles.

"Yeah, but you're the easiest one to rile up."

I smile as I observe the brothers, suddenly feeling homesick for one brother in particular. I walk around Chase to start preparing my tea when I notice both of them go silent. I finish filling the kettle with fresh water and pop it on. Then, I turn around, crossing my arms.

"Go on. Say it," I tell both with a serious expression.

Chase looks at Liam quickly before rubbing the back of his neck. "He's been sleeping at the office, Stella. The poor guy is practically limping because he's curled up on his tiny, leather loveseat all night."

I hollow my cheeks and look away, chest aching. "He has a perfectly acceptable bed at the castle," I answer weakly. "It's not my problem if he's being stubborn."

"He refuses to sleep there without you," Chase adds.

The kettle whistles, so I distract myself with making a perfect cuppa. Once it's done steeping, I turn back around to face the two of them.

"What do you think about everything?" I ask Chase.

Now he looks even more uncomfortable. "I mean, I completely fucked up with Juliet a few months ago. I know the feeling of being willing to do anything to win the love of your life back."

The love of your life.

"Am I the love of his life? I haven't heard from him since I left," I admit, feeling silly.

"He's giving you space," Liam interjects. "Listen, we're both on your side. I hope you understand that. I know Miles does, and it's why he's feeling so shitty, because he knows he fucked up. But he is sorry."

"Truly," Chase says, smirking. "Especially because he's hobbling around all prideful and grumpy and snapping at anyone and everyone. It's pitiful."

I snort at the image of that. Something inside of me melts just a tiny bit.

"You can tell him I'll be at your wedding reception tomorrow," I say carefully. "We can talk then."

Chase and Liam high-five, and I try not to roll my eyes. A second later, Chase slides a small gift bag over to me.

"It's from him. He asked me to give it to you."

Furrowing my brows, I set my tea down and walk over to the small black bag. "What is it?"

"Well, I'm not sure how they do it in England, but in America, when you're given a gift, you have to open it to find out."

Chase ducks as I throw my soggy tea bag at his head, laughing.

"Don't be an arse." Snatching the bag up, I grab my tea in my other hand. "I'm heading upstairs to work. If you need me, you know where to find me." I walk over to Chase and give him an air kiss. "See you tomorrow. I hope you know that my present is going to be the most obnoxiously large gift on the table because you're so cheeky," I chirp, and the guys are still laughing as I walk away.

By the time I get into the bedroom, I close the door with my heeled foot and set my tea down. Then, I walk over to the bed and sit down, staring at the bag. *A gift?* What could it possibly be? What could he *possibly* say with something material?

I remove the black tissue paper and stare into the bag, brows pinched in confusion as I pull out a pair of socks with ...

Little pygmy goats all over them.

And the kicker is, they're personalized.

Estelle + Lucifer 4ever.

"What a prat," I mumble, grinning. Setting them aside, I reach in for the black card, pulling it out.

The front is personalized to me in gold ink.

To my wife.

"Why are you so perfect, Miles Ravage?" I whisper.

Opening the envelope, I pull out a piece of black cardstock. Written in the same gold ink is a note.

Estelle,

I bought these for you earlier this week
and wanted to give them to you.
I miss you.
(And so does Luc)
Xo,
Miles

Short. Simple. And yet ...

I swipe at my cheeks as I sit up and walk to my desk. I scratch out a note before I change my mind, because quite honestly, a very small part of me hates the thought of him being miserable.

Miles,
What's your favourite colour?
Xo,
Stella

I quickly walk back down to the kitchen, where Chase and Liam are hovered over two plates of omelets. I hand Chase the letter to Miles without another word before heading back upstairs to work on social media for VeRue.

A couple of hours later, I get my first ever text from my husband.

MILES

It used to be green, but now it's blue.

ME

What shade of blue?

MILES

The color of your eyes when you're laughing.

CHAPTER TWENTY-NINE
THE GROVELING

MILES

I check my tie a dozen times in the bedroom mirror, making sure it's perfect. Smoothing a hand over my hair, I grab my whiskey and polish off the rest of the crystal tumbler. Not enough to inebriate me, but *just* enough to quell my nerves. Chase mentioned that Estelle would be in attendance tonight, and I can't help the tiny, miniscule spark of hope working through me. Seeing her in person gives me another chance to apologize.

And fuck, I have a lot to apologize for.

But the main thing is the lying. And the betrayal.

I've spent the last six days making vows with myself about the kind of husband I want to be. I've had several moments of reckoning while I shiver alone in my office in the middle of the night. I don't deserve her, but I'll do everything in my power to become worthy of her.

My phone vibrates in my pocket, and when I pull it out, my stomach drops.

Here goes nothing.

"Father," I murmur, my free hand curling at my side.

"What the hell have you done, Miles?"

"Something I should've done a long time ago."

"You can't possibly think Prescott Deveraux is going to trust you after everything that happened—"

"Actually," I interject loudly. "He already does. As of this afternoon, Prescott Deveraux is my newest client."

"You can't just poach my clients."

"Oh no, that's not what's happening at all, father," I drawl, smiling cruelly. "In fact, I'm saving you. Because I'm trying to be a good person. A *better* person. It would really be a shame to be charged with another crime, wouldn't it?"

"Are you threatening me, son?"

I laugh. "You lost a lot of money. Again. The courts aren't going to look upon you very favorably, I'm afraid. Especially because Prescott Deveraux was able to track where his money went."

"There's no way."

"Where there's a will, there's a way," I reply, my fingers drumming along the mahogany dresser. "Luckily, I know some very important people who were able to dig into his portfolio a bit more, at least, the part you tried to hide. When I asked you last week if you'd lost the money, I never expected to find it in one of *your* offshore accounts, father."

"You can't touch that money," he growls.

"I don't want the money," I bite back. "I guess it's a good thing that I donated *two* million dollars to Prescott's various charities."

"He can't invest that—"

"I know. But he can invest the money I gifted him as an apology for getting tangled up with you. He's now *four* million dollars richer. And I'll tell you the same thing I told him: this time, I will ensure his money grows. This time, he can trust the person handling his hard-earned assets."

He's quiet for several seconds.

"And for what, Miles? A little pussy?"

"Don't you dare talk about my wife like that," I growl.

"Is she really worth all of this?"

"Of course she is. She always was." I check my watch as my jaw feathers angrily. Ten minutes until the reception. "I have somewhere to be, so I'm only going to say this once. Never contact me again. Never contact Estelle or Prescott again."

"Miles—"

I grind my jaw and close my eyes. "If you do, I will hand everything over to the authorities. Every receipt. Every bank statement. Every email between you and Prescott."

"You can't possibly be serious."

I laugh again. "I've never been so serious in my life, Charles."

I end the call with shaky hands. After taking a few steadying breaths, I pour myself another finger of whiskey, downing it in one gulp.

I told myself the next time my father called, I'd give him the ultimatum. I wasn't lying about Prescott being my newest client, either. If I couldn't fix the past, I sure as hell wasn't going to fuck up the future. The least I could do was bring Prescott on, make a massive donation in good faith, and reimburse him for my father's indiscretions. In fact, I flew him to California yesterday as a surprise to Estelle.

I want nothing to do with my father.

I'm done trying to see the good in him.

For so long, I clung onto the fact that he was family, but now I know that was never the case.

I have my brothers and Juliet.

And of course ... Estelle.

I leave the living quarters feeling more free than I ever have.

A few minutes later, I'm talking to Orion and Malakai near the bar when Chase and Juliet enter the room. The crowd goes wild, and Chase pulls Juliet in for a long, inappropriate kiss. I can't help but smile as I clap for my younger brother and his new wife.

And then I get a glimpse of the most stunning shade of dusty, royal blue—the exact same shade as my wife's eyes.

My eyes travel up from the bright pink heels to a pair of delicious looking calves. The dress is tight, and it hugs her curves beautifully, cinching her waist and draping over her chest. Tiny straps hold the whole thing up, and when my eyes get to her face, she's already watching me with a small smile. Her hair is wild and curly—and *fuck* I missed her. It takes everything in me not to run up to her and kiss her.

Not to get down on one knee and propose right here, right now.

Not to ask her to marry me *for real.*

I slowly walk over to her, my hands in my pockets. As I get closer, I notice the *R* necklace around her neck.

That's a good sign.

Just as I stop in front of her, she hands me an envelope.

"For you," she says, her cheeks going pink as her eyes survey my face, my neck, my chest. It's nice to know that I'm not the only one affected.

I take the envelope and smirk. "What's this for?"

"Just open it," she drawls, rolling her eyes.

"Estelle." I sigh, taking a half step closer. *Needing* to be near her. "I'm so sorry. For everything. I promise you, no more lies. From here on out, no more secrets."

Her lips twist to the side. "Okay."

I narrow my eyes. "Okay? That's it?"

She shrugs. "Yeah. I've had a lot of time to think, and the truth is, I don't care about the money, or the fact that you lied. I understand why you did it. You thought you were doing the right thing. You thought you were protecting and supporting me. And when I thought about it from your perspective, it made sense. I *know* you. I know how you learned how to make an English fry up for me. I know you requested the chef to make me my favorite meals. I know you made an effort and offered to go on my morning walks with me."

Hearing her say all of this ... it envelops me in something warm. Something comforting that I've never had before. *Something I never want to let go of again.*

"I know you surprised me by flying my father here tonight," she adds. "We spent a long time talking earlier. Thank you."

"Anything for you," I tell her honestly.

She pulls her lower lip between her teeth. "And, I know you showed me a part of yourself down in the cellar that I'll never get enough of," she says, her voice low. "I know how it feels to have someone cuddle up behind me for three days when life doesn't feel worth living," she adds, her voice a whisper. "I know how it feels to not be alone anymore."

Her eyes water.

My chest cracks open. "God, I missed you so fucking much."

She shakes her head as her eyes flick between mine. "I missed you more."

I kiss her before I know what I'm doing, and she lets out a tiny, satisfied gasp as my lips crash against hers. My fingers get tangled in her curls, and my tongue parts her lips easily. The other hand comes to her waist, and I pull her close to me. I need to feel her, need to touch her. One of her hands comes to my neck, and I moan when she runs her small fingers over the ultra-sensitive skin of my scars.

She pulls away before I can drag her into the next room.

"Open your present," she says, smiling.

Gods. When she smiles, her eyes shine the *exact* shade of blue—

"Miles."

I smile, the words on the tip of my tongue. When I unseal the envelope, I pull out a note card.

> *IOU.*
> *Good for one trip to see Lucifer.*

"What is this?" I ask, my heart pounding in my chest.

She laughs and crosses her arms. "I decided I would give you one opportunity a week to go see Lucifer with me," she starts, looking chagrined. "I don't like it, but I know that scary little beast means a lot to you, so I'll figure out a way to deal with it."

I drop the note and pull her into me, kissing her fervently. She groans when my hand snakes around her waist, dipping down to her ass and squeezing.

"Miles—"

"Stop fucking talking and let me tell you that I love you," I whisper against her lips, my hands moving to her hips as they dig into her skin. "I love you so fucking much that I don't even want to sleep under that fucking duvet without you." She laughs, or cries, against my lips before kissing me again. She smells like her ... like jasmine and Chanel No. 5. I inhale as warmth spreads through me. "I don't want to do this without you. I'm sorry. I'll keep telling you I'm sorry for the rest of our lives."

"I know, darling," she murmurs. I shiver at her words. "I love you, too."

Running a hand up to my face, she pulls away and looks at me with everything—every emotion, every morsel of hope I never dared let myself feel before I met her.

"Come home," I beg her.

"Louis already has my things," she says, kissing me again.

"So willing to forgive me, wife?" I ask, trying to keep my voice casual.

Please say yes.

"I wanted to be prepared," she murmurs against my lips. "Just in case you said all the right things."

"And? Did I?" I ask, pulling away from her slightly.

This time, the pleading tone is evident, and Estelle pauses for a second, her hands running down to my neck.

I don't bat an eye, because it's *her*. I'm so completely smitten with her that I don't care where or how she touches me—just that she *does*. No one else.

Only her.

"Yes, Miles. You did."

I let out a shaky breath. "I need you," I say, grinning. I run my hands down her sides and tug her close.

"I know. But I need to mingle for a little bit."

Groaning, I let her go. "Fine. I guess I deserve to wait."

"I have a surprise waiting for you in the cellar," she teases, giving me a coy smile.

And then she pulls away from me and re-enters the crowd in the next room.

She knows what she's doing.

This is her version of punishment for what I did, and truth be told, I deserve it.

For the entirety of the next hour, I say hello to anyone and everyone I can, knowing I sure as fuck won't be available once I get my hands on my wife later.

Once I'm able to show her all the ways I'm sorry.

Every few minutes, our eyes meet across the room, and I swear, I don't think my cock has ever been this hard for this long.

I'm leaning against the fireplace in the lounge sipping my whiskey when a small hand wraps around my waist.

"Let's go," Estelle murmurs.

Before I realize what's happening, she's leading me away from the party and through the kitchen. When we get to the door of the cellar, she looks over her shoulder at me.

"Ready for your surprise?" she asks, a mischievous smile on her face.

CHAPTER THIRTY
THE EXHIBITIONIST

STELLA

I don't know why I'm so nervous, but my hands are shaking as I lead Miles down the narrow staircase to the cellar. After speaking to my father earlier and realizing what he'd done for him, I realized that I wanted to do something *for* Miles. Not only did he somehow manage to bring my father on as a client, but he also made a sizable donation, and gifted my father his money back four times over.

Through this whole ordeal, the money didn't matter to me, but I did worry about my father's investment.

I should've known Miles would take care of it.

So, this is for him.

A proper thank you.

The note about Lucifer is just a cheeky idea to celebrate our one-month anniversary, but this?

I know he'll love this.

"Estelle, what the hell are you doing?" he asks slowly.

I open the door to the voyeur room, smiling as I hold it open for him.

"I believe there's another entrance for me," I purr, going up on my tip toes and kissing his cheek. "Go wait for me on the sofa, please."

"Estelle—"

I walk away from him before he can change my mind.

I'd asked Luna to help me with this part of my plan, and I was delighted to discover the secret passageway from the back of the castle to the glass room. The way Miles built it was ingenious—it's discrete and private, ensuring the people performing are comfortable.

I walk back upstairs, saying a quick hello to a few of the people who were at our wedding reception.

I walk out the back door and around the side of the castle to the discrete, nondescript entrance to the glass room, trying to quell my shaking legs. Walking down the stone passageway, I think about how Miles said he loves me. How I admitted I love him, too. How this was all so convoluted and backward, but how it felt right, somehow.

From that first day in the fountain—to now. How my interest in him never wavered. How our chemistry was always off the charts.

As I open the door to the bedroom, I take a deep, steadying breath.

This feels right.

"I had Luna reconfigure the speaker system so we can talk," I say out loud.

"Did you?" Miles voice replies, coming out of the new speaker she set up on the bedside table.

I grin. "I figured you could tell me what to do."

The low growl comes through the speaker and sends a shiver down my spine.

"Fuck, Estelle," he grits out. "You're going to kill me."

"What do you want me to do first, darling?" I ask, kicking my shoes off and walking over to the part of the mirrored wall that I know faces the couch.

"Strip for me, butterfly. Let me see that perfect body."

I swallow as I hook one finger under the strap of my dress, letting it fall to my shoulder.

"Fuck," Miles rasps. "I'm already touching my cock. You make me feel out of control."

Pulling my lower lip between my teeth, I do the same thing to the other strap, letting the top of my dress fall past the bright pink bustier I have on.

"Christ," he says hoarsely. "I need to see you without the dress. Take it off."

Reaching behind my back, I unzip the dress the rest of the way, letting it fall to a pile at my feet. Stepping out of it, I twirl around once slowly, showing off the bustier and matching high-rise thong.

Smirking, I bend over to pick up my dress slowly, and I hear a low growl come through the speakers.

"You're lucky that punishment isn't my thing, butterfly. Stop taunting me and take everything off."

"Are you sure?" Twisting around, I turn to face him, my hand reaching back to unclasp the bustier. Slowly —slow enough to torture him a bit.

I wonder where he is in there.

I wonder if he's sitting on the couch.

Is he touching himself?

"Are you sitting on the couch?" I ask, unhooking the clasps but not letting my bustier fall just yet.

"No." Suddenly, I see the outline of a hand right in front of me, but because this room is lit and the cellar is dark, I can't see anything else. "I'm right in front of you."

My heart races inside of my chest as I pull my bustier off, discarding it on the floor.

"Get on the bed," Miles commands.

I turn around, walk to the bed a few feet away, and lie down.

"I want you to spread your legs. Face me, please."

I smile as I do as he says, my right hand coming between my legs and grazing my damp knickers. My other hand reaches over to the nightstand, pulling out a dildo.

I hear Miles release a shuddering breath over the speakers. "Fuck, Estelle. I need to see you fuck yourself with that. Please," he adds, his voice frayed.

I inhale sharply at the need in his voice—at the way he sounds so completely unhinged and on the brink of ruin.

A very, very small part of me wants to torture him.

"Yeah?" I ask, shimmying out of my knickers, lifting my hips, and pulling them down my legs. Then, without another word, I slowly begin to coat the dildo by running it up and down my slit. The soft, silicone head rubs against my aching clit, and I arch my back slightly. "Tell me what to do," I gasp out.

"Spread your legs wider," he growls. "I want you to fuck yourself with the dildo," he adds, his voice fractured.

"Are you touching yourself?" I ask, my skin heating at the thought of him getting off just feet away, unable to get to me.

"Of course I am," he answers. "You make me crazy."

A low, warm hum works through me at his words. I place the head of the dildo at my opening, pausing to drive him a bit crazy. When I look up at the glass, I see the hand he placed against the glass curl into a fist.

"Wife," he grits out unevenly.

I smile as I press the dildo inside of me, arching my back as I do and letting out a low groan the same time he does, making the most delightful, low rumble of sounds.

"God, I wish this was your cock," I tell him, slowly removing it before pushing it back in just as slowly.

"You have no idea," he grumbles.

I push the dildo in deep, looking between my legs before looking back over at where Miles's hand is. I'm panting now, my core aching with need.

"Don't stop," he begs, voice ragged. "Keep fucking yourself."

I move my hand faster, my muscles coiling with tension at the idea of turning him on by doing this.

"Miles," I whimper.

"You have no idea how much I wish I could break this glass just to be inside of you. How much I need to be inside of you right now. My cock is pulsating for you, butterfly."

"Oh god," I breathe, my hand working faster.

"How I wish I could be that glistening piece of silicone, sliding in and out of your tight cunt, coated in your juices," he mumbles.

"Have you always had such a filthy mouth?" I ask, my words stilted and jerky.

"Do you like it?"

"Yes," I moan, throwing my head back.

"Good girl," he growls. "I love watching you fuck yourself. Watching the way your swollen lips suck that toy into yourself, how pretty they look wrapped around it."

I gasp. *Dirty, filthy—*

"But you know, I think I prefer the way they stretch just a bit farther for *my* cock. How perfect it feels being inside of you, like I'm wrapped up in heaven."

"Miles—"

I'm properly fucking myself with the dildo now, working the tip against the button inside of me as my other hand comes to my clit.

"Look at that pretty, pink bud. I want to suck and nibble that little clit for the rest of my life, Estelle," he rasps. "Fuck, I'm getting close."

"M—me too," I stutter.

My abdominal muscles contract as my toes curl. Lifting one leg a bit higher, it shifts the dildo just enough to make me cry out, to make my hips jerk off the bed.

"Miles," I gasp.

"Come for me. Give me a show."

"Oh, God," I cry. "I–I'm going to—"

The next swipe of my finger against my clit makes my body slowly start to convulse, and my pussy clamps onto the dildo in electrifying waves.

"Fuck yes," he mutters. "Look at that glistening cunt. Keep going. Push yourself over the edge, butterfly. I need to see it."

His words cause me to let out a low, keening moan as the pressure builds up, causing me to remove the dildo and flail around on the bed as a second, more powerful orgasm sweeps through me.

"Yes," he grits out. "Fuck, I'm coming so hard—"

I'm still gasping for air when I see his cock press against the glass for me to see. When I see the way his cum streaks against the glass, rope after thick rope, dripping heavily.

A few seconds later, I hear him audibly zip himself back into his trousers, the heavy breathing mixing with my panting breaths.

"Get dressed and meet me outside," he says gruffly, and then I hear the clacking of his shoes.

I sit up, feeling somewhat alarmed. That's it? After I had this room rewired for the speakers, after the whole dildo performance ... and he just walks out?

I quickly get dressed on shaky legs, wondering if it was somehow not enough for him—if maybe I did something wrong.

If maybe I said something wrong.

I have to clean myself up with a towel, and then I step into my pink heels and walk out of the room, trying to calm my nerves. I don't think I said anything that would piss him off ... or maybe he freaked out because we've been gone so long? As I push the door to the back garden open, the cold, November air makes my skin pebble. I wrap my arms around myself and look around, adjusting to the darkness.

Did he want to meet me here? Or did he mean outside in the castle, as in *outside* the cellar? I look to my left and right but it's so dark that the only things I can see are the sliding glass door to the castle kitchen on my left. Just as I take a step away from the door, I see Miles push the sliding door open and then closed behind him, marching to where I'm standing, shivering in the cold darkness. Goosebumps break out on my skin as I watch him walk with purpose to where I'm standing. He looks ... agitated. Or ... something else I haven't ever seen on his face.

Possessed. Galvanized. *Provoked*.

As he gets closer, I open my mouth to ask him what's wrong, but before I can, he presses me against the side of the castle, pinning me against the stone as his face comes within an inch of mine. He's still breathing heavily, and I can feel his erratic heartbeat against my chest.

"You," is all he says, almost angry.

And then he kisses me, groaning as our lips meet. The kiss tells me everything I need to know.

I did everything right.

My mouth parts to let his tongue in. His hands come to my thighs, and he rucks my dress up quickly.

Hear the click of his belt coming undone.

Taste the whiskey on his tongue as it explores my mouth.

I moan as he drags my dress up over my hips. My hands come to his neck, and I'm pleased to feel how damp he is with sweat, and the thought of working himself into a frenzy down in the cellar *because of me* makes me moan again.

"Miles," I whimper, tugging him closer. "What are you—"

"What is it, butterfly? Did you think I was done with you?"

CHAPTER THIRTY-ONE
THE VIDEO

MILES

"What?" She gasps as one of my fingers hooks underneath her panties. "No, I—"

"I. Can't. Get. Enough. Of. You," I mumble against her lips, pulling roughly on her panties until the elastic snaps, and they fall to the ground.

Without another word, I move my hands to her ass and lift her, smoothing my palms over her thighs as she wraps her legs around me. And as I sink into her hot, wet cunt, I press my lips against her neck, a low groan leaving my lips.

"Fuuuuck."

I lift my head up and find her needy mouth as I thrust up and into her roughly. Her breath brushes against my cheeks as I press my tongue between her lips.

"Yes," she mewls.

I sink deeper into her, letting gravity pull her down onto my cock. I let out a low, rumbling growl from my chest, the feeling of her tight, velvet cunt bringing me closer to my climax than I'd anticipated.

One of my hands comes to her hair, and I fist it roughly, pulling her head back so I can kiss her neck.

"I'm crazy for you," I murmur against her impossibly soft skin.

"The feeling is mutual," she says slowly, and just then, I pull out and slam back into her. She screams and her swollen pussy begins to flutter around my cock.

She gasps out a string of curses.

"If you stay, I won't ever get enough," I warn her, pulling my face away from her neck so I can look at her. "I won't ever feel satiated."

"God, Miles," she whispers, her fingers coming to my hair as I pound into her again. And again. And again. Her eyes widen each time I do, and she gasps for breath—like I'm somehow knocking the wind out of her with each thrust.

The slapping sound of her sweet, wet cunt bounces off the stone walls, and I fucking love it. I love everything about her. About us.

"I love your dirty mouth," she whines, squeezing her eyes shut.

"Good," I mumble, running the hand that was in her hair, down her neck and to the strap of her dress. I tug it down her shoulder, and then I work my way to the other one, tugging it down as well, so that I can see her tits bounce as I fuck her. "I love these," I groan, palming one of them as my other hand shifts her hips slightly, bringing her core forward and closer to me. "And I love you."

"I know," she breathes. "I love you, too."

"Remember that," I add, my thumb brushing over her nipple.

"What do you mean?" she whispers, her eyes hooded. Her cunt clamps around my cock as I pinch her nipple. She's so fucking reactive to my touch.

My cock.

Like she was made for me.

"Remember that I love you, butterfly," I rasp. "Because I can't help but want to fuck you like I don't."

She comes, her inner walls milking my cock.

"Miles," she cries, hands gripping my jacket as she rolls her hips along my cock, taking what she needs from me as her orgasm works through her. I growl, *so* close to losing it. As soon as she's done, I pull out of her and lower her legs onto the ground. "Wait. What about you?"

I press down on her shoulders, removing my phone from my pocket at the same time.

She must realize my intentions, because she gives me a coy smile as she lowers herself onto her knees as I press record and turn the flash on, highlighting her flushed cheeks.

"That's it," I grumble as she reaches for my aching cock. "You know what to do," I tell her, watching the way she looks up at me with a mix of surprise and yearning.

And then she wraps those perfect, pink lips around

my glistening cock, moaning when she tastes herself. My fingers tangle into her curls, and I fist her hair in my hand, driving farther into her mouth.

"You have such a perfect fucking mouth. Such a perfect fucking cunt. And one day, I'm going to be inside of your perfect fucking ass." She stills slightly, looking up at me with those wide, blue eyes. She pulls back and swirls her tongue around the tip of my cock.

"Really?" she asks, using one hand to stroke my length as her tongue swirls around the swollen head of my shaft again.

I pull away from her, placing a hand on the top of her head. "How many times do I have to tell you? I want you—everything about you. I want to fuck you every which way, in every hole, in every room of this castle, every single day for as long as you'll have me."

She swallows, and I watch her throat bob as she does. "I want that, too." And then *my wife* opens her mouth, tongue flat.

I hiss as I plunge between her lips, looking at my screen briefly to ensure that I'm recording this. I don't anticipate ever needing it, but just knowing I have pictures and videos of her, of us, sends a shiver down the base of my spine, drawing my balls up tight as my orgasm gets closer.

One of her little hands continues stroking me as her lips swallow me, and the other comes to my balls.

"Fuck," I groan. "I love watching you suck my cock," I tell her. "Look at you, on your knees for your husband like a good little wife," I say, and she moans at my words.

I smirk. *My wife has a praise kink, does she?*

I sink deeper into her mouth, loving the sound of her gagging. "Take it all the way," I command. "I know you can."

She moans again as she looks up at me, and *fuck*.

I lose it completely.

"Fuck, that's my girl," I murmur. "I'm going to come." She doesn't relent. Instead, she intensifies everything, suctioning her mouth slightly. "God, yes!"

My hips jerk as I spill down her throat, mouth falling open as she swallows every single drop of my cum. As my cock pulses against her tongue, as she slowly draws her lips off my sensitive cock, milking the last drop out of me before smacking her lips.

I end the video recording, putting my phone away and helping her up. Peppering her with kisses, she giggles as she kisses me, wrapping her arms around my neck.

"Why are you so fucking perfect," I say against her lips.

"It's truly exhausting," she teases, smiling.

I pull away and clean us up, helping her with her dress and putting my cock into my pants as I buckle my belt.

Once we finish, I hold my hand out for hers. "Ready?"

It's one word, but for me, it's just the beginning.

She gives me a radiant smile before placing her soft hand in mine. "Ready. Also, that was totally a ten out of ten. Just saying."

I'm drinking a glass of water when Juliet saunters over to me, a rueful smirk playing on her lips. She pokes me playfully, and I frown at her.

"Don't touch me," I say, glowering.

"Oh. Right. Sorry. I forgot that your *wife*, the one you *love*, is the only one allowed to touch you now."

I sigh and run my hand over my mouth. My eyes wander over to Estelle, who is having a heart-to-heart with her father. "Your husband can't keep his damn mouth shut, can he?"

She giggles. "Look, I'm very happy for you." Her expression turns contemplative. "I adore Stella. I think she's perfect for you. She came into your life so fast, but I think you fell so hard that she softened you in the process."

I take another sip of water as I let her words wash over me. I've always liked Juliet. She kept Chase on his toes, called him out on his bullshit, and refused to let him go when he got scared.

How Chase and I ended up with women who wanted to fight *for* us is beyond me.

I give her a small smile as I sip my water. "Thanks."

"I'm sad that I lost the bet to Kai, but it is what it is."

I nearly choke. "*Kai?*"

"Actually," Liam interjects, sauntering over to us. "*Technically*, I win."

"Like hell you do," Malakai adds, following Liam.

"I thought you weren't allowed to swear?" I tease,

nudging his shoulder. "Also, what the hell are you all talking about?"

Juliet looks between my brothers. "We—um—sort of placed bets on when you and Stella would fall in love at your wedding." Then she pulls her phone out. "I kept a list so we could all remember what we said. I also have them listed in order of probability, with mine being first, of course," she adds.

Chase walks up to us then, wrapping an arm around Juliet's waist.

"If she has a list, she means business," he tells us.

"Right, so I said six weeks. Chase said five weeks." She kisses her husband on the cheek. "So close. But also the wrong answer." He bursts out laughing as Juliet continues down the list. "Malakai said four and a half weeks. Orion said seven weeks. And Liam said twelve weeks," she finishes.

"Right," Liam says gruffly. "So, I was the closest."

I sip my water with an amused smile as my eyes flick between my brothers and Juliet. "How do you figure?" I ask my oldest brother.

Liam shrugs as he sips his beer. "You fell in love with her the first time you met her. Technically, that means I'm the winner," he finishes matter-of-factly.

His words knock me over, and I grip the glass a bit harder. Is he wrong? I don't know. I was intrigued by Estelle that night—mesmerized and captivated by her bright smile. But did I fall in love with her?

It's possible.

I never stopped thinking about her.

I wish I'd gotten her number. Or her name.

But love?

My eyes wander back over the crowd, finding my wife watching me already as she speaks to her father. I can tell she's speaking French because of the way she's speaking quickly and quietly. She shoots me a large smile.

Something inside of me thaws out completely.

I don't know if I loved her that night a little over a year ago, but something about that night, about *her*, changed me.

She was the bright sun in my darkness.

The golden girl to my villainous, immoral soul.

"Fine," I concede, and Liam makes a victorious gesture. I flip him off. "What do you want? A cookie? Estelle has an entire tin full of cookies," I tell him.

He laughs. "Actually, yes. Thank you."

I grumble as I walk over to the tin and pull the top off, offering cookies to everyone.

"It's like you caught the bouquet at the wedding," Juliet says excitedly.

"What do you mean?" Liam asks.

"You're next," she says cryptically.

He huffs a laugh. "Yeah. Right. Because I have so many women beating down my door."

Juliet narrows her eyes. "It'll happen when you least expect it."

Then she flounces away. Chase just gives Liam a knowing smile before following her. Malakai pats me on the arm before following them out of the kitchen.

"They're full of shit," he says, taking another sip of his beer.

I grin as I set my glass in the dishwasher. "Yeah. I thought the same thing a month ago."

Winking, I walk into the other room just as Estelle turns away from her father. Without thinking, I open my arms and pull her into me, hugging her tightly. Kissing the top of her head, I look up to see Prescott Deveraux watching us with a knowing smile before tipping his hat and walking away.

"Did you have a nice talk?" I ask her.

She pulls away, her hands not leaving my sides. "I did."

"Tired?" I ask, my voice hopeful.

She arches her brow. "For sleep?"

I wiggle my eyebrows, and she laughs. "Oh my god. You really are insatiable."

"I warned you," I say into her ear as I lead her away. "And I have the perfect video we can watch. *Together.*"

She's still laughing when I drag her toward the elevator.

CHAPTER THIRTY-TWO

THE PICTURE

MILES

One month later

"Oh god. Miles, I don't think I can do this—"

I squeeze her hand as she stares ahead of us. "Come on, butterfly. It's Christmas. We talked about this. You can do it."

She takes a step forward. "Fuck. Of all the animals you could've rescued, it had to be a goat?" she whines, taking another step into Lucifer's pen.

I chuckle. "He's very excited to meet you."

She turns around and glares at me. "And how would you know that? He could be plotting to murder me for all I know."

Nudging her forward, she gives me one last glowering stare before taking another step inside the pen. She looks so fucking cute in her black leggings and an oversized red flannel. Even more so with the green hat on her head, despite it being temperate today. But no, my wife insisted on full Christmas attire.

I jokingly make a bleating sound, and I laugh when Estelle jumps about three feet in the air.

"Bloody hell," she grumbles, glaring at me. "Are you trying to make me even more afraid of that demonic little beast? Let's get this over with."

"Maybe you should stop calling him a beast," I offer.

"Oh, fuck off," she tells me. "Get the camera ready. I'm only doing this once."

I pull the DSLR, a Christmas gift from my shameless little minx of a wife, from around my neck, adjusting the settings as much as I know how. I drag the tripod over to the front of Lucifer's house, screwing the camera in and ensuring I have the remote in the front pocket of my matching red flannel.

Because yes, we are a walking cliché in matching shirts and kitschy knit hats.

"Miles," she says slowly, peeking into the house. "Look. He's sleeping."

I leave the camera as is, walking to the door of the tiny house. Lucifer is curled up on his bed, eyes closed, nose tucked underneath his pillow.

"See? Look how cute," I say softly.

She pouts and crosses her arms. "Fine. He's cute when he's asleep. Wake him up so we can get our picture."

Smiling, I move her to the log I have set up for us to sit on, right underneath the sign she ordered that says, *Happy Holidays from the Ravage Family.*

"You sit down. I'll bring him over."

"Joy," she grumbles.

I slowly rouse Lucifer, and he bleats softly. "Merry Christmas, little guy," I tell him, patting the back of his head. "Let's take a quick picture, yeah? Don't mind your peevish mother. It's not your fault she can't separate reality from a silly children's show—"

"Excuse me, I can hear you!" Estelle says loudly from nearby.

I guide Lucifer out of the little house and go to sit next to my wife, pulling the two green hats out of my pocket as well as some treats.

I quickly hold my hand with the treats out, smiling at Estelle as she frowns at me.

"Come on," I tease. "Smile for the camera."

I get Lucifer to stand between us—much to Estelle's chagrin. I even manage to get a picture of him in his silly, little hat.

After we get our shot, Estelle hovers near the front door of his house as I pack up the tripod.

"Ready?" I ask.

She looks at me before looking back at Lucifer's house.

"It's just ..." she trails off, biting her lower lip. "It's Christmas."

I cock my head. "So I've heard. I still have the disgusting taste of mince pies stuck in my mouth."

Her mouth drops open. "Hey. I'll have you know that those are a very festive English treat on Christmas morning." I laugh as she looks at Lucifer's door. "I just meant that ... it's Christmas. And it's supposed to get cold tonight. Maybe ..." She swallows, and I see her fists curl at her sides. "Maybe he should come into the castle for the night?"

My lips twitch as I walk over to her. "Is that so? Even with his glowing red eyes?"

She growls as she turns to face me. "Not. Funny."

I laugh as I pull her into a tight hug. "I'm sure he'd love to come inside for the night."

"Not—not in our living quarters," she clarifies. "But ..." she chews on her lip. "Maybe we can make him a warm little home for the night in one of the guest rooms—"

I lean down and kiss her before she can say anything else, and my heart swells with pride.

"You're amazing," I tell her, my breath against her lips.

"One night," she mumbles, her hands coming to my collar and curling around the material. "Just one night."

"Fine by me."

————

Later that night, my face hurts from smiling so much. Chase and Juliet are over, as are Liam and Zoe, who is home for Christmas. I met her briefly at her parents' funeral, and she seems to be doing well. She's mature and charming. Her time at her boarding school and the unfortunate events of a couple of years ago have turned her into a very intelligent young woman. She tells us all about her upcoming trip to Mexico this April for her eighteenth birthday, and when I look up at Liam, surprised he'd allow her on a trip like that, he just glares at me before staring at the wall.

Like hell he's going to let her go on that trip.

Chase and Juliet tell us all about her new position at a university in Northern California—where they're headed in January.

Lucifer bleats happily anytime someone laughs, and it's really fucking adorable.

Estelle jumps every single time, and I think I fall even more in love with her.

Once we've all filled up on our Christmas feast and those disgustingly sweet mince pies, Estelle and I say goodbye as people filter out of the living room to the three guest rooms we've made up for them—one for Chase and Juliet, one for Liam, and one for Zoe.

I watch Estelle as she cleans up since she refuses to let me help her. To be fair, I cook our dinner most nights, finding that I love to cook as long as it's something that she loves to eat. Her hips sway as she hums a Christmas song, and *fuck* I want to memorize this moment forever.

I drag my new camera over and quietly click through the settings before holding it up to my face and taking a quick picture.

Estelle turns around quickly, pink gloves on her hands as she glares at me with soapy fingers.

"Did you just take a picture of my arse?"

I smirk. "Maybe."

Rolling her eyes, she presses her lips together and turns the water off, setting the gloves off to the side.

"You're having too much fun with that camera," she teases, walking over to me.

I spread my legs on the stool I'm sitting on, and she comes to stand between them. Pulling her close, I inhale the scent of her hair.

"Marry me?" I ask quietly.

She pulls away and shoves against my chest. "Very funny."

"No, I know we're already legally married," I say slowly, running a hand through her curls. "I mean ... for real. A big ceremony. Lots of people. A goddamn cake would be nice."

Her eyes widen slightly. "Really?"

I huff a nervous laugh. The idea of marrying Estelle again is something I've been thinking a lot about. So, why not?

"It's not like you can say no," I murmur, kissing the tip of her nose. "You can't *un*marry me."

Her eyes flutter closed. "Of course. You know I'd love that, darling."

I grin as I kiss her, placing my hands on either side of her face. When I pull away, I take her left hand—where the amethyst ring sparkles against the lights of the kitchen.

"I think a real wedding would make her proud," I tell her, knowing she'll know who I'm referring to.

Estelle sniffs and takes a step back, looking down at her hand. "I think it would."

"Do you think she would've liked me?" I ask, having been wondering this for weeks.

She looks up at me—her cheeks flushed, hair

tousled, flannel shirt unbuttoned enough to expose the lace of her neon green bra.

"She would've loved you," she says slowly, her expression emotional and soft. "Because you love me. She would've been able to see that love, and she would've loved you for it." Looking once again down at her ring, her eyes then flick back up to mine. "Another wedding? Really?"

I shrug. "Why not?"

Grinning, she rushes forward and collides with my body. "Okay. Let's do it."

I kiss the top of her head. "You plan it this time. Make it exactly how you imagined. Go crazy."

"What-if we ..." she trails off, and she shakes her head.

"What?" I ask, pulling away.

She gives me a sheepish smile. "What-if we have it in Paris?"

My face breaks out into a grin. "I can't think of a better place. I wonder if they'd let us get married in the Jardins du Trocadero?"

"We're probably banned for life," she admits.

"Yes, the French don't care for people swimming naked in their public fountains."

"Let's do it," she says excitedly. "Maybe not this next year, but the year after. I can launch my line, we can settle down a bit, and then ... we can plan the perfect wedding."

"Sounds perfect," I purr.

And then I kiss my *fiancée* and wife—wholeheartedly and unabashedly.

EPILOGUE
THE FOUNTAIN, PART TWO

ESTELLE

Five months later, Paris

"Where are you taking me?" I ask Miles, trying to peek through the black, silk ribbon he has tied around my eyes. Just as the words leave my mouth, the car comes to a slow stop, and I hear Miles get out on his side, opening my door a few seconds later.

"Watch your step," he says, placing an arm around my shoulder as we exit the black SUV.

"Are you choosing to ignore me, or are you going deaf in your old age?" I tease, referencing his birthday dinner with my father from earlier tonight. We were celebrating a few things. The launch of VeRue next week, Miles's birthday, and our six-month anniversary.

"Thirty-seven is not old." He sniffs, and I can't help

but smile as I blindly walk ... somewhere. "And yes, I am choosing to ignore you."

"Fine," I retort, clutching onto his white dress shirt. "But if I fall on my arse because I can't see—"

"I'm not going to let you fall, butterfly," he grits out. "There's a step here," he says quickly, slowing us down until I'm over the curb.

"Having my eyes covered is making me nauseous," I say quickly, feeling slightly motion sick.

"We're almost there."

Pressing my lips together, I take a few deep breaths to settle my stomach. A minute of walking blindly later, he slows us down, and I hear water splashing nearby. He lets me go, and I hear him begin to walk away.

"Miles," I warn.

"One second," he says from several feet away. "I'll tell you when to untie your blindfold."

I smile as I wait for his command.

I know where we are.

I knew where we were going when he said he had a surprise for me.

It's sweet, and though it's a little predictable, I can't help but fall in love with him even more.

"Okay, take it off."

I do as he says, already smiling when the Fountain of Warsaw at Les Jardins du Trocadero comes into view —as does the twinkling Eiffel Tower behind him.

"The lights!" I squeal, pointing to the tower. "God, it's so dreamy when the lights are on, isn't it?"

When I look at Miles, he's watching me with consternation, and he's completely naked.

"I'm not sure if I should be offended or amused that you noticed the Eiffel Tower before me, but—"

I bark out a laugh and cover my mouth. The lights are shining down on the water and my husband in it, sparkling against his scars and lighting up his eyes. He looks ... nervous. And a little bit uncomfortable. There are a lot more people around tonight than there were a year and a half ago, so a few people have already stopped and stared at Miles as he ducks down beneath the surface, eyes narrowed.

There's a pile of discarded clothes by the edge.

"Darling, I'm so proud of you," I coo, walking closer to the fountain.

"Are you going to get in with me, or am I going to have to show my cock to the entirety of Paris alone?"

"Well, I'm sorry to disappoint you," I say slowly, setting my purse down on the ledge. "But you're alone in your cock-wielding activities, because I don't actually have a cock—"

Before I can finish my sentence, Miles lurches forward and pulls me into the fountain, fully clothed.

"Miles!" I screech, laughing and grateful that it's a warm spring night. "You bloody arsehole!" I splash him with the water, and an expression of disgust graces his features.

"This water is probably going to give us Giardia."

I cackle, wrapping my arms around his neck. "Probably." Someone whistles behind us, and Miles flips them off. "Be nice. They're just playing around."

Miles frowns as his eyes dart over my white tank top. "Poor judgment on my part. Now everyone can see what only I'm allowed to see."

This makes me laugh louder. He's so bloody predictable and brooding. And I can't help but really fucking love and adore it.

"Did you bring towels?" I ask, grinning.

He swears under his breath. "No. But you're going to wear my shirt when we get out."

"Am I?" I purr, kissing his neck.

"Yes. Otherwise everyone in Paris will see your perfect tits."

"Well, it wouldn't be the first time," I muse, swimming away from him.

And by swim, I mean crab walk, because the fountain is only a meter deep. Miles is so tall that he has to sit on his bottom to hide himself properly.

Miles follows me, a mischievous glint in his eye.

"Speaking of," he says slowly, one hand coming up to my nipple and twisting it. I wince in pain. "Are you wearing a different bra?" he asks, pulling me close again. His erection presses against my hip, and a flash of white-hot heat works through me when I think of how randy he's been feeling all week. All month, really. I have no idea what's gotten into him—not that I'm complaining.

"No, why?" I ask, kissing him softly.

He groans as his hands come to knead my breasts through my shirt. Luckily, we're under water enough to cover any indiscretions.

"They seem bigger to me," he murmurs against my mouth and squeezing my nipples.

"Ouch, too hard," I tell him, slapping his hands away. "It's probably from all of the delicious French food you've been plying me with all week."

His eyes bore into mine when he pulls away. "I love you," he says softly.

"I love you too." Looking around, I can't help but wonder about that night. "What-if we never met here?" I ask, slowly wrapping my legs around his hips in the water.

"Get a room!" someone yells in French.

Miles smiles and ignores them. One of his hands brushes my wet hair away.

"Well, then we would've met at the restaurant," he says matter-of-factly. "Our fathers would've still brought us together."

I worry my lower lip between my teeth. "How would you have perceived me?"

"Beautiful. But that's a given," he starts.

"If you're trying to get me to shag you, I can tell you right now that it's working," I tease. "What else?"

He smirks as he kisses me, looking over my shoulder as he does to ensure no one is staring too hard. "Smart. Witty. Independent. Adorably feisty. That dress you were wearing brought out the blue of your eyes. You were, and still are, entirely mesmerizing."

"Keep going," I beg him.

"I would have agreed to the marriage, I think."

I stiffen. "Really?"

He nods. "As much as I didn't want to go through with it at first, I wouldn't have been able to deny how much you bewitched me. How intrigued I was. How I would've wanted to help you with your situation."

I smile against his lips. "But I had to go and ruin it all by staring at your scars," I whisper. "I still can't believe you thought I was repulsed by you. I mean, just look at you."

Now he's the one smiling. "What would *you* have thought about me?"

I shrug. "The same as I always did. Buttoned-up and grouchy, but with something else underneath the surface. Even if things didn't end up the way they did, I still would've kept picking away at the ice until I got inside, don't worry," I add, placing a hand on his bare chest. Suddenly, a memory comes back to me. "Did I ever tell you about the time I watched you wank in the shower before we got together?"

He makes a half-choking, half-surprised sound. "What?!"

I giggle. "Yep. I'd left my vibrator out, and when I went to hide it, you were wanking in the shower."

His eyes are sparkling with intrigue. "And? Did my wife enjoy the show?"

I grin. "I did. Very much so."

"Let's go," he says suddenly, swimming away.

"W–what? Why?"

He stands up and quickly pulls on his pants and trousers, giving me a pointed look.

Oh.

Staring down at me with darkened pupils, he cocks his head slightly as he holds his shirt open for me.

"Because I need to be inside of you."

I laugh as he helps me out of the fountain, my body flooding with warmth and arousal. Something about the way he can't ever seem to keep his hands to himself …

I peel my wet tank top, shorts, and knickers off as he wraps his white shirt around me. Buttoning it up, he collects the rest of my clothes and hands me my sandals and purse.

We're half-walking, half-jogging toward the black SUV that's parked nearby, Miles holding onto my hand and tugging me behind him.

"Did Chase slip you Viagra again?" I tease as he pulls my door open.

He gives me a withering glare as he helps me inside. "Very funny. I thought we agreed we wouldn't talk about that night?"

I'm still laughing when he comes around to his side, thinking about the night a couple months ago when Chase slipped both Miles and Liam Viagra unknowingly.

As he climbs in, he knocks on the window separating his driver from us. It slides down slowly.

"Please take us back to our apartment. Oh, and if I were you, I'd keep the partition up for the journey."

My mouth drops open as the driver chuckles, complying with Miles's request. "Are you out of your mind?" I hiss once we have privacy.

Miles chuckles, leaning over and placing a kiss on

my neck. "I believe *you* were the one who jumped my bones in that taxi, Mrs. Ravage," he murmurs. "I'm just paying it forward."

"Blegh, you smell like fountain water," I whine, pushing him away.

"Didn't stop me from kissing you back that night. Grin and bear it, wife."

The scent of the water continues to assault my nostrils, and I push him away harder. "No, really. All I can smell is swamp water and your wet, wool pants."

He laughs as he tries to kiss me again, and the car lurches forward in such a way that it feels like I left my stomach behind. Nausea roils through me, and I place a hand over my mouth.

"Stop the car," I tell him.

I think I hear Miles knock and tell the driver to pull over between the rushing of blood in my ears and the deep, calming breaths I'm taking, but I'm not sure. All I know is a few seconds later, the car stops suddenly, and I'm just throwing the door open when my stomach tosses its contents onto the pavement outside.

Once I'm done, I feel much better. Miles—*bless him*—massages my back as I wipe my mouth with the back of my hand.

"Food poisoning? Again?" he asks gently, helping me into the car.

"I guess," I mutter, frowning. We'd been in Mexico with Liam and Zoe for her eighteenth birthday a couple of weeks ago, and I'd spent an entire evening hugging the toilet.

It was *not* fun.

"I hope not," Miles says, pulling me into his side as he kisses the top of my head. The driver slowly continues, and I close my eyes to quell the queasiness. "Let's get you home and into bed," he adds, placing a warm, protective hand on my thigh.

"I hope I'm not sick for the launch," I say quietly.

"You'll feel better by next week, butterfly. Don't worry."

The alarm on my phone goes off. "Can you hand me my purse?" I ask him.

He does, and I quickly swallow my birth control pill, drinking the smallest amount of water possible so that I don't upset my stomach further.

Suddenly, realization dawns on me. "Oh, duh," I say, laughing. "I bet it's the new birth control. It's my hormones evening out."

When I look over at Miles, he looks relieved. "Makes sense. But if they're going to make you sick, why not just get one of those spring things again—"

I laugh. "It's a coil, darling. And we talked about this. They last five years, and if you want to knock me up next year after the wedding, it's not worth getting another one put in," I remind him. "The insertion is quite painful," I add, wrinkling my nose.

I'd gotten my coil out last month and switched to the pill. Miles and I are eager to start a family, but we also want to wait until after the wedding next August. It made sense to switch to something a bit more temporary.

"Fine, fine," he says. "I just hate seeing you sick." He kisses the top of my head again, and I hear him smell my hair. "See, I don't smell the fountain water at all. I think you smell like fucking heaven. Whatever those hormones are doing, they're making me feel crazy."

I laugh as we pull up to our flat. And by flat, it's really the entire top floor of the building. I say goodbye to the driver as Miles and I head upstairs.

I'd been worried about coming back to Paris with Miles, especially because Charles Ravage still lives here. But Miles kept his word and hasn't spoken to his father since their conversation almost six months ago. I know my father is very happy at Ravage Consulting Firm, and all's well that ends well, I suppose. Maybe one day he'll forgive his father, but knowing Miles, probably not.

He unlocks the door of our flat and closes it behind me, locking the deadbolt before pulling me into our bedroom.

"Why don't you undress," he says casually. "I'll run you a bath."

I stand by the bed as I slowly unbutton the white shirt I borrowed from him. He disposes of my wet clothes in the laundry basket, and then he walks into the bathroom, sitting on the edge of the bath as he waits for the water to heat up in the clawfoot tub. It hits me then. He's shirtless. That he gave me his shirt without a second thought. That he walked through Les Jardins du Trocadero with his scars on full display. And he had absolutely no reaction to doing so.

"Do you want some lavender bubble bath or eucalyptus bubble bath?" he asks, and the question causes me to burst into tears.

He comes running over to me a second later, scooping me up into his arms and carrying me to the bed, setting me on his lap.

"Estelle," he murmurs, petting my still-damp hair and brushing his thumbs along my cheeks as I sob. "Did I do something wrong? I don't have to run you a bath. We can just go to sleep."

I hiccup and laugh before sobbing again, and Miles's concerned expression makes me cry harder.

"I—don't—know—why I'm—crying."

He pulls me close to his body, murmuring softly and soothing me with his words.

Once I'm done, I sniff and rest my face against his neck before wrinkling my nose. "God, that fountain water is wretched," I say, pulling away.

He smirks down at me. "Feel better?"

I nod. "I suppose. I have no idea what that was about. I think I'm just emotionally wrung out from the launch. I mean, I've been so busy, and then we flew from Mexico to Paris, and I haven't had a second to really sit and digest that my clothes are going to premier next week, and then I have to do all the wedding planning because absolutely *nothing* has been secured except the venue and the dress," I add, heart racing. I start crying again as it all washes over me, and I feel so ... out of control.

"Estelle," Miles murmurs. "Deep breaths."

"And on top of it all, you just walked around Paris without a shirt." The notion is ironic, considering how different he was just six months ago. I swing from uncontrollable crying to laughing. A bubble of amusement bursts out of me—almost like when I used to get laugh attacks in primary school. Suddenly, I can't stop. "You—did it—for me." I am wheezing, doubled over as I try to catch my breath.

Once I finally do, I look up at Miles, who is watching me with a puzzled, uncertain expression.

"Um." He tentatively touches me. "How much did you drink tonight?"

This makes me laugh harder. It feels like my emotions are playing tug-of-war, and I can't control anything. Taking a few steadying breaths, I finally get myself under control.

"Barely a sip. Ever since Mexico, I haven't wanted alcohol," I tell him glumly. "Once you chunder up three margaritas, the smell of alcohol becomes much less appetizing," I add.

He's still watching me with a cautious, bewildered look. "Is it possible you could be pregnant?"

His words slam into me, and my heart gallops inside my chest in surprise. "No. Absolutely not. I had the coil for years, and then immediately switched to the pill. I mean, at this point I should probably print you a copy of my medical records so you can remind yourself—"

"Right, but you were sick two weeks ago. Maybe ... the pill had less of an effect? Because you, as you so elegantly put it, *chundered* up three margaritas?"

My blood turns to ice, and then I'm suddenly hot all over as the idea washes over me.

"But, you can miss one pill. Even if I *was* sick ..." I trail off as I count. "My period is due tomorrow. There's no way ..."

When I look up at Miles, he's watching me with a sickeningly hopeful expression on his face.

"I'm going for a walk," he says suddenly, walking to his closet and pulling a dark blue shirt down from his hanger.

I cross my arms. "A walk?"

He nods, dazed. "I need to know, Estelle."

I press my lips together. "Right now? At bloody midnight? And where are you going to find a pharmacy open at this hour? This isn't California. You can't expect—"

"You think I won't find a pharmacy open twenty-four hours?"

Sighing, I lean against the bed frame. "Fine," I tell him, smiling. "If it'll make you feel better."

"It will," he says matter-of-factly. He walks over to me and kisses me on the forehead. "Be back soon."

———

I'm freshly showered and listening to an extremely smutty stepbrother book when Miles comes back, out of breath and soaking wet.

"It started raining," he says, but then he cracks a grin and holds up a small box. "But I found a pharmacy that was open in the eleventh arrondissement."

"Tu es un imbécile," I mutter in French, frowning. "You're going to get sick," I add, watching as my soaking wet husband walks over to the bed and hands the box to me.

I snatch it from his hands and throw the duvet off me before walking into the bathroom. Miles follows me, and I glare at him as he shuts the door, locking us in the large ensuite together.

"This is absurd," I grumble, taking a test out and pulling my pants down so that I can piss on the damn stick.

"Is it?" he asks, looking excited and ... nervous.

I tilt my head. "I mean, I suppose it's possible it happened in Mexico. There was the *Night of Five Times*."

He huffs a laugh. "I'd like to think I filled you so full of my cum that your birth control just gave up."

I snort. "That's gross. Don't be gross."

"*Five Times*," he repeats, giving me a cocky smile.

When I'm done peeing on the stick, I place it on the counter and pull my pants up.

"Now what?" he asks, eyes flicking between me and the test.

I shrug. "I reckon we wait a couple of minutes." My hands come to the hard, muscled plane of his chest. "Care to get out of these sopping wet clothes, darling?" I unbutton his shirt.

When I look up at him, he's watching me with tenderness. And maybe a bit of awe.

"What?" I whisper, my hands pausing on the third button.

"I hope it's positive," he replies, smiling.

I furrow my brows. "When we had *the talk* last month, I had to practically beg you for kids."

"I changed my mind," he murmurs, reaching up and tucking a curl behind my ear. "I want kids *with you*. And I want them *now*."

I shove against his chest playfully. "Well, personally, I'd prefer to wait until after we're married."

"We *are* married, butterfly."

"You know what I mean. We've done things so out of order—"

"So?" His eyes are glittering with happiness. "Who fucking cares?"

"Miles ..." My voice quivers.

"What does the test say, Estelle?" he asks, nodding his head toward the counter.

I pull away from him and walk over, picking the white stick up.

And then I proceed to throw it across the bathroom.

"No," I say quickly, covering my mouth. "Give me another one. That one's faulty."

Miles snatches the test up and stares at it for a few seconds. My hands start to shake, and my heart pounds inside of my chest.

"Two lines is good, right?" he asks, looking at me with that same damn reverent expression that makes my heart feel as if it's going to crack in half.

I glare at him. "Two lines means I'm bloody well knocked up, Miles! Fifteen months before our wedding! One week before the launch of VeRue, and, and *fuck* this is not how it was supposed to happen, and *shite* we have Taylor Swift tickets for next summer, and I can't bring a baby, and *oh god* what's the *point* of birth control if it's just going to fail when you need it to succeed—"

Miles is right in front of me now, and he looks so, so happy. I'm panting, chest rising and falling, a million thoughts racing through my mind as panic begins to settle deep in my chest. My stomach roils with nerves, twisting and lurching. Reaching up, Miles grips my chin between his thumb and index finger. It feels nice, despite my weak knees and shaking legs.

"Estelle, calm down—"

"I think I'm going to be sick."

And then I proceed to chunder all over his signature Dior loafers.

————

Miles

A couple of hours later, once I've gotten Estelle calm enough to sleep, I climb out of our bed and walk to the window. It's nearly three in the morning, and I think of the last time I was restless at three in the morning in Paris. Glancing at Estelle, who is curled up in a fetal position, white-blonde curls wild around her face, I can't help but feel a tug of emotion deep inside of me. How captivating she was that night in the fountain. How much I grew to love her. *Fuck*, I love her so much, and I can't fucking wait to have babies with her.

I never considered having children of my own. Not after experiencing the shit show of Charles Ravage. But with Estelle, I can't imagine *not* sharing the love I have for her. I can't imagine *not* experiencing this with her.

And yes, we're doing things all out of order, but that's okay.

In a way ... having a baby at our wedding somehow feels perfect. Like it was always meant to be.

And I know she'll come around. I know she wants kids.

I smile when I think of two weeks ago—how sick she'd been our second night in Mexico. We'd all gone out for a fancy dinner to celebrate Zoe turning eighteen. Liam had been in a strange mood—surly and acting way too overprotective of Zoe. She had two of her close friends with her, *bad influences*, he'd said, and there was some kind of power game happening between the two of them. Estelle and I had too many margaritas, and then she ended up being sick all night from something we ate.

But the next night ...

Liam had locked himself away, Zoe and her friends were out on the town, and Estelle and I had taken advantage of our private villa over the water. I'm not sure what came over me, but it was a night I'd never forget.

Five Fucking Times.

Smiling ruefully, I walk back to bed and curl up against Estelle, nuzzling my nose into her curls. So, it's *not* just my imagination. She smells different lately because she's pregnant. My cock instantly hardens as I get a whiff of her new hormones.

"No," she groans. "I'm tired. Put that thing away."

I chuckle. "Did I wake you?" I ask.

"No. I can't sleep." She twists around to face me, and though it's dark in the bedroom, I can see the worry etched across her expression. "What-if ..." she trails off, biting her lower lip. "What-if I'm not a good mum?"

"Are you really worried about that?" I ask, placing my hand on her lower abdomen—right over where she's growing our baby.

Our baby.

She shrugs softly. "I don't know. I didn't have one. I don't—I'm not sure how to do it," she says, her voice wrought with emotion.

I take her hand and bring it to my lips. "I didn't exactly have the best father," I tell her gently. "We can figure it out. Together. Okay?"

She swallows, placing her hand over mine. "I already love this little baby so much," she whispers.

I squeeze my eyes shut, pulling her close to me. "Me too, butterfly. Me too."

"We're really doing this?" she asks, nuzzling her face against my neck.

"We're really doing this," I tell her.

"Even if my hormones go crazy?"

"*Especially* if your hormones go crazy. That little fit earlier was hilarious to watch."

She groans. "Very funny." She's quiet, and I can

practically hear the wheels spinning. "Even if this–causes me to have a really bad episode?"

I swallow. "I'll make sure my hands are warmed up for backrubs."

"What-if—*oh God*—my wedding dress, Miles."

I huff a laugh. "What about it?"

"Well, I'm probably going to gain weight and then my breasts will be the size of melons if I breastfeed ..."

I moan, squeezing her hips. "God, I *hope* your breasts are the size of melons."

"I'm being serious, Miles! The dress is ordered, and if I don't fit—"

"It's a good thing you make clothes for a living," I tease.

She's quiet as she considers it. "Yeah, I guess you're right."

"Anything else?" I murmur, my voice sleepy.

"If it's a boy, do you think he'll get your grumpy attitude?"

"Watch it, wife," I warn her.

Her laugh turns to quiet contemplation, and then a few minutes later, she's snoring lightly against my body. I reach down for her arms, finding her hands fisted around my T-shirt. My throat clogs with emotion as I kiss her forehead, thinking of everything we'd overcome—and everything still yet to come.

For better or for worse ...

Forever.

———

Thank you so much for reading Marry Lies! Are you ready for Liam's story?

You can preorder it here:
mybook.to/WardWilling

If you want to sign up for Ward Willing release news and updates, as well as receive excerpts and teasers before anyone else, **you can join my mailing list here:**

www.authoramandarichardson.com/newsletter

(You also get a free student/teacher novella as a thank you for joining!)

ACKNOWLEDGMENTS

Thank you so much for reading Marry Lies! Truth be told, this book had a rough start. I diligently outlined their story but when I went to sit down to write, the characters wanted nothing to do with the boxes I'd placed them in. I had about 10 different starts to the prologue and first few chapters, and it finally clicked into place once I stopped forcing them to behave. So, this is the product of a fully character-driven book, lol!

I have so many people to thank. My readers for already loving this world and begging for more books. I am far from done, and I'm so glad you love the Ravage brothers as much as I do. There's sooooo much more where these two books came from! I got the ideas for these brothers LAST summer, so you can imagine my joy now that I can write in their world.

There are so many people to thank for making this book what it is!

To my husband, who can be a huge grump sometimes. Like Stella, I enjoy pestering him and cluttering up the kitchen counters. ;) However, he is the reason any of my books get written. Thank you, Peter. I love you! And to my boys, who have told me (at 3 and 5) that they want to be writers like mummy when they grow up. I do all of this for you, and I'm so glad the three of you are on this journey with me.

To Brittni Van, you are such a wonderful friend and resource for this series! I cannot tell you how much your input helps me. From your alpha reading to our plotting sessions, you've really helped me hone in on these brothers. Thank you, thank you, thank you.

To Tori Ellis for the outline and editing help. I can't believe I've just discovered your editing prowess. I am forever in your debt. Sorry about all the em dashes.

To Erica, Brittni, and Macie, THANK YOU for the ever fantastic alpha reading feedback! Seriously, you guys are so pivotal to the story. Just knowing you're there with me, reading as I write... the days I spent in the writing cave didn't feel as lonely. Your suggestions and excitement kept me going on the hard days.

To Lo, thank you for the sensitivity read. You've become such an invaluable person to have on my team. I'm so glad we connected!

To Jess, Jasmine, and Chanel, you guys are the best beta readers around! Thanks for always giving such great feedback.

To Lacie, we finally got to meet in Chicago, yay! You've always been so supportive and I'm really happy that I added you to my beta team! Thank you for all of the wonderful suggestions.

To Emma, for the cover. The scars! Omg. I am obsessed. You brought Miles to life. Thank you.

To Rafa, for the gorgeous photo!

To Michele, for the proofreading. Thanks for loving my stories!

To my Keyboard Whores... I'm so glad I met some of you in person this past July. It felt like we'd always been friends. For so long, I struggled to find my people, but you are it for me. <3

ABOUT THE AUTHOR

Amanda Richardson writes from her chaotic dining room table in Yorkshire, England, often distracted by her husband and two adorable sons. When she's not writing contemporary and dark, twisted romance, she enjoys coffee (a little too much) and collecting house plants like they're going out of style.

You can visit my website here: **www.authoraman-darichardson.com**

ALSO BY AMANDA RICHARDSON

CONTEMPORARY ROMANCE

Ravaged Castle Series (MF):

Prey Tell

Marry Lies

Ward Willing

Step Brute

Holy Hearts

Ruthless Royals Duet (Reverse Harem):

Ruthless Crown

Ruthless Queen

Savage Hearts Series (Reverse Harem):

Savage Hate

Savage Gods

Savage Reign

Darkness Duet (Reverse Harem):

Lords of Darkness

Lady of Darkness

Love at Work series (MF):

Between the Pages

A Love Like That

Tracing the Stars

Say You Hate Me

HEATHENS Series (Dark Romance, MF):

SINNERS

HEATHENS

MONSTERS

VILLAINS (coming 2024)

Standalones (MF):

The Realm of You

The Island

PARANORMAL ROMANCE

Shadow Pack Series (Paranormal Romance, under my pen name K. Easton):

Shadow Wolf

Shadow Bride

Shadow Queen

Standalones:

Blood & Vows (K. Easton)